BEACH BLUES

ALSO BY JOANNE DEMAIO

The Denim Blue Sea

Blue Jeans and Coffee Beans

True Blend

Whole Latte Life

Wintry Novels
Snow Deer and Cocoa Cheer
Snowflakes and Coffee Cakes

beach blues

A NOVEL

JOANNE DEMAIO

This is a work of fiction. Names, characters, places, and incidents are either the product of the author's imagination or are used fictitiously. Any resemblance to actual persons, living or dead, events, or locales is entirely coincidental.

ISBN: 1532874693
ISBN 13: 9781532874697

www.joannedemaio.com

To Point O' Woods

A Connecticut beach forever promising summer,
a place where I find endless stories in the sand
and in the sweet salt air.

one

If a little beach cottage could look forlorn, this one does. Though she's not sure why. It's just a bungalow, really, in need of a fresh coat of white paint. Still, that's not it. Celia considers the cottage before her. It sits on a small hill, so the sea breezes will reach into its windows. And those sheer curtain panels on the top of each paned window look like white sails, puffing in the wind. It all perfectly suits the cottage name: Summer Winds.

Yet there's some wistfulness about the beach bungalow, or regret, because this cozy place must have long been someone's dream. A family made a lifetime of memories right here. Evenings on the screened front porch, lanterns lit, cool drinks being sipped. Or sunny mornings, walking out the front door to the sandy roads, hauling tubes and towels and umbrellas, flip-flops flipping. Even that cottage name, Summer Winds, evokes the promise of easy, breezy days.

But now, the dream is over. Celia stands beside a FOR SALE sign in the front yard. The family's time together on the beach—in the salt air and sea breezes, amidst sunsets and sandcastles—has ended. The day has come when it's all for sale: the home, the nostalgia, the anticipation of another summer. Someone is letting go of a dream and saying goodbye to their weathered cottage.

Before she opens the front door, Celia gives one more look, taking in the curls of peeling paint and dried-out wooden stairs leading to the screened porch. New folks will decide whether or not this is the place for their own summer dreams. They'll walk through the rooms, picturing life close to the sea while contemplating buying this cottage—and Celia's task is to convince them. She turns the key in the painted door and steps inside, breathing in the musty air that, as only in a cottage, has an endearing quality. Stopping in the living room and giving the stiff windows a shove to let in the salty air brings life right back to the stale space. She touches a conch shell on the mantel, then a clear lamp filled with sea glass, aware that she has staged plenty of homes. But staging a beach cottage is a first, and is not the same.

Because selling a cottage seems sad. She can feel it, the melancholy over a dream being sold.

Yet her one first gesture, throwing open the windows, already brings hope. A hitching breeze off Long Island Sound makes its way inside, carrying the cry of cawing seagulls. She pulls a notebook from her tote, takes a deep breath of the sweet salt air and starts jotting ideas.

Elsa can tell already. This is going to be one of those long, hot New England summers—starting early and holding on well into September. After cuffing her jeans and slipping on sandals for the walk, she steps outside into the mid-June sunshine. The brightness has her pull down big sunglasses from the top of her head. And since the empty cottage is only a block away, she decides to bring her own watering can. Even though one was left behind there, it leaks, dripping on her toes as she gives the flower boxes a drink.

Not that she always minds. There are times when she actually kicks off her sandals and wiggles her bare toes in the green grass, delighted to be living here at Stony Point after so many years overseas. Transforming her run-down beach house into a future

inn, or tending this neighboring bungalow … it's all become the simple pleasure of her days. So much so that she's added trailing ferns to the peeling window boxes at the little cottage for sale, and finally the delicate green plants cascade over the box sides. She approaches them now, dipping her fingers into the soil to check for moisture before heading around back. A lone robin chirrups in a maple tree, accompanying Elsa's humming at the spigot as she fills the watering can. Too bad there isn't a sound of clinking dishes from the kitchen inside; instead the cottage is sadly empty these sunny days, its family long gone now.

At least she *thought* no one was here. While tipping her watering can at a side window box, a woman in the living room catches her eye. She's pacing indecisively, with a large lamp in her hand. Elsa gives a friendly knock at the window frame.

"Oh!" the woman says, turning quickly with a hand to her heart.

"I'm so sorry, I didn't mean to startle you. Just saying hello! Are you buying this lovely cottage?" Elsa asks through the screen.

"Buying?" The woman looks around the room, sets down the lamp and approaches the window. "No. Not that I wouldn't like to. But no." A quick smile gives away her shyness as she pauses. "I'm staging the place, for the listing agent?"

"For Eva?"

"Yes. Do you know her?"

"Eva is my niece! She's on vacation, so I'm doing her a favor watering the window boxes. Don't mind me!" Elsa lifts her spouted can before pulling off her garden gloves. "I'd shake your hand, but …" She motions to the window.

"Come around, I'll meet you on the porch."

Elsa hurries along the side of the cottage, past a birdhouse hanging from the branch of a dogwood tree, and turns onto the stone path in the front yard. "Well, hello again," she says as the porch door opens. "I'm Elsa." She perches her sunglasses on her head. "Elsa DeLuca."

"Celia," the woman answers, tucking back a strand of auburn hair and extending a hand. "Celia Gray."

"How nice to meet you." Elsa shakes her hand and glances into the screened-in porch. Dusty conch shells and faded hurricane lanterns line a high shelf, and a collection of glass pitchers stands on a wicker table in the corner. "I'm always so intrigued by these storybook cottages, and how charming they can be."

"I know. Every cottage *can* tell a story, right? Though this is the first I've ever staged. Your niece lined me up with a few jobs."

Elsa nods. "So you live at Stony Point?"

"Temporarily, for a month or two. And I checked with the realtor to see if there was interest in my services while I'm here. You know, dressing up properties that have been sitting on the market."

"And where are you staying?"

"At a friend's place, on the side street along the marsh. It's the silver-shingled cottage, last one in the turnaround. Maybe you've seen it? With the tall peak in front?"

"I'm not sure. I'm still getting acquainted with all the beach roads, myself. But I do know you'll love it near the lagoon. It's such a magical spot, with the swans paddling by. And those sweeping marsh grasses always swaying and whispering. Last summer, I stayed at a tiny place called Hydrangea House. Changed my *entire* life, those few months! You are so fortunate to be here."

"Well thank you, Elsa. It's nice to meet a friend and have someone to chat with."

Elsa considers this Celia who seems to have uprooted some home life to come to the Connecticut shore. Okay, so it's not only cottages that have a story; there must be one Celia's not telling, too. "Beach chats are always fun." Elsa looks past her then, into the living room. It's small, but comfy. The one paneled wall is dark with age and sea dampness. "How sad it must be to sell a gem like this. What will you do to stage it?"

Celia joins her gaze around the room. "For starters, declutter. And look, they have a gorgeous vintage trunk all covered up." She lifts a blanket from a distressed blue-painted trunk used as a coffee table. "It's nautical and should be seen. So things like that. Rearranging, adding a few accessories, painting walls." She quiets then, almost uncomfortably.

But one thing Elsa does see is that Celia has a keen design eye; even her slight touches make a difference. So she tries to set her at ease with more friendly talk. "I own that rambling cottage near the water. The one with all the construction scaffolding. Let's see, it's only Tuesday. Why don't you stop by later for a lemonade on the deck? I'll tell you the right spots to visit while you're here."

Celia tips her head. "You'd do that?"

"Well, you're my new beach friend," Elsa says with a wink. "Give me your phone number and I'll call you with the time."

Celia writes her cell phone number on a paper scrap and asks Elsa to jot down hers, as well.

"Is your family with you?" Elsa asks while doing so. She tears her number from the page and hands it to Celia.

"Family?"

And there it is again, that quick smile that's uncertain, maybe? Regretful?

"No," Celia continues. "I'm here alone. I'm actually recently divorced, and since my friend can't make it to her cottage, she said I should use it. For a change of pace. So I'm keeping an eye on the place while I do some life regrouping."

"That is exactly what I did last year," Elsa tells her while tucking Celia's number in her pocket. "I came to Connecticut for a wedding, from Italy—where I'd moved after college, gotten married and raised my son. Two weeks here and I ended up starting my whole life over. And in my late fifties, imagine? But you know how it goes ... It was only going to be a brief stay, and now look at me. Sold the house in

Milan, and that old property I've bought here? I'm turning it into a beach inn! Maybe you're starting over, too?"

"Oh." Celia walks to one of the paned windows, the little white topper puffing in the breeze like a sail on a boat. "I'm not sure about that yet."

"Well, dear. What I *am* sure about is this: The best place to start over is somewhere by the sea."

two

JASON BARLOW TAKES A LONG breath and rolls his neck. Whenever he's immersed in a building design and comes this close to nailing it, he sits stock-still at his drafting desk for hours—so intent on concentrating he's practically inside the design.

But he's got good reason to get this one done, and it stems from the only bad part of being a cottage architect at Stony Point: the Hammer Law. Starting on the first day of summer, through Labor Day, all construction must cease as vacation season arrives at the shore. And even though Elsa's beach inn turret will not be built anytime soon, he's feeling the pressure of that dreaded Hammer Law. A construction crew is at the inn site nearly round the clock, trying to make progress on its renovation prep before everything comes to a halt—the hammers silenced to let through the sound of waves and gulls and sea breezes.

It doesn't help that Maris has been travelling for her job. He glances at the framed photograph beside his computer. Maris leans into him outside the Vermont A-frame where they honeymooned last year. Her brown hair is tucked behind an ear, her finger hooked into one of his belt loops, her smile genuine. Though she's in Europe now for fashion inspiration, wouldn't he like to be there in Italy with her—staying in a stone villa, strolling a piazza—instead of being in his barn studio by himself, again.

Sometimes the quiet is too reminiscent of the isolation he felt before she came into his life, so it's better not to dwell on missing Maris. He reaches over and touches her photo, then gets busy, spinning around on his stool and heading over to the side wall. His brother's canvas and leather-bound journals spill from the bookshelves. He pulls one from the shelf and skims the passages, feeling pieces of sand beneath his finger dragging down each page. It's hard to believe Neil's been dead nine years now. But if his brother hadn't walked the beach all those years ago and noted his seaside thoughts and ideas, Jason's not sure he could pull off his architecture business renovating cottages, solo now. With Neil's timeworn journal collection in the room, it often feels like his spirit is right there, looking over Jason's shoulder at his designs.

Outside the double entry doors, the leaves rustle in one of those sea breezes that blow here on the bluff. Folding the journal closed, Jason turns and listens. His brother's voice comes when he's alone like this, with no distractions, no sound of Maris, no touch, no looks. And he doesn't want to miss it drifting in on the summer wind. That connection with the past is why he finally refurbished his father's old barn into his architecture studio.

Because Jason first heard the voice here two years ago, when he cleared out the grimy tables and masonry tools. Dust swirling in the sunlight stirred up memories of his father and Neil and himself, together behind the house, their hands and minds at work with building plans. When Jason opened the doors and windows to air out the space, his brother's hushed voice came in on a sea breeze: *You can do it.*

Sea breezes, ghosts … they're all one and the same. Visiting upon him, nudging him, whispering. So Jason heads toward the door now, still holding Neil's journal. Outside, morning shadows slant beneath the trees as the sun rises higher in the eastern sky. During the few years that he and his brother restored cottages together, they'd work morning-to-night, deliberating rooflines or wall angles or structural purposes best suited to a dilapidated bungalow or crumbling cottage.

"Elsa likes the idea of adding a turret to the inn," Jason says. He stands at the slider screen and looks out on rays of sun glinting through the leaves.

In a moment, that warm breeze lifts those leaves on the towering maple tree. "I can't believe you're even putting a turret on Foley's old cottage, man. Seriously?"

"It works, wait till you see it," Jason says into the wind. "Once I included it in the design, it's like it was meant to be, the way the original cottage walls fit perfectly around it."

"And now she wants to change it?" Neil asks, or a wave breaks out on the rocky bluff. "How so?"

"She's tinkering, you know how that goes. What do you think of a copper roof, just on the turret, not on the cottage?"

"No way." The words blend with a raucous call of a blue jay. "Too upscale, too attention-grabbing."

Then, nothing. Just the rhythm of the waves breaking at the bottom of the bluff. But Jason knows; if he waits long enough, Neil's voice will come through with some answer. The waves keep rolling in, the tempo of the sea steady today.

"Time and a place for a copper roof." A larger wave breaks on the distant rocks, the spray hissing as it falls back to the sea, fading. "Except not on Foley's joint, man. Keep it beach chic. More on the shabby side, but nice."

The words prod Jason back to his designs and papers spread beneath the work lamp on his desk. On the way there, his cell phone dings with a text message. If he hadn't been alone for almost two weeks, he probably wouldn't get spooked thinking it's Neil, texting some last thought to him.

Got five minutes, Barlow. Jason instead reads the text message from Kyle. *Waiting for the grub to cook through. Shit, it's mobbed here.*

He can picture his friend standing in the one spot he loves most: behind the big stove at his diner, chef apron donned over his black tee, a spatula in each hand.

Pork Chop Special today, with farm-fresh beans. I'll save you a plate? With your wife gallivanting in Europe, someone's got to keep you eating your greens.

Jason checks his watch. He's got a full day ahead of him, meeting with several clients before stopping at the salvage shop. *Be there later*, he texts Kyle back. *Grab a brew at The Sand Bar afterward, catch the game.*

After setting the phone aside, he angles the swing lamp over his drafting table. And then, he does it. It's subtle, but he shifts in his chair before putting pencil to tracing paper, turning his head toward the open double doors. Just in case Neil says anything more about Elsa's turret.

Rays of late-day sun cast a mystical spell on the dark tunnel beneath the stone railroad trestle. Lauren slowly drives through to the other side, passing the guard shack and waving to Nick dressed in full uniform, clipboard raised. He motions for her to stop, so she does, rolling down the passenger window and leaning across the front seat.

"Hey, Lauren. Surprised seeing you this fine Tuesday." Nick taps his shiny new clipboard. "I've got to log every visitor, no matter who."

"But you've known me for, let's see, twenty years now?"

"New beach commissioner. Real stickler for the rules."

"Seriously?" As she says it, her old friend is scribbling down her name and license plate number.

"You have no idea. The guy's a piece of work. Checks my logs every day. So where you headed?"

"I'm on my way to Foley's."

"You mean to Elsa's place? She did buy the property, right?"

"She did. But it's always Foley's, to all of us anyway. Well, maybe *you* were too young to appreciate it, back in the day."

"Yeah, I get it. Go on, move along then."

Lauren puts the car in gear, taps the horn and drives the narrow beach streets toward Elsa's. No matter how many times she's driven these roads, it always feels like the first time. The painted bungalows sitting on stone foundations, the shingled colonials with windows open toward the sea, the beach grasses and hydrangea bushes brimming beside front porches, wind chimes jingling in the sea breeze … If she had to name it, it would be a little slice of heaven, oh yes it would. Her memories from this place are that sweet.

Including the ones of Foley's old beach hangout. She relives a memory every time she sees the big cottage, like right now: Someone's standing up on the deck off the back room, waving, so happy at her arrival. If the low sunlight shines a certain way, it could be a young Eva, or Maris. She parks her car and gets out now, this time waving to Elsa up on that deck. Beyond, scaffolding rises along one side of the cottage where decaying wood shingles are being removed. Sawhorses litter the yard, along with large white buckets filled with workers' equipment—scrapers and rope and such. While climbing the deck stairs, the sound of hammering comes to her from the front of the cottage. She supposes a skeleton crew is working late, trying to beat the Hammer Law.

"Lauren! Come, come, sit and relax," Elsa says before giving her a hug.

"It's so good to be here, Elsa. Now I can't wait for my vacation coming up." Lauren leans her portfolio against a bistro table leg, then slowly spins around on the second-level deck. "Three—fingers crossed—sunny beach weeks with the fam."

"Oh, perfect. But in the meantime, I'm glad you could make it for this impromptu business meeting. I saw a staircase mural in one of my decorating magazines and instantly thought of you!"

"I was excited to get your text, and already have a few ideas in my portfolio." Lauren glances at the hangout room around which

Elsa strung white twinkly lights. "But I've never painted on stair risers before, so I'm a little nervous."

"I've seen your work, and I have no doubts. Here, sit." Elsa pulls out a chair at the bistro table, where Mason jars filled with seashells and candles shimmer in the waning light, wine goblets sparkle, and two plates are covered with pastries.

"Elsa? I thought this was just a drink-and-think meeting. With lemonade?"

"I wanted to try out some pastries I baked, too. It's the perfect way to practice for when the inn is eventually open for business. So these are raspberry-*lemonade* cream puffs."

"And this sinful-looking delight?" Lauren points to a golden-crusted pie on a white cake stand.

"Lemon cheesecake. You and Celia will be my test guests."

"Celia? Do I know a Celia?"

"No, hon." Elsa sits beside Lauren and glances out to the street. "I met her today. She's a friend of Eva's apparently, and stages cottages for sale. She's new to Stony Point, so I asked her to stop by for a visit." Elsa looks past her, over the deck railing. "There she is now!"

Lauren turns to see, first, a grand bouquet of hydrangeas nearly blocking the view of this Celia. Her auburn hair is long and straight, her cuffed jeans and blue-and-white striped top perfectly beachy. And her expression as she looks up at them? Hesitant, until Lauren does it. She relives that teenaged memory from warm summer evenings decades ago on this very deck—and gives a sweeping wave hello.

———

Elsa can clearly see it. Oh, it's so close, she can reach out and touch it. With the sun setting on the horizon, the candlelight flickering like fireflies, and the June air soft on their skin, she knows that her decision to turn this run-down cottage into a beach inn was definitely the right one. Two nearly empty pastry platters and two glasses of wine later, no one wants to move from their deck-top table. A year from now, she can picture the entire deck filled with tables, and guests lingering long into a candlelit night.

Yet there's still so much to do! Renovating, drawing up plans with Jason, and decorating. Elsa sips her wine, remembering the summer before when the boardwalk twinkled with driftwood centerpieces in the dusky evening light. "Lauren, sitting here like this in the candlelight, reviewing your mural mocks, I'm wondering something. Those centerpiece driftwood arrangements you made for Maris' wedding would be perfect for the dining room here at the inn."

"Really?" Lauren asks.

"Yes." Elsa turns to Celia. "Maris is my other niece, Eva's sister. I reunited with them after thirty years apart, right before Maris and Jason's wedding. Their evening reception was on the beach last summer."

"*On* the beach? It must have been enchanting. This was the wedding that had you leave your home in Italy?"

Elsa nods and looks to Lauren again. "Actually, there are many projects here that could use your artistic touch, and that's why I invited you today. Here's my thought: I checked with the realtor covering for Eva. Come to find out, your cottage is available to rent through Labor Day, so I negotiated a deal for a *much* lower rent—*if* you stay on, which I'd love for you to do. Stay in that cottage you rented for a few extra weeks."

"But I could never! The rent will still be way too much. Kyle and I could barely swing our own weeks."

Elsa holds up her open hand. "Wait. I will pay you a stipend that covers the additional rent as part of your pay. Because, Lauren, there are activities here to keep your children busy while you work. And more importantly, you'll be *nearby* to paint my projects, all while letting the sea air inspire you. Deal?"

When Elsa extends her hand, Lauren slowly shakes it. "Just let me check with Kyle?"

"Of course." Elsa sits back and dabs a few cheesecake crumbs with her fork. "You talk it over with your husband."

"I'm sure he won't mind. Anything to earn more money." Lauren squints at them both. "Because, okay. I'm going to tell you two a secret. But you have to *promise* not to tell anyone!"

"Our word is good," Elsa assures her. "Right, Celia?"

"Oh, I *love* secrets. My lips are sealed." Celia draws two fingers across her pursed lips.

"Okay." Lauren gives in to a big smile. "Kyle and I have started looking at houses. Here."

"At Stony Point?" Elsa asks. Beyond them, the sun has sunk below the horizon, leaving a swath of red and orange painted above the distant sea.

"We want to move here," Lauren whispers, her eyes actually tearing up. "Shoot, look at me getting all emotional."

"You want to uproot?" Elsa leans closer and clasps Lauren's hand. "Sell your home in Eastfield?"

"Do we ever. We've so outgrown it, not to mention I definitely need a studio if I'm serious about my artwork. And if we have to move, well, where else would we possibly want to live?"

"I absolutely get that," Elsa tells her. "This place has a magical way of drawing people in."

"That's wonderful!" Celia adds. "You must be so excited."

"We are. But I probably shouldn't have said anything. Please don't tell?"

"It's a beach secret, Stony Point style." Elsa points to faint glimmers in the now-dark lavender sky. "Made beneath the stars."

"It's just that this is such a special place. And I get the feeling you're going to make this beach inn its grand destination spot, Elsa," Lauren says then. "Has your son seen it yet?"

"Salvatore? Once, right before I bought it. He came for a long weekend last August, when Jason and Maris were on their honeymoon."

Lauren reaches over and adds a splash more wine to their glasses. "They didn't get to meet him? Did Eva?"

Elsa shakes her head. "Eva and Matt took Taylor to Cape Cod that weekend." She turns to Celia. "Taylor is Eva's daughter. They wanted a little getaway before she started high school."

"Does your son still live in Italy, Elsa?" Celia asks.

"No. Sal grew up in Milan, but went to university in the States and then never went back, except for the sad year when my husband died. Which is another reason I'm glad to be living in Connecticut … I get to see my son more often. Sal lives in Manhattan now, where I visited at Christmas. And it would be so nice if he could see the progress on the renovations here, but his schedule is very busy. He works on Wall Street, and busy comes with the job."

"I can only imagine." Celia looks out in the direction of Long Island Sound. "What a different life he must lead than yours here, living at the sea."

"Elsa. Speaking of living at the sea …" Lauren quickly stands. "I have a fun idea."

"What is it?"

"We should give Celia a tour of Stony Point. You know, with all the inside scoop."

"I'd love to. When?" Celia asks.

"As my son says, there's no time like the present. And the beach roads are so pretty in the evening." Elsa reaches for each of their hands and gives a squeeze. "We'll take my new golf cart for a spin!"

"You bought one?" Lauren hurries to the deck stairs to look down at the driveway. "Now *you're* a woman of secrets."

"It's a great way to get around here. Just be sure to buckle your seatbelts," Elsa warns, "or you'll be violating Ordinance 3.00B62, or something like that. Believe me, I *know.* The new beach commissioner is such a nitpicker, he had the guards fine me twice in one week. I owe twenty dollars already!"

But twenty dollars or not, Elsa doesn't mind driving past the softly illuminated cottages with lanterns on the porches and lace curtains wafting in the breeze; pointing out Maris and Jason's imposing home on the bluff; cruising Sea View Road with its eastern view of the horizon showing a moon rising over the misty water; and finally arriving at Champion Road—notorious for its golf cart races beyond the boardwalk—where she parks the cart with a sigh.

"Let's get out and walk, ladies. Breathe some of that sweet salt air."

As Lauren strolls beside Celia along the wooden boardwalk, she tells their new friend one of Stony Point's best-kept secrets. "What you'll find out sooner rather than later, Celia, is this." Lauren takes a long breath of the damp sea air. "That salt air Elsa mentioned? Someone very special once told me of its magic, and I've always found it to be true." She squints into the shadowy light, gazing down the sandy beach. "Whenever you need a little positivity, a little happiness, simply take a deep breath of it, because, well … it cures what ails you."

It's officially summer when the entrance door to The Sand Bar is propped open to the evening. And with the warm days they've had, Jason isn't surprised to see that door wide open. Passing traffic sounds blend smoothly with a jukebox tune about cruising the highway on long, hot nights. And then there are the greetings: familiar voices calling out as though everyone just returned from a fishing voyage and stopped in to rest their weary bones over a nice cold one. It's that kind of laid-back vibe that suits the local tavern, and everyone in it. Someone even hauled out the beach umbrellas. With twinkly lights glowing along their spokes, one umbrella is set at either end of the long bar.

"Can't believe summer's here again." Kyle Bradford tips his glass of beer to Jason's. "Cheers, man."

"What are we toasting?"

"Life. Beautiful life." Kyle sips his beer. "You saved mine, been two years now, on a night that started right in this very bar. And I'm here to tell you, it's good to be alive, man."

"Kyle, you have to let that go."

"Never. I owe you." He raises his glass again and holds it aloft.

"Okay, okay. Cheers to you." Jason takes a long swallow of the brew.

"Hear from Maris?"

Jason nods. "Her company's sending her to Milan now, which has Elsa thrilled knowing Maris will be in her old stomping grounds. Saybrooks' Italian design counterparts are there, and Maris is pretty stoked to see what vision they'll bring to her whole denim scheme."

"Make sure you keep in touch. Shit, you're only newlyweds. Not supposed to be apart like that."

"Works for us." Jason grabs a handful of pretzels. "We're both so busy, so we get it. Get each other. You know what I mean?"

Kyle eats a pretzel or two, apparently mulling over the situation in between bites, his eyes glancing at the ballgame on the wall-mounted TV. "Well, be sure to message her. A lot. And don't forget. It's not good for you to be alone and brooding in that big old cottage."

"Brooding?"

Kyle shrugs and pulls Jason's phone over to his side of the table. "You didn't start up with those cigarettes again, did you?"

"No, I'm done with that shit. I quit last year, remember? On my wedding day. With you."

"Yeah, broke the pack in half." Kyle squints while typing a text message on Jason's phone. "Keep it that way," he says while sliding the phone back.

In the bar's dim lighting, Jason reads the words Kyle texted to Maris. *Ciao Italia.* He adds a line of his own—*Miss you, sweetheart*—then sets the phone to the side. "What's going on with you and *your* wife?"

"Lauren? Nothing, why?"

"You renting a cottage this summer? It's quiet at the beach with everyone away. Maris. Matt and Eva on their cross-country trip."

"Damn, still can't believe they rented an RV. Awesome machine, man. Nicer than my cottage, which we *are* renting, yes. A few weeks later in the summer. Jerry's covering the diner for one week I'll take completely off, and I'll be back and forth to work the others."

"Same place as last year?"

"Sure is, the little yellow one over on Hillcrest Road."

He eyes Jason while pressing his hand to his perspiring forehead. In a brief pause when there are only voices laughing, and traffic sounds as cars pass the open doors, Jason knows. Something is about to spill.

"Want to know a secret?" Kyle finally asks, leaning closer while dropping his voice.

"Oh, no. Don't get me involved."

"No, no. It's good. It's all good, guy. Just between you and me, though. You know, since I was your best man. Because seriously, I'm not supposed to say anything. Lauren would *kill* me if she knew I was telling you."

"Okay, then. Spill it already, would you?"

"We're thinking of moving to Stony Point."

"Really? You'd leave Eastfield?"

"We're outgrowing our Cape Cod there, and fast. Lauren needs an art studio, and with the kids getting older, we're running out of space. Plus the schools are better in Stony Point, not to mention it'll save on my commute to the diner."

"Commute? It's only twenty minutes from where you live now."

"Yeah, well. We've been talking about it."

"You'd live at the beach? I mean, let's face it, you two have lots of memories there, some not so good." Jason glances out the dusty window beside their booth, where a few miles away, a lot of drama went down with Kyle over the years. That one Connecticut beach can spell trouble sometimes.

Kyle shoves a handful of pretzels in his mouth, looking around the bar as he does. "It is what it is, Barlow. The past, you know? But the beach, and that salt air. Well, you remember. Cures what ails you."

"If you're sure." His friend does have a point, though. If it wasn't for that one beach nestled in a crook of the Sound, Jason might not be sitting in this booth tonight, downing an easy drink or two. "But I can't be bailing you out all the time. The last few summers were enough." He finishes his beer and lifts the pitcher to pour more. "I'll keep an eye open. If any cottages go for sale, I'll give you a heads-up."

"Perfect. But listen, it's not definite. We need to save up more cash, first. Maybe within the next year. So don't tell anyone. Not even your wife." Kyle feels his shirt pocket as though looking for a smoke, but pulls out his cell phone instead, checking for messages. "And I mean it. If Maris knew, then Eva would. Then word would get back to Lauren. You know how the women are chatty and all."

"The women are chatty? Jesus, Kyle, you're almost as bad as they are."

"Yeah, well. Keep it under wraps, would you?"

Jason tips his glass to Kyle's. "You got it, dude."

three

Though she can't see him from where she stands in the kitchen, Elsa knows right where Jason's heading this Wednesday morning—straight to the backyard patio table that overlooks the distant water. She notices that about him, how he always wants to see that sea.

"I brought coffee, Elsa," Jason says loud enough for her to hear through the open kitchen window. "Okay, and cinnamon pastries, too."

Elsa sets the last of the cantaloupe on a plate and puts on her favorite cat-eye sunglasses. "Have you heard from Maris?" she asks while carrying the fruit out through the side door into the bright sunshine.

"Last night," Jason answers around a mouthful of cruller. "She's done at the textile show and is off to Milan for the inspiration part of her trip."

"Wonderful!" As she sits with Jason, he sets two doughnuts on the edge of her fruit plate. "Pastries?" she asks, nodding to the plate. "*Really?*" When he only shrugs, she takes one, feeling the sugary grains beneath her fingers, and breaks the soft doughnut in half. The early morning sun is warm already, and the light breeze carries the caw of seagulls. When Jason dunks his cruller in his coffee, she does the same. "Mmm. *Magnifico*," she says behind closed eyes. "Freshly made?"

"Always, from the convenience store past the railroad trestle. And before I forget, Maris gave me a message for you to watch your email today. She's going to stop by your old shop in Milan. Said she'll send pictures."

"Oh, I can't wait! It's so quiet with her and Eva gone this summer. I miss them both, even though they send me updates on their trips. But it's not the same." Elsa wavers then, between a slice of cantaloupe and another hunk of sinful cinnamon *pastry*. She chooses the doughnut, cups it beneath her mouth and bites in. "How do you handle it?" she asks around the food.

"Handle what?"

"Being without your wife nearby."

"That's the nature of our lives, Elsa. We're both crazy busy, catching up after last year. You know, with the wedding and all that. But it's always good to hear her voice. Maris keeps me grounded."

Elsa pulls in her chair and coffee-dunks the rest of her doughnut. But she saw it, the way Jason dragged his knuckle along the scar on his jaw, just at the mention of Maris being away. Beyond them, out toward the beach, the dune grasses have filled in, softening the view with their green feathery blades. "When I was first widowed, it was hard to be alone in my villa. And with your wife travelling, well, I don't want you to be lonely, like I was. So why don't you come over for dinner this week? I promised Maris I'd look after you and make sure you eat right." She briefly lifts her sunglasses and raises an eyebrow while nudging the cantaloupe slices closer. "So Friday, okay?"

"I don't know."

"You must make time for *famiglia*, Jason. And I'm your family now." When Jason raises his coffee cup in agreement, Elsa tips her cup to his. "I'll tell you a secret," she says, "since we *are* family. Word is you might be getting another new neighbor here at Stony Point, and soon."

"No kidding."

She looks past him at the construction crew arriving—hard hats on, tool belts slung around their waists—then lowers her voice. "Just between us, Lauren told me that she and Kyle are house-hunting here. But promise you won't say anything!"

"Elsa, really? That's old news."

"What?"

"You know how it is … there are no secrets at Stony Point. Kyle already told me about looking for a house, over a beer at The Sand Bar."

"Oh, shoot."

"What?"

"I never get to be that person. You know, the one with a secret no one knows."

"Well, I'll tell you one. Right now."

Finally—a real secret. She rubs her hands together and waits for him to spill it.

Jason stands, slips his cell phone in his cargo pants pocket and grabs his coffee. "That Hammer Law is days away and I'm worried not enough will get done here before then. Let's go in and see where you want that turret so we can move forward with the plans."

"That's it?" Elsa pulls off her sunglasses and sets them on the top of her head while following Jason around sawhorses, then through the rambling cottage to the old teen hangout room. "That's your secret, that you're *worried*?"

"It is. Because I have a difficult client to deal with otherwise."

"Who, me?" She gives Jason a gentle shove before opening the door into the dusty room stuck in a time warp. And, apparently it is to stay that way; she's been told in *no* uncertain terms. Creaking wood floor and nicked restaurant booths and retro pinball machine and all. "The water view is best right here. We have to take advantage of that, so the turret is a statement feature of the inn, Jason. Maybe with wraparound windows to bring in the sea. Can you do that, while keeping the integrity of this, well to hear you kids talk about it, this *shrine*?"

"That's right. And don't you go messing with it."

"Ahem, Mr. Barlow. Who put down a hefty sum for this beach dump?"

"Okay, okay. I get it. It's *your* inn, but they're *our* memories." He paces the room. "So the point is to see that distant water from here?"

"Absolutely." Elsa looks out the screen window to the inn's grounds, which are a chaotic mess of a construction site, much to her frustration. She's not used to running a business in complete disarray. Her boutique in Italy was meticulous: every piece of clothing hung perfectly so, the floors and countertops spotless, the sidewalk outside inspiring with her chalked messages. "But I'm having a hard time envisioning this all coming together, Jason. Especially if we want the inn up and running next year."

"Don't panic yet. You need to see a sketch Neil once did. It's of a grand cottage, and included a turret. The sketch is loose, though, so we can imagine *your* details and I'll work them in. It's in my truck. I've got a few minutes, if you can take a look."

Elsa checks her watch. "I'll walk you out. The geranium pots are dry around back and I want to give them a drink. Okay, okay, and wipe the construction dust off them. Meet me there with the journal?"

The sun is nearly white as it rises higher in the morning sky. Even the birds are quiet beneath its warmth today. Jason stops before the scaffolding and examines the weathered shingles there. He still can't believe Elsa actually bought Foley's old cottage. Especially since it's been neglected for far too long and is showing signs of wear. He hopes the workers can temporarily patch places where the building sustained water damage, before that Hammer Law descends.

When he rounds the corner to the front of the inn, a man is standing near the street as a taxicab backs out of the driveway. Jason squints through the glare of that brilliant June sunshine. Two suitcases are at the man's feet, and he wears a suit jacket and skinny tie with cuffed jeans and boat shoes. Really, he could be straight out of Maris' denim campaigns.

"Can I help you with something?" Jason asks, shielding his eyes against the sun. "The inn's not open for business yet. Be another year, still." He gives a whistle for the departing taxi to stop.

The man turns to him, hand outstretched. "How you doing? And you might be?"

Jason shakes his hand, noting the expensive watch on this guy's other wrist, above the hand holding onto a cell phone. "Jason Barlow. Architect managing the site here. Can I help you with something?"

"Sure. Hang on a sec."

The guy approaches the idling cab and pulls out a wad of bills for the driver. And Jason knows it's a hefty tip simply by the way the driver raises his eyebrow at the weight of it.

"To compensate for your delay," this casual stranger assures the driver. "Just now." He knocks on the car roof and waves him off.

Watching all this go down, Jason also notices that the guy seems tired. It shows in his eyes when he turns back. "Maybe you don't understand," Jason explains, sidestepping a pile of roof shingles stripped off the front peak. "Inn's closed."

"Is the owner around?"

"But you can't stay here." He motions to the two suitcases still set on the yard. "So what difference does it make?"

"A big difference, actually." The man squints at Jason. "Matter of fact, you and I might be related."

There's something about this dude. He's arrogant as hell with his serious watch and tie, and an attitude like he owns the place. "Come again?" Jason asks.

The guy points between himself and Jason. "Family, man."

"Wait." Jason eyes him closely. "Shit. Sal? You're Salvatore?"

"You got it, cousin. Through marriage, right? Aren't you Maris' husband?"

Okay, so Jason hasn't been around extended family much these past few years. Because when he shakes Sal's hand again, clasping his arm, he's a little thrown when this cousin pulls him into a hug and pats his shoulder.

"How do you like that," Jason says when he backs away, still eyeing him. Sal's probably about his age—mid-thirties—tall, his hair dark, his clothes obviously good threads. Heck, he's a Wall Street hotshot, and that swagger has a way of showing through. But so does something else, a hint of being worn around the edges, maybe.

"Sal DeLuca," Jason says, watching this mysterious cousin of his. "Nice to finally meet you, man. I've heard a lot about you."

"Thanks, same here. My mother's pretty impressed with this place, the people especially. Now, I'll ask you again," Sal says, this time with a ready smile. "Is she around?"

"Sure is, but she didn't say you were coming." He signals for Sal to follow him.

"She doesn't know."

Jason stops and turns around. "Seriously?"

Sal nods, slightly.

"Shit, she'll be damn floored to see you."

"I know."

"Come on. And watch your step around the construction," Jason says, lifting one of Sal's suitcases. "She's around back, watering the geraniums."

"Ah, that's my ma. Always in the *giardino*, tending the plants."

When they turn the corner of the old cottage, Jason motions for Sal to stop. Elsa is busy lifting a large watering can and sprinkling the red blossoms. Her sunglasses are on and garden gloves cover her hands.

"Elsa," Jason calls. "You won't believe it. Someone was out front, looking for a room. Your first customer."

"Too bad we can't accommodate them. I hope you told them to come back, maybe in the spring?"

"He was pretty insistent."

"Excuse me," Sal says from behind Jason. "Is there *any* way I can finagle a room here?"

"Well, I'm sure my friend told you …" Elsa begins as she sets the heavy watering can on top of a sawhorse.

It's when she stops moving for a second that Jason knows. He knows that Elsa knows, and he watches her slowly turn while lifting her sunglasses on top of her head, the tears already lining her face.

Salvatore steps forward then, grinning with a twinkle in his eye, holding his hands open wide. "*Ciao*, Ma."

four

"PORTAMI AL MARE."

Later that morning, Elsa cuffs her jeans and walks alongside her son at the water's edge. She convinced him to kick off his boat shoes and walk barefoot in the lazy breaking waves, too. "Take me to the sea?" she asks.

"Yes. The words came to me in a dream, Ma. I heard a voice, soft. Or distant, maybe. *Portami al mare.* It was like a sign, so I did it." He stops and looks out past the big rock and the swim raft, to the vast water of Long Island Sound. "I came to the sea."

"But what about your work? You've been so busy."

"I have. But I also haven't taken a vacation in years. Years, Ma. So now, I am. Finally."

"You're staying for a week? That's wonderful!"

"No, longer than that."

"Two weeks? Amazing!"

"Ma." Sal picks up a flat stone and skims it over the rippling water surface. "All summer."

"*What?*"

"I'm spending the summer."

Elsa reaches up and presses the back of her hand to her son's forehead. He looks fatigued, and his hair is already turning wavy in the damp sea air. "Are you feeling okay? Be straight with me, Salvatore. I need to know."

"Yes, just tired. I've been working nonstop with no vacation, no relaxation, and this is a good time to kick back. With you opening an inn."

"But what about your job? You're not quitting?"

"No. I'm taking a short leave, that's all."

They meander around sand chairs and an umbrella set near the water, nodding to the family there. "No one just walks away from Wall Street like that, Salvatore. What's really going on?"

"I'm telling you! Do you know how much money I've made for that company? Whatever you imagine, I can assure you that the figure is too low. I've made them tons, and they know it. And part of the reason is that I'm always there, working *ridiculously* long hours for years and accruing lots of unused vacation time. Management does not want to lose me, so they've given my time off the nod of approval. It might be reluctant, but it's there."

For a few seconds, there is only the slow, easy splash of lapping waves, the water hissing as it retreats across the sand. "Why don't I believe you?" Elsa finally asks. "You're telling me that you up and left New York to hang out here at the beach … with your mother?"

"For a while, yes. And not just hang out, I want to help you get this inn off the ground."

"I'm not complaining, believe me. But this is real sudden, Sal."

"Listen. For all these years with my nose to the grindstone working with people's money, I often ended the day with one thought: If I could find some way to buy time, pure empty time, I would. Because *weeks* would pass and it felt like I never left the office. So I invested and saved enough money where now, I can. You know me, Ma. I've put plenty of cash away for retirement, or for whenever I'm not working regular anymore."

"So you're here until Labor Day?"

"Or thereabouts. It's open-ended. At least in my mind. Because I'm thinking about making a change, too."

"A change? You're the second person to tell me that this week." Elsa can't help but have a passing thought of Celia, looking withdrawn as she puttered about the little white cottage, Summer Winds. "A woman I met told me she came to the beach for the exact same reason."

"It's a good place to be when you're burned out. Maybe I'll feel better with your cooking, and breathing this salt air. Damn," he says, taking a long breath as the waves break at his feet. "It's such a tonic."

"It is." Elsa motions to the bend at the end of the beach where the coastline curves around a rocky outcropping and patch of woods. "This beach is perfectly nestled in that crook of the coast. See it? The jetty and trees act like a wall keeping the salt air hovering here."

Sal looks down the length of the crescent-moon-shaped beach, glancing along the high tide line.

"I used to hear it last year, from time to time," Elsa explains. "And it's true."

"What's that?"

"The salt air here? It cures what ails you, Salvatore. So breathe ..." She gives her son's hand a quick squeeze, then picks up a few seashells, bending to rinse them in the cool seawater. "Works like a charm."

It's a pretty sound, and one Celia hasn't heard in a long time. The wind chime on the outside deck jingles lightly in a sea breeze, making her look up from the unruly paper on the kitchen table to see the swaying grasses of the marsh. She takes a deep breath of the salt air, then presses the wrinkles out of the fold-up tourist map she found in a kitchen drawer. The streets wind this way and that, Hillcrest and

Sea View, Brightwater and Champion, Sandpiper and Bayside, names so charming they seem straight out of a summery fairy tale.

The problem is, the curving nooks and crannies make it hard to pinpoint the exact locations of the next three cottages on her list to stage.

"Bayside Road," she whispers, dragging her finger along the street situated near an inlet by the railroad tracks. Any house near train tracks will need some decorating magic, she presumes, so that buyers won't even *see* the tracks.

When her cell phone rings, Celia is glad it's her new friend Elsa calling. Maybe she can help her find these cottages.

"Sal is here," Elsa says.

"Your son?" Celia shifts the phone as she turns the map, still distracted by it.

"Yes! And he'll be staying at the inn, so I need to go shopping in Westcreek. There's a vintage shop where I hope to find some furniture to cozy up the place. You want to come along? Maybe pick up accent pieces for yourself?"

"Would I ever. If I bring my local map, can you help me find the cottages I need to stage?"

"Of course. There's a diner close by, so we'll stop for coffee. And a bite to eat. I want to talk to you about something, first."

"Everything's okay, I hope?"

"Oh yes," Elsa assures her. "I just have a question for you."

It's the next line, though, that has Celia fold up the map, hurry to get her sandals and wait on the front porch this Wednesday afternoon. Something about Elsa saying her surprise question is more a fun, over-coffee proposition, which is *so* what she needs right now. Anything to get Celia's mind off of all the beach road names making her life seem rather inadequate, the way they suggest that life is but a lovely dream at Stony Point.

—

Blue pendant lights hang over the long countertop. They're a soft, swirled blue, very much like the muted blue of smooth sea glass. It makes Celia think of her father's sea glass collection, and the way he's forever walking any beach he finds in search of the elusive blue pieces.

"This is Lauren and Kyle's place. They bought it two summers ago," Elsa says as she settles across from her in the booth.

"Really!" Celia glances outside at the quaint shops across the street and sailboats bobbing in the distant harbor. "What an ideal spot for a diner." Inside, along The Driftwood Café's countertop, folks sit on red-cushioned stools, and at the far end, a glass pastry case overflows with blueberry muffins. Celia notices, too, the driftwood paintings displayed on a shelf on the side wall. There are lighthouse and pier and seagull paintings, all done on curving wood washed in by the sea.

"Elsa," a voice calls out, and Celia turns to see a tall, happy guy wearing a white apron over a black tee and black pants.

"Kyle," Elsa answers, waving to him. "Hello!"

Kyle saunters over, wiping his hands on a towel, then shakes Elsa's hand. "Good to see you, Elsa."

"Thanks, and this is my friend Celia. Celia Gray. She's working for Eva staging cottages over at Stony Point."

"Celia, how do you do? I think Lauren mentioned meeting you, last night."

"Yes, over dessert yesterday, at Elsa's. She asked me to keep an eye open for any new properties for sale."

"She told you two?" Kyle asks, looking from Elsa to Celia.

"Kyle," Elsa insists. "Don't you know there are no secrets at Stony Point?"

"Yeah, but still." Kyle shakes his head. "Ah, heck. We're just looking, anyway. Nowhere near ready to buy."

"Are those Lauren's paintings there?" Celia points to the display shelf.

"Absolutely," Elsa says. "She sells them as keepsakes."

When a whistle sounds from the busy kitchen, Kyle backs away, hands up. "The stoves call. Enjoy your afternoon, ladies."

"What a nice guy," Celia remarks. "He and Lauren make a cute couple."

"Don't they?"

"And I love what they've done in here. I mean, those miniature glass fishing floats hung in the windows?" Celia motions to the red and blue and green globes strung with rope. "So pretty!"

"Lauren adds her artistic touch to the space, definitely."

"If you don't mind, Elsa, I really want to look at her paintings on the way out. They might be something I can use staging the cottages. You know, to bring the beach right indoors. Do you think she'd consider leasing them?"

Elsa sits back and eyes Celia. "Now you see? That's exactly why I want to hire you."

"What? Hire *me*?"

"Yes. Remember I had a fun question for you? That's it. I want to hire you. Look how you instantly saw staging potential in Lauren's driftwood art."

"I don't understand."

"Listen. I have so many ideas for the inn, but need someone like you, with a trained design eye, to keep it all cohesive. I need a firm conceptual plan for now, so that once the reno is complete next spring, the décor can be quickly implemented."

They pause as their waitress sets down a carafe of coffee and two mugs, then breezes on to the next table.

While lifting the carafe and filling their cups, Elsa says, "I'll pay you, of course. We'll need to discuss fees and my budget. But I already like what I see in your work."

"You're aware that staging is different from decorating, Elsa? Because I'm not sure if what I do is what you really need. In staging, my work is meant to showcase the *structure* of the house, so potential buyers can picture their *own* furniture in it."

"Precisely. Have dinner at my place, Friday night. I'll give you the grand tour. And when you see what my amazing architect is drawing up for that old beach house, you'll understand that you are *perfect* for the job. I want the actual walls and windows of my inn to speak for themselves, and not be lost to the furnishings."

Celia looks at Elsa and wonders how it is that when life seems to change, it always happens so fast. Like it did with her marriage ending, and now this—coming to Stony Point and having a world of new opportunities open up. She extends her hand across the table.

"Deal?" Elsa asks, taking her hand.

Celia gives a firm shake. "Deal."

five

ANOTHER DAY IN THE BOOKS." Later that week, Kyle taps the keys on his desktop calculator, slaps the ledger shut and checks his watch. Whistling a tune, he heads out to the diner counter and arranges a place setting, carefully lining up the flatware on a paper napkin. Finally, it's off to the refrigerator to check the plate overloaded with meatloaf, mashed potatoes and beans, gravy on the side, before going back to the diner door and looking to the parking lot—where Jason's SUV is nowhere in sight. He flips The Driftwood Café's OPEN sign to CLOSED and tugs on the locked door. Only then does he pull out his cell phone.

"Yo, man," he says in a voicemail. "Where you at? Diner's all closed up and your food's ready. Come on, I read in the paper the blues are biting. Lauren's home with the kids and planning Elsa's mural, so it's a good night for fishing. Hurry up."

He disconnects and walks over to the door again, shielding his eyes from the setting sun's rays while scanning the parking lot. Nothing. No Jason, no SUV. "Let's go, let's go." He dials Jason again to leave another brief message before pacing to his office where he lifts off his T-shirt, swabs his face and neck, and—as always—balls up the fabric and gives it a hook shot straight into the trash can. "Score," he whispers while opening a three-pack of new black tees and pulling one on over his head, right as his cell phone rings.

"Barlow, where the hell are you? Your food's getting cold. Working this late on a Friday?"

"Man, I completely forgot, Kyle. I'm at Elsa's, having something to eat."

"Seriously?"

"Sorry, guy. Can you pack my plate? I'll have it tomorrow."

"Fine. We still fishing?"

"Yeah. Where we casting off? I'll meet you there in a while."

"On the rocks. And get a move on. Tide's been going out all afternoon."

"It's low? Okay, good. I'll call you as soon as I'm freed up, and I'll bring the dog. She needs to burn off some energy."

When Kyle hangs up, he grabs a pile of old fishing net from the back closet. Maybe it wasn't so bad when it used to hang on the wall, the way it gave the space that down-home coastal feel. Before Kyle bought the diner, it was The Dockside, more of a local dive. The thing is, ever since his old boss, Jerry, gave him the chance to buy it—and to go from part-time cook to proprietor—Kyle doubts every decision, including the new diner name. Is The Driftwood Café too upscale for a casual beach eatery?

"Jesus, relax," he tells himself, hooking the ropy net up against a large wall across from the booths.

Celia's not really sure why Elsa invited her tonight, of all nights. Sure, she needs a room-by-room tour to better understand Elsa's vision for the inn. But from the looks of the intimate dining room in the old cottage, Elsa needs no help decorating. Seashells are casually placed around flickering lanterns atop the long, wood-planked table. Add that to the French country chairs painted distressed navy, and the chipped-paint built-in cupboard lined with mismatched china pieces—anchored with white pitchers filled with dried lagoon grasses—and, well, it all gives new meaning to seaside shabby chic.

But it's the easy way conversation flows among the dinner guests that has Celia feeling like a fish out of water. Until Elsa sets her at ease while announcing that she's rehearsing for Sunday dinners at her future inn.

"You're all my practice guests this evening," Elsa tells them, with a wink at Celia. "And if you don't like the menu, please say so."

Not like the food? From the sublime taste of the breaded chicken breasts stuffed with spinach and cream cheese, to the side of grilled zucchini slices, Celia's ready to book a reservation and doesn't hesitate in letting Elsa know.

She's also intrigued to finally meet this Jason Barlow: Elsa's nephew-in-law and apparent architect extraordinaire. But as comfortable as Jason is chatting at the table, doesn't he have a story somewhere inside him? Hints of it show, from the prosthetic limb below his left knee, to his wavy dark hair hitting his shirt collar, to his unshaven face. Glimpses of shadows there cannot be denied.

But it's Elsa's son, Salvatore, who's keeping them all on their toes. He gives a running commentary on the beach lives to which Elsa and Jason are so accustomed, and they are startled at his perception of it. It's *his* words to which Celia most relates.

"I dream of a simple life like this, so often lately," Sal remarks when he sips his wine during dinner.

Oh, and doesn't Celia dream it, too, especially after the divorce that's left her unhinged for months now. Though she doesn't dare say so, and risk being psychoanalyzed at this beach dinner table.

"Simple life?" Jason asks as he throws a glance at his cell phone dinging with another message. "If you could've seen the day I had, you might think otherwise." He tips his wineglass to Sal's as he says it.

"Yeah, but listen. Does it matter what *type* of day you have when it ends with dinner by the sea, salt air drifting in the windows?" Sal sits back with a deep breath. "When I'm busy on the Street, this is the stuff of my fantasies."

"The Street?" Celia asks, without letting on that she totally gets his cottage-dinner fantasy. Because lately, this type of evening only happens in the movies she's been watching, alone.

"Wall Street, which is where I work." Sal forks a piece of chicken, holding it aloft a moment. "And when I say eighty-hour weeks are common, unfortunately you can believe me. Some companies actually insist their analysts take off one weekend, a month."

"A *month*?" Celia asks. "Not every week?"

When Sal reaches for the zucchini serving plate, Elsa nudges it to him. "Well," his mother says, "that's just crazy. One weekend a month?"

"I kid you not, Ma. Nothing like Italy," he says while spearing several zucchini slices. "That's where I grew up," he tells Jason and Celia around a mouthful of food. "Seriously, time is what I miss most with my work. Time like this, tonight. It's very sweet when it's fleeting. Or when, by the time Friday night rolls around, you're too damn exhausted to enjoy it."

"But you've got job security, guy," Jason counters while grabbing a warm roll. "Sure the market's volatile—and if the stock market collapses, so goes the world's finances. But what government is ever going to allow the world's monetary system to collapse? None, so you'll always have work." Jason rips his roll and drags half through the spinachy cream-cheese concoction on his plate. "And let me tell you as someone who hustles for his next project, that job security's pretty sweet, too."

"Hustle? You? Don't tell me clients aren't knocking down your door. Because anywhere I turn around here all I see are Barlow Architecture signs on every other front lawn. Shit, you've got the Connecticut shore all sewn up. And that's no easy feat."

"No. But it's all I know." Jason says it so matter-of-fact, there's no mistaking that it's all he'll *ever* do, too. "Been at it for years."

"Even before the war?" Celia asks, leaning her arms on the table, her fingers wrapped around a wine goblet. In the pause then, a lone robin holds onto its song outside, late into the evening.

"War?" Jason asks.

"I wondered, too," Sal says. "Afghanistan? Iraq?" He points to the dog tags hanging from a chain around Jason's neck. "You lose your leg at war?"

Jason looks to Elsa, then back to Sal. "Your mother didn't tell you?" he asks.

"No, I didn't, Jason. Sal only just got here ..." Elsa tips her head, a slight, apologetic smile on her face. "I didn't want to overstep my place."

Jason nods as his hand reaches to the dog tags, which he holds for a second. "These were my father's, actually. He fought in Vietnam, and died a few years ago. I wasn't in the war; my leg was injured in a car accident."

"Shit, I didn't know. I'm really sorry to hear that," Sal tells him. "Has it been long?"

"Nine years now." Jason glances to the open dining room windows where an evening sea breeze makes its way to them. As he says the words, his cell phone dings with another message.

"Oh, how awful." Celia leans over and gives his arm a quick squeeze. "I had no idea ... I'm truly sorry."

"Don't apologize. It is what it is, and you acclimate, you know. Not to mention that, thankfully, technology's given me back much of what I need to get around." When he motions to his prosthetic limb, his phone rings this time, so he stands and excuses himself to handle the persistent caller.

"It must be Maris," Elsa tells Celia and Sal. "He's always waiting for her to check in. She's in Italy for work."

"Ah, *il bel paese*, the beautiful country." Sal sips his wine and holds up his glass in a toast. "I look forward to meeting this Maris, Ma."

Clearing her throat, Celia stands to collect the dirty plates from the table. "I'll help you clean, Elsa." She heads out of the dining room with an armful of dishes, feeling less awkward by keeping busy. Something about Jason leaving the room made the dining space feel too personal. In the kitchen, oregano, basil and sage spill from tiny red pots lining the wide windowsill over the sink. Celia rinses the plates and loads them in the dishwasher before returning to the dining room for more, passing the living room as she does. Sal sips his wine, Elsa forks a piece of food, and only the clatter of Celia stacking dishes breaks a new silence there—one that gets her to say something, *anything*, to comfortably get through this dinner. "I love where you put those vintage buoys we bought in town," she says while reaching over the table for another plate.

"Me, too," Elsa agrees as she heads into the kitchen. "Right where you told me, alongside the fireplace."

Sal slides his chair away from the table and leans back enough to see into the living room. "Interesting design choice."

"It's to bring the idea of the sea inside," Celia explains, looking first to Elsa standing at the kitchen dishwasher, then to Sal. Sal, who's got his steady—and God damn it—attentive gaze locked on her. "It's a staging trick." While talking, Celia's scooping up pieces of silverware, and a fork clatters to the floor. Sal reaches for it just as she does, both bending close. And of course, his hand lands on it right beneath hers.

"Allow me," Sal says so softly, she's not certain he said it all as he gives her the fork.

But there's more. His look has her tuck a strand of hair behind her ear before turning—naturally, in the wrong direction—then turning again, to the kitchen.

That is, until she catches sight of Elsa returning to the room. "Please sit and relax, Celia. I'll get the rest later." As she says it, Jason approaches the table again, his phone call apparently over.

"On second thought, I have a better idea." Elsa motions to the rest of her cottage. "Let's leave the boys here to their man talk while I give you that tour of the rooms I promised."

"Wait, Elsa," Jason interrupts as he stands behind his chair and pushes it in. "I really have to get going."

"Before dessert?" Elsa asks.

And Celia almost laughs at the horrified expression Elsa tosses Jason's way.

Sal reaches over and pushes Jason's chair back out. "Jason, my friend. You haven't been around my mother all that long."

"Oh, I have." Jason slowly sits himself down in his chair. "I know, I know." He sets his cell phone on the table again. "*Famiglia*."

"That's better." Elsa taps his shoulder as she breezes past him with Celia. "We'll put on coffee, too, and won't be long."

"Make it decaf, Ma," Sal says. "It's late."

While waiting, Jason pulls over the chicken platter, spears another piece and forks off a mouthful. "So how long are you staying? The weekend?"

Sal lifts the empty wine bottle, then sets it down. "No, much longer, actually. I'm helping my mother with the inn business. Not to mention, the grind at work's got me beat, which I don't dwell on with her. You know how she can be, getting worried and whatnot."

Jason nods while spooning up the spinach cream-cheese mixture from the platter edge. "She'll keep you well fed anyway."

"No shit." Sal stands then, and calls out as he heads to the kitchen. "How about a beer, Jason? We'll have it on this significant deck I've been hearing so much about."

With a quick thought of Kyle waiting to fish, Jason checks his watch before following Sal. They climb the outside stairs to the upper-level deck, where a sliver of moon hangs low in the midnight-blue sky, far over the distant water.

Sal leans his elbows on the railing, beer bottle in hand, facing the night. "You've got your work cut out for you refurbishing this beach joint, cousin." He takes a long swig of the beer. "And from what I've been hearing, my mother's not to tamper with this deck and that back room, there." He waves his bottle in the direction of the old teen hangout, shadowy in the evening light.

Jason looks over his shoulder at the infamous room. Nothing's changed—its windows are dusty; the screen door squeaks and slams; the wood floor inside is still gritty with sand. "Back in the day, this place was called Foley's. Downstairs, the cottage was a market, basically, stocking food and essentials for the beach community. Foley and his family lived upstairs." Jason motions to the second floor behind them, so Sal turns and faces the building now. "The old man's grandson lived there, too. The kid was a little rough around the edges, so Foley put on the addition to keep an eye on him, and all the Stony Point teens. Turns out, this spot was pretty popular. A few generations of us locals spent summer nights of our youth right here."

"To sweet memories, then." Sal swigs his drink while considering the dark windows, the screen door and dried-out shingles of the addition tacked onto the rear of the cottage. "So how do you redesign it while keeping that history intact?"

"I get a nostalgic vibe in lots of my clients' cottages. So I reference my brother's journals. My studio's got shelves of them, with all Neil's writings and notes on the sea and beach life, relevant to different summer homes he'd come across, either in person or in old photographs. He tapped into the story *inside* the walls and had a way of bringing that character to the structure."

"I'd like to meet this Neil. He sounds all right, man."

"He was."

At those two words, Sal turns and looks Jason straight on, silently.

"Neil was pretty amazing, actually," Jason tells him while glancing away. A tall oak tree beside the deck rises like a shadow in the night, its branches looming over them. "But that accident when I lost my leg? I was on a bike, Neil's Harley. We were both on it, just cruising, when a car drove straight into us. My brother didn't survive the crash. He was only twenty-seven, Sal. Twenty-seven."

"Oh, shit. Shit, shit, that's tough. I am so sorry."

"Me, too. You know? Neil was my kid brother. But man, he was also my carpenter, a historian and a bit of a writer. Thankfully I've got tons of his journals, like I said. Pages and pages of his thoughts and words. We worked together those days, before the accident."

"You've travelled a tough road, man."

"To hell and back," Jason says. "My brother and I were very close, and it hasn't always been easy since. Your cousin—Maris—helped turn my life around, got me to see things straight." Exhaling a long breath, he runs his knuckles across the scar on his jaw. "She means the world to me."

"I'm sure she does."

"And what about you? Got a lady waiting for you back in the city?"

It surprises Jason, the way Sal laughs at his question. "No. No one waiting. Women don't really get it, what I do."

"How so?"

"On the Street, you get addicted to the pace. It's a rush. Before you know it, your life becomes very narrow … and then it can kind of close in on you."

Elsa's voice calls for them then, stopping Sal. Before heading inside, he leans again on the deck railing and looks once more out at the night.

"Elsa, what is this topping?" Celia lightly touches the sparse sprinkling of crystals on the chocolate brownies.

"Salt. Sea salt, actually. To suit the venue here."

"Mmm, I love it." Celia looks to Jason, who is chewing with his eyes closed, and then to Sal, reaching for another. "You're on seconds already?" she asks.

"I have to be quick, before my cousin gets to them." He hitches his head to Jason, who is wiping his mouth with a napkin.

"Is that caramel inside these?" he asks Elsa.

"Yes, I think Maris will allow you to have a dessert treat, since you ate a nutritious meal first." She turns to Sal and Celia. "I've specifically been asked to keep an eye on my nephew-in-law in Maris' absence, to keep him eating healthy."

Jason waves her off as his cell phone vibrates on the tabletop. Sal reaches for it as Jason bites into a second brownie.

"Who is this dude?" Sal asks, reading aloud a text message. "*I'm on the bench, let's go already.*"

"That's Kyle," Jason says around a mouthful of brownie while wiping his hands on his napkin. "Friend of mine."

"Lauren's Kyle?" Celia asks, leaning closer to Sal to read the text. "I met him the other day."

"Nice fellow," Elsa says. "Has he been the one calling all night?"

"Yes, he has. Guess he's waiting at my place. That bench is out on the bluff, beyond my house." Jason stands then, still eyeing the brownie plate. "He's getting impatient."

"For what?" Sal leans back in his chair.

"We do this fishing thing, every week. Friday night fishing."

"Really?" Sal sits straight, looking up briefly at Jason behind him. "Fishing?"

"You know … Fish, shoot the shit, have a brew."

The cell phone buzzes with another text message, which Sal reads out loud. "*Five minutes and I'm gone.*"

And then, much to Celia's surprise, Sal starts texting Kyle.

"What the hell are you telling him?" Jason watches Sal quickly type.

"Listen, cousin. It's all about the deal. Always. On the Street, at the beach. I'm negotiating—in your name, of course. I told him, *Fifteen minutes, and I'm there.*"

Jason snaps his fingers for his phone. "Elsa, I had a wonderful dinner, but I can't keep my friend waiting any longer."

"Hold on." Elsa stands while patting a napkin to her mouth. "At least bring some brownies and coffee to enjoy while fishing."

"Only if you're fast, Elsa. I don't like to leave Kyle alone for too long."

"And why's that?" Sal hands Jason his cell phone.

"Long story, for another time," Jason tells him while glancing at his phone.

Celia stands then, too, and calls out to Elsa already in the kitchen. "Elsa, I have to leave as well. I've had a lovely time, but really need to get an early start tomorrow."

"What happens tomorrow?" Jason asks as he heads to the kitchen for his food package.

"There's this little cottage that needs some TLC before an open house on Sunday."

"Is that Summer Winds, where I met you watering the flower boxes?" Elsa asks from the other room while pouring coffee into a thermos.

"That's the one. I have to paint the front door, at the very least." Celia loops her bag over her shoulder. "So I better be on my way."

"Did you drive?" Sal asks.

"Drive?" Celia glances from him, to Jason standing in the kitchen doorway. "No. No, my cottage is only a couple blocks …" She pauses, finger to chin, and turns to the right. "That way," she says while turning, seeking a target to point at.

Sal stands at the window. "It's dark, a lady shouldn't be alone on these roads."

"*What?*" Celia clasps her tote close to her side. "We're at the beach, not the city! I can look out for myself." She slowly backs toward the door.

Sal holds his hand up for her to wait. "I'll grab two coffees from my mother and walk you, so you'll be safe."

"Really, Sal. It's barely a few minutes from here."

But it happens then. She finally gets it, kind of, this camaraderie she's been witnessing all evening. Somehow, they've sucked her right into its vortex when each and every one of them—Elsa included, moving into that doorway behind Jason—eyes her sternly. Silently, but sternly.

Celia reluctantly looks to Sal, who is still standing and waiting. With a slight smile, she shakes her head. "Okay, okay. Fine."

six

The air is different here. Back home in Addison, Celia would wake up in the morning to find dew sprinkled across the green lawns and over the cornfield at the end of her street. But at the beach, the damp arrives in the evening, a faint silvery mist hovering, often to the sound of a distant foghorn. The mist gives a vague hue to the cottage lamplight shining in the windows they pass.

"Now tell me the truth," Sal says. "What's a girl like yourself doing here alone?"

Celia sips her coffee, silently thanking Elsa for it as it buys her a moment's pause. "You really want to know?"

"Sure. You must have an interesting story going on."

Celia looks up at him. There's something about the way Sal watches people, as though he's unaccustomed to the everyday life of folks like her, living far from the Street. Though he wears a button-down shirt with the sleeves casually folded back, he also wears his jeans cuffed, so she sees the attempt at a beach-life transition. There's this contradiction to him: a large gleaming watch strapped around his wrist, contrasted with worn boat shoes on his bare feet. He wavers between two places.

After another sip of coffee, Celia answers Sal's inquiring words. "Interesting story? Me? I'm not sure if I'd call being recently divorced interesting."

"Depends. Find something interesting about it to tell me."

"Okay. How about this? I signed the papers right on my thirty-second birthday. This past December."

"On your birthday? Now that's awful. You couldn't change the date?"

"No. It was set in stone."

"Everything's negotiable, Celia. Somehow."

"Ah, well." They pass a cottage with thin white starfish propped in the square panes of the front windows, and she makes a mental note of the coastal look. "*C'est la vie.*"

"I hear you. That's life. I've told myself the same thing at times. Especially when I left Italy to come to the States. *That's life, Sal.*"

"I can't begin to imagine starting over in a foreign country!"

"It wasn't *too* bad, Celia. My mother insisted that since she uprooted and left America behind for her husband, her son had to at least have an American-style education. She had me attend international schools in Italy, which assured I'd be fluent in English."

"Maybe she hoped you'd one day live here?"

He nods. "It might have been her secret wish all along. And knowing the language made a world of difference when I came here for college. It helped me settle in and regroup."

"Which is exactly what I'm trying to do, take this year to regroup." Celia glances up at the sky, where the sea mist softens the stars' sparkle. "To think about this second chance I have to start a part of my life over again."

"A good friend of mine in the city says second chances are God-given. *Molto speciale.*"

"I don't understand."

"They're very special. So think carefully about it, this second chance of yours."

They pass cottages, some still dark and empty this early in the season; others with lanterns glowing on porches, rooms inside softly illuminated. It's the time of day when Celia loves to be nosy, stealing glimpses inside people's homes. Because doesn't life have a way of seeming charmed by lamplight? When she looks back to where the road forked, she realizes her curiosity carried her away. "Hmm, I think we may be lost?"

"You don't live down this street?"

"No, I don't think so anyway." She glances at the road behind them once more. "Gosh, these winding streets throw off my sense of direction. Isn't that the boardwalk over there?"

"It is. Your cottage isn't close by?"

"I'm afraid not. I think we may have zigged somewhere when we should have zagged. Should we turn back?"

"Not yet. I don't mind zigging with a pretty woman tonight."

She can't help it; Celia smiles at this Wall Street guy's play on words. They veer onto a side road behind the beach, running from the boardwalk to the lagoon at the far end. Dunes cover the sandy hill on the beach side, and cottages line the other. "I think this is Champion Road. Your mother tells me some intense golf cart races happen here, in the dark of night."

"Is that what my ma's been up to lately, burning out with her new wheels?"

"What a sight that would be, though I suspect it's probably the guys racing. Not that I wouldn't put it past your mother!"

And it happens again, the unexpected turns her life has been taking. Because suddenly they're strolling across the long boardwalk, their feet pressing on the wood planks, the grit of sand beneath their shoes. Across the sand, lazy waves lap along the deserted beach, and behind the boardwalk bench, the boat basin is filled with rowboats, cabin cruisers and small motorboats, all tied in their slips. With the pull of the tides, the boats rise and fall against the pilings, making creaking noises in the night. When Sal glances over his shoulder, not once but three times now, Celia turns to see what he's watching.

"Must be Kyle." He points to a hazy flashlight beam on the rock jetty at the far end of the beach. "Didn't Jason say they'd fish off the rocks?"

"He did." Celia tries to make out Kyle, shielding her eyes in the night and squinting to see before looking up at Sal. "You're going there, afterward, aren't you?" The way his stare is so darn steady in the misty beach air, it has her glance away, then back at him.

"I think I might, after I get you home. Maybe try this Friday fishing thing." He takes her elbow as they pass a young couple sitting there. "Hey, check it out."

Celia steps off the boardwalk onto the sand and reads a sign tacked onto a dock post. As she does, Sal's voice comes from behind.

"Want to go?"

"What?" She looks from Sal, back to the sign. "To a beach party?"

"You bet," Sal says, moving closer and bending to read the details. "It's Stony Point's first-day-of-summer celebration. Now that's a nice way to kick off the season. They've got music and dancing. Sand games. We can have some laughs together?"

"Oh. Well, thank you, that's awfully nice of you." She reads the sign again. "But I think I'll have to pass."

"Why? Are you busy Sunday?" He motions to the date on the sign.

"Well, no." She gives a quick smile and wonders how this keeps happening here, this funny way of life tipping her days on edge. "I'm sorry, it's not you, honestly. You're a nice guy and all, but I'm not really ready to date yet."

"We can stop by for a little while, maybe?"

"Sal, it's just that, you know … " Oh, why did she ever agree to take on Elsa's job? Look what it's brought into her life: men, and dates, and summer shindigs, and boardwalk strolls. All she wants is to be sitting in her cottage, maybe watching a *movie* about all this romantic pursuit on a misty night at the beach. *Watch* it, not live it. "I'm not looking to get involved with anyone right now."

"Perfect," Sal surprises her as they head off the beach toward the cottage-lined streets again. "Because neither am I. There's no time for love on Wall Street lately, I can assure you that."

"You won't take it personally?"

"Absolutely not."

"Oh, I'm so relieved you understand."

"I do. So we'll go to the beach party together, then." Sal looks at her for one quiet second before adding, "With no strings attached."

The beam from Gull Island Lighthouse sweeps across the dark water. The light briefly illuminates landmarks caught in its path: the swim raft and big rock behind it, the last cottage on the point, the wood pilings strung with heavy rope at the end of the pier leading to the boat basin. It all situates Jason, sitting on the rocks, casting his line out into Long Island Sound.

When a motion far out on the jetty catches his eye, he hooks his fingers in his mouth and gives a whistle sharp enough to stop his German shepherd in her tracks. Madison turns at his whistle and scrambles closer to where he sits with Kyle. "She's been acting up lately," Jason says. "I think she misses Maris." He zips his sweatshirt halfway, then pulls a biscuit from the pocket and tosses it to the dog. "She keeps her in line."

"The dog's not the only one your wife keeps in line." Kyle tugs at his fishing rod before reeling it in. "She keeps *you* in line, too. Man, you were over an hour late tonight."

"I'm telling you, Kyle. It just happened. Elsa wanted to give me something to eat, and I'm sure report to Maris on my well-being, so I agreed to stop by. And the next thing? Well, they're wonderful people, the DeLucas. And the food is great. But really, don't have dinner there unless you don't mind three hours of dining. It's one delicious course at a time, and they savor every damn minute of each one. Sitting around, talking, drinking. Shit, it was nice, but Stony Point is no Italy. We don't have time for that here."

Kyle sets aside his fishing pole and snaps open a can of beer. "I get it. At least you brought me dessert." He shoves half a brownie in his mouth. "Man," he says around the food. "All is forgiven, that's good stuff. What am I tasting in this morsel?"

"Elsa said something about sea salt."

"Yeah, but there's something else." Kyle finishes the brownie. "She added some secret ingredient and it's driving me crazy. I want to know." He swipes the crumbs from his hands, clears some seaweed from his line, stands and casts off again. "Well, I wrapped your meatloaf dinner and loaded it in the cooler in my truck. Promised Maris I'd look after you, too. Keep you fed and all that."

"Thanks, I'll have it tomorrow." Then, nothing. Just small waves and thick salt air that lull Jason until he feels a tug on his line that has him tug it right back, then let it out again. "I'm so crazy busy, I cannot believe tomorrow's the last day before the Hammer Law kicks in. Got three crews working overtime to beat it." He turns to Kyle. "Toss me a brew."

Kyle does, and they sit quietly. Gentle waves lap easy on the rocks below. "How's your leg, in the damp here? Okay?" Kyle asks.

"It's all right." Jason snaps open the can and shifts his prosthetic leg while sitting on a low boulder.

"There's a bigger rock, to your left." Kyle shines a flashlight beam directly on it. "It's up higher, so it's drier, too. Why don't you move there and be comfortable?"

Sometimes you know you just can't win. When that flashlight beam stays locked on the other rock, even though he *wants* to stay put, Jason can't help but give in. "You got it, Doc." He takes his gear and sets it up on the dry rock that admittedly *is* better for him, anyway. The last thing he needs is an ache settling in for the weekend.

"Always got your back, man," Kyle says in the dark.

Madison takes the commotion as an excuse to wander to the lower rocks covered with seaweed, but exposed by the low tide. A sliver of moon hangs in the sky; its light, faint. When the dog gives a growl, Jason turns to see a dark silhouette stumbling on the rocks as someone makes their way over from the beach.

"DeLuca? Is that you?" he calls out.

"Yeah." Sal's footing slips on the wet, uneven surface. "Shit," he says.

Madison rushes over, her head dropped, tail down. "Her name's Madison," Jason tells Sal as his cousin reaches down and pets the scruff of the dog's neck. "She won't bother you, except to play fetch. Toss a piece of driftwood on the beach and you've got a friend for life."

"Atta girl," Sal says while the dog sniffs at his feet, tail slowly swinging.

Jason gives a low whistle and the dog returns to him. "Sit now, Maddy. We're fishing."

"Catching anything?" Sal raises a fishing pole he holds.

"Just nibbles so far." As Sal slowly approaches, one hand outstretched for balance, Madison whines while keeping a wary eye on him. "Have a seat, guy," Jason says while reeling in some line and watching for his bobber in the water.

Sal stops and looks out at Long Island Sound, then finds a large boulder to lean against.

"Hey Sal, this here's—"

"Kyle. Got to be Kyle."

"That's right," Jason says with a glance to Kyle. "Friend of mine."

"*Friend?*" Kyle stands and leans over to shake hands with Sal. "Try recent best man, bro. Good to meet you."

Sal squints at him through the misty darkness. "Any friend of Jason's is a friend of mine."

"Well, grab a brew, Salvatore," Kyle tells him as he settles in with his fishing pole again. "There's a cooler there. And I see you brought your own gear?"

"Not really." Sal sets a fishing rod against the rock before he reaches for a cold beer. "Found it in the pickup, parked out on the road. Figured the truck belonged to one of you."

"It's mine." Kyle casts out his line.

"Thought I might try my luck with this Friday night fishing," Sal's saying as he gives the reel a spin.

"You came to the right place." Kyle shifts his rod to unwrap another brownie.

"Tackle box is over here," Jason tells Sal as he lifts the box beside him.

"Man, Kyle." Sal opens the tackle box and fingers through the lures and sinkers. "Those are some nice wheels you've got."

Which gets Kyle to nearly choke on that second brownie. "You're kidding me, right?"

"Not at all. Love those old trucks. What's on the engine?"

"Over a hundred thousand."

"Is that right … Seeing how far you can push it?"

"For now, anyway. Gets me back and forth to work."

"Where's work?"

"You'll have to check it out, Sal." Jason raises his beer can in Kyle's direction. "Kyle owns the local diner, great cuisine."

"No shit."

And there it is, that food obsession Jason witnessed earlier around the dining room table. The mere mention of a *diner* gets Sal hurrying across the rocks to sit beside Kyle.

"I love diner food, the way it tastes like home cooking." Sal casts his line over the dark water. "What do you serve up, man?"

"The usual fare. Breakfast menu, all-American meals from burgers to meatloaf to pork chops and onions. Oh, and one mean grilled cheese."

"Damn, the best. Not too many places like that in Italy, let me tell you. How's business? Good?"

Kyle slips Jason a skeptical look, before eyeing Sal. "Sure, you know." And apparently that's all he's revealing, at least while distracted by Sal's fishing line. Something is tugging at it enough for Sal to stand and try to reel it in. "Wait," Kyle tells him. "Wait! Might just be a nibble. Let the sucker have a good bite to snag him. Fishing's all about patience, man."

"*Pazienza*," Sal whispers as he sits again. In a moment, his line goes slack, so he manages a swig of his beer.

"Guess it's the one that got away," Jason says as a ripple swishes across the water, farther out, but close to the jetty. He reels in his line to cast in that direction.

"Think it's a blue? Chasing in the minnows?" Kyle asks.

"Could be." It's that kind of a night, with a little pursuit going on. So Jason stands and gives a side cast while whistling to the dog scrambling too far out on the rocks. The night is dark with the hazy crescent moon dropping only faint illumination, so he remains still, listening for any more telltale splashes. But the only noise comes from the steady small waves lapping at the rocks—and even that sound is slight as the tide ebbs, about to change.

seven

"GUESS WHERE I AM."

"Maris! I'm so glad you called." As Elsa says it, a lumbering dump truck carrying a load of stones pulls in beyond her deck. She turns and goes inside Foley's back room, shutting the door against the construction noise. "Now, where could you be?" she says into her cell phone. "Give me a hint."

"Okay. Well, this is my one day off before I visit Genoa tomorrow, the birthplace of denim. So I wanted to come here, the perfect place to be on the first weekend of summer."

"No!" Elsa sits in one of the padded booths and gazes out the dusty window, picturing precisely where her niece is. "Is it what I'm thinking?"

"Bagni Sillo."

"I knew it!" Elsa takes a deep breath and imagines being there, too, at the tiny slice of paradise by the sea, nestled into the cliffs on the Ligurian coast.

"But I'm calling you to be sure the sea is here? I just got off the train from Milan, and now I'm on this winding path of cobblestones. And there are tall stone walls on either side of it, all damp and covered in vines."

"Ah, yes. You are on your way."

"Really? I mean, I can definitely *smell* the sea, but I still don't see it."

"Oh, you will." A cloud of powdery white dust that rises into Elsa's window view has her stand and return to the outside deck. The dump truck has dropped all the stones into one large pile.

"I'm passing a tree growing inside the old walls, and there's a bend in the path now, where there are stairs. But there aren't many people around, Elsa."

"Bagni Sillo is a well-kept secret, dear. Only the locals know about it, not the tourists. You keep walking, I'll wait. And tell me what you're seeing."

"I'm a little nervous, actually," Maris says.

Elsa merely listens, an expectant smile on her face. And she knows Maris has arrived the moment she hears the gasp.

"Oh my God! It's the sea, Elsa. So beautiful!" Maris describes the rocky walkway and the roped handrail while she makes her way to a small stone balcony.

Her words—*blue, and emerald green, as far as the eye can see; spectacular; twinkling ocean stars*—bring Elsa memories, both happy and bittersweet. With closed eyes, Elsa is back in Italy, at the place she'd stood with Sal when he was a boy, and even before that, the place where she found solace after her sister June's sudden death.

"Elsa?"

"I'm here," she answers while wiping a tear from her cheek. "But how I wish I was with you." Instead, she turns at the sound of wood siding being ripped off her beach house, followed by the thud of hammering.

"Is now a good time for you?" Maris asks. "It sounds awfully noisy there. Crews are working on a Saturday?"

"On this one, they are. It's the last day before the Hammer Law takes effect."

"Of course. Stony Point's noisiest day of the year."

Elsa leans on the deck railing and looks off to the side to watch a few workers, hard hats and tool belts on. They nail a sheet of plywood onto the outside wall now stripped of siding. "Jason's pulling in as we speak, Maris."

"He'd love it here."

And in the wispy lift of Maris' voice that comes over the phone lines, over the continents, Elsa knows that her beloved Bagni Sillo has mesmerized her niece. "He would. I can just envision where you are. So many times, my husband and Salvatore went all the way down the cliffs to the water, and I would sit under an umbrella with my journal. I'd watch Sal—oh, how he'd swim! Couldn't get him out of the water, the way he'd jump and flip like a dolphin."

"I'm going to get a seat now, Elsa."

"Don't forget to order the strawberries. Strawberries and gelato, so divine."

"I can't tell you how many ocean stars are sparkling on the water. It's simply stunning."

"Make a wish, Maris! Your first summer wish, right at the sea."

After a second, Maris softly says, "Done."

Elsa touches her star necklace and closes her eyes. Breathing the Stony Point salt air, she's transported right to the Ligurian Sea again. And yes, there! She hears the waves breaking over the cliff rocks. It's where her peace comes from, having heard that sound over the years and knowing in her heart that the waves always break on the cliffs, always come to shore … no matter where she is. She stays in that moment, until footsteps grow louder. It's Jason, coming up the deck stairs holding a thin box.

"Jason! Hurry, Maris is on the line." She lightly cups the phone. "Is that a pizza?"

"Elsa?" Maris asks. "Did you say pizza?"

"What?" The last thing Elsa wants is to rat out Jason, who first sets the box on the deck table, then quickly puts a finger to his lips and shakes his head. "Your husband," Elsa says to Maris, "he brought me beautiful new designs for the turret room, which I'm about to review."

"Elsa! I *heard* you say *pizza*. He needs to eat right, because I know he gets really lazy about that."

Elsa lifts the pizza box lid. "There aren't even any greens on it, Jason!" she whispers.

"Shh," he whispers back before taking the cell phone. "Hi, sweetheart."

Oh, he's smooth, Elsa thinks while setting out plates and half listening to the conversation.

"It's so good to hear your voice, I'm missing you like crazy," Jason says, leaning on the deck railing while watching the construction crew. "What? No, I brought side salads, too. Don't worry."

From his salad lie, and from Jason turning up a hand toward Elsa, it's apparent that Maris is pestering him about his menu choices. But nothing will stop him from getting to that food as he cleverly evades the topic. "Do I ever have something to tell you. But it's a secret. You have to swear you will *not* tell your sister. Eva will never hold it in."

Well. One thing Elsa can't deny is that the pizza looks scrumptious. She cuts two slices and sets them on the plates at the bistro table. The sun is rising higher in the sky, so she also cranks open the umbrella so they can eat in the shade, but still within sight of that distant water she wants included in the turret design. As she twists open the bottle of soda Jason brought, she smiles at the secret that's actually becoming a news headline here.

"Not until you promise me," Jason says. After a pause, he continues. "That's better. So here it is. Looks like we'll be having new neighbors." He throws Elsa a wink as he spills the secret. "You'll never guess who's house-hunting here at Stony Point."

———

Standing on the front porch, Celia first removes a brass doorknocker, then dips a brush in blue paint and spreads it over the cottage door. The brush bristles make a swishing sound reminding her of when she was a child and her father painted a room, or the house itself. He'd fill a can with clear water and give her a paintbrush, too, so she could "paint" a wall of her own while he was close by. It's why the solitude of painting soothes her.

So when a voice calls out, "Knock, knock!" she jumps before turning around to see Sal opening the porch's screened door. He wears cargo shorts, a tee, work boots and sunglasses, which he's lifting to the top of his head. His face is shadowed, as though he didn't shave in his attempt to transition to beach living. There's always some contrast about him, like the way he still wears his big, serious business watch but also carries a striped lunch tote straight from his mother's kitchen.

"Surely you have an extra paintbrush for the help?" he asks.

"What?"

"The help. I'd like to pitch in here. It'll give me something to do."

But it's the twinkle in his eye that gets her guard up. "No, that's okay, Sal. You're on vacation, I can't let you work like that." She swipes the back of her hand across her forehead, and when she glances at that blue-spattered hand, realizes she probably dotted wet paint on her face.

"Two people get the job done twice as fast." Sal sets his tote on the front porch. "More time for relaxing then, no?"

She takes a quick breath, looking first from her half-painted cottage door, then back to Sal—waiting for her answer, hands turned up.

"Time's a-wasting," he says.

"Sal." The day is very warm, and she must look a mess with her sweaty tank top and denim cutoffs, her sneakers loosely tied, her hair pulled into a messy bun with strands escaping and clinging to her perspiring face. Really, it's not how she cares to be seen, especially by this single city slicker trying to fit in at the beach. She opens her mouth to send him on his way, but stops when he tips his head with a ready smile. "Fine," she says, relenting for the second time in so many days. "I'm set up to paint an accent wall in the living room. You can work on that, if you insist."

"Absolutely." When he walks by her, he scoops up a rag from the stoop and dabs the wet paint off her forehead.

"Thanks," she says, grabbing the rag from him. "You have to stir the paint before you begin. It's the beige can over there." She points through the doorway and moves aside so he can squeeze past her.

"Okay, boss." He steps over the threshold and gets busy, lifting off the can lid, mixing and pouring sand-colored paint into a tray. "You must have a steady hand," he calls out.

Which gets Celia to observe her hand moving down the door in a long sweep.

"You don't tape?" he asks, all while pushing a roller over the living room wall with untaped edges.

"No." She brushes paint on a streaked spot on the door. "I painted with my dad when I was little. Well," she says, eyeing the now-blue front door, "I painted with *water*, but still. He showed me all the right techniques. You know … how to load the brush, how to cut in close, follow the grain. We still do projects together; he helped paint my house two years ago."

"It's why you stage, then."

"What do you mean?" Celia asks while finishing up the front of the door.

"Your dad. He taught you to appreciate your home, and you bring that to your work."

"Oh." Celia considers this. "Could be. I loved tagging along on Saturday hardware store runs, or while window puttying. Or painting." It's true; her father was expert at keeping their home comfortable. "What about you?" she asks.

"What's that?"

Celia sets her paintbrush across the top of her paint can. "What makes you live a life of numbers?"

When Sal looks over his shoulder at her, she notices his face is perspiring. The cottage is warm inside, so she walks to a side window and lifts it open, giving the sticking sash a shove as he considers her question.

"Blame it on my mother."

"Elsa?"

"You better believe it. Talk about a numbers obsession. From when I was a boy, every single birthday was a *huge* occasion. I know all moms love their kids' birthdays." He pauses while freshening his paint roller and sweeping the beige paint down the wall. "But for my own ma, she takes it to an extreme. I guess it's her *thing*," he says, air-quoting the word with the paint roller in one hand. "There's always a candle on the cake for *every* single year. Even now, I can assure you. Each birthday would be a national holiday, if she had her way."

Celia tips her head with a small smile. "That is so sweet, actually."

Sal pulls another rag from his back pocket and presses it to his face. "It's warm in here, no?"

"Little bit." Celia goes to the kitchen, runs a cloth beneath cool water and brings it to him. "You look kind of pale," she says, touching the cloth to his face. "Maybe you should sit down."

He does, settling in a plaid club chair beside the paned window. "I'm practically in air conditioning around the clock, in the city. Not really used to this beach heat."

"But there's a nice sea breeze, don't you feel it?" She lifts the window higher, then takes the wet paint roller he's still holding. "I'll see if there's a fan somewhere around here."

"No, no. I'm okay." He's quiet then, until he catches Celia glance at him. "So, Celia. Are we still on for the shindig tomorrow night?" As he says it, he presses the cool cloth to his forehead.

"I guess," she answers while dipping the roller in the paint tray.

"Good. That's good. I'll swing by your place and we'll walk there together."

Then, there's only the sound of Celia rolling wet paint onto the wall. It's a growing trend, having these accent walls, and she needs it done for the open house. After a few more swaths are painted, she looks back at Sal, still sitting in his chair. "Maybe you'd like something to eat?"

He nods. "My ma always says, *Mangia, mangia, che ti fa' bene.*"

"Eat, eat, I get. But the rest?"

"Eat, it'll do you good."

"Lunch, then?" Celia raises the roller high on the wall.

"I think so. I'll get the sandwiches and meet you out back. Is there a place to sit outside?"

"Yes. On the deck. The owners left a few chairs behind."

When he walks to the front porch for his lunch tote and heads around back, Celia quickly rolls a few more swaths of paint, then returns the roller to the tray.

Okay, and she also pinches her arm, just to be sure. Because on days like this, her life feels like it's playing out in one of those movies she loves to watch. The backdrop in this one? A charming, but nosy, New England beach town. The plot? Two wash-ashores adjusting to time spent by the sea. She imagines a camera panning to Sal, who's a little worn around the edges from city life, setting out napkins, followed by wrapped sandwiches, on a cottage deck. There's a small bowl, too, maybe of cut-up fruit. Then comes the wine, a bottle he'd brought in that tote, and pours now into two glasses.

And like the leading lady in one of those movies, Celia's feeling utterly vulnerable about it all. Especially when she steps onto the deck and Sal turns toward her, unshaven, his dark hair wavy in the heat as he lifts his wineglass in a toast in such a way that she takes her own glass and touches it to his before sipping—all on a quiet summer afternoon.

eight

FROM WHERE JASON STANDS, DISTANT tiki torches and strings of white lights glimmer in the twilight. On the far end of the beach, they illuminate banquet tables covered with checked tablecloths and barbecue food with all the trimmings. The catering grills smoke with hamburgers and hot dogs, chicken and ribs. Around them, people mill about in shorts and sundresses, light jackets and sandals. Jason stands alone, near the rocks, and watches the festivities underway at Stony Point's annual Summer Shindig.

"I can't believe another year's gone by," he says. After a few seconds, he starts walking on the packed sand right below the high tide line. The firmness of the ground there feels good on his gait. "Maris said I'd get so much done while she's away for these weeks, but I'll tell you, Neil. It's lies, all lies."

"Slacking off, bro?" Neil asks as a wave gently splashes on the rocks.

"You shitting me? I'm working harder than ever. It's just that no one leaves me alone, making sure I'm happy. And healthy, and have a full belly."

"Tough life."

At least Jason *thinks* he hears the words, or else it's the dune grass rustling in the breeze. "Who am I kidding?" He stops to pick up a flat stone. "Life's good, actually. Better than it's been, anyway. My biggest issue is that damn Hammer Law."

"Love that quiet time when the hammers are silenced," Neil says as a breeze lifts off Long Island Sound. "It's when I did my best research, remember?"

"You bet." Jason skims the stone over the dark water. At the horizon, the sky fades to lavender. Further down the beach, the kids' party is happening, hosted by the camp counselors at Parks and Rec. Beach balls are being tossed, a sandy tug-of-war begins. Off to the side, a few boys are making a sand fort near the water. One of them is Evan. "Your son's gotten so big, Neil. He's eight years old now, going into third grade already." Jason stops, squinting into the evening light and seeing more than Evan. With the boy's moppy hair, dark shorts and striped tee, it's like he's looking straight at a memory of a young Neil. "Remember when we'd build sand forts and pretend we were in Vietnam, reenacting Dad's war stories?"

"Those were good times, Jay. Lying in the sand, directly on the front lines. Thought we were invincible."

Evan is making a trench, pushing the sand in a wall on one side of him. He looks up at a low-flying seagull that gives a squawk as it soars past at sunset. But that's not what Jason is seeing. No, he's watching his *brother* at eight, ducking into their sandy foxhole, throwing a rock grenade out into the encroaching waves bringing in the enemy. "Shit," he whispers, looking longer at Evan, then walking again toward the shindig. "I know you had a falling-out with Kyle, but he's doing right by your son. Don't worry. Kyle's a stand-up guy."

Then, nothing. Because what can his brother say to that? Continuing along the packed sand, Jason passes the still-unlit bonfire pit, and ahead, a dance area is roped off. Above it, small light bulbs are strung in a crisscross pattern.

"First day of summer, Neil," Jason says while walking toward the boardwalk. "Wish you were here."

Kyle hooks his fingers in his mouth and gives a whistle sharp enough to cut through the festivity noise. "Barlow!" he calls out while laying a rope across the sand, shielding his eyes to see Jason at the water's edge. "You in?"

"What do you think, Bradford?" Jason yells back as he nears.

Celia takes it all in as Sal walks her down the boardwalk. "Look," she says, pointing ahead. "There's your mother, sitting with Lauren. That's Kyle's wife."

"Sal! Celia!" Elsa calls out, waving them over.

"What a beautiful evening," Celia tells them, looking at the white lights strung beneath the boardwalk pavilion.

"It is," Elsa agrees. "And Sal, come here. You must meet Lauren." Elsa hooks an arm through Lauren's beside her. "Lauren will be at the inn often this summer, painting a stair mural."

"Lauren." Sal walks to her and takes her hand in his. "It's so nice to finally meet. My ma and Celia have told me a lot about you."

"All good, I hope," Lauren answers with a grin.

"Of course. So you're Kyle's better half, then?" Sal asks with a wink. "I fished with your husband the other night."

"Oh, those two," Lauren says, nodding to Kyle and Jason talking on the sand. "They're obsessed with Friday night fishing."

Sal turns to look out at the beach. "And what is all this?" He motions to the people lining up nearby, close to the boardwalk lights.

"It's a competition, and a very heated one," Kyle interrupts. He grabs a megaphone and hands Sal a clamshell. "Vie to be the Stony Point Clamshell Champ?"

Sal takes the shell. "You are on, my friend. How do I do this?"

"Get in line behind the rope and I'll explain," Kyle tells him. "You playing, Ell?"

"As if." Lauren grabs three large clamshells and stands beside Celia in the wavering line reaching across the beach. "Elsa? How about you?" she calls out.

Elsa relaxes on the boardwalk bench. "I'll be a spectator this time around."

"Okay, if I can have your attention," Kyle announces into the megaphone as people stretch and shimmy to loosen up. Celia does the same, giving her arms a quick shake. "You get three tosses," Kyle tells them while pacing the sand, "and they must be *underhanded.* Don't need anyone getting clipped in the head. And anyone crossing *over* the rope while throwing a shell is also disqualified."

"What's the prize?" a man asks, sounding a little too excited.

"It's just your thing, Vincenzo," Kyle answers. "Food. Winner gets a voucher for two free ice creams off the truck."

Random applause breaks out with a whistle or two, right as Celia notices Jason getting in line on the other side of Sal. Kyle personally delivers Jason's clamshells.

"*You're* refereeing this thing?" Jason asks him.

"Bet your ass I am."

"How'd that happen? You don't even own a place here."

"Hellooo, I have rights, you know. This competition was entrusted to me by our resident state trooper—Matt Gallagher—who was very sorry to relinquish his referee responsibility due to his vacation."

"Well, okay. Then keep an eye on these two." Jason points to Sal, who is standing behind Celia now and guiding her arm in a practice toss. "They're planning some sort of clamshell collusion," he tells Kyle while sending a wink Celia's way.

"Listen you guys," Kyle warns them. "No horsing around or I'll have to eject you." He takes his place in front of the crowd. "Now the point of the game is to get as many of your three clamshells in the sand pails lined up here, or as close as possible."

But it isn't until after he begins the competition by blasting a pocket air horn that the mania ensues. Celia's never seen anything like it as clamshells take flight across the beach.

"Hey, hey," a voice yells amidst whoops and hollers. "Ref! Cheating here."

Kyle rushes to a man in his late twenties who stands fully over the line while trying to nail the toss. "Really, Nick?" Kyle calls as he approaches. "Out!" When the tosser ignores him, Kyle steps his six-foot-two frame closer, hiking his thumb. This offending Nick skulks onto the boardwalk.

"Keep the shells low," Kyle loudly warns, glaring at the cheater, then ducking at a misplaced toss. "*Low*, and easy does it!"

Celia wonders if the competition always gets aggressive like this—seriously, for free ice cream? But the tosses are strong and fierce in the evening tiki-torch lighting. She takes careful aim, holding a clamshell up in her line of vision, then swings her arm back to toss it.

"Nice throw, but check this out," Sal tells her, casually giving his shell a fling into the air; it lands with a thud in the sand beyond his pail.

Before Celia can say anything, Kyle sounds his trusty pocket air horn, its three toots blaring. "That's it, time's up! Hold your shells!"

With that, the ruckus quiets and Kyle walks the line of sand pails, coming upon one pail with two shells in it, and one shell leaning against it. He squints into the glare of the boardwalk lights to see whose it might be.

Celia follows his gaze just as Sal lifts Jason's arm.

"The champ," Sal calls out. "I'm rubbing elbows with the best."

"It was close," Kyle tells the crowd. "But Barlow edged out DeLuca by a snail shell. Congratulations, man," he tells Jason as he hands him the ice-cream certificate, then looks at Celia. "Would you mind," Kyle says, giving her his cell phone. "I need a picture with the winner for the beach newsletter."

Celia snaps the picture precisely as Sal photobombs it, because, really, would it be any other way? And of course, before she can take a redo, the bandleader taps his microphone.

"Time to dance, folks," he announces. "Ringing in summer with an old favorite."

As the band strikes up the opening notes of *Auld Lang Syne*, a woman nearby says, "Oh, I *love* this song. Vinny, remember when you proposed to me right on New Year's Eve?"

"That's Paige," Lauren leans in and tells Celia. "Jason's sister. She and her husband are staying with Jason for the weekend. With their kids, too."

Celia nods as this Vinny, all lanky and spontaneous, gets down on one knee in the sand and takes Paige's hand. "May I have the honor of this dance?"

Here we go again, Celia thinks. Someone might as well have the camera rolling, with the movie director sitting in his chair, leading the cast in their appropriate romantic-comedy roles in some nostalgic summertime movie. Celia sees it all: the twinkling white lights, the pale paper lanterns looking like full moons strung over the dance area, the tea-light candles glimmering inside silver-wire minnow traps. Beside her, Kyle gently takes Lauren in his arms, close enough for Celia to overhear his now-gentle voice. "Come on, for everything, Ell," he says, sweeping his fingers across her cheek. "Everything."

All of it—the dancing and misty beach illumination—well, it all leaves Celia feeling like the out-of-place single girl at any New Year's Eve party, wanting only to be at home instead of alone and awkward in an intimate lovers' setting.

Until someone touches her shoulder and she turns to see Sal. His face is shadowed, his touch light, his eyes smiling.

"Would you like to dance, Celia? To a summer when we become old acquaintances?"

She hesitates, then steps into his arms on the candlelit beach. They slow dance on the outskirts, much the way she sometimes feels here. On the outskirts, not quite enmeshed in the decades-old beach friendships that hold on at Stony Point.

They continue dancing, his touch on her back holding her close. And in the magic of the song of acquaintances and good times gone by; in the hiss of waves lapping along the night beach; in the sea breeze gracing her skin, she has to wonder. When she surprisingly tells Sal how she wants the night to never end, does he really answer her, his mouth near her ear, agreeing? *Me, too*, is what she swears he whispers.

But she'll never know for sure, because just when the familiar tune comes to a close and leaves her feeling a little sad, the night changes. The whole summer-to-come changes, actually. All in one moment. All when Sal brushes his fingers across her face, his touch as light as the sea breeze itself. It's a touch that gets her to look from the shimmering water reflecting the white lights and bonfire flames, to his dark eyes as he leans down and gives her one long, tender kiss beside the sea.

nine

EARLY WEDNESDAY MORNING, THE SUN is low in the sky. By its color alone, Jason can tell it's going to be a hot one. He whistles to Maddy on the leash. "Let's go and get breakfast set up." The dog walks beside him, snorting the fresh salt air. If Jason had to pick—and it wouldn't be easy—he'd say this time of day is his favorite on the beach, with late night being a close second. But something about the empty morning beach is vast, with all that sand stretched out, the waves lapping easy, a seagull sweeping low over the water ... and just him.

So he's surprised to see someone at the other end of the boardwalk, until he recognizes Nick, patrolling. You can't miss him with that new Stony Point guard uniform all pressed and shining: the khaki button-down shirt with black epaulets and those black shorts.

"Nice threads," Jason says, raising an eyebrow while lifting a wrapped egg sandwich out of a bag. "Looking sharp, Nick."

"Shit, it's that new commissioner. You know how everyone says this place never changes? He put a stop to that, changing *everything*." Nick pulls a ticket pad and shiny pen from a cargo pocket. "Speaking of which, Barlow, you're violating Ordinance F1. No food on the beach." He motions to the sandwich right as Jason tears open a ketchup packet with his teeth.

"Are you kidding? It's breakfast. Elsa texted me to meet her here to talk business." Jason lifts the top of the roll and squeezes ketchup on the egg. "I have one for her, too. So it's work-related."

"Sorry." Nick checks off boxes on his violation pad. "Rules are the rules, that's the new security motto."

Jason takes a bite of his sandwich. "But I just got it," he says around a mouthful. Maybe if he acts chummy with Nick, he'll toss the ticket. Crumple it up and give it a hook shot into the trash. "Over at the convenience store. Past the trestle?"

"I know exactly where you got it." Nick merely glances at him, then gets back to the business of busting his balls with a fine, his pen moving over the pad. "The three ninety-nine special? Eat them all the time. But not on the beach." He tears off the ticket and hands it to Jason. "I had to fine you double, because of the second one. For Elsa."

"Shit. That's the most expensive egg sandwich I ever ate." Jason shoves the ticket in his pocket.

"I'm supposed to fine you for the dog, too." Nick bends and gives Maddy's neck a scratch.

"Madison?"

"Between you and me, I'll let it go this time. Since she's on the leash."

Jason pulls the dog away from Nick. "I'll tell you who's on a leash. It's *you*, Nick. You're on a leash to that commissioner."

"Hey, just doing my—"

"Yeah, yeah. Get out of here now," Jason tells him, waving him off when Nick calls over his shoulder something about seeing him around. Then Jason presses the paper food bag flat on the boardwalk bench and sets Elsa's wrapped egg sandwich on it, along with two ketchup packets. If there's one thing he's learned, it's that his aunt-through-marriage likes to douse her food.

"Hey, Jason," a voice calls from behind him as Madison lopes down the boardwalk, the leash dragging. "Is Elsa around?"

Jason turns to see Celia—straw fedora on her head, tote slung over her shoulder—stopped to pet the dog. "You got the text?" he asks. "I thought it was just me."

"Got it yesterday." Celia drops her tote on the bench. "It was kind of cryptic, no?"

"Definitely. And that's Madison. She's friendly, wants to say hello." As Celia talks to the dog, a motion catches Jason's eye. "Looks like Lauren got the text, too."

Wearing a blue maxi dress, flip-flops and big sunglasses, Lauren ambles down the boardwalk. "What's up, guys?"

"Elsa summoned you, too?" Celia asks.

"Sure did. Hey, Maddy!" Lauren gives the dog a pat before looking out at the rippling water. "What a beautiful morning."

Okay, so it's apparent Elsa is up to something. Jason takes another bite of his sandwich, then sips his coffee. "What do you suppose this is about? Elsa change her mind about the inn?"

"I hope not!" Lauren turns quickly to him. "I'm right in the middle of designing her mural, plus she wants the same driftwood centerpieces I made for your wedding. It feels good to be busy with my artwork again."

"Same here," Celia chimes in from where she sits on the bench, her head tipped up to the sun. "I love collaborating on her cottage décor."

"*Buongiorno!*" Sal calls out from the far end of the boardwalk, where he climbs the stairs carrying a fold-up table beneath his arm.

"Morning, Salvatore." Jason raises his coffee cup in a toast. "*Come stai?*"

"Hey, hey. Not bad, my friend." Sal leans the table against the boardwalk bench. "I'm good," he says, clasping Jason's arm. "You've all been beckoned by my mother?"

Jason helps him open the table beneath the shade pavilion. "What's this about, Sal? Any idea?"

"I've got the inside scoop, but I'm sworn to secrecy." He zips his fingers across his lips while glancing up at the small, cross-beamed shade roof in the center of the boardwalk. Then he moves the table into the sunshine before turning to everyone watching. "Your boardwalk is like the piazzas, back home. We're all gathered to talk." His eyes land on the wrapped egg sandwich placed on a paper bag on the bench. "And eat, apparently." He reaches for the food.

"Hang on, that's for Elsa."

Sal lifts the wrapping and takes a look inside. "But it's greasy, man. My mother doesn't eat this stuff."

"You kidding me?" Jason asks as he pushes the last of his breakfast into his mouth. "Then she's a *closet* junk-food junkie. Been feeding me grinders, specialty potato chips, all kinds of grub since Maris left."

"Seriously?" Sal lifts the top of the roll. "What's this on, a croissant?"

"Yeah, her favorite."

"No shit." Sal tears open a ketchup packet and swirls it on the egg.

"I see the apple doesn't fall far from the tree." Jason pulls a plastic knife from the bag. "Here, let me cut half off for your mother." Sal sets the sandwich down on the paper, and Jason drags the knife through it. Suddenly, a shadow hovers behind him.

"That looks good," Lauren says, standing so near she's crowding him. "Can I have a bite?"

Jason glares over his shoulder at her. "Just a piece." He hands her a small corner, and gives Sal the rest of the sandwich half before safely wrapping up Elsa's.

"Mmm. Got a piece for me?" Celia moves closer to Sal. "Something about this salt air makes my appetite crazy."

Sal holds up his half, eyebrows raised as she nods enthusiastically. So he cups it and she places her hand on his wrist, bites the sandwich and closes her eyes with the taste. "Oh, sweet heaven."

"Jason," Sal says, taking another bite and slowly chewing. "You did all right, man. Where the hell is this from?"

It's how he says it, asking carefully between that savored chewing, that has Jason laugh. The DeLucas have a way with food, that's for sure. "The snack counter in the convenience store."

But something about Sal's expression has Jason move right next to Elsa's sandwich half, ready to guard it. "Get away," Jason warns them. He whistles to Madison and the dog promptly moves to his side, ears alert, head tipped. "Sit," Jason says while slipping her a biscuit from his shorts pocket, "and don't let this motley crew fool you, either. Guard that sandwich with your life."

—

"Good morning, and thank you for coming!" Elsa wears a flowing chambray tunic over white-denim clamdiggers. Celia notices how she takes care of herself, with a floppy straw hat and cat-eye sunglasses protecting against the bright sun. "I'm so happy and blessed to see you all here," Elsa continues. "But you might be wondering why I summoned you today." As she says it, Elsa sets on the table a framed photograph with a lacy scarf draped over it.

If Celia were watching this in a movie, sparkling stardust would be swirling as Elsa pulls out a handful of sea glass from her tote and sprinkles the pieces around the covered picture frame. All the while, Sal is lighting a candle in a Mason jar. And in the middle of this mystical beach moment, Lauren's cell phone rings.

"Oh, I'm *so* sorry," Lauren says with a glance at her phone. "Can you hold that thought, Elsa?"

Elsa nods and turns to the wrapped egg sandwich, lifts her sunglasses and winks at Jason, then removes the croissant top and squirts ketchup on the egg as Lauren talks. When Elsa holds up only the remaining half, she whispers to Jason, "*Where's the rest?*"

Jason waves to the others. "Vultures."

And Celia sees how Elsa can't help herself; even as she nods to Jason, she's biting into the ketchuped egg sandwich. But Celia' distracted then, by Lauren's conversation.

"Oh no," she says. "It's just not a good time." Lauren stands and walks away a few feet. "You're breaking up, Kyle." She holds the phone high above her, apparently trying to not lose the signal. "Okay, okay. Calm down. I'll be there in fifteen minutes."

"Sounds like a minor emergency," Sal says in Celia's ear, nudging her arm as he does.

"Elsa, I'm really sorry." Lauren slips her phone into her canvas bag. "You planned this beautiful morning and I have to leave. The diner's mobbed with lots of tourists and Kyle's short-handed. One of the waitresses called in sick." She walks over to give Elsa a hug.

"I understand, dear. Sometimes you have to trade your paint smock for an apron smock."

"Good thing my mother has the kids. I'll be waiting tables all day. We'll talk later?"

Sal suddenly stands up. "You stay put, Lauren. I'll go to the diner."

"What?" Lauren asks as all heads turn to Sal.

"Hey, I waited tables in college. It was fun. Where is this Driftwood Café?"

"No," Lauren insists. "I cannot impose on you like that."

"It's no big deal." Sal motions to Elsa. "I've heard Ma's story my whole life, and it's more important for you to hear it today."

Lauren checks her watch and eyes Sal. "It'll be a long day, and I'm warning you, Kyle's tense."

"Just be chill with him," Jason says. "Blow past his nerves." He raises his coffee cup in a toast. "And good luck with that."

Sal turns to Elsa, who is pulling keys from her tote. But right before he turned, Celia felt it, the way he brushed her shoulder with his fingers. She briefly grabs them and gives a slight squeeze.

"Take my car," Elsa says while tossing him the keys. "And don't rush," she calls after him as he hurries down the boardwalk.

Celia watches him go, and when he gets lost in the glare of bright sunshine, the magical movie, starring Elsa, continues.

"Now, where was I?"

When Elsa lifts the silky scarf off the framed photograph, years of time lift away, too, as she remembers that special day …

June's hair was wavy in the damp sea air that long-ago morning. Elsa sat with her sister on the very edge of the boardwalk as their father snapped the picture. They were teenagers—their jeans faded, their tank tops fitted, their bare feet set in the sand. Long Island Sound glimmered across the beach, an egret rose from the distant misty lagoon, and a school of minnows swished along the water's surface in the boat basin behind them. Life was as peaceful as their surroundings.

But it was the view that mesmerized Elsa. As the sun rose, it sparkled on the water, giving the illusion of thousands of twinkling stars.

"You'll only see them there in the early morning," June told her. "You know why? They're stars that fell from the sky, overnight." And Elsa watched those stars rise and fall and shimmer atop the gentle waves while her sister continued softly, giving her fingers a squeeze. "Ocean stars. They float on the top of the sea, twinkling like that, until they regain their strength and rise back up to the sky later in the day."

Now, decades later, Elsa reaches over and lightly touches the photograph while telling her sister's story. "*But ocean stars are just as magical as the night stars*, June whispered to me that morning, a morning as bright and clear as this one. *So make a wish*, she said."

Everyone silently looks out at the sparkling water of Long Island Sound. Thankfully, it's as Elsa had hoped: the morning as tranquil as can be, the sun casting stars on the sea. While they look, she dabs the scarf on her cheek, wiping a wistful tear.

"It's important for you to know that my sister, June, walked this *very* boardwalk all those years ago. And her daughters, Maris and Eva, live here now. So June once was, and still *is*, a part of this beach. And my hope is that all your inn designs reflect her star story, even in some small way."

Jason, so like his brother, jots notes in a leather journal he'd brought along. Oh, doesn't Elsa have the best team working on her dream beach inn. When Celia reaches over and squeezes Elsa's hand the same way June did that day on the boardwalk, Elsa finally makes her grand announcement.

"Lauren," she says, then pauses. "First, I'd like to commission you to create a painted sign. It is to be special and wondrous, as it will bear the name of my beach inn by the sea. Which is the ultimate reason I gathered you all here today, to formally announce the inn's name."

When Elsa gazes at Jason and Lauren, their strong ties to this beach are apparent in their damp eyes. Elsa, with her own tears escaping, touches June's photo before motioning again to the stars flickering on the water and repeating her sister's words, once more.

"*Ocean stars*," she whispers. "And thus, in honor of my sweet sister … The Ocean Star Inn."

ten

Kyle peels off his black tee, blots his perspiring face and neck, then slam-dunks the damp shirt into the trash can. He glances at his watch before pulling on a clean T-shirt from the package on his office shelf. "Lauren, where are you?" he mutters while putting his apron back on and rushing out to the big stove. The chatting voices, clinking silverware and scraping chairs in the diner mean only one thing: The place is packed. He quickly starts two breakfast orders, and mid-flip of the pancakes, hears a voice behind him.

"Got an extra apron?"

Kyle looks over his shoulder and nearly drops the spatula. "Sal? Hey, you here for some chow?"

Sal walks over to a back wall, away from the stoves, and grabs a white half-apron from a hook. "This'll do." He picks a menu up off a small stack and skims the pages.

"You'll be waiting on section two, in the far corner," one of the waitresses tells him. "The tables near Lauren's driftwood."

"Whoa, wait!" Kyle lifts the pancakes off the stovetop and onto waiting dishes. "Hang on!" he calls after his head waitress. But she's long gone, having grabbed warm plates of food to deliver. So he turns to Sal, who is also breezing right past him while dropping an order pad and pencil into his apron pouch.

"Catch you later, boss."

"Wait. What the—" But when another waitress clips three new orders to his carousel, he grabs them and starts sizzling bacon and cracking eggs before things get ahead of him. And it doesn't take long for that to happen, not with the way Sal keeps clipping orders on the carousel, which he then gives a spin before turning back to his customers. So Kyle wants to witness this Wall Street dude working the floor, waiting tables. He steps back from the stove and sure enough, there's Sal in the diner: laughing, talking, patting folks on the shoulders. Kyle shakes his head and gets cooking, doubling up on the eggs—sunny-side up and scrambled—and waffles and buttermilk pancakes, sprinkling them with powdered sugar and chocolate chips, getting the home fries crisp, and adding extra toast slices.

Sal continues back and forth, grabbing the plates, until Kyle stops him. "What's up, man? What's with the king-size orders?"

"Can you keep up?"

"Keep up? Of course, but what gives? Haven't cooked this much in ages."

"Shit, it's all about engaging with your people." Sal glances into the mobbed diner, eyeing the touristy crowd. "They're coming in for a bite to eat, but there's more, you know? They're stopping in on the road of *life*, man."

"Are you serious?" Kyle asks, scooping scrambled eggs off his griddle.

"Of course. And hey, smile, guy." Sal loads four plates onto his tray. "Smiles equal sales."

Kyle waves him off, but then takes a break from the stoves and saunters out into the diner, listening to this city slicker in action with his customers. *Where you staying? And who's this cupcake?* At that one, Kyle has to turn and see; the last thing he needs is some harassment lawsuit filed against him. But the cupcake is an eighty-year-old woman, all aglow at Sal's attention. *Nice shirt, where'd you pick that up?* he remarks while checking out some teenager's button-down. *You come in on that Vespa?* he asks a young couple with helmets set on the table. *I rode them in Italy.*

If it's the road of life his customers are stopping in on, Sal's getting right on that road with them. As he walks back to the stove, to his overflowing carousel, Kyle hears something else. It's slight at first, but grows louder as everyone wants Sal's attention.

Waiter! Oh, waiter! Can I get seconds? More juice over here?

And it's music to his ears as Kyle sets his order-carousel spinning and turns to his constantly, endlessly, beautifully sizzling stovetops.

—

"It's perfect. I love that name Elsa chose," Celia says, her sandals flip-flopping on the sandy road. One thing that never gets old here is the charm of the bungalows and cottages, looking straight out of a summer fairy tale with all their flower boxes and porch swings and silver shingles and white-paned windows.

"The Ocean Star Inn," Lauren muses as they walk slowly in the heat. "Wow, she nailed it."

"What a visual it conjures, those stars sparkling on top of the sea."

The sun is high in the sky, and a blue jay caws from a tall maple tree. "The wind chimes are still." Lauren points to a collection of white seashells strung with fishing line on a front porch. "Not even a sea breeze today." As Celia lifts her fedora for a look, a golf cart toots its horn when it speeds past them. "Hey!" Lauren calls after it. "Speed limit *fifteen*, Jason!" They see Elsa give a friendly wave as Jason brings her and her folding table back to the inn, with Madison sitting in the backseat happy as can be, snorting the salt air.

"Seems like Elsa's keeping Jason plenty busy while his wife is away," Celia remarks.

"Oh, she is. Everyone is, keeping an eye on him, keeping him fed."

"He and Maris have no children?"

"No, it's just the two of them. They're so cute together, a perfect match."

"I don't know what makes some marriages work, and others not." And what surprises Celia is that her next thought isn't a thought at all; the surprise is that she's comfortable enough with her beach friend to actually *say* it. "I'm still getting over my failed marriage, and it's been months."

"At least you had no children?" Lauren gives her a sympathetic smile as they continue along the winding beach road. "They take it so hard."

"No, no kids."

"So how are you holding up? I know a couple summers ago, Kyle and I hit a rough patch, and I looked at duplexes, considering moving out with our two little ones. But I felt so depressed."

"I think what's hard is that me and Ben—that's my ex—we stopped caring to even try." Until now, Celia's only talked about her divorce with her best friend from back home. Funny how that reluctance has been fading away like the morning sea mist. "We didn't argue, or disagree. We just grew apart."

"That actually might be what kept me and Kyle together. We cared enough to seriously keep trying—boy, did we try—and it worked." They pass a rustic rowboat leaning on its side in a cottage front yard. Someone filled it with dirt, and added petunias and red geraniums, with vines draping over the boat sides.

"That's my cottage!" Celia reaches into her bag for a slip of paper with an address on it. "Yes," she says, stopping in the street and eyeing the blue two-story colonial with a screened side porch.

"You're staying here?"

"No, it's next on my list to stage, and I couldn't find it before." Celia walks across the yard to the front door, thinking she'll change its paint color and add a wreath. "Showed up when I least expected it."

"Kind of like your new summer romance?" Lauren asks from behind her.

"What?"

Lauren waggles a paint-spattered finger at her. "I saw Sal kiss you the other night, dancing on the beach. So are you two seeing each other?"

"No! Oh no, I only just met him." As she says it, she puts her code in the lockbox. "I mean," Celia continues while retrieving the cottage key, "he seems so nice and everything … good-looking, fun to be with. And that's my red flag—a guy like that is still single? It's hard to believe, so what's his flaw?"

"No flaw," Lauren says. She snaps off a marigold blossom from the rowboat planter and tucks it behind her ear. "It's the Street!" she declares, finger-quoting the words while spinning around, her maxi dress flaring at her legs.

"Oh, that *Street.*" Celia laughs and sits on the stoop, patting it for Lauren to join her. "If it's a flaw, I still don't know. But it could be."

"Now wait a minute," Lauren says in all seriousness, sitting beside her on the step. "Give him a chance. Because lots of love happens at this little beach. Actually, everyone you've met got together right here."

"Everyone?"

Lauren nods gravely. "It's a proven fact that when you drive under that railroad trestle *alone*, you will one day leave here with either a ring, or a baby, *or* a broken heart. Something. Please remember that."

"Jason and Maris? Met *here*?"

"Oh, yes. In their teens. We all summered here as kids. Some families owned a cottage, others rented. A few, who we were totally jealous of, lived at the beach year-round. So back to Maris and Jason. Well, after *years* of going separate ways for college and careers, they reunited and had their wedding reception right on the boardwalk last August. It was a beautiful night, with all the Mason jar candles and twinkling lights. So," she says, "just be aware that there's something in this sweet salt air."

"You and Kyle, too? You met here?"

"Well, yeah ..."

"Wait a minute! You're hiding something. What's your secret, girlfriend?"

Lauren gives a small smile and checks her watch. "I've really got to get to Elsa's, she's waiting for me," Lauren says while standing. "Another time, maybe."

Still sitting on the stoop, Celia studies her new friend heading toward the road, a flower behind her ear, and now a sadness in her eyes.

"I'm telling you, there's so much history here, Celia. You have no idea," Lauren calls back. "But we're all about as tangled up as that seaweed running along the beach."

~

At The Sand Bar that evening, the waitress lifts a pitcher of beer and four tall glasses off her tray. When she starts to pour, Jason stops her. "No worries. I got it." She nods and takes the empty tray to the bar.

"So how do you keep the flame alive?" Sal asks as Jason fills his glass.

After a moment's silence, Jason glances at him. "You asking me?"

"Yes. You know, with your wife gone. How do you keep the flame alive?"

Jason considers him while leaning over the table to fill Kyle's glass now. What is it about this guy, that he can smoothly put a question like that out there and no one blinks an eye? He looks at Kyle, who shrugs just enough for Jason to notice. "Not that it's any of your business, Salvatore, but my wife and I are doing fine in that department, don't worry. After our wedding plans last year, we lost a lot of ground at work, so Maris is kicking her career into overdrive for a while." Jason fills Nick's glass, then his own. "We're both busy catching up this year, trying to get ahead."

"Yeah, but you know what they say." Kyle takes a long swallow of his brew. "All work and no play makes Jason a dull boy."

"Shit," Jason says, leaning back in the dark booth and eyeing his best man. "From you, too, I'm getting this interrogation?"

Sal pulls his beer close. "Come on, you and Maris are *newlyweds*, man. You should be burning up the sheets." With that, he tips his glass to Jason's.

"I gave you some good advice last year, remember?" Kyle raises an eyebrow at Jason. "When your wife gets back, take her up to Little Beach. Talk about curing what ails you. A little skinny-dipping goes a long way."

"What?" Sal interrupts. "What's this Little Beach? There's more to this place?"

"Little Beach, it's up the path through the woods," Nick explains. "Why? You got someone you want to head up there with?"

"Won't the bull be calling you back, DeLuca?" Kyle asks. "Seems like you should be charging forward like that three-and-a-half-ton bronze bull in your city, making money for good folks out there."

"Careful now." Sal sits up straight and points at Kyle across the table. "That charging bull was designed by an Italian fellow."

"Yeah, we're all paisans here," Jason tells him. "Relax."

"I'm taking the summer off, anyway," Sal explains, reaching for a handful of pretzels. "Helping my mother start her business."

"You bullshitting?" Jason asks. It's warm in the dark bar, and he wonders why no one's opened the door for some fresh air. "I still can't believe any employer gives that much time off." With that, he leaves their booth, gives a whistle to the bartender and points to the door to which he's headed, motioning that he's going to prop it open.

"Wall Street waits for no one, guy," Kyle is saying when Jason returns to their booth. "My guess is there's a line of young pups fresh out of business school, pulling at the leash for your job." Kyle slides the pretzel basket across the table and tosses a few in his mouth. "What gives?"

"What gives is that I'm paying my mother back. She's done so much. You know, when I was growing up, she opened her boutique in Milan really just to be available to me."

"Oh, come on. That's why you're here?" Kyle asks.

Nick squints across the table at Sal. "Cue the violins."

"Hey, watch it," Sal warns. "She lost a lot in her life … her sister, her relationship with her nieces. Not to mention that her husband, my father, died a few years ago. So now that she's finally reunited with the family she loves," Sal clasps Jason's shoulder, "I'm repaying her."

"Well, aren't you a nice guy? But you're also full of shit," Nick says while still eyeing Sal.

"I don't buy it, either," Kyle adds.

Sal holds up both his hands. "That's the truth, boys. And if the firm lets me go, well … do you have any idea how much money I have?"

"I'd rather not know." Kyle tips his glass up for the last few drops, then sets it down hard. "Just pretend you're one of us. Speaking of which, need a part-time summer job?"

"At your diner?" Sal asks.

"Absolutely. After the day you put in hustling tables and bringing in business, it's the least I can do to buy you a drink tonight." Kyle touches his now-empty glass to Sal's. "So can I put you on the payroll?"

Jason watches this closely. "Really?" he asks Kyle. "Sal's going to *work* at The Driftwood Café? The Wall Street mogul is going to schlep around, with you?"

"Listen, DeLuca," Kyle tells Sal. "I had a ten percent increase in business today. The tip jar was overflowing. You can fill in on staff vacations."

"On one condition." Sal leans forward.

"Careful, Kyle," Jason says. "Everything's a deal with this guy. He's not going from white collar to blue unless there's a serious payoff."

Sal holds Kyle's gaze. "Show me your books. I want to see your latest quarterlies."

"Hey, that's qualified information," Kyle answers, glancing to the bar when someone there calls his name.

Jason turns to see a woman with heavily lined brown eyes—eyes that he can't forget—set her gaze on Kyle, throwing him a flirty wave from her barstool. Having walked in on her and Kyle together last summer, Jason gives Kyle a warning kick beneath the table. Still, Kyle hitches his head to her with a discreet hello, then barely shrugs at Jason before turning back to Sal, who is now turning toward the bar to see what just went down. "And what would you need to know my numbers for?" Kyle asks him.

"Wait, what's going on with her?" Nick motions toward the woman.

"Seriously," Sal says. "Not a bad-looking little dame there."

"Listen, we're talking business or I'm out of here." Kyle starts to stand.

"Okay, okay," Sal tells him with another glance back at the bar action. "I saw some places at your diner where you can increase traffic *and* those book numbers."

Kyle slowly sits again. "How?"

"Listen, your eatery is filled with tourists this time of year. And tourists want souvenirs." Sal points to the faded concert tee Jason is wearing. "They want to *prove* they went somewhere. Where the hell are your diner T-shirts? Even the waitstaff could wear them. It's free advertising, man."

"I'd buy one," Nick pipes in. "You should get on that, Bradford."

"What else?" Kyle asks with suspicion.

"Nope. Got to see your financials first, then we'll talk business."

Kyle squints at him for a long second. "Okay." He finally reaches across the table to shake Sal's hand. "Stop by tomorrow before I open up and we've got a deal."

"Whoa, whoa. Not so fast," Jason says, setting his drink down so quickly, some splashes out as he reaches over and stops the handshake. "You don't have to work at the diner. I'm swamped. You interested in a summer internship? I'll keep you busy prepping a cottage teardown *and* designing your mother's inn. You come by *my* place in the morning and shadow me. See if you'd like it." He extends his hand to shake.

"Stop the presses, man." Nick reaches out and prevents the handshake. "What about me? Don't you want to ride shotgun in a security car, get the lowdown on Stony Point rule-breakers?" He extends his hand to Sal.

"Okay, DeLuca." Jason divvies up what's left of the pitcher into their glasses. "What's it going to be? Diner, Barlow Architecture, or guard duty?"

"Oh, no. You guys decide where I'm working tomorrow." Sal sits back and raises his glass to them.

"Golf cart race?" Nick asks while scratching the side of his chin. "You'll work for the winner."

"Hey, guy." Jason reaches over and gives Nick's chin a quick rub. "You're looking very sensitive tonight. Where's the goatee?"

"Oh, Jesus. That new commissioner's such a prick. Had to shave off the *scruff*, as he called it. All the guards must be clean-shaven, to set a good impression. Says we can't be looking like hoodlums patrolling."

"No way." Kyle rubs his own chin. "He's polishing you up sweet, like a pretty boy now."

Nick shoves Kyle hard in the booth. "Shut up, asshole. Now we racing golf carts or not? I'll whoop you but good."

"Nah," Kyle says, finishing his beer. "It's late, and I'm beat. I've got to get home."

"Darts?" Jason asks, motioning to the back room of the bar.

"It's too warm in here for darts." With that, Kyle lifts his arm to his forehead. "Let's go outside."

"Outside?" But Jason sees it, as Kyle stands. The pressure's on and so is Kyle's sweating—clear evidence that he wants to win Sal, bad.

Kyle sets his hands on the table and leans over it, saying with utter solemnity, "I've got Evan's Wiffle bat in the truck. Whoever hits the ball farthest wins the Italian."

"Evan," Sal says, standing too. "Who's this Evan?"

"That's Kyle's son," Jason tells him as they leave the booth.

"Evan," Kyle explains while pulling a handful of bills from his wallet and leaving them on the table. "He's eight years old and loves baseball."

"No shit." Sal finishes his beer while standing, then hurries behind the others toward the propped-open door. "You've got a *son*, that's awesome. Someone to follow in your footsteps. Good for you."

"He's a great kid, and won't mind if we use his gear." Kyle heads outside and down the bar's few stairs to the parking lot. "Let's take a swing at the ball and decide who gets you tomorrow, once and for all."

And Jason knows, as Kyle grabs a plastic ball and yellow bat from his truck bed. He knows as Sal takes his position on a pseudo-pitcher's mound at the far end of the lot, as Nick crouches to catch, as Kyle stands the bat against his legs—stretching his arms, twisting his waist—then taps the bat to the ground before getting into swing position, the bat circling up over his head. Yes, what Jason knows is this: All baseball hell is about to break loose.

eleven

"I LOST."

Lauren opens her eyes and turns to Kyle beside her in bed. His arm is flung over his face, blocking the early morning sunlight. He slept with no shirt on, wearing only his pajama bottoms. "Who got him?" she asks while touching his shoulder. "Nick?"

"Jason. Hit that damn ball right out of the parking lot." With that, he gets up and walks over to the window air conditioning unit, punching the button twice before it kicks on. "It's hot in here."

"What time is it?" Lauren asks, and even though she's dozing again, nothing stops the late-June sunlight from brightening the bedroom in their little Cape Cod in Eastfield … the *east*-facing master bedroom, with persistent sunrays reminding them every morning.

"Five o'clock."

The mattress shifts as Kyle settles on the bed again. When he's quiet for a few seconds, Lauren manages to squint an eye open to see what he's up to. It's just what she thought: scrolling through the real-estate app on his cell phone.

"New notification, Ell. Something came up for sale at the beach. Four bedrooms, so space for an art studio."

"Nice." But she can't help it, her eyes flutter closed again. "Go back to sleep, it's early still."

"Only one bath. Huh. Maybe Jason can add something."

She swears she fell asleep then, for the briefest of moments, until Kyle's voice starts again. "I booked a showing, for this morning."

That's all it takes to fully wake her. "I can't." Everything on the day's itinerary runs through her mind, starting with a quick trip to Gull Island Lighthouse to get inspired for Elsa's stair mural. So she sits up, straightening her striped satin sleep-shirt and running a hand through her mussed hair. "I have to drop the kids at Mom's, then catch a ferry to Gull Island. And you have to work."

Kyle's already tapping a number as she says it. "Jerry?" he asks into the phone while closely watching her. "Yeah, sorry to wake you. Can you cover for me this morning?" In the quiet pause, he shrugs at Lauren, then says, "Oh man, great." After talking the details, he leans over and sets his cell phone on the nightstand. "I need to live where there's a sea breeze cooling me off," he tells Lauren, then collapses back on the bed, pressing his arm on his damp forehead.

Yup, and now *his* itinerary begins when he glances at Lauren, reaches to her and gently twists a strand of her hair. "I'll go with you to Gull Island, after we look at that house."

"You're playing hooky?" Okay, so she's all huff, but no resistance. Not with the way Kyle's stroking her hair, then sliding his fingers with a feather touch along her arm. He takes her wrist and tugs her closer as he turns on his side. "If we're looking at a house first," Lauren whispers while sliding lower in the bed, "then we're really running late." Her hands glide up Kyle's back when he slips up her sleep-shirt and moves over her so that, yes, she gets it: This is *first* on his itinerary. "No time for fooling around," she adds after he kisses her, then nuzzles her neck. But her words barely make it out when he presses two fingers on her lips.

"There's always time." He drags his fingers down her chin, along her neck and to her breasts. "Come on, two in the shower this morning?"

"Kyle!" She sits up and grabs the robe from the foot of the bed.

"What?"

They're so behind schedule, all she can do is swat him with the robe before slipping it on and getting off the bed.

"Oh yeah," he says, never taking his eyes off her as he slowly follows her toward the shower. "That feels good."

It's the yellow color that does it. That gets Jason to look twice while checking his voicemail messages. It's the color that gets him to put his cell phone on the kitchen counter and walk to the slider with his morning coffee. But it's what's beneath the color that gets him nearly sputtering on a mouthful of the hot brew. It's Sal, wearing a bright yellow hard hat, walking up the sloping driveway. Jason gives a whistle. "Back here," he calls out through the slider screen, watching this Wall Street dude wearing serious construction boots clomp through his yard.

"I'm all yours today," Sal says walking in and greeting a tail-wagging, prancing Madison. "You won me, fair and square."

Which gets Jason to shake his head and drag a hand over his mouth, down his chin.

"What? Won't these work?" Sal extends a foot and shows off his new boots. "Genuine leather, with a nice padded collar on top. I went with the darker brown so they wouldn't show too much dirt."

But it's the tool belt that finally gets Jason to laugh. "You're just *shadowing* me today, DeLuca. And I'm the architect, not the site foreman. What's with the gear?"

"Hell, you might as well put me to work. The hardware store opened at the crack of dawn, so I stopped in and got my supplies." He lifts a hammer from a tool-belt loop, then drops it back in place. "You're the boss."

It's apparent Sal means business, what with the measuring tape, screw drivers, chalk line, punch, wrenches, and God knows what else he tucked into each leather pocket and loop of the spiffy tool belt strapped over his cargo shorts.

"Listen, Sal. There's this thing called the Hammer Law here. No heavy construction is allowed in the summer months."

"None?"

"None." Jason can only hide his grin behind another sip from his coffee mug.

"No shit. Isn't it your busiest time?"

"Well, yeah. But lots of vacationing happens at Stony Point, and folks don't want to hear a racket. So you can at least lose the hat."

"Damn." Sal lifts off the hard hat and gives it a sharp knock with his knuckles. "Was looking forward to trying it out."

"Sorry. Hey, I have some last-minute things to do before we head out." Jason reaches for his cell phone. "So grab a coffee and make yourself at home."

"I'll pass, not big on caffeine. Wall Street gets me hopped up enough." Sal snaps his fingers for Madison to follow him as he leans into the kitchen doorway and surveys the house. When he eventually spots the jukebox in the living room alcove, he turns around with a question on his face.

"It's from Foley's back room," Jason explains while waiting on hold for his construction foreman. "That's the bona fide real deal, from the good old days."

"What's it doing here?" As he asks, Sal's drawn to the record selection, his hand brushing over the glass.

"Last summer, when Foley's was still on the market, everyone hated to lose that piece of machinery. So they bought it and made it a wedding gift for me and Maris."

"Now that's one event I'm sorry I missed," Sal says right as Jason's phone call resumes.

And minutes later, it's the silver color that catches Jason's eye. That gets him to end his call and slip his phone in his pocket. That brings back bittersweet memories. "Belonged to my father," he says as Sal returns carrying a vintage pewter hourglass. "It's been on the mantel for decades now."

Sal sets the hourglass on the kitchen island and sits on a stool. "What a great piece. The patina's magnificent."

It is, Jason has to admit. Over the years, the pewter's darkened, its shadows telling their own story of life in this cottage. "When my father's tour in Vietnam was over, he bought this place for the peace of it." Jason motions around the room. "Mom was so glad he was safely home, she had that hourglass filled special with the finest Stony Point sand, then gave it to him as a gift." He reaches over and turns the hourglass so the sand grains begin flowing into the bottom bulb. "An hourglass is all about time passing, and after what my father'd just come out of in the jungle, well … This signified every single minute they'd now have together, at the beach, by the sea."

Sal pulls the hourglass closer, running his hand along the pewter and studying the grains of sand silently falling to the bottom. "Fascinating," he says, almost under his breath.

It's happened to Jason, too, the way those falling specks of sand entrance you. There's something powerful about them. He pours another coffee into a travel mug before grabbing his keys. "It's late, we better get moving. I have to make a quick stop in my studio."

"Close by?" Sal asks as he turns the hourglass again, obviously taken with it.

"Not far." A sharp whistle gets the dog running as Jason opens the slider. "Let's go," he says to Madison while pointing to the barn out back. Weathered fishing buoys hanging on the outside of it add a splash of faded color to its brown, rough-hewn walls. "One of the things my father did when he moved here was to make the barn his workshop," Jason says to Sal as they cross the backyard. "He was a mason and had lots of tools and equipment."

When Jason opens the barn doors, the faint scent of old wood dust and tools meets him, as though it's a permanent part of the structure. "I finished renovating it last year. This is my studio here," he says, motioning to the vast downstairs. Sunlight streams in through the skylights; one wall is covered with framed photographs of his redesigned beach cottages and seaside homes; further in are his drafting tables and computer desk, beside which a few engineering scales weigh down recent sketches. "And Maris works upstairs when she doesn't have to go to Manhattan." He nods to the large loft where mannequins wear various blue jean pieces, and bolts of denim are stacked against a wall, and inspiration easels are opened beside her sketching desk.

Sal takes it all in with a low whistle as he walks the wide-planked barn floors. "That's one big-ass desk you've got there." His work boots lightly thump along while he checks out the loft. "Quite an operation going on up there, too."

"Definitely. Maris is director of women's denim for Saybrooks Department Store."

"What a gig. Thus the European inspiration trip? She designing a new line?"

"Something like that," Jason tells him. And he notices Sal's raised eyebrow giving away his awe. But as Sal talks, the first place that actually draws him is the wall of shelves filled with Neil's journals.

"Your brother's?" Sal asks with a glance back.

"That's right."

Just like his father's hourglass, the timeworn journals and photo albums intrigue Sal. He chooses a brown leather one, opens it and brushes through the sandy pages. "You weren't kidding when you said Neil liked to pen his thoughts." He looks over at Jason, then at the pages again. "Incredible stuff, here."

"He had a way with words, Sal. But for now, I need to grab my duffel and get going. Lots of stops today. First up, checking in with the foreman on the teardown on the hill."

Sal gently sets the journal back in its place and follows behind Jason. "Hey, man. What's up with the moose head?"

Hell, that mounted head hung on the wall at the top of the stairs—the moose's massive antlers reaching to either side—means the world to him. Maris pats its nose whenever she passes it, as though it's some sort of good-luck charm. "Long story, Sal. For another day, over a good stiff drink." Jason grabs his duffel and holds the door open.

"Damn," Sal says as he walks outside into the bright sunlight, his tool belt creaking. "Lots of stories I'm waiting to hear from you beach folks."

~

"The houses are really close." Kyle bends and peers out the dining room window. "The neighbors can literally see right in."

"Now remember, this is primarily a beach community, with many seasonal cottages on *small* yards," their realtor begins. From where she stands across the room, there's a hopeful lilt to her voice that Kyle suspects is trying to keep them upbeat. "Not too many year-round homes at Stony Point, though we have been seeing more conversions from cottage to home lately," she continues. "So keep an open mind."

"Plus it has four bedrooms," Lauren reminds him when she approaches the window and winces at the sight of the neighboring cottage. "I can have a studio. And three of the bedrooms are upstairs, so Evan won't have to sleep alone downstairs, like at home."

Finally, they make their way up the narrow staircase to the second floor. Kyle's been in enough of these shanties with their knotty-pine paneling and exposed-beam ceilings and stuffy air to make an educated guess as to what they'll find.

"There's only one bath," the realtor says over her shoulder. "But it's upstairs and central to the bedrooms."

So Kyle hooks a sharp left into that one bathroom—and it's just like he thought. He stops in front of the claw-foot tub. "There's no shower."

Lauren stands beside him, silently, but meets his frustrated gaze when he glances down at her.

"Well." The realtor joins them beside the white tub, motioning to the faucet handles. "It's got one of those hand-held numbers."

"Here's the real test." Kyle slides the wraparound shower curtain to the side, climbs into the tub and squeezes down to sit, his arms tightly holding his folded-up knees. Then, and only then, he looks up at the realtor.

"You have to keep an open mind!" she insists.

"No good. This won't work." He unfolds himself and stands to get out of the tub.

"Jason can design a bath downstairs, or maybe redo this one." Lauren takes his hand to help him out. "He can probably tack on an outdoor shower, too."

"You know someone who does handy work?" the realtor asks as she moves on to the too-small bedrooms with sloped ceilings and drafty, single-pane windows.

"Kyle's good friend, Jason. Barlow Architecture?"

"Oh, sure. Lucky you. He seems very in-demand with all his yard signs I see at remodeled cottages." Their realtor opens a tiny closet door.

"Lauren, this house is already at the top of our budget." Actually, Kyle's not sure he'd even want Jason to see this overpriced shack. "And Jason doesn't work for free."

"Maybe we really can't afford to move yet," Lauren says as they all tromp down the narrow stairs.

Once outside, Kyle can't miss the moldy shingles on the front of the house. He touches them, then steps back and surveys the roof.

"I know it can be discouraging, but you have to think about the potential." The realtor joins his gaze at the dated roof. "I can show you one that recently came up, but it's not in the system yet. It's over on Hillcrest Road, not too far from the cottage you're renting next month."

"I don't know." From everything Kyle's seen, it's hard to summon any hope. Not until Lauren nudges him, and he reluctantly agrees. "It'd have to be quick, we're catching the ferry to Gull Island Lighthouse."

"Okay!" The realtor returns the cottage key to the lockbox. "But there's one thing. It's a three-bedroom."

When the slightest groan comes from Lauren, Kyle closes his eyes and shakes his head.

"Wait! There's a side porch you could convert into Lauren's … *studio*, is it?" their eternally optimistic realtor asks. "Just keep an open mind!"

twelve

As she picks up a silvery shell from the high tide line, sand slips through Celia's fingers. It's just like the summer, she thinks, slipping away one day at a time—a week of days having passed already since Elsa announced her inn's name. The thought gets her to scoop up a handful of the sand and slowly spread her fingers to let it first trickle, then stream out of her hold. She's only got two months of days here before it'll be time to drive beneath that train trestle to leave.

And according to Lauren, it'll be with one of three things. A piece of green sea glass glints beneath a retreating wave, so Celia gingerly picks that up, dips it in the sea and swishes it three times, saying with each swish, "A ring, a baby, or a broken heart." After dropping the glass in her sand pail, she starts walking along the beach again. The morning sun is warm, and the beach is crowded; families and guests are arriving for the Fourth of July holiday weekend. Children stand in the shallow waves wearing their floaties; colorful umbrellas line the beach like a row of swirling lollipops; sand chairs sit at the water's edge, the sunbathers staying cool, seaside.

When Celia ambles to the far end of the beach, past the swimming area and the lone gray cottage on the sand, she adds a seagull feather to the pail. The water is calm here, where the beach curves like a crescent moon along the stone jetty. It looks like a good spot to sit on a big rock and soak up some sun. Until a puttering sound interrupts the lapping waves reaching her toes.

"Ahoy, Celia!" a man's voice calls out.

She turns and squints against the sun at the people on the beach, but doesn't spot anyone motioning to her.

"Where've you been lately?" the voice asks, but that puttering motorboat engine muffles it. "Over here!"

When she turns again, someone waving catches her eye—waving from the little boat in the water, moving along parallel to her beach walk.

"Oh, Sal!" she says, shielding her eyes. "Hi there."

Sal shuts off the engine in what looks like a rowboat, floating not too far offshore. "Haven't seen you around. No boardwalk strolls lately?"

The way he says it, Celia wonders if maybe he's been hanging out on the boardwalk, *waiting* to see her there. "Time just gets away from me sometimes," she tells him while tucking her flip-flops into the pail and wading out in the water. "I had to finish Summer Winds, and now I'm on to the next cottage to stage."

The boat drifts further away, so Sal lifts the engine out of the water and grabs a couple of wooden paddles, dipping them in and rowing toward shore. "Catch anything?" he asks, nodding to her sand pail.

"Catch?" Celia glances down at the seashells she's collected.

"Were you crabbing? On the rocks there?" He points to the jetty where a few people are huddled, dropping their crabbing line into the shallow water.

"No! Oh, no crabs. This is staging stuff." Celia shields her eyes again. "I'm looking for seashells, sea glass, that sort of thing." Tipping the pail his way, she wades deeper to show him.

Sal paddles the boat closer at the same time Celia tiptoes in his direction, careful not to get her frayed denim cutoffs wet. The boat's paint is faded, with streaks of natural wood showing through, though its hull seems to be brick red.

"Do you have a few minutes?" he asks. "Care to go for a ride?"

"A ride?" Celia looks over her shoulder to the beach, then at her pail. How easy it would be to decline. To say she's busy working on a deadline, before waving him off and heading back to her cottage, alone. But when he lifts his sunglasses to the top of his head, well, maybe it wouldn't be easy saying no, after all. Not to those dark, twinkling eyes, to that smile, to those upturned hands. She slightly shrugs at herself, a little confused about this guy from the Street wanting to putter around on Long Island Sound. With her.

"I'll paddle in and meet you, so you can climb aboard."

By the time she gets to the shallows, Sal's there—standing in the boat, reaching for her and giving a hoist as she steps up over the edge. "Oops, careful." His hands grab her waist as the boat rocks. "Okay, now?"

"Yes!" Celia says, throwing him a quick smile. The first thing she notices when she looks back at him are the whiskers on his unshaven face, and his dark hair wavy in the damp sea air. Then, well then she tucks her hair behind an ear and looks around, left to right. The rowboat's interior is plain: planked bench seats, unfinished wood, a small outboard engine. Barefoot, she moves carefully aside with her arms outstretched to keep her balance before dropping on a seat, her knees bent close in front of her as Sal sits on the bench facing her. Their knees nearly touch; they're both quiet. Though he's barefoot, too, his leather boat shoes sit beneath his bench. It's still quiet when he dips the paddles in to get them to deeper water. When she catches his eye, he hitches his head toward her, smiling.

"Nice, no? Being on the water?"

"I didn't realize you had a boat," Celia says.

There's another silent second when he puts his sunglasses back on and finagles the paddles to turn the boat around and head it away from the beach. "This old rowboat came with Foley's, actually, when my mother bought the place. The previous owners had two years left on the lease of their marina slip, behind the boardwalk?"

"Sure," Celia says. "I love watching the boats docked there. They're all so pretty, bobbing in the water."

Sal nods. "So my mother showed me the boat this weekend. It was on a rusty trailer behind the cottage. A fellow on the construction crew helped me get it in the water, and I've been taking a spin here and there, especially after working with Jason these past few days. Man, he is one busy architect." He gives the paddles a good pull, and the Sound's gentle waves splash along the wooden sides.

"What does Jason have you do? You're not trained in architecture."

The paddles drip seawater as Sal lifts them and pauses. "I pretty much tag along, kind of like a kid brother. We went to a salvage company to purchase cast-iron stair railings, and spent time reviewing a teardown prep with his contractor." He nods toward a dilapidated cottage on the hill overlooking the other end of the beach. "Man, is he pumped about the new design that'll go up in its place."

It isn't until the boat reaches deeper water that Sal drops the engine and starts it up. They move along slowly, and Celia dips her fingers over the edge to feel the sea, dribbling some on her arms to keep cool in the bright sunshine. And as though he notices, Sal turns the boat and they head back into the boat basin, putter right through it and float beneath a low stone bridge, onto the saltwater channel leading to the shaded lagoon. There, among the swaying marsh grasses, he shuts off the engine and paddles again. The boat seems like it's on a cloud, moving slowly and smoothly around each bend. A white egret hunts on a nearby bank where the water is shallow, and further out, summer homes overlook the serene spot.

"This is so relaxing." Celia takes a long breath. "Look. There's my place." She points out the silver-shingled cottage with a tall peak on the side. "It belongs to my friends back home, George and Amy."

"It's the second one over, right?" Sal asks. "With the big deck?"

"Yes. I love sitting there. Sometimes the swans actually swim past."

Sal paddles into an inlet leading closer. "When I didn't see you around for a few days, I thought maybe you'd left Stony Point. So I actually walked by your cottage," he says, nodding to the back deck as he paddles. The oars creak; the water drips when they lift out of the lagoon. "I heard someone inside playing a guitar?"

"That was me." Celia tucks her hair behind an ear and gives a small smile. "I like to strum a tune."

"It sounded nice, hearing that near the sea."

"You should've knocked! Don't be a stranger." She looks over at the deck, seeing the empty Adirondack chairs, the small table. "I was sitting right there, with the fire pit going, playing a few songs."

The boat drifts past, so Sal reverses the paddles to keep her cottage in sight. "You are a woman of many secrets, Celia Gray."

"Well, I'm not that good. Mostly I write my own little songs, that's all." The midday sun is warm now, even here on the calm water. But the birds are busy, flitting among the tall grasses, and a kingfisher warbles from a low tree branch in her cottage backyard. "Never mind about me, what about you! You must be about ready to get back to the Street?"

There's a pause then, when she looks more closely at Sal as he lifts a paddle and glances to her cottage. His forehead is lined with perspiration, and he seems winded from the constant rowing against the lagoon current. "Let's drop anchor," he says. To do so, he walks past her to the front of the boat, touching her shoulder as he does, before releasing the anchor into the lagoon waters. "You okay here?" he asks while sitting on his bench again, this time turned sideways toward the cottage.

"Of course, it's perfect." And before it can get too quiet again, she clears her throat and presses him. "So you were telling me about going back to New York?"

"Well, it won't be anytime soon, Celia. I've got lots of vacation weeks, and want to help my mother get this inn thing off the ground."

"That's really nice of you, Sal. Her heart seems set on turning Foley's into something wonderful."

"Which she will do, I have no doubt. Her drive is amazing. I'm putting together an extensive business plan and advising her financially. Plus, I'm just taking it easy for now. Started to feel really burnt out, so this is good. I can telecommute, get in some conference calls, do market research. You know, keep my feet wet, so to speak."

The boat drifts, pulling against the anchor line. Celia glances from the cottage, back to Sal, who leans forward then, a sunhat in his hand. It's denim, with a patchwork fabric on the underside of the floppy brim.

"Here, you're getting a sunburn." He touches her cheek, then gently tugs the hat on her head and tucks her hair back. It's when his hand touches the side of her neck, brushing wisps of her hair, that he stops moving, though.

And he doesn't move again—she feels it, that stillness that lasts until she shifts her gaze to the lagoon beyond and then straight back to him. When she does, his head tips slightly, as though he's trying to read her, before he leans close and kisses her beneath that floppy hat brim. Around them, the kingfisher trills again, and a fish makes a small splash in the calm water, and the anchor line softly creaks. Celia hears it, while beneath her hat she feels his fingers tangle in those wisps of hair, feels him pull her to him, feels his hands embracing her neck, his mouth soft on hers at first, until it grows more insistent, just for a moment or two.

Until he pulls away, his thumb stroking her face as he looks only at her eyes—not at the cottage behind them, not at the egret taking flight, not at the water subtly shifting the boat. And while still looking at her eyes, his fingers fix the hair strands he'd mussed, tenderly combing through them.

"Word on the beach street," he whispers to her in their wooden rowboat, "is that Kyle has some bottle rockets for the Fourth of July, after a cookout at Jason's."

Still looking, she notices. His eyes don't waver one bit from hers. "Would you like to go with me?" he asks.

"Oh, Sal. I'm headed home to Addison for the weekend." She takes a long breath and looks over at her cottage on the banks of the lagoon. "Because I'm not sure I'm ready for another big get-together here. So I thought I'd lie low. My friends George and Amy … the ones I'm cottage-sitting for," she says, nodding to her summer home-away-from-home, "they're having a barbecue, next door to where I live."

He leans back then, but his dark eyes stay locked on hers. "Would you believe that I've never been to a July Fourth barbecue? You know, in a shady yard with a smoking grill, a big picnic table covered with macaroni salad and deviled eggs. I've always stayed in the city." And then, he simply touches her arm for a second.

"Sal." Her gaze stays on that one spot of her tanned arm that he touched, until she finally looks at him. "Why are you interested in me?"

"Is there a reason I shouldn't be?"

"Well, no. It's just …" Celia turns on her bench seat, and her foot clips her seashell pail, which tips over and spills shells on the boat's bottom. At the same time she bends to scoop them back in, Sal reaches down and picks up a few shells, along with the one piece of green sea glass. When he reaches his hand over to drop them in the pail she holds, he leans in and kisses her again. No hands this time, no feel of his fingers tangled in her hair. Scarcely a kiss as light as the breeze lifting off the salt water. "I wouldn't mind being at that barbecue *with* you, Celia."

Her eyes drop closed as she smiles and shakes her head, just for a moment. Then she touches his unshaven face. "That would be really nice."

"Okay, it's a date." He moves to the bow of the boat and pulls the anchor in, then takes his seat again and picks up the paddles. "I'm helping out at Kyle's diner tomorrow, but he closes early on Fridays to do that fishing thing with Jason. So we can get an early start on Saturday." As he rows away, he tugs her patchwork hat. "What time should I be at your cottage?"

—

Her laugh is short-lived. First, Elsa reads the back of the postcard, which elicits a smile. *This coffeepot made me think of all the coffee that you, Maris and I have poured together this past year. So many sweet, sweet cups of java, along with beautiful words and seaside memories. Love and miss you, Eva, Matt and Tay*

Before she flips the postcard over, Elsa runs a finger across the words, truly missing her nieces. With Maris in Europe and soon out on the West Coast, and Eva and Matt taking their daughter on a cross-country RV trip, things are awfully quiet around here. So she turns the postcard and sees a soaring water tower against a backdrop of sky somewhere in the midwest. The funny part that makes her laugh, though, is that the water tower has been designed in the shape of the biggest coffeepot she's ever seen!

But her smile and laughter and longings and reminiscing are gone in a flash. All it takes is for Elsa to tear open the one envelope in her mailbox. The one from the dreaded new beach commissioner. The one requesting details on her recent fence delivery. The one clearly stating that other than living hedges, no fences are allowed at Stony Point. The commissioner goes on to note the number of picket fence sections delivered to Elsa's inn, and reminds her that they have to pass board approval for installation. So far, they have not, and the fine is two hundred fifty dollars.

"Ohh!" Elsa flips the paper over, then back again. "Oh, oh … damn it!" She looks at her cottage wrapped in scaffolding and surrounded by sawhorses, then rushes inside for her tote and golf cart key so she can drive straight to that commissioner's office and give him a piece of her mind. Of course, with the strictly enforced, non-negotiable, fifteen-mile-per-hour speed limit on these roads, she'd probably get there faster on foot. But heck, driving slowly gives her time to call the commissioner's new rules and regulations every foul name in the book.

When she arrives at his office—if you'd call it that; the white, flat-roofed modular unit is nothing more than a gussied-up trailer, with its sliding windows and four steps leading to a steel entry door—she stops. Then she gives two sharp raps on that industrial door before walking right in, the legal notice gripped in one hand, her keys in the other.

"Is Mr. Raines here?"

The man sitting at the reception desk wears a gray button-down shirt with the sleeves casually cuffed. His salt-and-pepper hair is more silver than black, and faint circles shadow his, okay, his blue eyes.

"In a sec, I'm on the phone," he says, holding up a finger as he turns away to finish his conversation.

When he hangs up, after about three huffs from Elsa, one of which might have included a stamp of her leather-sandal-clad foot, the phone immediately rings again. But she doesn't give him a chance to answer it. "I'm tired of these fines." Elsa slaps the notice on his metal desk. "I'm not breaking ordinances. You issue these violations to me without even learning the details."

"Mrs. …"

"DeLuca. It's DeLuca. With a *capital* L, so maybe I should fine you for not spelling my name correctly on your form. I mean, it is a *legality*, after all."

He throws her a quick smile, and what? Is that a twinkle in his eye? It's hard to tell beyond her seething anger.

"Mrs. DeLuca, with a capital L." He glances down at the violation. "Since the fence has not actually been installed yet, the best I can do is reduce your fine to one twenty-five. But you have to petition the Board of Governors to repeal it fully."

With that, he leaves the reception desk and goes into a small office off the visitor area. Elsa hears a printer flipping and printing pages. "Complete this petition request form," he's saying as he returns to the lobby of his pathetic beach trailer, "and return it in time for the next board review."

"But I'm telling you right here and now. Most of the fence is decorative, to complement my hydrangea landscaping. Why do I have to write it all out?"

"I'm sorry, but that's Stony Point procedure. And the rules are the rules." His hand still holds out the form in her direction. "This way you can think about your argument in support of the fence."

So they are at a crossroads. She can stand there and argue with his authority, or she can concede and fill out the form. "Oh, I'll give you something to think about," she says while snatching the paper, turning on her heel and slamming out the front door to her golf cart. She puts on her big sunglasses and stuffs the form in her tote, which she tosses on the passenger seat. After a glance back at Commissioner Raines' glorified trailer-office, her foot is heavy on the gas, making the golf cart's wheels spin and the vehicle shimmy—nearly crashing into Jason walking his dog.

"Whoa! Whoa! Elsa, easy does it!"

Elsa screeches the cart to a stop beside them. "We'll never get this inn opened, not with all these God damn violations."

Jason glares at her, pulls Madison close on the leash, walks around her golf cart and approaches the driver's seat. "Move over."

"What?" Elsa whips off her sunglasses and glares right back at him.

"You're too hot under the collar to drive." He settles his dog in the back, then returns to Elsa's side and hikes his thumb at her. "I'm driving. *You* need to cool down." He hands her a bag—wait, a bag from the convenience store that is warm on the bottom, and has a wonderful aroma. When she opens it to take a peek, he tosses a warning her way. "Hands off. That's *my* snack for out on the bluff."

So Elsa tsks, crumples the top of the bag closed and sits straight in the passenger seat. While Jason drives her cart off the lawn it ended up on, he glances at her—she sees it out of the corner of her eye.

"Are you going to tell me what's gotten you driving around here like a madwoman?"

"Ooh. My blood is boiling!" Elsa throws him a glance, then brazenly pulls the bag of chips from his bag, rips it open and starts eating. On her second mouthful, she reaches into her tote and holds up the violation letter.

"Great." Jason slows the cart. "I recognize that letterhead." Apparently it's enough for him to pull a U-turn. She assumes it's to return to the commissioner's office, until he drives the cart straight past it, heading for the train trestle. "Don't worry," he's saying while driving beneath the railroad bridge, then pulling into the convenience store parking lot not far beyond it. "Violations are a part of the remodeling process. I see this all the time," he assures her as he takes the paper from her while parking. When he gets out of the golf cart, he merely skims the notification before folding it up and putting it in his cargo shorts pocket.

Regardless, Elsa's still peeved, but it isn't until she sees that Jason's busy inside the store, buying her an egg sandwich, she's sure, that she plucks two potato chips from the bag and holds them over her shoulder. "Sorry about before," she says. When Madison quickly licks the chips off her hand, she gets her a few more. "Sit now, your master's coming out," she sternly tells the dog, who obliges.

"I see violations in every single project. They're to be expected." The way Jason instantly picks up the thread of conversation, you'd think he never left the golf cart. "It'll all work out." He hands her the new bag. "You're not feeding Madison this stuff, are you? It's not good for her digestion."

Elsa briskly shakes her head, before throwing a casual wink at the dog still eyeing her.

As Jason drives back to his cottage, Elsa barely notices the flower barrels cascading with geraniums, petunias and vines; she scarcely sees the sunlight glinting off silver-shingled cottages; hardly notices the scent of the sea as they park in Jason's driveway and walk to the stone bench out on the bluff. It's awfully hard to be aware of anything more than her inn's stalled progress.

"If you don't want to fuss with ordinance details," Jason says while unwrapping his bagel sandwich on the stone bench, "I'll visit this new commissioner. Tell him to forward me the violations." He rips open a foil packet with his teeth, squeezes ketchup on his egg sandwich and takes a bite. "I can handle him," he says around a mouthful.

"Oh, no." On the bluff, down below, waves are breaking. Their rhythm, steady and slow, calms Elsa such that she takes a deep breath of the salt air. Paper wrapping covers her lap, and her egg sandwich is gripped in her two hands. She raises it for a bite, but pauses before digging in. "I can handle Mr. Raines, just fine."

thirteen

A RIBBON OF SOUND FLOATS THROUGH the evening air, light as a summer mist. Kyle's jangling his key ring, trying to find the diner's key, when he hears it. Hears Sal whistling, and slowly walking on the parking lot's gritty pavement while waiting for him to lock up.

"Friday-fishing tonight?" Sal calls out.

But he sounds distracted, enough for Kyle to glance over his shoulder. Sal is eyeing the front of the diner while untying his waiter bib behind his waist. Finally Kyle turns the key in the lock and pulls on the door, twice, to be sure it's secure. "No. Not tonight."

"Why not, man? It's a perfect night, the fish'll be biting."

"Too busy with the holiday." Kyle hurries down the stairs, looking back once. The diner's silver walls gleam in the setting sunlight; inside, hurricane lanterns on timers glow, showing a hint of the red padded window booths. It all has that retro feel, like an old-fashioned diner straight out of another era. "Kids are excited about the barbecue at Barlow's. I've got crab bait for Evan," he says while holding up an insulated bag, "and a bubble wand for Hailey."

"Nice. You'll bring your kids on the beach, then."

"What about you, DeLuca?" They walk across the parking lot together. With the distant violet horizon, it's sure to be a hot one tomorrow. "You going to Jason's, too?"

"Not sure. Maybe later in the day."

"Ah, shit." Kyle stops in his tracks. "Damn it, I got a flat." He points to his pickup truck parked in a space off to the side. Parked and leaning a bit, with the bad rear tire.

Sal walks over to it and gives it a kick, nudging the soft rubber. "Yup. Flat as a pancake. Got a spare?"

"Always, with this bomber." Kyle hauls out his spare, bouncing it twice before leaning it on the side of the truck. As he does, Sal is already grabbing the tire-changing tools, setting the jack beneath the axle and rotating it. When he steps back, Kyle starts with the lug wrench. "I promised Maris I'd keep an eye on Barlow, so it's good I'll be there for the cookout. Kill two birds with one stone: a little holiday celebrating, a little checking up on Jason." With that, he gives the wrench a spin and starts removing the tire's lug nuts.

"Now Jason Barlow does not strike me as someone who needs looking after. He does a good job of taking care of himself, from what I can see." Sal bends down then, grabs the tire and pulls it off the truck.

"He does." Kyle checks his watch, then lifts the fabric of his black tee and wipes off the perspiration on his forehead. "But only since Maris came back into his life. Trust me on this one, Sal. She's the light of his life, since he lost Neil."

"His brother." Sal sets the flat tire in the truck bed.

"That's right."

"In the wreck."

"They were on Neil's Harley." Kyle crouches with the new tire, trying to line up the spare with the bolts. He stops and looks up at Sal. "A man driving had a heart attack at the wheel and drove his car straight into them." He finagles the tire into place and holds out his hand for Sal to give him a lug nut.

"No shit. A heart attack."

"Yeah, it was pretty bleak. Happened nine years ago, and took many of those years for Jason to recover." Kyle hand-spins the lug nuts, tightening each one. When he stands and wipes his palms on his black pants, Sal grabs the wrench, bends down and finishes tightening each nut, giving a few good pulls and pushes. "It's Maris who turned his life around after that day," Kyle assures him.

"Ah, Maris. The elusive cousin I've yet to meet." Sal gives the tire a spin. "Okay, we're good to go."

As Kyle lowers the jack, Sal says something that is hard for Kyle to believe, not coming from this guy straight off the Street. "*Love* this vehicle, man."

"You kidding me?" Kyle asks after setting the jack into the truck bed. "Here, then." He underhand-throws his keys to Sal. "I'm beat from standing at that stove all day. You drive to the inn."

"You sure?" Sal catches the keys with a snap of his wrist.

"No problem."

"All right. And on the way," he says as Kyle gets in the passenger side and buckles his seatbelt, "we'll discuss that outdoor patio you're going to open at this here beach diner."

In the dark truck cab, Kyle looks over at him. "The what?"

"You heard me, Bradford." Sal starts the engine, revving it before putting it in gear. "I was checking out your property. There's a nice spot for outdoor tables, in the front, toward the side."

Kyle whips around and looks out the passenger window he's cranking down.

"Want to increase the dollars in your books?" Sal is asking. "Buy your wife a nice beach house? Maybe turn your family of four into five? Dining alfresco, my friend. Folks will be lining up for a seat." Sal pulls the pickup out of the parking lot, chirping the tires as he shifts the gears. As he does, Kyle throws a quick glance to the side mirror where his diner is looking mighty fine, but is closed up tight on what should be a busy Friday night.

Jason waited on the bluff until late. With the holiday weekend here, lots of people lingered on the boardwalk long into the night. Now, at this hour, all's finally quiet. He stops in his barn studio and grabs a black sweatshirt from a hook before taking his German shepherd down to the beach. Just like he'd hoped, the ache in his left leg fades while walking the packed sand beneath the high tide line. Something about the firm seaside ground soothes his gait. The waves break easy, and the nearly full moon drops a swath of silver on the water. Maris would love it, seeing the silver and deep blue blending; it's a color she'd bring straight to her denim designs.

But with Maris still overseas, the whole evening's felt like it did a few years ago when he was totally alone: his brother and father dead, his sister away, Maris living her own life across the country. And tonight, slivers of phantom pain let him know he's veering into that familiar loneliness. He picks up a few stones, skimming them over the water and watching the ripples in the moonlight. When his leg gets stiff standing there, he continues down the beach toward the rock jetty. Madison runs far ahead of him, her nose to the driftline, her tail wagging behind her.

"You out there, Neil?" Jason's hand reaches to the Vietnam dog tags hanging on his neck, and he slides them on the chain. "Maybe I should've gone to Italy for a few days."

"Missing your wife?" he hears as a wave splashes close to his feet.

"Shit, yeah. Could've holed up in a little villa somewhere and had a nice time. Got all tied up with work instead, and now it's too late." If anyone gets that, it would be Neil—who always worked well into the night, reviewing Jason's blueprints, reading up on cottage histories. "Not so much the job keeping me here, as Maris' cousin. Sal," Jason says under his breath. Near the rock jetty, a small patch of woods—tall oaks and pines—darkens the beach with night shadows as the branches block even the stars. "He's been coming along to the sites, and having someone to bounce ideas off of, well, feels like the old days. Remember?" He glances toward those pines, their scent blending with the salt of the sea.

"Good times, bro." The breeze rustling the pine needles can sound exactly like a gentle wave breaking; it's hard to decipher the two.

"So I took him to a new job," Jason quietly says. "Starting teardown prep work with the contractor. Getting the utilities shut off, disconnected, the works."

At the jetty, the small waves splash on the rocks. "What cottage, man? Not too many teardowns around."

That's Jason's cue to turn and walk back down the beach, in the direction of his most recent job. "The gray one," he says, pointing to the cottages at the far end. "The dump on the hill." At night, it's always the one that's pitch black. All the neighboring cottages have golden lamplight spilling from their windows, the people inside relishing their time beside the sea. All except for the one cottage.

"You mean the Woods' house? Old Maggie Woods' cottage?"

"That's the one. It's such an eyesore, new owners want to start from scratch and build something in its place." He walks closer, seeing only a shadow of the neglected building, which never had the coastal look of a beach cottage to begin with. "It's a huge job, on top of everything else. Including the inn."

Jason walks further, and another wave breaks ahead of him, the foam hissing. "You complaining? Goin' wussie on me?" he hears, the words so soft they could be imagined.

"Shut up," Jason says before waving off Neil's spirit. A light breeze rustles the beach grass beyond the jetty. Jason picks up a piece of driftwood and flings it far down the empty night beach, his dog running right after it, her collar jangling. Though there's plenty of moonlight, the water outside its path is dark, as is the sky. But a motion catches his eye: a rowboat drifting into the moonlight on the water.

So he stops, then walks a few feet down the beach, watching. It's the same boat that's been out there recent nights. Whoever it is seems to be alone, floating in the darkness. And as Jason well knows, only one thing drives a person to the water in the black of night—some tormented thought to be worked out.

Tonight's different, though. Instead of just floating, whoever's on the boat starts a small outboard engine. It gets puttering, and the boat moves through the water, heading toward the boat basin.

Well, once and for all, Jason wants to know who else obviously can't sleep. So he trots across the dark beach to the boardwalk, quiets Maddy and stands in the shadows. A few mounted lights shine in the marina behind the boardwalk, scarcely illuminating the boats. The water there looks like glass; he's not sure when he last saw it this still.

"Slack water," his brother's voice returns on a sea breeze and it distracts Jason. "Tide's about to change."

"Jesus Christ," Jason says under his breath. He shakes his head, then squints at the vague sight as the rowboat moves into its boat slip. "Sal," he tells himself. "It's Sal."

fourteen

WHAT IS IT ABOUT HIM? How does Salvatore DeLuca take a Fourth of July started with trepidation and turn it into bliss? Seriously, from the moment he arrived—mooring his rowboat at the ramshackle dock behind her cottage and lifting a wicker picnic basket from the boat—it's been simply charming. Then came the stop at the gas station, after which he tugged her hand to the neighboring beach shoppe. Like two kids, they loaded up on cheap sunglasses; a bag of penny candy; a hat for him that says *Beach Bum*, and bright, foamy flip-flops for her. Finally, Sal bought two sailor's knot bracelets, then made Celia wait in the car as he purchased and hid a surprise in the trunk. All that before they even hit the highway toward Addison, while she's done nothing but smile.

And it feels good. If she wasn't actually driving now, why she might kick off her sandals and stick her bare feet out the window—wind blowing, music cranked. Just like in the movies she loves to watch, oh yes. Instead, she opens the car's sunroof and ups the music, only a notch, right before she discreetly pinches herself on the arm. When Sal catches her doing so, she merely sticks that arm straight out the open window, hand cupped to catch a happy breeze while cruising down the highway.

But when his cell phone rings, she pulls that arm back in, partially closes the window, lowers the radio volume and puts two hands on the wheel, returning to reality.

"Everything okay, Ma?" he asks into his phone. "Okay, good. I'm sure Jason will grill up a storm for you all today."

He's quiet then, listening to Elsa ramble on about something. Celia stifles a smile when she deciphers that it's still food they're talking about. "A bag of *marshmallows*? That's what you brought?" Sal moves the phone slightly and tells Celia that Elsa has a clandestine fondness for s'mores and now she's trying to get Jason hooked.

Celia shakes her head, listening still. "Right, Ma. Riiight. They're for the *kids*, I'm sure. Listen, got to go. You have fun on the beach today, okay?"

After he disconnects, Celia puts her window all the way down again and a wisp of hair escapes her French braid and blows across her face.

"You're very beautiful," Sal tells her as he brushes the hair aside while she keeps her eyes on the road.

She manages the briefest of glances, then turns back to her driving. The highway hugs the Connecticut River on the right, curving and winding along with the road. Rays of morning sunshine sparkle on the water, reminding her of Elsa's ocean stars. Goodness, goodness, that's all Celia feels today. "Do me a favor?" she impulsively asks Sal as she brushes away another windblown strand of hair.

"Sure, what's up?"

She looks at him again, then back to the road, then back to him. He wears two polo shirts, white over navy, the buttons open, the collars casually up. "Drive?"

"Your car?" He lifts his cheap sunglasses to the top of his head. "Now?"

She nods, hits her blinker and carefully pulls onto the shoulder. "Would you mind?"

"Not at all." He unlatches his seatbelt and they both get out, run around the car and switch places. "Just point me in the right direction."

"North, keep following the highway north." Celia motions ahead as Sal merges into traffic while slipping his big sunglasses back on. "Oh, this is perfect," she says, grinning at the puzzled look on Sal's face. "Absolutely perfect." She cuffs the sleeves of her striped seersucker blouse, presses out a wrinkle in her white distressed-denim shorts, then bends down to slip off her new flip-flops. Before doing anything else, she buys some time and wiggles her toes, contemplating. Then, okay … she does it. Pulling her braid over her shoulder, she leans back on the headrest, reclines the seat—just a little, not enough to seem risqué—and props up her legs and hangs her bare feet out the window. At the same time, she drops her eyes closed and lives purely in the moment, seeing behind her lids the director, sitting in his movie set chair, megaphone to his mouth, yelling, *And … Action!*

Even better, as she relaxes in the first truly fun day she's had in months, suddenly Sal tunes the radio a little louder, playing a catchy song about summer days and lonely sailors and harbor towns.

But that's not the clincher. No, the clincher is when she feels his hand take hers. First, his thumb runs along the pale yellow sailor's knot bracelet on her wrist before he simply wraps his fingers around hers and doesn't let go for the rest of the drive. First stop? One of the nicest summer spots she knows: Addison Cove.

—

It's delightful, of course. Their worn, slivery picnic table sits beneath the shade of a maple tree. Sal spreads a red-and-white checked tablecloth over the planked tabletop and they enjoy a snack, waterside. It's not seaside, but the lapping cove water calms just the same. A few pleasure boats are anchored on the water, and as if on cue, a small sailboat—its sails white as a cloud—floats past.

Sal cuts slices from a block of cheese, and Celia sets a piece on a cracker and bites in. This is definitely turning into a day for the senses: the salty taste of the cracker, the sight of the silver cove, the sound of lapping waves and a quacking mallard duck, the touch of a summer breeze.

"What's in there?" Sal asks, pointing to a large brown barn sitting on the far banks of the cove.

"Back in colonial times, this was a busy shipping port and the barn was a warehouse for goods from all over the world. Now?" Celia gives a fond look at the weathered barn. "Well now it's a magical Christmas shop. Snowflakes and Coffee Cakes, with the wonder of the season brimming from every nook and cranny inside, all year round."

"So this is your hometown?"

Celia shakes her head. "No, it's Ben's. That's my ex, and we moved here after we got married. So Addison's only been home for a few years."

"I really like it. But it seems awfully quiet for a holiday weekend, no? Where are all the people enjoying the cove?"

"Oh, you don't know Addison. We have lots of festivities here, and today it's the Yankee Doodle concert on The Green. The whole town goes. You know, it's pure Americana … families and food and horseshoes and mini flags in the flower barrels and music."

"Sounds nice, but I'm liking it right here. Wish I could paddle my boat in that water," Sal muses. He pulls his cell phone from a pocket in his cargo shorts and takes a picture of the view, before snapping a candid of her. "It's very serene."

"I've always loved this spot," Celia agrees. She turns and looks back at the road leading to the cove, a street lined with saltbox and Dutch colonials, picket fences and towering trees. "It's Addison's secret treasure, the way you drive down that winding historical street that suddenly curves into this …" They sit side by side with a panoramic view of the cove, and a comfortable quiet settles on the late morning. "There's a blanket in my trunk, if you'd like to sit on the grass close to the water. We have time before my friends' barbecue."

Sal gives her arm a squeeze before heading to her car, returning with not only the blanket, but with the guitar she'd tucked in the trunk this morning, too, as well as her straw fedora. He hitches his head toward the water as he passes the picnic table and opens the blanket, flipping it high and letting it float gently onto the grass. Celia wastes no time, grabbing the wine bottle and their two cups and settling on the blanket beside Sal. He gently moves aside her braid before tugging the straw hat on her head, then leans back on his hands, legs crossed in front of him, boat shoes kicked off, of course, and *Beach Bum* hat pulled low.

"Play me a tune," he says softly, sliding her guitar case closer.

Celia shifts her position and sits cross-legged, settling the guitar in her lap. And what happens is that the chords she strums, simple and light, mimic the day. The sounds her guitar pick elicits are the steady rhythm of lapping water, the changing chords of a blue jay swooping branch-to-branch, the vibrato rustle of green leaves. When she looks up from her strumming, Celia's surprised. She'd thought Sal was taking in the water view, relaxing in the July day's warmth. But he isn't. He's watching only her. Again, he reaches over and tucks a loose strand of hair, his hand softly brushing her ear, her cheek. She holds his gaze, the pick in her fingers, her hand rising and falling over the strings.

"You're a natural, Celia, and make it look so easy."

"Want to try?" she asks while drawing out a chord, plucking the low note before strumming the strings.

He tips his head with the thought, his eyes dropping to her strumming hand.

"Come on," she insists, lifting the strap over her head. "I'll teach you."

Sal sets his sunglasses on the blanket, takes the guitar and sits it across his lap. First he looks down at the instrument as though studying its every function, then uses his fingertips to awkwardly strum.

"Watch," Celia says, moving beside him. "Use this." She hands him her guitar pick. "Curl your fingers, and hold it between your thumb and first finger."

When his fingers fist tightly, she touches his hand. "No tension. Easy." So he takes a long breath before loosening his grip. "You're going to let that pick glide across the strings." Her own hand moves up and down to demonstrate as she hums along. "Ready?"

"What about this?" Sal asks, wiggling his left hand fingers that hold the guitar's neck. "How do I find a chord?"

"Here." Celia gets up and kneels close behind him, her left arm reaching around his side. "Your thumb," she explains, "goes behind the neck. Like this." She puts her hand in position on the neck. "Then wrap your fingers around to the strings, like this, arching your fingers." While talking, her voice gets softer with each phrase, her body leans closer. She notices how Sal lets go of the guitar's neck and merely watches *her* hand get into position. "Okay," Celia relents. "We'll do this together." She lifts off her hat and sets it on the grass before starting their unique duet: she chording, he strumming. "Now give me a steady rhythm. A few downstrokes."

Sal shifts his position, subtly, but enough for her to comfortably reach around and manage the finger work on the chords while he strums.

"Any time," she says while on her knees and leaning gently into his back, her hand in playing position on the guitar neck. "Slowly, so I can keep up with you."

And they do it; Sal plays his first tune, with Celia behind him, shifting her fingers on the strings, her face nearly resting on his shoulder. She chooses a song she'd written this past winter, not long after her divorce, but doesn't dare sing the words. Hearing his tentative strumming brings back the memory of sitting alone in her living room, strumming as uncertainly as Sal does now while she put together the tune, and began putting together her life. Never, not for one second that long-ago cold night, did she think that only months later, the meaning of her lonely song would change.

But it does, when Sal turns his face toward hers and stops mid-strum. Neither of them moves, not until Sal silently lifts her sunglasses to the top of her head, reaches his hand to her face and kisses her, beside the cove. When his hand slips behind her neck and pulls her close, he deepens the kiss, his body turning toward hers on their picnic blanket in the shade. When he moves, the guitar slips off his lap and he shifts onto his knees, both hands now framing her face as though he can't get enough of her, his kiss almost greedy in its surprising intensity. He leans into Celia as they kneel together, and though it's all she can do to not go with it, to not lie back on the blanket beneath him, her hands instead reach around his waist and take his touch, his insistence, for only a few moments longer.

"Sal," she finally manages to whisper.

He kisses her two, three times more before pulling away, pressing back those persistent wisps of hair, his fingers outlining her jaw and dragging along her neck, his voice low. "I'm so glad to have met you." He shifts and sits on the blanket, his knees folded, his arms wrapped around them as he takes in the cove sight in front of them.

If Celia could describe the feeling, it's as though this lazy Saturday moment is all theirs, with the rest of the world spinning outside of it. She touches Sal's hair, draws her finger across his back, shoulder-to-shoulder. Then, well then she picks up the guitar, glides the pick across the strings and begins to strum. This time, she hums along so softly, but she thinks he hears when he glances at her, then lies down on the blanket—his hands folded behind his head, the sky open above him—and merely listens.

fifteen

SOMETIMES YOU JUST KNOW, AND Celia does. Though the rest of the day is wonderful; though it is filled with backyard picnic tables laden with salads and burgers and hot dogs and corn on the cob and watermelon slices that Sal's only dreamed of; though he got to experience his very first honest-to-goodness Fourth of July backyard barbecue; though he laughed with George and charmed Amy and gave piggyback rides across the green lawn to her daughter, Grace; though he had a turn flipping burgers at the grill; though he played a mean beanbag toss with George and his friends, taking a flying leap to make a hole in one; though he took Celia's hand when they walked to her yellow bungalow next door to Amy's late in the day, Celia knows that things changed between them.

"Look," Sal says, pointing toward Amy's side yard. A lace wedding gown hangs from the clothesline there. "Seems like it's dancing in the breeze." The gown slightly moves, the fabric shimmering in the sunlight. "Are Amy and George married? Is that her gown?"

"No." Celia keeps walking and doesn't look back. A simple thing like that gown brings too many sad memories. "Amy sells vintage wedding gowns at her shop, Wedding Wishes," she explains while opening the latch on her picket-fence gate. "When she gets in a new batch, she likes to air them out in the sunshine."

"So what's the matter?" Sal asks from behind her.

"Nothing, really. I'm just tired."

"Tired?" He walks through the gate, silent for a few steps. "Or sad?"

"What?" Celia looks from him, to the gown. "Oh, damn. Sometimes the whole marriage thing can get me down. It sneaks up on me, that feeling, when I see things like that." She motions to Amy's gown waltzing on the line.

"What do you mean, it gets you down?" Sal sits on the top step to her front porch, considering the lone gown off in the distance.

"You know. That idea of promising love and commitment, till death do you part. It's all a sham, really, and kind of dramatic, don't you think? I mean, look at me. My marriage just quietly unraveled after I wore *my* beautiful white gown."

Sal pats the step beside him and so she sits there. His arms rest on his knees, his hands loosely clasped. He wears a big watch on his left wrist, his new white sailor's knot bracelet on the right. And it's the sailor's knot with which he fidgets, turning it while he talks. "Maybe you're looking at the situation all wrong."

"Wrong?"

"Yes. Maybe your divorce is more about second chances, instead of failure. My friend Michael," he says, then stops and traces a finger over a knot in his ropy bracelet. "Michael Micelli, a mounted police officer in the city. He's the one who tells me all the time that second chances are God-given, and he should know. A bullet missed his heart by inches."

"Well." Celia takes a long breath because, okay, that's a little different.

"I know what you're thinking. That it's different. But it *isn't*, Celia. A second chance is a second chance. And when you see your friend's gowns out there ..." He nods toward Amy's farmhouse next door. "They're a reminder."

"Of what?"

"Life's downright complicated, and most people never get a second chance at a happy marriage. But you actually have the chance to try again." With that, he taps her pale yellow sailor's knot bracelet.

"Maybe." She stands and nudges the welcome mat closer to the front door. "Listen, we should get going. I need decorating pieces from out in my garden shed. Well," she explains, "it used to be a garden shed when this house was built. The yards are so big, people did lots of gardening back in the day. But I use the shed to store staging inventory now. Anyway … I'll find my things and we'll take off?"

Sal gets up from where he sits and studies her.

"I'll be right back," she whispers, looking away with sudden tears in her eyes, then stepping down the porch stairs. But when Sal grabs her arm, she stops without turning.

"Why don't we have a glass of wine first, out on your deck?" his voice says behind her. "It's a beautiful evening, Celia."

"We don't have time." She turns and looks from his face, down to his hand on her arm. "It's getting late."

"Late? What are you late for?" He moves to the step she's on and leans on the handrail. "Time is *meant* for this. Come on." He touches her chin. "*Sorridi.*"

"What?" she whispers just as, damn it, one of those tears escapes. And yes, he sees it. Sees it and catches it with his thumb.

"Smile," he whispers back. "It means smile. Even when you're sad."

She rolls her eyes, quickly, and okay, a sort-of half smile comes then.

"Aha, I see it!" He lightly kisses her cheek. "Right there."

"Oh, Sal," she says, shaking her head.

"It helps, trust me." His hand lifts the long silver chain around her neck to see her turquoise pendant. "My father taught me that all my life. To smile when I'm sad."

"Right, like what did you ever have to be sad about?"

He raises his eyebrows, just enough to suggest that doesn't everyone have something: a failed marriage, a parent long gone, a regretful decision, a missed chance … something. In other words, she's not alone.

"Okay." The twilight sky is violet at the horizon, the air warm, a lone robin sings its song. "Okay. Here's the key," she says while nodding to her front door. "I have to run out to the shed, and if you get the wine in the kitchen, I'll meet you on the deck." She skips down the remaining stairs, then turns back to see him still standing and watching her. "And thank you, Sal."

All he does is turn up his hands, as if it's that easy. Just smile.

~

She sees it from a distance. Her kitchen light is on at this dusky hour and Sal opens her slider to the deck. He steps outside, a full wineglass in each hand, and on his way to the patio table, looks toward her garden shed. It's when he catches sight of her carrying a mantel clock across the lawn that he bumps into the table and spills wine all over his white polo shirt.

Celia sets the clock down and rushes over with a rag from the shed. "Here, let me get that before it sets." She presses the rag on his chest, right over the stain.

Sal takes the rag from her and turns toward the kitchen light. "I'll go inside and put water on it," he says as he walks toward the slider.

Before the dewy lawn does any damage to her staging clock, Celia hurries back for it, then returns to her house. "Use hot water," she calls out while sliding the screen door closed. "It'll stop the stain." But when she turns around, Sal is not at the sink. So he must've gone into the guest bathroom. The door is partially open, the light on. "How's it going in there?"

"Not bad." Sal's voice is distracted, as though he's busy soaking and blotting fabric. "I'm okay."

"Ben left behind some old shirts when he moved out," Celia says as she passes the bathroom toward her bedroom. "I'll get one so you can at least put on something dry. You don't need me, do you?" But instead of waiting for an answer, she hurries to her bedroom and stops at a small painted dresser. Where the heck are those shirts? She rummages through a few piles in the bottom drawer, then slams it shut and goes to the closet. Ben's side was long ago taken over by Celia's own clothes, but, if she's not mistaken, some shirts may still hang in the back. She slides several blouses and skirts over and sees, behind everything, a couple of button-downs. She holds one up and considers it in the dim closet light.

"I found a shirt you can borrow," she calls as she brushes off the dusty fabric and leaves the closet, nearly bumping into Sal. "Oh! Oh, Sal." She holds out the hanger, looking past him, then back at him.

"You asked me if I needed you."

"What?" Celia tucks a loose wisp of hair behind her ear.

"Back there." He takes the shirt she holds and sets it on her bed. As he's talking, he's removing his two polo shirts, pulling the stained white one over his head, followed by the damp navy one beneath it. "You asked me if I needed you," he repeats as he removes Ben's shirt from the hanger and slips into it, folding up the cuffs. It's not until he's buttoning it that he looks at her again.

"What I meant …" She glances to his soiled shirts on the bed, then back to Ben's shirt buttoned out of order. "Here," she whispers, stepping closer. "You missed one." Celia tentatively reaches out and undoes a few buttons to straighten out the shirt. The problem is, Sal's hand covers hers as he wraps his fingers around them and folds both her hands to his chest. Now, though, she won't meet his look and so watches only his hand, with its ropy sailor's knot bracelet at the wrist. Did that really happen only hours ago, their fun stop loading up on beach trinkets as the day began?

Sal moves closer, his other hand hooking a finger beneath her chin as he bends to give her a kiss. It's barely a kiss at all—as light as the summer breeze wafting through the window—but enough of a kiss to get her to look at him. To see his dark eyes and notice a bit of weariness there; to see the shadow of whiskers on his face; the curl of hair against the shirt collar. She raises a hand to touch it, that one curl of hair, her finger toying with it.

And he does the same, reaching for her French braid. He pulls it to the side, over her shoulder, and removes the elastic. His fingers slowly unravel it then, slipping through one thick auburn strand at a time, gently tugging through her hair, bottom to top, the sensation on her neck and scalp as unexpected as this hushed moment she never saw coming. When the braid is fully undone, he sets his hands on the back of her neck and lifts his spread fingers up through her hair such that her head drops back, her eyes close, and he kisses her neck first, then her mouth.

Okay, so the question of who needs whom is negligible. Because in this one moment—the one when the sun has scarcely set and a lone robin trills; the one when leaves rustle in the tree outside her window; the one when Amy's wedding gown on the clothes-line shimmers in the shadows of dusk; the one when Celia's tangled feelings about wedding gowns and love and possibility and second chances seem as knotted as a sailor's bracelet—she hasn't needed anyone more.

While he kisses her still, Celia surprises even herself. Her hands drop and begin unbuttoning the seersucker blouse she put on hours ago, when the day began. But her surprise pales beside Sal's. His kiss stops, he steps back and tips his head, a question on his face as he strokes her hair.

"Let me?" he asks.

And so her hands fall to her side, her gaze shifts and she watches as his hands—the big watch on one, the ropy bracelet on the other—slip the tiny blouse buttons through the nearly sheer fabric. When those hands finish, they first stroke the long silver chains hanging from her neck before lifting the blouse and dropping it off her shoulders as she pulls her arms through. And still she just watches, waiting for what the entire day has led to as her fingertips hook through the belt loops of Sal's cargo shorts and tug him closer now. At the same time, she backs toward her bed and Sal follows in what feels like an intimate July dance. When Sal lies down on the patchwork quilt beside her, she sees the half-shutters over her windows, tilted open to let in the summer air. Above them, the moon rises high, casting a large tree in silhouette against the sky. The bedroom walls, painted paneling, are the same hue as the moonlight, pale cream. On one wall, silk scarves hang from a pegged rack, and dried cattails spill from a floor vase. Summer and light and ease, feelings Celia had thought only months ago were long gone, return.

"I adore you, Celia," Sal says then as he slips her lacy bra straps from her shoulders, reaches around her and takes it off completely. "Every beautiful bit of you."

There's no denying it from his touch, a gentle touch that never stops, not when he slips off her shorts, not when she undresses him. In the dark, his hands run the length of her body, soothing Celia in such a way that any feelings tangled up in her heart unravel as she loves him right back. The ease of it all—of feeling the weight of him moving over her beneath a cool sheet, of reaching her hands behind him and stroking his back, his shoulders, then moving to his face—get her to smile beneath his kiss, enough that he feels it.

"Now that's more like it," he says, pulling away and touching her lips with his fingertips.

"What do you mean?" she asks, her fingers tracing along his jaw, back around his ear, then dragging around his neck.

"Smile," he whispers. "Look how wonderful it makes everything, Celia."

But there's something in his own smile, through it all, that says otherwise. What it is she's seeing, she can't be sure. And he won't let her scrutinize it any longer as he kisses each cheek, each eye, her collarbone, and finally, the soft of her neck, moving down the length of her body then back up again, his mouth and tongue being sure that wonderful isn't enough of a word.

"Sal," she whispers when he kisses her mouth once again.

"Celia," he barely murmurs back, seeming unable to stop now. The kiss deepens while his hand slides beneath her back and lifts her to him, not giving her a chance to say more. The July moonlight simply shines down on them through the slatted window blinds, its light muted and soft as she hears him whisper her name in the shadows, his breath near, his touch unmistakable.

—

"Let's try this again."

Celia lowers a match to light two white lanterns on her deck just as Sal, slowly, pours red wine into two glasses. "What a perfect day it's been, Sal," she says as she sits beside him and looks out at the yard. It's dark, the neighborhood quiet now, and only crickets chirp. "Thank you."

Sal leans over and kisses the side of her head. He wears Ben's old shirt over his cargo shorts, and if she must say so, that shirt never looked as good as it does right now, on Sal.

"Look." She points to the far corner of the yard.

"Is that a deer?"

"Yes. There's a cornfield at the end of the street, past the big red barn. It draws the deer out at night."

They watch as the doe raises her head, ears straight, before leaping off into the darkness as though it had never even been there.

"I have a surprise for you, before this holiday is done." Sal's hand reaches out and takes hold of hers. "Where are your car keys?"

"Inside, in the kitchen. Why?"

"Never mind." He stands to get her keys, grabbing the grill lighter on his way. Minutes later, he returns, except not through the slider; no, he walks around the side of the house in the darkness, illuminated by one twinkling sparkler he gives to Celia. Before she can say anything, he motions for her to wait there on the deck as he walks out into her vast backyard. She squints to see him crossing the lawn, setting up something on the grass.

Suddenly, he flicks the lighter and quickly walks back across her yard, lighting two dozen tall sparklers set in her lawn. Once they are all fizzing and shining, he returns to Celia's deck and sits beside her again, taking her hand as she silently watches her own personal Fourth of July light show flashing and glittering in the night. She's silent, but oh is her smile wide until each and every sparkler burns to its very last flicker.

"Pinch me," she whispers.

"What?"

Celia slides her chair even closer to Sal's and holds her arm over his lap. "Pinch me."

"Okay." He runs his fingers along the length of her arm, stroking her skin softly before very lightly giving a squeeze near her wrist.

A few sparklers flare and flash a moment longer, and then the summer night is dark again. The candlelit deck throws the only light now, Celia's lantern glimmering on the patio table, another on the deck railing. She leans close and kisses Sal, once, twice, then again, before settling in her chair and sipping her wine, her hand never letting go of his.

sixteen

"Excuse me." While holding his cell phone to his ear, Jason lightly touches a woman's arm and squeezes past. "Excuse me, please," he says again, this time pointing ahead of a man standing in line with a young boy. "Just need to get by." The man moves aside and Jason still can't believe it. For a Wednesday morning, The Driftwood Café is mobbed; the line of people waiting for a table reaches out the door. So he heads to the counter and sits on one of only two empty stools. "It's shingled, then?" he asks his client on the phone. "Nantucket style?" Beside him, folks are eating eggs and pancakes and sausages—and it's enough to make him want a heaping plate himself. "Okay, I really can't say without seeing your cottage. I'll have to stop by for a predesign consultation."

"Hey, Barlow." Kyle walks out from the diner's kitchen wearing his white chef apron over a black tee and black pants, wiping his hands on a dish towel. "What's up, man?"

"Coffee to-go today. I'm busy." Jason holds up a finger for Kyle to wait. "Yeah, sorry," he says into his cell phone. "I'm not in my office right now, so can you do me a favor? Call back this number, and when you get the voicemail, leave me your cottage address. I'll get back to you with a date." All the while, he's aware of Kyle hovering in front of him like a shadow.

"Eh, you've got five minutes," Kyle finally says. As Jason ends the call, Kyle's pouring two mugs of coffee.

Well, there's apparently no arguing with his best man, so Jason sets his elbows on the counter, his thumb finding the scar on his jaw as he scans the headlines of a newspaper left behind.

"Here you go." Kyle sets down a cup of black coffee along with a cinnamon cruller on a plate. "So what's happening? How's the leg treating you?"

The thing is, since Friday night's bout of phantom pain, Jason's kept himself too busy to notice. If he's learned one thing since losing that leg, it's that there are varying ways to medicate. Keeping ridiculously busy is one. "It's good, Kyle." He pauses when his cell phone rings, prompting Kyle to snag it and tap the decline button. "Had a little episode the other day, but other than that—"

"What do you mean, an episode? Everything okay?"

"Just some phantom pain bull. I walked it off."

"You sure? Need to call your doctor maybe?"

"No, nothing like that."

"Your wife know about this episode?"

"Maris? No, she doesn't, and we're going to keep it that way." Jason sips his hot coffee, and what that does is make him miss his wife, even more. One of their favorite things to do is sit on the deck summer mornings, early, and have coffee together before they get too busy to even catch up. "I'm not going to worry her over in Italy."

Kyle nudges the cruller plate closer to Jason. "Then have something to eat, keep your strength intact. I read that cinnamon gives you energy. It's a good way to kick-start the day." He crosses his arms in front of him, leans back and eyes Jason.

"Want to take my temp while you're at it?" Jason asks.

"No. I'm just saying to eat up, okay?"

And when Kyle steps closer, his crossed arms revealing sizable muscles that could shove that cruller anywhere he wants, Jason waves him off. "Okay, Doc. You've always got my health covered."

"Besides," Kyle tells him, "your continental breakfast's on the house. Courtesy of your best man."

Jason lifts the cruller in a pseudo-toast and bites in.

Kyle obliges the toast, taking a bite of a blueberry muffin in return. "Wait, it's Wednesday, isn't it? I thought you had Sal today," Kyle says around the food, wiping the back of his hand across his mouth and throwing a quick look toward his overworked kitchen when one of the harried cooks drops a pan. "To help with your workload. Where's he at?"

Jason takes another sip of coffee. "I stopped at Elsa's place, but he wasn't there. She thought he might be at Celia's cottage."

"Celia's? Over on the marsh?"

"Heads up," comes from behind Jason. He turns just as a waitress hoists a large tray filled with dirty dishes and stacks of empty coffee cups ready to topple.

"That's right." Jason pulls in to the counter as she passes by.

"Really, now." Always the gentleman, Kyle presses the rest of his muffin into his mouth before taking the tray from the waitress and walking it into the kitchen. "Was Sal there?" he calls back.

"I'm sure he was." Jason breaks off a hunk of his cruller and dunks it in the coffee. "But I didn't go." When Kyle returns, wiping his hands on his apron, Jason eats the remaining cruller piece and slides his phone closer to check his messages. "If those two have something going on, I'm not about to walk in on them. Had enough of that last year," he says, raising an eyebrow.

"Yeah." Apparently Kyle still isn't over *that* episode, as he chokes on a sip of coffee. "Shit," he says, setting down his cup, then picking it up again. "Women."

"Hey, you should get back to your stove. You've got a full house."

"Nah, Rob and Jerry can handle it."

"And what the hell's going on in your parking lot?"

"Didn't I tell you?" Kyle looks out the window, then leans over and gives a yell toward the kitchen. "Yo, Jerry! I'm taking five."

"Not a good time!" Rob's voice calls from a stove.

Jerry hurries out, still holding a spatula. "You go," he says to Kyle, and when he spots Jason, walks over to shake his hand. "Good to see you, Jason. You hanging out with this bum today?" He swings his thumb toward Kyle.

"Come on. Grab your joe," Kyle tells Jason, before turning to Jerry. "Back in a flash, okay?"

"You bought the diner from me how many years ago now?" Jerry asks as Kyle heads toward the door. "Don't need my permission, Captain."

Kyle salutes him while Jason grabs his phone before they walk past the line of waiting customers toward the exit. "You're not going to believe this," Kyle is saying while pushing the door open and stepping out into the sunshine. "It was all the Italian's idea."

"Sal?" Jason's trying to put together his image of the slick guy from the Street with the quaint patio he's seeing: a small area of the parking lot surrounded by rope swim line secured to wooden dock posts. The rope is strung with fishing buoys of red, green and yellow. On one side, Jerry's old fishing net décor hangs from makeshift fence panels giving relief from the rays of sun. A half-dozen round tables are set up, their navy umbrellas open, folks in shorts and tees and sunglasses sitting on folding chairs around each one.

"That DeLuca. He made it seem like such an obvious thing to do. But this is a temporary setup. I'm having a concrete pad installed so the tables are raised off the pavement. And actually, these tables and chairs are rented, until Lauren and I pick out what we want. But Sal thought we should," Kyle adds, waving to the outdoor crowd, "cash in on the summer surge. *Avanti tutta*."

"Say again?"

"Full speed ahead. You know, Italian lingo."

"Amazing." Jason tips up his mug to finish the coffee. "Patio dining. Good for you, man." He shakes Kyle's hand. "Maris and I will stop by for breakfast, when she gets back." His cell phone dings with a message. "It's work. A door came in I've been waiting on, at the salvage company. So I've got to hit the road."

"No prob." Kyle glances at the crowd eating outdoors and presses his arm to his perspiring forehead right as one of his cooks hangs out the door and gives a sharp whistle. "And hey, find Sal. Get him to The Sand Bar tonight. We'll wheedle that Celia story out of him."

Celia carries a sand chair and tote while quietly walking up behind Lauren on the beach. Her silence isn't intentional; it's just that she's mesmerized by what she's seeing. An easel faces Long Island Sound, and Lauren stands at it, wearing a long white cover-up over her bathing suit, a damp blonde ponytail hanging down her back. But it's what's on the easel that catches Celia's eye—and breath. Streaks of blue depict seawater, with sparkling constellations of silver ocean stars sprinkled on the rippling waves.

But still, Celia can't hold back as she nears her beach friend. "You didn't tell me it would happen this fast!" she calls out.

Lauren stops mid-stroke and turns, shielding her eyes from the sun. "Hey, Celia." She hurries over and gives her a light hug, careful to not get any paint on her.

Celia sets down the tote and opens the sand chair beside Lauren. "What a nice day!"

"Wait … What happens fast?" Lauren asks, already back to her painting.

"Happens amazingly fast. The change you told me about." Celia tips up her fedora and watches Lauren paint.

"Change?" Lauren pulls back brush bristles dabbed in silver and flicks the paint on her paper.

"You arrive under the trestle at Stony Point as one person … and leave as another?"

When Lauren spins to face her, the cover-up swirls around her legs. "Really? Sal?"

Celia nods, and she's sure that's all she has to do because doesn't she just *feel* the sparkle in her eyes and, okay, the unstoppable smile. "He stopped at my place earlier for breakfast on the deck, before I headed to the inn to work."

"Yes!" Lauren's fist, clenched around a paintbrush, punches the air. "Spill it, girlfriend!"

A perfect word choice—*spill it.* Because it's all Celia can do to not have the story pour out. "First things first," she says instead, holding up a finger. "When I got to the inn to take my staging notes and room measurements, Elsa asked me to bring you a snack." She opens the tote and lifts out a wrapped pastry, still warm from the oven.

"Ooh, what is it?"

"Something heavenly, I'm sure." Celia hands her the food with a plate. "Elsa was going to bring it herself, but wanted to email Maris and Eva before it got too late." She looks up at Lauren and raises a thermos. "Coffee?"

"Definitely, I'm ravenous! And still waiting," she adds, tapping her bare foot impatiently in the sand.

When Celia hands her a cup of steaming coffee, she glances around. "Where are your kids? I thought they'd be here, too."

"They're with my mom while I paint ideas for the inn stairs," Lauren explains around a mouthful of pastry, which she washes down with a swallow of coffee. "She recently retired and babysits for me now. Wouldn't I love to find a home with an in-law apartment, so she and Dad could spend more time with us." She takes another bite, stuffing in the last of the pastry. "But enough of that. I want to hear about you and Sal!"

The thing is, it's the kind of story that can't be discussed while sitting in sand chairs. Oh, no. Not with a true beach friend, you can't. So Celia cuffs her white jeans and tells her Fourth of July story—everything from riding with her feet out the window, to Sal's sparklers twinkling on her lawn—all while they walk the beach. Gentle waves break at their feet; a sandpiper scoots along ahead of them as though listening in. Every now and then a piece of sea glass catches Celia's eye, and she picks it up and drops it in her pocket, her heart so full, her life finally, well, so fine.

"It's funny," Celia says when they reach the rock jetty at the end of the beach and turn back, "because I thought I'd stay at Stony Point, stage a few cottages, strum a few tunes, regroup and leave when the time was right. But now, well, now there's Sal. And everybody. Those sparklers said it all, twinkling in the dark that night. Everything's just magical."

"Does Elsa know?" Lauren asks as she skims a flat stone over the calm water.

Celia finds a stone, too, and pauses with it in her hand. "I think she might. I mean, we *were* away for the whole weekend." Toying with her skimming stone, she rubs her fingers across it. "Elsa didn't say anything, but she had that knowing look when I was there this morning. And she was so sweet, with hot coffee and toast with fresh jam waiting for me outside on that deck, off the back room." With that, Celia gets into position and gives a good side-arm throw, watching her stone skim across the water's surface. And yes, she does it: While counting the skips across the rippling Sound, she's counting her blessings, too.

~

Wednesday evening, sunrays glint through the window, casting hazy light on The Sand Bar. "Hungry?" Jason asks, sitting across from Kyle in their regular booth.

Kyle tips the pretzel basket to its side and empties a few crumbs into his hand. "New listing came up at the beach. The realtor squeezed in a quick tour before Lauren had to get home to the kids. And I'll tell you, that salt air gives you an appetite."

"How was the house? Doable?" Jason asks. He lifts his foot on the booth's bench seat and leans against the wall, the window there open, a salty breeze hitching in.

"No garage, wood paneling everywhere. Straight out of the forties." As a waitress passes their table, Kyle lifts the empty pretzel basket and asks for a refill.

"Going to keep looking?"

"I guess. It's not too promising, though. We need more cash. Speaking of money," Kyle says, lifting the brim of his *Gone Fishing* cap and glancing toward the bar door propped open to the evening. "You ever find your paisan today?"

"Sal?" Jason tips his glass for a swallow of beer. "No. But when I stopped home to get out of my work clothes, I left him a voicemail to meet us here."

Kyle does a double take and points to the doorway. "Speak of the devil."

"Hey, guys," Nick calls out, with Sal close behind him. They squint a little, coming in from the still-bright evening sunlight into the dark bar. Sal stops at the jukebox near the door and drops in a few coins before heading to their booth and sliding in beside Jason.

"Hey, man," he says, extending his hand for a shake. "What's happening?"

"Glad to see you finally showed up *someplace* today," Jason tells him.

"What are you talking about?" Sal asks.

"Your mother sent me on a wild-goose chase to find you this morning, mentioned something about Celia's cottage?"

"She did? Shit, how would she know?"

No one says a word then. Not one syllable. Only a couple eyebrows are raised, just as the waitress sets down a plastic basket heaping with pretzels.

Kyle lifts a pretzel, then drops it back in the basket. "Oh, miss," he calls after the waitress. "Can you bring me a cheeseburger? Deluxe, all the extras."

"Make it two," Nick says. He drops a large key ring on the table.

"Three," Sal adds, holding up three fingers as she jots the order down on a pad.

Jason turns up his hands when they all look at him. "What?"

"You eat dinner yet?" Kyle asks.

He shakes his head. "Four," he calls out.

"And what about you?" Kyle asks Sal.

"Didn't you hear? I got one, too."

"Not that." Kyle waves off the waitress. "It's Wednesday, you were supposed to work today."

"I did." Sal twists a big watch straight on his wrist. "What a day, *Gesù, Santa Maria.*"

"He worked the afternoon shift with me." Nick salutes Sal. "Good job, dude."

"You worked with *him*?" Jason asks. "You were supposed to work with me."

"You never showed up to get me. From Celia's." Sal lifts Nick's heavy-duty key ring and gives the keys a jangle. "So I walked the beach with Nick, rode shotgun in the security car."

"Funny thing," Nick tells them while tossing a handful of pretzels in his mouth. "He pulled over a speeding golf cart—and it turned out to be his mother!"

"Elsa?" Kyle asks. "Oh, classic. She must've loved that."

"*Merda*," Sal says under his breath.

"English, guy." Jason hits his arm. "Say it in English."

"Shit. You know, it was my ma, and she wasn't too happy that I fined her. So … *shit*." Sal shrugs then.

"Seriously?" Nick asks. "That's *shit* in Italian? You've got to teach me a few choice words."

"Next time I'm on your payroll," Sal says. "For now, I'm famished. Where's our food?"

"Come on, already!" Kyle half stands, looking for the waitress.

"*Dai!*" Sal says, and when they all turn up their hands, he explains. "Okay, translating! It's what Kyle said … *Come on, already!*"

"Hey." Kyle leans over the table and taps a rope strapped on Sal's right wrist. "What's this, a bracelet?"

Sal holds up his arm, elbow on the table. "Nautical bracelet," he says and gives it a spin. "Sailor's knot."

"No kidding." Kyle leans closer and pushes up his cap. "Hey, I was a shipbuilder, back in the day. And those sailors' knots are like, unbreakable. They're used for hitching ships, so that's strong stuff, man. Where'd you get yours? I'd like to have one."

"Got it with Celia, Saturday."

"On the Fourth?" Kyle still considers the ropy band Sal wears.

"And I suppose Celia has one, too?" Nick asks. He picks up Sal's arm and eyes the rope.

Kyle sits back in the booth and hits his forehead. "Oh, *merda.* I get it now."

"What?" Jason asks. "Get what?"

Kyle points to Sal. "Unbreakable bonds? I think we've got a summer romance going on here."

"Is that right?" Jason looks over at Sal.

"Never mind me," Sal tells him. He reaches over and rubs Jason's whiskered face, then touches his ratty college tee. "What the hell's going on with you?"

"With me? Why?"

"You're like a mountain man these days. When's the last time you had a decent shave and cut your hair? It's looking a mess."

Jason runs his hand through the unruly waves in his hair. He knows damn well he's overdue for a cut. But the only way to keep himself distracted is with work, lots of work. No time to sit in a barber's chair and get all pampered.

"When the wife's away, Jason will play?" Nick pushes him.

"What? I'm having a brew, okay?" A song starts on the jukebox, one he figures Sal must've chosen, if he's got a new romance going on. It's all about the Fourth of July and a beautiful day in the park. "One drink and I'm gone. Got a lot to do in my studio tonight."

"Yeah, well word around this beach town is that you can't take care of yourself in the pretty lady's absence." Sal looks him dead-on, waiting for his rebuttal.

"What?"

"Nice out." Sal hitches his head at him. "Maris is gone, and everyone keeps a watchful eye on you. What gives?"

"You *are* looking gaunt," Kyle tells him. "Need a grocery store run? I'm the guy to go with."

"I eat here and there. You know."

"Hey." Kyle grabs a handful of the pretzels, popping one in his mouth. "You've got an anniversary coming up. Got any plans?"

"Plans?" Jason grabs a few pretzels, too. "It's a little early for plans, the anniversary's not till next month."

"You American boys are so clueless. The love of your life's anniversary, and you have no plans? *Mamma mia*," Sal says, shaking his head.

"Clueless?" Kyle asks. "Speaking of the love of your life, when are you going to tell us about yours? You and Celia really a thing?"

"There truly are no secrets here, are there?" Sal sits back, waiting for someone to answer.

But they don't. None of them. They just look at him as though he's the one who's clueless. And they don't relent, not until the waitress arrives with a large tray weighed down with deluxe cheeseburger dinners, and they sort out the food, add ketchup and mustard, grab fries and onion rings, devour pickles.

"Oh, man," Nick finally says after taking a bite of his dripping burger. "So good."

"Careful," Kyle tells him. "Wouldn't want to get that grease on your spiffy uniform."

As Nick glances down at his epaulet-topped shoulder, the burger dribbles on his chin, which he wipes off with the back of his hand. "Pa-ra-dise."

"Paradise is a cheeseburger?" Sal asks, dousing his fries with ketchup.

"Sure is," Nick explains, taking another double bite. "Especially after patrolling your *paradise* beach community. They're whacko there in July. Commandeering a boat, flying past No-Speeding signs, red cups of liquor on the beach."

Jason watches them deliberate while he eats. "Paradise is open to interpretation," he finally says.

Sal motions his laden cheeseburger across the table. "What's yours, Kyle?"

"Easy." Kyle takes a long swig of his beer. "Standing at the big stove, cooking up a storm. You know, food from *my* diner makes people happy? Ain't nothing better."

Sal raises his mug in a toast to Kyle, to which Kyle reciprocates, tipping his glass. "What about you, dude?" Sal asks, nodding to Jason then.

Jason sets down his burger, wipes his mouth with his napkin and sits back. He runs his knuckles along his scarred jawline, thinking. "Sunday mornings in bed with my wife."

"Good answer," Sal says.

Jason finishes his beer. "Yeah, waves breaking out on the bluff, seagulls calling, a salty breeze coming in the window. Paradise."

"When's the Mrs. coming back?" Kyle asks.

"Couple weeks still." Which is at the root of his being busy. Being alone and quiet in that house invites too many demons in the shadows, in the creaking wood, the reflections.

"So what's it been while she's gone? Sunday morning sexting?" Nick asks.

"None of your God damn business, punk. And watch what you say before I kick your ass." When Nick just shrugs, Jason turns to Sal. "What about you? Paradise something on the Street? Hustle and bustle, the city grind?"

It's a moment when the bar quiets. The jukebox songs stop, the guys at the table are all busy chowing down. Sal bites into his burger, stuffing in the last piece. “It’s funny,” he begins, talking around the food. “Never thought I’d say this, what with pretty much having everything I want. Seriously, I’m not bragging. Worked fucking hard for the past decade to get there, to have money, a good life in the city. And yet,” he says, taking a long drink of his beer, “I’m finding paradise right here in this little seaside town.”

No one says anything for a long second. Finally, Kyle takes his glass and tips it to Sal’s. Nick and Jason do the same, at the same time.

“Hey, man,” Kyle tells Sal then as he snags onion rings off of Jason’s plate. “Come to some open houses with Lauren and me. See something you like? You never know, you might stick around.”

seventeen

THE NEXT WEEK, ELSA FINISHES watering the red geraniums outside her cottage, the sun warm on her back, morning birds lightly twittering. While reknotting her tie-front blouse, she thinks that if it wasn't for the salt air filling her lungs, she could believe she was in Italy again. As she kneels on a floral-print foam kneepad now, her hair tied back with a rolled bandana, the feeling persists … that she's back in Milan. Oh, it's undeniably like so many years ago when she'd write an inspiration message on the walkway outside her boutique there, the day beginning as she'd hear the distant tram clanging past. Down the street, green patio umbrellas would open on the tables at an outdoor café, and next door, someone watered concrete planters filled with shrubs and vines.

She considers the old stone patio Sal cleared for her here, in front of her future inn. Over the weekend, he yanked the weeds, swept up the sand and edged the border. It's only temporary, but the small stone patio will suffice. A wooden planter box on wheels does the trick for bringing in greenery, as does the ornamental dune grass she planted along the side. Sal also added a few large conch shells to the border, placing them decoratively on the stone edge.

"Seashells," Elsa whispers, looking at the blank patio, chalk in hand. With one sweeping motion, she writes the day's inspiration in grand cursive across the stone: *Seashells and Hellos!*

"I believe that's classified as graffiti."

Elsa whips around at the sound of the voice; a familiar voice, no less. But one she doesn't particularly care to hear. "Are you kidding me?" she asks, lifting her sunglasses to the top of her head and glaring at the beach commissioner.

"Ordinance G1. No graffiti permitted, in any manner, within the confines of Stony Point. That there is unauthorized writing on a public entranceway."

"*Public?* This is my private property!"

"For now, but once it's an inn, it becomes public, Mrs. DeLuca."

"And it *will* be an inn. Do you know how much zoning red tape I had to go through?"

"Yes, I do sit on the board. And when your inn's opened, graffiti is not permitted."

"But it's a friendly message, how is that *graffiti*?"

"Doesn't matter if it's friendly or not. What matters is that it's unauthorized."

"Ooh." Elsa sets down her chalk and stands, squinting through her anger, hands on her hips. "This is my *inn*-spiration! At my boutique in Milan, I wrote sidewalk messages every day. People always smiled, something you might consider trying, Mr. Raines. Not to mention, it's ... it's just *chalk*!"

"Mrs. DeLuca, please. The rules are the rules."

"This is so unfair." She swipes her hands together, brushing off the chalk dust. "If my husband were alive, you wouldn't say these things to him, calling this art graffiti. And if you did, well, he'd give you a piece of his mind!"

"But the graffiti isn't why I'm here now. I actually tried to catch you yesterday, but no one was around."

"Monday? I was out shopping with my decorator, Celia."

"Well, I'm glad you're here today. It's about the sign."

"Sign?" Elsa glances toward where she foresees placing Lauren's painted inn sign. "It's not even made yet."

The commissioner nods toward her cottage. "In the window. I believe it's in violation of Ordinance SI.03."

If this keeps up, Elsa's sure to get a nice case of whiplash, the way she spins herself around to see what the hell this man is talking about. Now she can't miss it, that one small BEACH INN – COMING SOON sign propped in a front window. "Seriously?"

Sunlight shines on the beach commissioner's salt-and-pepper hair while he clearly points a finger at her sign, his eyebrows ever so slightly quirked so that, really, she has to look twice to see if he's joking or not. "Rules forbid residents from posting signs advertising future businesses."

"Future? Well it *would* be open now if it wasn't for your damn Hammer Law." Elsa steps closer to him, pointing her own finger at his chest. "Wait. Was *that* a violation?" she asks, breathless from her exasperation. "My using a *swear* word?"

Mr. Raines looks up from—what? From writing another ticket? He peels it off his pad and holds it out to her, the Tuesday, July 14 date duly noted, along with yet another monetary fine, underlined twice. "No need to lose your temper, Mrs. DeLuca. This is just a formality."

—

This part comes easy, this sketching the beach scene on each ascending stair riser inside the inn. Lauren has the sea view memorized from all the times she's stood on the end of Stony Point Beach. But the Gull Island Lighthouse she adds to the sketch is actually a view she remembers from a *different* vantage point: from the fishing shack beyond Little Beach where she spent time with Neil years ago, when they were in their late twenties. Gazing out at the distant lighthouse from their hideaway, they'd whisper secret hopes and plan their next secluded outing.

So while bent low on the staircase, each pencil line of her sketched dune grass, each outlined hydrangea along one side of the lower risers, each hand-drawn gentle wave … captivates her. All of it brings Lauren so deep into faded memories—of Neil boating her out past Little Beach on warm summer days, of the two of them sitting in folding chairs outside the shack there, holding hands in the sun, taking in the sea and soaring gulls—that she doesn't hear the clatter coming down the stairs. Doesn't realize Sal is about to crash straight into her, nearly toppling over as he stops himself from the collision.

"Whoa, whoa, Lauren! I didn't see you there," he says, grabbing onto the banister to prevent his fall.

"Oh, Sal! You nearly gave me a heart attack." Lauren stands, one hand to her heart, the other holding two pencils at once.

Sal glances back up the stairs to where she's sure his bedroom is, then turns to Lauren again. "Well then, you must have been *very* lost in thought, with all the racket I made trying like hell to get out of here on time." He steps around her and looks up at the stair risers covered with her seaside sketches, then back at her face. But he doesn't just look; he reaches out and brushes aside one lone tear. "Okaay, so you've been lost in one pretty powerful thought here."

"What?" Lauren slaps her hand to her face, surprised at the tear he'd found. Damn it, Neil *still* does that sometimes, catching her so off guard. But with this painting, one depicting an intimate part of her life, and then, well then Sal walking straight into her personal memory in his cuffed jeans, moppy hair, partially tucked shirt—remarkably like a casual Neil walking up to her on the beach—well, she's surprised there's only *one* tear. "It's nothing. Just feeling sentimental today. Or spooked." She gives him a quick smile. "Long story."

"That tear is more than sentimental, and I'd love to hear why." Sal checks a big watch on his wrist and twists it straight. "*Merda*, I am so late to Jason's. I really have to go." He hurries down the rest of the stairs, turning back once he's at the bottom. "But you owe me a story now, Lauren. Because no pretty lady should harbor sad tears like the one I just saw."

—

It's one of those Tuesday mornings, a typically busy mid-July workday. Jason's cell phone rings for the third time, but he's sitting at the kitchen table, and the phone is plugged into the charger on the counter, and he doesn't much feel like getting up to see who it is. Doesn't help that his leg is seriously bothering him today, so much so that he still hasn't put on his prosthesis, and uses his crutches instead. When he does get up, it sure as hell won't be to answer his phone; it'll be to head straight upstairs to the medicine cabinet for a few aspirin. A walk to the bathroom might get him to shave, too. When he runs the back of his fingers across the scar on his jawline, it's surprising to feel how much his whiskers have grown in. What's it been, two days without a shave? Three, since Saturday?

Before he has time to remember, there's a quick knock at the patio door, right before Sal slides the screen open and walks straight into the kitchen, his overloaded tool belt creaking as he does.

"Hey," Jason says while grabbing at Maddy's collar as she rushes toward Sal, a growl in her throat, all while his cell phone rings again. "Make yourself at home, why don't you," he tells Sal.

"Thanks." Sal points to the phone on the counter. "Want it?"

"No."

Sal steals a look at the caller ID, then sets his yellow hard hat on the table and pulls out a chair, giving the dog's neck a good rub. "That dude Rick is calling, from the salvage yard?"

Jason lifts his coffee and squints past the rising steam. "Said I didn't want to know."

"Hey." Sal holds up two hands, fingers outstretched, and leans his chair back. "Sorry." He looks over at the countertop. "Got any breakfast around here?"

Jason hitches his head toward the half-eaten box of powdered doughnuts near the stove. "I see you're ready to work, all geared up today."

"Bring it on," Sal says on his way to the counter. He lifts a doughnut, then drops it back in the box. "Question is … You ready?"

It's a line that Jason could've figured was coming. Whenever Sal's worked with him, Jason's pretty much had a phone to one ear, manipulating two conversations—one to whoever was on the phone; and the other to Sal, or a job foreman, or a client who stopped by. So Sal's accustomed to seeing him chomping at the bit. But today, the phantom pain is acting up enough to slow him. He tried exercising, doing stretching repetitions before getting out of bed, to no avail. Sometimes wrapping his upper leg in scalding hot towels helps, the actual pain of it eliminating the phantom pain. It didn't work this morning; the pain persists.

"Give me a few minutes. Still waking up, man." With that, Jason picks up the crutches from the floor beside him, stands, slips the cuffs on his forearms and walks toward the living room. He also hears Sal talk under his breath.

"*Shit.*"

"You got it, Salvatore. That about sums up how I'm feeling," Jason says without looking back. Of course, Sal hadn't realized he's on only one leg this morning, not until he clearly sees the limb missing when Jason stands in his cargo shorts and tee.

Sal's tool-belt gear creaks as he follows behind Jason. "That cannot be easy, your leg a reminder every *day* like that."

Now, Jason stops and looks back at Sal. "You mean, my stump?" Though Sal winces upon hearing it, in all these years, Jason hasn't come across any other word for the reality of his left leg ending just past his knee.

"Yes. Your, well … it's such a constant in your life."

Okay, so Sal can't even say the word, stump. Won't go there. "And it's bothering me today," Jason tells him as he continues walking with his crutches. "Which usually means something else is bothering me, and it manifests itself in phantom pain."

"Phantom, so … in your missing limb?"

"That's right."

"Well what's bothering you? If you take care of it—"

"Seriously?" Jason asks, whipping around the best he can with the crutches. He stands there, not moving, and feeling the pain in the missing limb while staring at Sal. "*You've* got the cure for me? You're completely ignorant, dude. So shut the fuck up."

"I just thought … Hell, Jason," he says, turning up a hand. Sal's eyes scan the living room then, which is looking pretty messy with Maris gone for all these weeks. Jason knows it, and now Sal will too. Newspapers are tossed on the sofa; empty coffee mugs sit on the end tables; boxes of still-unpacked wedding gifts line one wall; the floor hasn't been swept; a sweatshirt hangs from the back of the upholstered chair in the corner, the chair to which Jason's now headed.

"Don't get me wrong. You're lucky to be ignorant," Jason says. "The thing is, I know what will help, and that's to get this day over with. Either that or drown it out with a few potent drinks."

Sal stands at the mantel and gives the pewter hourglass a flip. "That bad?"

"It'll pass. Eventually. So let's get started. We're going to stop at the Woods' teardown, be sure the electrical is all off before any work continues."

"Isn't that the site foreman's job?"

"It is. But on some jobs, I act as project manager, too, when I like to keep a handle on things. And this is one of them, believe me. The crew's got some quiet interior work to do: taking down doors, ripping off molding. That sort of thing, to start gutting the cottage." Jason sets his crutches aside and sits in the upholstered chair, takes a long breath and rubs his hand across his whiskered jaw. "It's what comes afterward that's the problem." He looks over at Sal. "That's effing up my leg today."

"Really."

"We're driving down the coast twenty miles, to Sullivan's cottage at Sea Spray Beach. A custom salvaged door was delivered there, and I want to see it. Close to wrapping up that job, and it was one of my toughest. Ever."

"And why's that?"

Jason picks up the silicone liner for his limb and rolls it over his stump, carefully adds a sock to it, then fusses with the liner and sock as he presses them up onto his thigh. "Sullivan is the guy who drove his car into my brother and me."

Sal leans back with a small laugh. "Wait. You renovated the house of the guy who killed your brother?"

"I did," Jason assures him when he reaches for the prosthetic limb leaning against the end table. He pulls it onto his stump, then stands to test that all is secure.

"*Gesù, Santa Maria*, I'm sure all your sins are absolved."

"Maybe, maybe not. Maris still doesn't like that I took the job. It practically derailed our wedding last summer."

"No. No, Jason. Don't tell me you went against your beautiful bride's wishes."

"Wasn't easy, and it's been an ongoing source of contention."

"Shit, you're one brave man. You risked losing the love of your life like that?"

Jason heads back into the kitchen to pack his work duffel with a few papers, a thermos and something to eat. "Maris doesn't like it, but she understands. She knows Sullivan is the only other person who really gets what happened that day. He was there, man. He saw what no one else did, no one on the planet."

Sal stands in the kitchen doorway. "But he killed your brother. He's the enemy, Jason."

"I used to think he was, too. But he isn't. Time was the enemy that day."

"Time?"

"If I had a few more seconds, things would be different today. Half a minute more, and Neil would be right here." Jason nods toward a chair at the kitchen table. "Time was my enemy, on attack. And it won. Simple as that. Now I'm left with a memory and my stump. And today, this humidity's a bitch. The stump's perspiring already."

"Stump. Stump. It seems so harsh." Sal walks to the table and sits in the same chair Neil used to sit in—just like Sal, actually, wearing his weighed-down tool belt, ready to work. "*Moncone.*"

"Mon what?" Jason asks, zipping his black duffel closed.

"*Moncone.* It's Italian, for stump. *Moncone.*" He looks up at Jason. "Mon-cone-ay."

"Mon-cone-ay."

"That's right," Sal says, standing when Jason hikes up his duffel. Sal walks to the slider, his work boots heavy on the floor, and pauses. "Sometimes you have to soften things, cousin. If only for yourself."

~

The cottage was built up on the hill decades ago, and no one's done a thing to it since. The gray shingles are faded, some rotting. There's roof mold, and white paint profusely peels off the eaves and trim.

"Come on," Jason says. "We'll go up the back way."

"Wow, how could someone let a beach cottage deteriorate like this?" Sal asks. "It's disrespectful, man. Especially to the neighbors who work so hard keeping up their places."

"No shit. Old Maggie Woods was that way, everybody knew it. Disrespectful. Inconsiderate of others. You know, did what she wanted with no scruples, no ethics, all to pretend she was someone she wasn't. A bit of a kleptomaniac, too. Someday I'll tell you a story about things she did to my family."

"Ah, another Stony Point story."

"Her life was a sham, really, and it finally came down around her just like the cottage."

They walk past the detached garage that sits on the roadside. Some of the garage's windows are broken and plugged with stiff cardboard, and its roof is caving in. They glance through an intact, but filthy window, to see utter disarray. Tools, yard equipment, an old car, bags and cartons—all of it haggard and neglected.

"My brother Neil always said a house never lies." Jason nudges aside a chipped terra-cotta pot left upside down behind the garage. "That you can judge a person's happiness by the condition of their home."

"If that's the case," Sal says when they pass an ancient charcoal grill left rusting beneath dead tree branches, "this person never knew a day of happiness. Or love, I'd presume."

Jason sets his duffel on an old picnic table up higher in the yard and pulls out his coffee thermos. "I brought some ideas I had in mind for the rebuild," he says, opening a roll of initial drawings and anchoring the corners with rocks from the unkempt lawn.

"Fascinating stuff, here." Sal traces his finger along the symmetry of rooflines and peaks, walls and windows. He glances up at the cottage, trying to place Jason's new image.

"Keep in mind that local building regulations stipulate I respect the existing cottage footprint, and can't vary much from it. So I'm limited in my design parameters."

When they hear a bell ring, it's a sound—*ting-a-ling!*—so unsuited to the cottage debris around them.

"Hey, hey," Sal says, glancing down the hill to the road. "It's Celia."

Jason turns to see Celia getting off a bicycle at the base of the hill. It's an old-fashioned cruiser bike with fenders over the wheels and a wicker basket clipped onto the handlebars. "Yo, Celia," he calls. "Nice wheels!"

She gives the bell another ring, then lifts something out of the basket and heads up the hill to their picnic table. "I found it in the shed behind my cottage." She looks back at the bicycle, her smile beaming. "Dusted it off and have been pedaling ever since." She walks behind Sal, bending to give him a quick kiss before sitting beside him. "Wow, nice design, Mr. Barlow," she says of the plans laid out on the table. "It's pretty grand, compared to what's here now." She looks up at the old cottage. "Don't know how it's even still standing."

"Won't be for long." Sal looks at it too, then gives Celia's hand a squeeze.

"Oh! I brought a snack for you guys." She unwraps a dish towel from around a golden loaf of bread drizzled with a sweet glaze. "This was my mom's favorite recipe, lemon-blueberry bread, which I made early this morning. Fresh out of the oven." She pulls a knife from her tote and slices off thick hunks. "Here, have some."

As Jason does, he notices how Celia slides a piece toward Sal beside her, then touches his shoulder before quickly combing her fingers through his hair.

Sal takes the slab of fruit bread and bites into half of it. "Oh my God," he says around the food.

"So good," Jason agrees, dunking his own piece in his coffee.

"What are your plans today, Cee?" Sal asks.

As if he reminded her that she's running late, she abruptly stands and brushes bread crumbs off her shorts. "I'm finishing up a staging for an open-house cottage this weekend, so I have to cut fresh hydrangeas from Elsa's. Then it's Operation Ocean Star Inn, drafting room concepts for your mother. How about you two?"

Jason tells her about the Sullivan reno twenty miles down the coast, saying they'll pick up Maddy first, since she loves to run on the beach there. "Sea Spray's more harsh than Stony Point. The surf is stronger, with lots of dunes and wild grasses."

"I'm always looking for new places to scour for sea glass." Celia leaves the bread for them and hikes her tote on her shoulder. "If you see any pieces, pick them up for me?" she asks Sal when he stands, too. "Especially the greens and blues, my absolute favorites."

Jason waits at the picnic table and pencils in notations on his designs until Sal gets back from walking Celia to her bicycle. That's when he asks Sal what *his* plans are.

"I'm yours for the day. Ready to reno."

"No, your plans with Celia."

They both glance to the street as Celia pedals off with a *ting-a-ling*. "It's only been a few weeks," Sal tells him. "No plans, really."

"You're so full of shit. When you're a kid, no plan works. What are you, thirty-three, thirty-four?"

"Turning thirty-six next month."

Jason raises his coffee cup to Sal. "Same age Neil would have been. And old enough to have a plan. It's obvious Celia's head over heels for you. So you sticking around here? You don't ever say much, but bringing a nice woman like that into the picture, well, I don't know if she's ready for another broken heart."

"That's not my intention."

"And I can't really read you, so what *is* your intention? When I saw Maris two years ago, I knew in minutes she was the one, and I wasn't going to let her slip away."

Sal twists open a bottled water he'd crammed in his tool belt, then looks out at the distant sea. "I think I like working with Kyle better. He doesn't ask prying questions."

Jason says nothing while staring Sal down. The only sound is the distant rhythm of waves breaking on the beach.

"You all look out for each other here," Sal finally says. "Don't you?"

The way he says it, Jason thinks he's almost offended. Though he's not sure why. But everything from Sal's elusive Celia answers, to his solo boat rides in the middle of the night—it all hints at shit he's not saying.

"That's right, we do. But don't get so defensive about it. We look out for you, too. You're family, guy."

When Sal waves him off with an *Eh*, Jason reaches across the table to shake his hand. "Hey, *famiglia,* I said. So listen, I'm not really sure what your story is, DeLuca, but if you need more time here, I can really use an assistant on some jobs. It's been great talking out ideas with you, like I used to with Neil." As he says it, Jason rolls up the cottage plans laid out on the picnic table and drops them in his work duffel. "Kind of like you'd be stepping right into my brother's shoes."

Works for me, Jason hears as a seagull swoops low, cawing into the breeze. "What's that?" he asks, turning back to Sal as they head up to the cottage.

"Nothing, didn't say a word," Sal tells him with a shrug.

eighteen

If there's one thing Celia misses from home, it's Friday night movies at Amy's farmhouse. Every week, they'd settle in with popcorn and ice cream and fluffy slippers—and pick a romantic comedy to get lost in. The best she can do this Friday is talk to her friend on the phone.

"How's the cottage holding up?" Amy asks her now.

Celia glances around the kitchen, her cell phone pressed to her ear. She's puttered in George and Amy's cottage for weeks: dusting off the painted tables in the living room, wiping the artificial peaches spilling from a ceramic bowl on the kitchen table. But the back deck is her favorite place, especially sitting there in the evenings with a glass of wine and hearing nothing but the babbling flow of marsh water and the rustle of tall grasses lining its banks. She opens the screen door to the deck and steps out into the late-day sunshine. The air feels nice on her skin, so she tugs down the puckered shoulders of her peasant blouse.

"Celia? Are you at least getting a sea breeze? Is it okay there in this heat?" Amy asks.

"Yes. Yes, it's absolutely lovely, Amy." The low slant of light adding a golden hue to the lagoon mesmerizes her, as always. She sits in one of the Adirondack chairs facing the view. "I can't thank you enough for letting me stay here. Please tell George that for me."

"Believe me, we're glad to have you there," Amy says.

Celia doesn't doubt that. In the pause of their phone conversation, she can tell that things are still unsettled in Amy's life.

"After last year," Amy tells her, "we still prefer to lie low. So we're relieved you can keep an eye on George's cottage. I'm glad it's doing fine."

At that, Celia has to softly laugh.

"What?" Amy asks.

"Well the *cottage* is fine, but I'm another story. This summer, it's actually *my* life that's spinning out of control."

"With Sal?"

"Yes, and it's completely out of the blue, exactly like those romantic movies we watch." As if on cue, a great egret gracefully swoops down into the marsh, the way it might in one of those same movies. "You don't think George will mind that Sal ties his rowboat to the dock here, do you? He sometimes comes over by boat."

"I'm sure he won't. Sal seems like such a nice guy, Cee. And gosh, after everything you've done for me, I can't think of anyone more deserving of a little happiness. It's wonderful that you and Sal can spend so much time together."

"Well, you'd think so, but between the two of us, we've been working a lot."

"Working? I thought he was there on vacation."

"He is, but he's getting Elsa squared away with the business-end of her inn. And then he does side jobs helping that architect George knows."

"Jason?

"That's the one. And he works with another guy, Kyle. Get this, Amy. Sal waits tables at Kyle's diner."

"What? Mr. *Wall Street* Sal? A *waiter*?"

Celia spins the sailor's knot bracelet on her wrist. "Isn't that cute? So he keeps himself busy, but all our *free* time is spent together. And I have to tell you, it's amazing. Something I never saw coming."

"So sweet. You're having a summer romance, which is really good for the soul—especially after your whole divorce fiasco. Any plans for tonight, Cee? It is Friday, after all, a big date night."

The way Amy's voice turns all sultry, Celia remembers how last summer the tables were turned and she'd ask Amy the same thing about George, hoping their relationship would work out. Celia painted Amy's nails, babysat Amy's daughter, Grace … anything to give those two a nudge toward love. And now, Amy's returning the favor.

"Date? Hmm. Well, he's coming over after his shift at the diner. We'll probably hang out on the beach, walk the boardwalk, things like that. Because, Amy? I've gone and done it."

"Oh, no. What now, Cee?"

"Relax," Celia says, standing and adjusting her white peasant top over her denim cutoffs. "I've only turned into a certified beach bum!" As she says it, she notices the horizon turning violet and so checks her watch. "It's getting late, I wonder where he is."

If Kyle has anything, it's patience. Life's tested it over and over again, going back almost a decade to when he waited for Lauren to come to her senses and go through with their wedding, after Neil died. And talk about patience, for years he endured the heavy physical work of union shipbuilding with all its ups and downs, feast or famine: double-shift overtime or pink-slip layoffs. Some would say he's got the patience of a saint, suspecting for a long time that his son, Evan, was actually Neil's, finding out only last year the truth of it all. And Lord knows he had patience for years—ten, at least—working temporary, part-time gigs at Jerry's diner, The Dockside. He glances over at it now from his stalled-out pickup in its parking lot—doubting if he should've renamed the diner The Driftwood Café after all, or left well enough alone. He wonders what Sal would've advised.

Sal—who is bent over beneath the truck's open hood, a greasy rag hanging from his back pocket. Sal's arm reaches out and he moves his hand in a twisting motion. "Try it now," he yells.

Kyle, sitting in the driver's seat, turns the ignition and hears a scratching whirr. "It's seen its day," he calls through his rolled-down window, then presses his arm to his damp forehead. "Shit, it's too hot to be working on it, DeLuca."

"Maybe it's the timing belt." Sal plucks some mechanic gizmo from the pathetic toolset Kyle drives around with. And Kyle *patiently* sits there, catching a glimpse of Sal engrossed in the fine workings of the old truck engine. Riveted, he'd call it, if he had to name the look on Sal's face. One thing's for sure, he wouldn't want to cross that determined face in Wall Street dealings. A few clangs and clinks sound from under the hood.

"Turn the ignition," Sal says without looking away from the motor. He just stands there in his cuffed jeans and now-greasy tee, hands on hips, watching it.

Kyle turns the key, presses the gas and pounds the dashboard—but nothing. So he gets out and walks to the raised hood. "Give it up, man. It's almost eight o'clock already, I'll call for a tow before it's too late. Supposed to bring Jason dinner."

"Bullshit, don't waste your money on a tow." And still, Sal can't take his eyes off the engine, or keep his hands off the tools and dipsticks and belts and hoses. "I'll get it started."

Kyle lifts a greasy wrench and drops it in his toolbox, then wipes the grease on his white chef apron, which he still hasn't removed. Damn, now he'll have to presoak the stain, wash it twice … or just toss it. "That's okay. Forget it."

"No way." Sal steps back and squints at Kyle. "I love this truck. If you treat it fine, it'll work. But you don't believe I can start it, do you?"

"My faith in that truck ran out a long time ago." Kyle lifts his apron off over his head, folds it up and presses it to his face and neck, blotting his perspiration, before lifting his arm and glancing at the damp circle on his black tee. "I'd like to believe you, DeLuca. Hell, I'd owe you big time if you got it going and saved me the tow-and-repair charge."

"Now we're talking, man." Sal wipes his grease-stained hand on his jeans, then extends it to Kyle. "Let's put something on it."

So it's all about the odds, it seems now, coming from someone who must master them daily. Kyle exhales a long breath, then reluctantly shakes hands.

"If I start it up," Sal says, "let's see." He stops, looks out at the darkening horizon, checks his watch, then looks at Kyle. "The truck's mine for the weekend."

"What?"

"I could use a set of wheels to take out Celia. You know." He hitches his head toward the truck.

"Fine. And good luck, you'll need it." Kyle turns to the diner and passes his now-empty outdoor patio, calling over his shoulder, "I'm going in to pack Jason's dinner." Which he does: a hefty Salisbury steak, mashed potatoes and peas, all of it loaded with onions and brown gravy. And he's no fool; there's no way that truck will start tonight. So after locking up the doors and pulling on them twice, he dials the local full-service gas station for a tow. With his stained apron slung over his arm holding Jason's dinner, his other hand holds his cell to his ear. "We're closed," he tells an approaching couple. "Closed at seven tonight." He walks to the truck then, slowing as he nears it. And as he hears the idling engine. "What the hell?" He disconnects the tow call and drops the phone in his pants pocket.

"Purring like a kitten," Sal says from where he sits—in the driver's seat.

"*Merda.*" Kyle walks around the truck while eyeing it, then gets in the passenger side. "How'd you do it?"

"Easy. Gave it a little lovin'." As though he can't help himself, Sal gently pats the dashboard. "You don't mind losing your vehicle for a couple days?"

"We shook on it," Kyle says while slamming the door shut and setting Jason's carryout bag behind the seat. "I'm good for my word."

So Sal puts the truck in gear and slowly cruises toward the parking lot exit. "Okay, then I'm going to have one mighty fine weekend."

It's the way he says it that has Kyle believe him. For some godforsaken reason, this old jalopy has Mr. Wall Street in some sort of trance; Kyle hears it, sees it in the way Sal tenderly shifts the gears, presses the clutch.

"Hey, just keep it clean. Don't be sullying my ride. And drop me off at Barlow's, would you?" Kyle checks his watch again. "He'll drive me home after we do some fishing."

Oh my God, Celia thinks when she recognizes Kyle's pickup truck pulling in front of her cottage. *Something's happened to Sal, and Kyle's here to tell me in person.* Quick, panicked thoughts of an accident, or illness, flit through her mind as she sets down her glass of water so suddenly it spills over on an end table. She leaves it and hurries through the living room, pushes the screen door open and trots along the lawn, her trembling hand to her heart.

The tears nearly come, but she fights them back with a glance up at the dusky sky, then back at Sal—yes, *Sal*—emerging from the truck. And it scares her then, how utterly distraught she was, thinking that some harm had come to him. How did this happen? How did she fall for him so hard, so fast? Especially after she'd sworn off love since her divorce, believing that it's all a farce. What she's most thankful for as Sal closes the truck door is that his back is to her as she fights one random, emotional sob, pinches herself and tries to get a grip. *Sorridi,* she tells herself. Smile.

"Hey, darling," Sal says when he turns. "Don't you look beautiful."

"Oh, Sal," Celia tells him as she walks closer, smiling and shaking her head. "You're looking pretty sharp yourself." She gently straightens the skinny tie he wears with a button-down short-sleeved shirt over his cuffed jeans. And yes, she notices how nicely pressed those jeans are, too. Her fingers move to touch a curl of his shower-damp hair while she still smiles, and her fingers still tremble.

"Grab your purse, Celia, because ..." He jangles Kyle's truck keys. "Tonight, I'm taking you out on the town."

And does he ever; Sal takes her out on the *beach* town. They order the best fried clams Celia's ever tasted at The Clam Shack, where they sit outdoors at a stone table and pluck clams and French fries from red-and-white checked cardboard cartons. She notices how Sal is just like his mother, dousing all his food—clams in tartar sauce, fries in ketchup. But not only that, he also relishes every single taste, every bite, his eyes sometimes closing with pleasure. The take-out joint sits at the mouth of the Connecticut River, which empties into Long Island Sound, and so the water runs deep and strong here. After Sal leads her to the causeway to drop in extra fries for the brave swans paddling against the current, the good times continue.

Cruising in Sal's weekend wheels, they head a few beach towns over—where tiny cottages are stacked on top of each other, and seasonal shops sell overpriced tubes and towels. An arcade there is packed with teens and family vacationers escaping the heat of the Connecticut shore. Sal and Celia venture in to shoot basketball hoops, wrack up zinging-and-clanging pinball points, and race padded bumper cars—where Celia's car gets jammed into a corner. For a consolation prize,

Sal stops at the stuffed-animal machine and maneuvers a mechanical claw to pluck a plush seagull from a pile and drop it down a chute, straight into her hands. And okay, her heart, too.

Later, he parks Kyle's old pickup truck at a roadside ice-cream shack for huge, gooey sundaes. Their outdoor table overlooks a vast marsh with saltwater inlets winding through it, and tall grasses whispering secrets in the night. Far above, twinkling stars glimmer against a moonless sky stretching beyond, over a night sea. All Celia thinks of is Elsa's story of ocean stars twinkling on the water, and how similar the two look: celestial and sea stars.

"I never want this night to end," Celia says, sitting beside Sal and scraping her spoon along the bottom of her empty ice-cream dish.

"Me neither." He briefly touches the gauzy fabric of her peasant top, then strokes her bare shoulder. "Maybe I can do something about that."

Well, if he has any way of wheeling and dealing with Father Time to stop the clock right here and now, Celia's all for it. A few couples sit at surrounding tables, their voices quiet. Crickets chirp and a salty breeze drifts off the marsh. And doesn't Sal do it then—stop time in his own way—when he approaches carrying one super-deluxe banana-split sundae-jubilee, dripping whipped cream and hot fudge and caramel sauce and chocolate sprinkles and cherries ... with two tall spoons set into it.

"This should take us a while," he says as he settles onto his chair and scoots it closer to Celia.

"What is this? I've never seen an ice cream this huge." Celia turns the long bowl sideways and studies it. "You're crazy, Sal!"

"Crazy about you. So I asked them to put something special together. They call this sundae ... Love Potion by the Ocean."

Celia can't help herself and laughs while slapping his arm. "You totally made that up! And are *such* a world-class flirt."

"You don't believe me?" Sal fills a heaping spoon with fudge-laced ice cream and holds it out to Celia's mouth, which she opens as he feeds her a taste of sweet heaven in the warm summer air, beneath the stars.

Love Potion by the Ocean? Maybe he wasn't lying after all.

Jason drags a slice of bread through the gravy on his plate and scoops up bits of mashed potatoes with it. The painted plank table is covered with their dinner plates, a pile of unopened mail, a tackle box and his cell phone. "Can't believe how the fish were biting tonight."

"Yeah, it was something." Kyle takes his empty dish to the sink and lets out a low whistle. "Bro, you can't let these sit here." He fills the sink with hot, soapy water. "The food will get all crusted on. When's the last time you washed dishes?"

"I don't know," Jason answers around a mouthful of bread that sopped up the last of his Salisbury steak. "Just been loading them in the dishwasher till it's full." He hears Kyle open the dishwasher behind him, then loudly clear his throat, pointing at the overloaded dishwasher. Jason turns up his hands and shrugs.

As if he knows there's no sense in arguing, Kyle wipes off the dishes in the sink and squeezes them into the dishwasher. "Hey, you calling your wife tonight?"

Jason checks his phone and calculates the time difference. "It's almost eleven. Too late, she'll be asleep. I'll send her a text for when she wakes up." He types in a few words about the night at the beach, and fishing with Kyle, finishing up with telling her he misses her.

"It's hot in here, man." Kyle bends and squints at the dishwasher controls, then hits a few buttons. "You never put central air in this bungalow on the bluff?"

There's no use explaining that with the schedules they keep, most of the time he and Maris aren't even home. When they do finally crash here, they're too beat to do much more than linger on the deck on summer nights. "Usually a sea breeze comes through." He glances over at the filling dishwasher. "Hang on, pause it," he says, standing and scooping up the last of his gravy-laden food scraps and finishing them in one swallow. "One more coming."

Kyle opens the dishwasher and waits for Jason to stuff his unrinsed plate inside. As he does, Kyle wipes his forehead with a dish towel, then drags it around his neck.

"Grab a couple brews from the fridge," Jason tells Kyle. "We'll go out on the bench."

"I'm on it." On his way to the refrigerator, Kyle pushes in the two chairs at the table, straightens the salt and pepper shakers, and snags Jason's phone.

"What are you doing?"

"Texting your wife, dude." Kyle's fingers fly over the phone keyboard. "She needs to know that you agreed to install central air here."

"Give me that."

"Done." Kyle tosses him his phone, gets two cold beers and goes outside through the slider, a panting Maddy close behind him. "Your poor dog's sweating, too. Do it for her, at least." He walks across the lawn toward the bluff, and the German shepherd veers to her kiddie pool filled with water. "Hey, Sal told me he met Sullivan the other day," Kyle says over his shoulder.

Jason follows behind him and sees how Kyle holds one of the frosty cans to his face. "He did."

"So he knows the story, then. What'd he say?"

"Not much. Shook Ted's hand. You know, he was polite."

"Yeah."

They walk on the lawn, a few twigs snapping beneath their feet. Jason catches up to Kyle and takes one of the beers from him. "Sal told me afterward he was surprised I didn't invite Ted to Neil's anniversary mass in a few weeks. Thought I should."

"Tough call." Kyle stops at the bench and snaps open his cold beer. "I mean, come on. We're talking *Theodore*. I know it wasn't his fault, but still. He drove his car into you guys."

"He did, but according to the Italian, it's the closure that matters. He wonders if I have it or not."

Kyle sits, and Jason joins him. Down below, waves break easy on the rocks. Jason likes that; no matter what, those waves always break, and if he stops whatever he's doing—no matter where—it always feels like he can hear them.

"Toured a house with Lauren today." Kyle swigs his beer. "The shower spigot came to my chin."

Jason hits Kyle's arm. "Check it out." He points at the water. "That's Sal now, over there." A lone rowboat moves slowly through the water. There's no moon tonight, so it's dark and the boat is barely a silhouette blending with the sea.

"Where?" Kyle walks to the edge of the bluff, squinting. "You sure?"

"He's in Foley's old boat. Remember that dinghy?"

It's enough of a memory to get Kyle to look at Jason in disbelief, then turn again toward the water. Jason picks up his can and walks behind Kyle while taking a drink of his beer.

"I see him out there, late," he tells Kyle, his voice quiet.

"No shit. What's he doing?"

"Drifting. Here. At the lagoon. When I'm on the beach late at night, he's usually somewhere out there."

"Strange." Kyle bends and shields his eyes against the darkness. "Is he alone?"

"Looks it."

"That's funny, because he went out with Celia earlier. Wonder if they had a fight."

"Who knows." Jason moves beside Kyle and they watch Sal. "What I do know is that something's up with him. Seriously, he just drifts in that rowboat. Sometimes he starts the engine and putters around out there. But mostly? Just drifts."

nineteen

IT'S LIKE A GHOST TOWN around here lately. Saturday afternoon, Elsa peers out the kitchen window at the scaffolding rising on one side of her cottage. A pile of large stones sits in the yard, having been pulled from the earth by a bucket loader clearing the land for the turret addition—if Jason ever finishes drawing up the plans. And the violating fence sections are covered with blue tarps now, since all construction came to a halt with the Hammer Law. So that look of commotion-stopped gives the property an eerie feel.

But at last, life! Out in the cottage, someone comes in the front door, and Elsa hears Lauren talking to whoever it is.

"Sal?" Elsa calls while rinsing her hands under the faucet. "Is that you? I was wondering if you'd stop by and visit your ma today." She shuts off the tap and sprinkles water from her fingers on her tiny red herb pails, all while yelling over her shoulder, "I'm making a zucchini quiche for dinner." Drying her hands on a dish towel then, a strand of hair falls onto her face, which she brushes away with the back of her fingers.

"It's not Sal. It's only me, clocking in a little early for our weekend design consultation." Celia stands in the doorway wearing faded denim skinnies with a white tank top. Her hand fiddles with a pale yellow sailor's knot bracelet. "But Sal's fine," she quietly says. "I had breakfast with him at Kyle's diner."

Something about Celia has Elsa walk over to her. It's a look in her hazel eyes, a little soulful but uncomfortable about being too forthcoming. Maybe it's the way she stands in the doorway, uncertain about entering the room. "Oh, hon," Elsa says as she gives her a hug. "When Sal's with you, I know he's fine."

Celia steps back, her head tipped down. "Did you know he took me out on the town last night?"

What can Elsa do except waggle her finger? "No secrets at Stony Point, remember that." When Celia rolls her eyes with a reluctant smile, Elsa takes her hand. "Come on in. Sit down, we'll get started on your questionnaire." They walk to the big table covered with bowls and cooking utensils. "But speaking of secrets, because there's always time for a little girl talk," Elsa says, "I do secretly hope Sal will stay on here. And maybe you're the charm that can woo him away from the city."

"Really?" Celia moves aside a dish and sets her tote on an empty chair. "But his career is there."

"It is, but he can do other things with his financial experience. I always hoped he'd live close by, and he seems so happy here, always talking about you."

Celia tucks her straight auburn hair behind an ear. "He does?"

Right as the timer beeps, Elsa nods her head. "Oh! My food's ready." She puts on starfish-print cooking mitts and pulls a pan from the oven.

"That smells *heavenly*," Celia says, leaning closer to see. "You're going to be such a good innkeeper."

"It's Sal's favorite, zucchini quiche." Elsa sets the pan on a rack on the counter. "We'll sneak a slice after it cools." She walks to the doorway and calls out to Lauren, who's been painting a sample view on the staircase mural. "Would you like some quiche, Lauren?"

"No thanks, Elsa." Lauren's voice carries through the cottage from whatever stair she's perched on, paintbrush in hand. "I'm finding a stopping point now, Kyle's picking me up soon. My mom's babysitting and I don't want to keep her waiting."

With a shrug, Elsa turns back to the kitchen and sees a change in Celia from just moments ago. There's a sparkle in her eyes as she sits at the table, hands clasped.

"Now I'm curious, Elsa. What exactly *does* your son say about me?"

Elsa sees the same sparkle in Sal lately, too, so that's that. These two are smitten with each other, a match made in beach-heaven. "Little things," she begins, pulling out a chair. "Like what you do together. And that you play guitar, and collect sea glass."

"Really?"

"Yes, and I must admit, I'm a bit jealous. You were my new beach friend, coming by for lemonade, chatting while I watered the flowers at Summer Winds, shopping with me … But now my son has snatched you away and I miss hanging out." She gives Celia's arm an affectionate squeeze. "Ah, such is life."

"Aw, Elsa. Don't worry. You'll be seeing so much of me now. I finished the Summer Winds cottage, and I'm wrapping up my last staging job. As of today, I'm all yours, planning the inn's décor and so much more!" She pauses when the wind chimes outside the kitchen window jingle in a sea breeze, the light seashells and beads clattering. "And to start, my first question is actually a personal one, to reflect *you* in the concepts."

"Interesting …"

"I actually got this idea from Sal," Celia begins. "Because he talks about you, too. About his childhood, and the things you've been through with losing your sister, and then losing touch with your nieces on top of it. I believe you are a very strong woman, Elsa. Especially now."

"Now? Why now?"

"You're a widow? Uprooting your life and starting over on another continent? Wow, do I admire that! Getting divorced completely derailed me, and I'd *love* to know what gets you through the difficult days. It'll help me to focus on the inn as a restful destination."

"That's easy, dear. One memory does." With that, Elsa walks into the living room and comes back with a Mason jar filled with sand; and seashells; and wisps of lagoon grass; and a dried hydrangea blossom, its petals tan and lavender now. A fine gold chain with a star pendant is entwined in the blossom. "Years ago," she begins as she moves a mixer aside and sets the jar on the table between them, "my sister, June, rented a cottage here at Stony Point for one September week. So I made the trip and stayed with her and her daughter Maris. One evening, June took old Mason jars from a dusty shelf in that cottage and we went to the lagoon together. The sun had set and the sky was royal blue, but the far horizon still held on to some of its pastel colors."

"The blue hour! My father taught me that, and how it's uncertain if that hour is night, or still day. Sometimes I watch it from my deck, facing the lagoon, and it's magical when the sky is that twilight blue."

Elsa can only smile, her eyes already tearing up. "That evening *was* magical, the air thick with salt, a pair of swans paddling by. And suddenly, out of the tall marsh grasses, twinkling lights floated toward the sky. They were fireflies! So we opened our jars—June, little Maris, and I—and we caught them, just for a few minutes, watching them flicker in the jars like candles in the night. And when we released them, the fireflies twinkled up higher and higher to that dark blue sky. *Look*, June said, pointing to all the fireflies rising from the grasses. *They're stars, dancing up above tonight.*"

"Oh, Elsa. What a beautiful memory you have."

"I do," she whispers. "In that moment with my sister, life was as sweet as it could ever be." When Celia hands her a napkin, Elsa takes it and blots her eyes. "So last summer, when I saw June's daughter Maris making one of these," she says, holding up the decorated Mason jar, "and calling it her *happiness* jar, well I knew I had to make my own happiness jar to commemorate that September night with my sister. It's a moment I return to whenever life is feeling sad, and it helps. So my advice to you, Celia," she says with a warm smile, "is to capture those sweet moments in your life. They are so fleeting, yet they give us the most strength. Some people keep a diary. I say to keep happiness jars."

"Hold that thought!" Celia pulls a notebook from her tote. "What a great story to build into your inn's theme. *Some people keep a diary. I say to keep happiness jars,*" she whispers while writing. "We can incorporate happiness jars into the décor, using that sentiment."

"What?"

Celia picks up the happiness jar, and the gold chain that was once June's glints in the late-day sunlight coming through the window. "Guests all receive a jar, on their nightstand, maybe. Maybe with a few words on a slip of paper, asking them to bottle their happiness during their stay? And they keep the jar as an inn souvenir. I can help you decorate them, Elsa, with burlap and twine, maybe a feather, or shells, and they'll be the heart of your décor."

"I love it." Elsa takes the jar and gazes at all inside it. "It's perfect."

Celia says nothing more. She simply reaches across the table and squeezes Elsa's hand, which just about melts Elsa's heart. Because isn't that hand-squeeze the very same thing June often did, to silently tell her that she loved her.

~

From halfway up the staircase, Lauren scans the top landing to be sure she didn't leave behind any sketch pads or tubes of paint. As she zips her supply tote, Sal comes in through the front door of the cottage.

"Your ride's here, Lauren."

"Kyle's here already?" She checks her watch. "Can you tell him I'll be a minute? I'm almost done cleaning up."

"I'm your ride." Sal steps closer, looking at the sample stair riser she painted.

"You? But Kyle has my car, so what's up?"

"The diner patio is so busy, he's still there. Decided to extend his Saturday evening hours to make some extra cash. I told him he'd be missing out on good money, otherwise." Sal looks at her sketched view of a ragged coastline, small whitecaps on the waves, dune grass swaying. "And since I have your husband's truck for the weekend, I'm driving you home." He gives the keys a shake. "Didn't you get Kyle's message?"

"No." Lauren unzips her tote and pulls out her phone. "Oh, damn. It's off." When she puts it on, there's the text message. "Okay, then," she says. "You're my ride."

He looks at the stair-mural-in-progress, again. "Nice work, by the way. No tears today?"

"Sal! That was one time, when I just felt sad thinking of something."

"Salvatore?" Elsa asks when she comes into the foyer. "Is that finally you? I haven't seen you in days."

"Ma! I was here yesterday."

"Well, it feels like days," she says around the hug she gives him.

"Ah." Sal steps back and opens his arms at the sight of Celia standing there, too. "All the beautiful women in my life—here under one roof. *Magnifico!*" As he says it, it's obvious that he can't take his eyes off of Celia, especially as his hands cradle her face when he gives her a tender kiss.

"Stay for a nice Saturday dinner? You and Celia?" Elsa asks. "Oh! I bought you some new shorts, too. You've been wearing the same couple of pairs since you got here. Be sure to try them on later."

"*Basta, Ma!* Enough, not in front of our guests," he says with a wink while standing beside Celia, his arm around her shoulder. "My ma convince you to have dinner already?" he asks, kissing the side of her head.

Oh, Lauren sees it, the way Celia's eyes drop closed with the kiss. New summer love … it's the absolute sweetest.

"I have some last-minute staging for an open house tomorrow, but I can finish it up in the morning." Celia gives Sal's hand a squeeze. "I'd love to dine here this evening. That zucchini quiche looks divine."

The funny thing, Lauren thinks, is that the talk has shrunken to only Celia and Sal, as though no one else is in the room. To them, no one else matters.

"Come for a ride first, while I drive Lauren home?" Sal hitches his head toward the front door. "There's room for three in that pickup truck, if we hold our breath."

And the touching continues, as Celia's hand runs up and down Sal's arm, her fingers dragging around his sailor's knot bracelet. "No, I'll help your mom set the table." Finally, Celia turns to Elsa. "Maybe we can slice fresh tomatoes for a side dish?"

"Yes! With sea salt and mozzarella! Some sprigs of basil from my herb pots, too. Lauren, are you sure you can't stay?" Elsa asks.

"Thanks, but another time. My kids must be getting stir-crazy at home with my mom."

"Okay, let's get going." Sal kisses Celia again, grabs his *Beach Bum* cap from a table, then picks up Lauren's art tote and holds the front door open for her.

"Don't be long!" Celia calls out as the door closes behind them.

twenty

SOMEDAY I'M GOING TO BUY this truck from your husband." Sal pats the dusty dashboard as he says it.

"Are you kidding me?" As they leave Stony Point and drive beneath the railroad trestle, Lauren glances into the messy truck bed at Kyle's fishing poles and toolboxes and baseball glove. "This old clunker?"

"Absolutely."

"Sal. I'm sure you have enough money to buy *three* brand-new trucks, fully loaded. What would you want with this hunk of metal?"

"Oh, man," he says while hitting the turn signal and taking a left onto the main drag. "There's so much history in these wheels. It's all about the story it tells, and where it's been, and living a very laid-back life travelling the roads like this."

She squints at him. "You're full of shit. *And* Eastfield's the other way. You took a wrong turn."

"I don't think so."

It's the sudden defiance with which he adjusts his *Beach Bum* cap that clues Lauren in. "Oh, no you don't."

"What?"

"I *know* what you're doing, Mr. DeLuca."

"Do you now?"

He tosses her a glance—one just long enough for her to nod with the same defiance. "Turn it around," she tells him.

He settles more comfortably in the driver's seat. "Seems like a perfect evening to hear a story. Your sad memory?"

"I'm sorry, Sal. You're a nice guy and all. But when you caught me crying while painting your mother's stairs, well … that story's personal. Those tears were not meant for you to see."

"But I *did* see them." He lowers his sunglasses, checks out the western horizon where the sun sits like a fireball, then puts his sunglasses back in place and turns onto a side road. "And it made me think of an old Italian proverb."

"Swell." Lauren crosses her arms and sits straight, looking out the windshield at the passing small homes set on lightly wooded lots. July's shadows grow long at this twilight hour, falling on swing sets, and birdbaths, and low stone walls edging front yards. "Okay, let me hear it."

"The saying goes … Tell your life in smiles, not tears."

She looks over at this New York hotshot telling her how to live. "I told you those tears were from a *memory*, not from my life now."

"Right. But life is too short to not *replace* those tears with smiles now, when you think of that memory. *Sorridi*, Lauren." He glances at her. "Smile."

The rural road curves as they pass a stretch of farmland. It's always surprising the way a sprawling barn and field of black-and-white cows suddenly signals the change from beach area to countryside in these sleepy New England towns. Wispy cornstalks sway in the low golden sunlight, and Lauren takes it all in before looking over at Sal. "What is it with you? You get under everyone's skin, yet you're everyone's friend."

"Something wrong with that? You know, I'm an only child, no brothers, no sisters. And I like everyone here. You're all a great bunch of people and feel like a big family. I've lived over a decade in Manhattan and haven't come close to finding more than a few decent folks there."

"Sometimes it does feel like that, that we're all one Stony Point family. I'll give you that much."

"*Si.* One family, and one that I keep hearing has many dark secrets, too."

"Too many, actually."

Sal takes a sharp bend in the road, and they pass a town library first, then a community center, the sign out front advertising a local art show. "So maybe it's time to let go of yours?"

"He brought me flowers once. Right from that little flower hut, there." Lauren points to an approaching farm stand. A rusty, squat red trailer is parked beside it. Using two-by-fours and metal flashing, someone built a peaked roof over the two-wheeled trailer, then covered the trailer bed with used wooden crates and hung a hand-painted sign advertising farm-fresh flowers. Old glass bottles filled with cut summer bouquets line each crate.

"Kyle did?"

Does every landmark have to hold a memory of Neil, even this old utility trailer, dented and rusting roadside? She looks at Sal and shakes her head, no.

"Ah," he says. "So the story begins."

He slows the truck and pulls into the parking area. When the tires crunch over the rutted dirt and gravel, even that sound evokes sadness for Lauren as she imagines Neil pulling in much the same way, and hearing the same sound. Sal parks off to the side, with a clear view of the quirky flower stand.

"It was one time, that he did that." Lauren takes a quick breath. "Brought me flowers. They were so pretty, picked fresh right there." She points to a small field lined with swaying summer blossoms behind the farm stand. "My bouquet, well, it was zinnias and snapdragons. Purple coneflowers. And one sunflower. Oh, and blades of green marsh grasses, all tied with twine in a jar. He said he saw my paint palette in the flower colors."

Sal crosses his arms over the steering wheel and eyes the brimming vases set beneath a red-painted FARM FRESH sign. "Just once? He gave you flowers only one time?"

"One time. So how can I forget them?" It happens then, instead of her eyes tearing up, she smiles. Sadly, but still. "In my twenties, I spent most weekends at craft fairs, selling my driftwood paintings. So I'd have to keep a large inventory, and he'd usually find me when I was painting down on the beach. At first, it was coincidental. You know, we just crossed paths. But we got to talking and then, I could tell, he'd come looking for me, sometimes saying how he'd missed me the past few days. That sort of thing."

"Wait." Sal sits back in the driver's seat and shifts toward her now. "So this is *not* Kyle?"

"No. This was when I was engaged to Kyle."

"*Gesù, Santa Maria.*"

When he looks from her, then back to the flowers, Lauren knows what question is coming next, and Sal doesn't let her down.

"Does this man have a name?"

She doesn't answer; not right away, anyway. Because when she says the name, she wants to see what happens to Sal's eyes, how they react. So she sits silently until his head turns toward her. Then, she surrenders it. "Neil."

And yes, his eyes say it all as they look down, trying to place the name with anyone other than the *only* Neil he's heard talk of. And when his dark eyes meet hers again, she is nodding as he asks, "Jason's brother?"

"It all began just talking on the beach while I painted, that spring when I was engaged to Kyle. Nine years ago now. I'd known Neil since we were teenagers, of course, hanging out at Stony Point with the gang. But that year, things changed. By the end of the summer, we were in love, Sal."

He simply shakes his head, then lifts the brim of his cap, watching her as she talks.

"The last time I saw him," she says, looking out at the dusky horizon from the front seat of the pickup, "was a rainy day in August. Four days before he died."

"And you were engaged to Kyle?"

"That day? Yes. Two days later, I broke off the engagement and started doing things to stop the wedding. Neil was still alive then."

"So you're telling me that you were going to be with Neil, *instead* of Kyle?"

"That was the plan." But this, she whispers. The more she talks, the closer Neil feels, and there's a sanctity to this unexpected moment when she gets to tell their story. Because, really, no one, nowhere, has ever heard all the private nuances and memories. No one. "The last time I saw Neil, we danced to the jukebox. In Foley's, of all places. It was a rainy evening and we were first trapped on the boardwalk, arguing a little. The wedding was coming up, and Neil was furious that I hadn't broken off with Kyle yet." If she looks out the truck passenger window and squints just right, can't she envision that day again. She thinks Sal can see it, too, merely in the soft desperation of her words telling him about the steady rain, and how Jason was at the Barlow home, and they couldn't get to the shack to stay dry and talk, so the only place to be *alone* was Foley's, which was empty that summer.

"We ran in the rain from the beach, to Foley's. Neil jimmied the lock and broke in to the back room, one last time together. It was pouring outside. But in that boarded-up room, it was dry, and that's where we had it out. He threw some things, his drumsticks—oh, he was so mad. But he wore me down, Sal, as he usually did, and we eventually talked, cried, played a few songs. Had one last sweet dance." Her eyes close, her body subtly sways with the memory of Neil's arms around her, dust swirling like stardust that day, in the dim light of only the jukebox.

"And then?"

"He made love to me, Sal."

"In *Foley's*?" His eyes don't leave hers, as though he's trying to envision all this drama going on in that shabby room. "My *mother's* place? That room everyone loves and acts like it's a shrine?"

"There's a reason it's a shrine. Every one of us has some private memory there. Every one of us."

"Man," he says as he starts the truck and pulls out onto the rural street. "I have to process all this. I mean, you? And Neil?"

They cruise winding, narrow roads off the beaten path of Stony Point's beach community. Here, the only sense of the sea is the distant sky, reaching to the far, violet horizon. Here, small gingerbread homes and country shanties replace cedar-shingled cottages and weathered bungalows. They pass the occasional front-yard sign advertising fishing bait for sale, or fresh tomatoes from someone's backyard garden.

"You asked for all this, Sal, but I don't think you really realized what you were pressing me to reveal."

"No, I absolutely did not."

"And I'm not done, so get ready. I'm going to tell you something else, which you will take to your grave, Salvatore. Promise me."

"Are you sure you want to do that, Lauren? Maybe some things are better left unsaid?"

"Don't think you're getting off that easy, now. You've heard this much, and you need to hear it to the end. So promise me that what I'm about to tell you never leaves this damn truck."

"Okay." He takes a curve in the road heading back to the main drag. The deep shadows of a forest fall across the pavement. "Okay, then. Lay it on me."

"Evan? My son? He's Neil's, actually."

"Now that's about enough." Sal pulls Kyle's pickup off the road onto the grassy shoulder. "I can't even focus on driving with this love triangle going on. You could write a *book* with your story, my God. Does Kyle know?"

"Kyle. And Jason, so I'm sure Maris does, too. Which means her sister, Eva, knows. So yeah, the way our secrets are here, it must've gone through the pipeline. And it's another reason I'm so glad your mother bought Foley's."

"Why? I don't get it."

And so Lauren simply raises her eyebrow at Sal.

"No."

"Yes. That's where I got pregnant, I'm sure." She nods. "That last night I spent with Neil."

Sal leans his head back on the headrest in disbelief.

The rest, Lauren whispers again—it's that special. "So after all these years, I have a place to go to sometimes when I miss him. That back room. A place to stir up the dust of the past, to feel Neil's spirit, listen to a song, time travel." She's quiet then, until he looks directly at her. "Remember his touch."

"In Foley's."

She shrugs. "We tried to go to the shack that day, for privacy. But the tide was out, so it was Foley's instead."

"You keep mentioning a shack, a shack. What shack is this?"

"You've heard of Little Beach, the hidden beach through the path in the woods?"

Sal only nods, listening.

"Well, you have to go way past that. There's an old fishing shack in a secluded spot, far around the bend of Little Beach. It's best to get there when the tide is in, high tide, to maneuver around a rocky ledge."

Sal immediately lifts his cell phone from the cup holder and taps the screen. "Take me there?"

"What! Are you crazy? I haven't been there, well, since Neil was alive."

Sal hitches his head in the direction of the sea.

"But I have to get home, Sal." Lauren checks her watch, noticing paint spatters on her denim board shorts and thinking of her day, and her kids, and Kyle. "It's late."

"*And* it's high tide. Right now." He shows her the tide chart he pulled up on his phone. "So it's now or never, Ell."

Hearing him call her that—Ell—upsets her. No one but Kyle ever calls her that name. Kyle, who she loves very much. More than ever, now. "I don't get you," Lauren says, turning toward her open passenger window and sneaking her fingers to swipe a tear off her face. "All this has nothing to do with you. It was just a tryst Neil and I had a long time ago. Why would you care?"

"A tryst?" Sal reaches over, hooks his finger beneath her chin and turns her face toward him. "Listen. I'm your *friend*, and that was more than a tryst. I sensed you carried something heavy from the moment I saw you cry on my ma's stairs. And if you don't let out a story like that one, well, you'll always be sad, let me assure you. So for tonight? I'm your shoulder to cry on, Lauren. And then, we're going to turn those persistent tears into smiles. Somehow … after all these years."

"No." Lauren shakes her head. "As much as I'd love to see that old shack, just one more time …"

"Why can't we?"

"Because I've told you enough. And I'll be in serious trouble if I *ever* got caught. Plus you can't get there on foot. You need a boat. The only way to find that shack is on the water."

"I have a boat."

"What? You are going to get me so screwed." The thing is, she says it while pulling her cell phone from her purse and dialing her mother. "Truck problems," she tells her while glaring at Sal. "Sal's tinkering under the hood, but he says not to worry. He's almost got it. Yes, Mom. I'm fine. And I have my phone. It's late. Why don't you take the kids to the diner for supper, and I'll meet you at home by the time you're back. Okay. Okay. Love you." She drops the phone into her purse. "What about you? Isn't Celia waiting?"

"And my ma. For dinner."

As he calls them from the truck, Lauren reaches behind the driver's seat and pulls out Kyle's dusty flashlight. It'll be nearly dark by the time they get there.

—

It's such a calming sound, one that she'll never tire of, not in all her livelong days. Seawater drips from the creaking oars now. And when Lauren closes her eyes, feeling the rise and fall of gentle swells beneath their boat, she's gone. That fluid motion erases nine years of time and if she inhales a deep breath of salt air, she's twenty-seven again, with Neil there, behind her closed eyes.

But she quickly opens them, knowing this stretch of the coast can be treacherous to navigate. After they rounded the bend leaving Little Beach behind, Sal lifted the rowboat's outboard engine and paddles now. The coastline here is rocky, with small boulders concealed beneath the high tide water. "There," she suddenly says, remembering as soon as she sees the sloping, wind-blown beach grass. "It's just beyond those dunes, which is why no one ever really found it."

Sal paddles the boat around one last bend, where a secret beach opens up before them. "Here?" he asks. "I don't see it."

But Lauren has no doubt, still, after all these years. It's a magical spot etched into so many of her dreams. As soon as the water's low enough to not get her shorts wet, she climbs out of the boat and wades toward shore. The current is stronger here, with the open Sound spread before them, and it pulls at her legs so that she struggles to get through it. But she keeps going, and when the water is only ankle-deep, she starts to run, shining the flashlight beam across the secluded beach. "It's there," she calls back to Sal. "Right there!"

twenty-one

If sunshine could be promising, that one morning nine years ago, it was. It brought to life everything its golden rays touched. Birds sang arias; butterflies waltzed; the sea breathed; the translucent wings of dragonflies quivered. As Lauren walked the narrow path that long-ago spring day, she heard his voice behind her.

"It's just over that hill, through these dunes," Neil had said. He wore a backpack filled with food, drinks, journals and his camera. "I think you'll like it."

Lauren's tote was slung over her shoulder, and she pushed aside wispy dune grass brushing her legs on the winding sandy trail. A slatted storm fence leaned against some of the sweeping grasses, keeping the trail somewhat clear. Neil had convinced her to leave Stony Point's main beach to take her *here* for a surprise? This wasn't the familiar Little Beach, the one beyond the wooded path at the far end of Stony Point. This was different, more ragged and overgrown. Some of the trail grasses clung to her floral-print gauzy skirt, the bottom of which was still damp from wading through the water when he'd helped her out of his old Boston Whaler. But when she finally reached the top of a gently sloping dune, the view stopped her.

Stopped her still, with just her skirt fluttering in the breeze. First, the colors caught her eye: the shack's weathered silver shingles, upon which lobster buoys of red and blue and yellow hung from rope, and then the greens of more wild dune grass. Textures followed, as she stepped closer: the deep wood grain of the shingles, and the seaworn-smooth surface of the buoys, not to mention the paint peels curling from the window frame, and the sweeping blades of beach grass brushing against the side of the shack, nearly concealing it.

"It's a nice place to set up an easel." The sound of Neil's voice—so close, his mouth was almost pressed to her ear—startled Lauren. "Whoa, easy there," he said, steadying her shoulders from behind when she jumped. They stood on the top of the dune, the grasses whispering around them, the old shack set to the side on the beach below. "It gives you a place to get out of the sun to eat, or rest, after sketching or painting."

She looked back at him, her eyes taking in his wavy hair, his unshaven cheeks, his dark eyes. He's giving this to her, she'd thought. A painting hideaway.

"Come on." He bent to cuff his jeans, the chain of his father's Vietnam dog tags slipping from behind his tee, then took her hand to walk down the sloping sand.

She had no words; it was all too good to be true. This was the fantasy of her wildest artist dreams. After years of visiting her grandparents' Stony Point cottage, she'd learned to paint on the beach off-season, before the summer crowds arrived. But even in the spring, there were always passersby on the main beach, folks curious about her easel, and the images she sketched and dappled. So now, to have this solitude? This secluded shack that looked like paradise? Already she envisioned her easel set up in front of the dune grass, overlooking the choppy surf.

"I fixed it up a little," Neil told her as he unlatched the door. It was wood planked, and covered with faded white paint, all battered from taking the brunt of sea spray. Beside the doorway was a weather-beaten four-paned window, with curls of paint peeling off the trim. Old fishing net draped over some of the hanging buoys on the shingles, and the shack looked as untamed and scraggly as the dune grass sweeping up along its side wall.

Until she stepped inside. Until she saw some of the original wood-boarded walls painted white, and the waxed hardwood floor, and rustic beamed ceiling. Hurricane lanterns and candles lined shelves on the walls, and small tables were covered with baskets and blankets, jars of shells and sea glass, journals and a battery-operated radio.

"I rebuilt the back wall." Neil pointed to the freshly painted wall topped with a shelf of whittled duck decoys. "It was in bad shape from the wind and seaside elements."

A couple of fishing rods hung on the back wall, too. And off to the side, a kerosene two-burner camping stove sat on a low shelf, as did a cooler. Neil slipped off his backpack and set it on a cushioned chair. "I brought out new windows, there," he said, pointing to the corner of the room. Two unfinished windows sat on the floor, beside a can of white paint. "I'll give the outside trim a fresh coat of paint, after I install them."

Lauren set down the sandals she carried and walked barefoot around the one open room. Sunlight streamed in through the paned windows, and a warm sea breeze wafted in through the open door. She moved along the perimeter of the room, her hand alighting on candles and Neil's journals, loose conch shells placed on shelves beside a typewriter, a black sweatshirt hanging from a nail on the wall. When she looked back at him, he still stood near the door, watching her.

"I should get going," she said then, setting down a piece of driftwood she'd lifted from a basket on the shelf. He caught her, she just knew it, caught her dragging her finger over its smooth surface, picturing what she might paint on it, inhaling deeply for a scent of the sea.

"Why? I have chairs, we'll set up outside for now. You can draw something, get a feel for the place."

He didn't wait for her answer, but instead pushed the painted door further open with his foot and carried two folding chairs out to the sand. Lauren didn't move; instead, she watched as he opened each chair, adjusting their angle until satisfied with their view. Then he turned and motioned for her to come outside before he sat himself in one of the sand chairs.

She hesitated, of course, still looking around the seemingly forbidden room. There was a salty mustiness to the secret space, giving it a ragged feel. Or maybe its pure mysteriousness did it, making this shack feel dangerous. She eventually walked outside with her canvas art tote. The breeze rippled her long skirt, and when she sat beside Neil, he didn't say anything, just nodded toward the water as two seagulls swooped low.

And that's what she sketched that first day in their fishing shack. Two seagulls, flying low over the choppy water, their wings outstretched, their feathered bodies hovering in the sea breeze. On the edge of the drawing, she added a side-view of the shack, penciling in a cluster of battered buoys beside the window.

"Do you *own* this place?" Lauren asked while her colored pencils scratched back and forth.

"No." Neil looked at the shack behind them. "It's nothing more than an old shack someone built years ago. A spot for fishermen to anchor and have a rest, get off the water. They'll do that, sometimes. Make a little shelter to maybe cook up something to eat, or take a nap."

"Just randomly, out in the wild like this?"

"Sure. When I came across it, it was pretty dilapidated. No one had used it in years, from the looks of it."

"So how did you do all this?" she asked while drawing. The breeze lifted off the water steady that day, blowing wisps of her blonde hair. "Paint the walls, install windows. Get all those supplies inside."

"A little at a time," Neil explained. "I have the tools I need from working with my brother, and I'd bring things out in the Whaler."

"Did Jason help you?"

Neil shook his head. "I didn't tell him about it. Thought maybe you and I could use it for now. You know, I could write here, and you could paint."

Lauren glanced up at another cawing seagull swooping over the water and felt something new, and confusing. The mere thought that she was *liking* this, was getting comfortable at Neil's desolate shack, scared her. "We should probably get going. No one knows where I am."

It seemed like he agreed, the way he stood up and walked to the water, first squinting over to the bank of dunes behind which they'd docked his boat, then wading into the water, still looking back beyond the sand and rocks. "Too late," he called over his shoulder.

"What?"

"The tide shifted, Lauren. I can't get my boat through those rocks; the water's too low now. We're stranded until the tide comes in."

"But that'll be hours!" She stood and trotted to the edge of the water, seeing for herself how the waves had already receded. "We can make it if we hurry, can't we?"

Neil simply shook his head, turning up his hands.

"What the hell? If I don't get home, people will start looking for me, Neil."

Neil walked to her then. The cuffs of his jeans were damp from standing in the lapping waves, and he wore a denim shirt loose over that black tee. "It's all right, you're safe here. So don't worry."

"It's not me I'm worried about. It's everyone wondering where I've disappeared to." She held back a strand of her blowing hair and looked over at the shack. "What if someone calls the police?"

"Shh." As he shushed her, he stepped closer, the sea breeze lifting his wavy hair, his shirttail flapping in the wind. "You have to relax, Lauren. Listen," he said then, stopping beside her. "Try this, it'll help. Close your eyes and really breathe that salt air."

She shook her head and rolled her eyes.

"No, no. Come on," he persisted, stepping even closer. "Deep breath."

The two of them stood there on that remote, windswept beach, in front of the run-down shack, as though they were the last two people on earth. The waves broke, the sun glistened on the water, and a sandpiper scooted past. Finally she looked directly at him and took a quick breath.

"No." He stepped closer still. "For it to work, you have to close your eyes and *leave* them closed. Then take at least three, maybe four, breaths, each one longer than the last. Go ahead."

She stared at him, and then gave in. Her eyes dropped closed, and she heard him whisper, *Good.* So she took a tentative breath, then another longer one, the salt air filling her lungs. And that's when it happened, when his hands cradled her face and he leaned in and kissed her. The first thing she noticed—before she opened her eyes with indignation—was that she kissed him back, not wanting to open her eyes at all. Not until he deepened the kiss and pure guilt had her step back—still kissing him, though, as she halfheartedly pulled away. Because it wasn't just Neil holding her face, his hands reaching around her neck beneath her hair, lifting strands of it. There was the salty touch of the breeze, too. And the sound of the sea, with rogue seagulls cawing. There was his body pressing against hers now, and his smile beneath their kiss, and okay, there were her hands reaching around his shoulders, beneath his unbuttoned denim shirt.

And there was Kyle.

"Jesus," Lauren whispered then, pulling away and smoothing the fabric of the fitted pale pink tee she'd put on that morning, thinking the day would be nothing more than a breezy, casual painting day. Now her hands weren't sure what the hell to do, until they suddenly dug her cell phone out of her tote. "I'm with Kyle, Neil. *Kyle.*" She flashed her diamond ring at him.

"Lauren, I'm sorry, it's just—" He stepped closer, reaching out for her.

"Oh no." She backed away, turning around and dialing her phone. "Shit," she said, shaking her phone. "Shit, shit, shit." She lifted it high in the air, walked briskly down to the water, then back to the shack. "Did you plan this?" she yelled with a glance at Neil. She shoved open the sticking door of the shack and went inside, pacing around the room while dialing her phone once more. But of course there was no cell-phone service here in this godforsaken, deserted hovel. There was only herself and Neil, and the undeniable truth that they couldn't hide from each other. So she sat on a chair beside a round table, where she put her phone so that both her hands could cover her face when she dropped her head into them.

In the absolute stillness in the shack, the sound of the waves came to her. Slowly, rhythmically. And she breathed—one breath, then a longer one—behind closed eyes. The breaths kept coming as she heard Neil open the creaking door and kneel directly in front of her. But her head stayed bowed in her hands, each inhale longer than the last as he told her getting stranded was *not* his plan. That he only wanted some quiet time with her. That he cared for her. More than he'd realized.

With the touch of his hand running along her arm, she finally lifted her head. With the touch of his fingers dabbing her tears, she smiled—slightly, and with sadness, too. With his hand pressing her windblown hair back, stroking her peacock-feather earring, she leaned forward. Just a little, but enough. Enough for that darn hand of his to reach behind her head and pull her close again. And when his mouth met hers, when she sighed into the kiss, her hands frantically slipped that denim shirt off his damn shoulders, right as his arms lifted her from that chair and got her to stand. By the time he'd led her to the bed near the side wall—a bed that was nothing more than a camping cot, really, with a soft, light blanket over it—his hands had raised off her pink tee, easily. And when they lay side by side on that narrow cot, she'd slipped down his jeans and tugged them off.

Breathe, he whispered again, just once, when the only thing left between them was the quickly lifted fabric of her floral skirt, and his silver chain—the dog tags against her breasts, his hand beneath her back, his body over hers.

~

Nearly a decade later, the salt air fills her lungs again as Lauren walks around the single-room seaside fishing shack. One breath, followed by another longer one. "And then I never wanted to leave," she tells Sal now. "After we'd made love a second time, I wished the God damn tide would never turn again."

Sal's flashlight beam shines along the dust-covered shelves. A life had been frozen inside these shingled walls. Lauren watches the light moving over salt-coated leather journals, and dusty mugs, and drumsticks. Neil's life idled, right here. In a way, part of hers did, too.

"It's unbelievable," Sal tells Lauren with a quick glance.

And she sees it, how even he can't keep his eyes off the personal artifacts that were never touched again, once Neil unexpectedly died. Sal picks up a journal and blows off the dust, then shines the light on some of the pages, thumbing through, before carefully setting it down.

"Neil always had a pen in his hand, or behind his ear, or in a pocket. Writing, writing. He was working on a novel, actually, and God, the journals he kept." Lauren brushes through a cobweb and steps beside Sal. "I'd forgotten all about these." She picks up a journal and her hand rests flat on its gritty cover. "But there's no way I can open it."

"Why not?"

"Why not? I'm in a good place in my life now, and I'm really afraid of what his words can do." When she shoves the journal back with the others, a scurrying blur, a mouse maybe, runs across the shelf above it. So she takes the flashlight and shines it on the rustic ceiling beams, the table and chairs, the cot—its blanket still neatly folded, the way Neil always left it.

It's the cot that draws her, and she sits on the very edge of it. "I never wanted to hurt either of them, Sal."

Finally, he turns and sits in a rickety chair that creaks beneath his weight, just listening. She can tell by his stillness.

"I loved them *both*, damn it. Always have. Kyle, and Neil." She shakes her head, her eyes burning with tears that she holds back the best she can. "It's like he's still here," she whispers so softly, she can't even be sure Sal hears.

"So who was the better man, Lauren?"

"What?" She whips around in the near dark.

"Neil? Or Kyle?"

"You have a hell of a lot of nerve." She laughs, then. "And only you, Salvatore, can get away with a question like that. Because you must figure that one outdid the other, and you're going to get me to admit it, aren't you?"

Nothing. No noise, no movement, except for the sea breeze coming in through the open door. She gets up and stands in the doorway, then runs her hands through her hair. It's all the same here, but time has left its mark on everything, with the salt and damp and mustiness. Before they came in, Lauren had lifted several of the fallen buoys outside and hung them back on the silvered shingles. She turns and looks around the room again. It's all his, all Neil's. Somehow, he is trapped beneath the dust, his life paused *right* here, because it's so obvious by the way he left things—canned food, and sweatshirts, and boat shoes, and the radio, and hurricane lanterns, bottled water, scrapbooks, notes, magazines, the drumsticks—he intended to come back.

"The better man?" She pauses and hears Sal turn to her. "Kyle."

"I thought you'd say Kyle."

"That's right. He's been by my side since I was seventeen, and knows me better than I know myself."

"And come on." Sal tips his chair back and watches her closely. "You have to love a dude raising another man's child and not saying a *word* about it. Upstanding, Lauren. I've spent time with Kyle at the diner. After seeing this, and seeing what he *must* have figured was in your life, well, he's a lot stronger than he ever lets on."

Sal stands; she hears him do so when she turns away and looks out at the night sea. The horizon is violet, the sky above black now, with stars just starting to glimmer. There's no moon tonight, no mid-July moonlight falling on the water, catching ripples of waves. And it seems intentional, as though the darkness is meant to cloak her longing, her memory.

"Are you sure you want to move to Stony Point, permanently?" Sal asks. He'd come up beside her and looks out at the water, too. When she barely shrugs, he seems to want to convince her. "You're one lucky woman, Lauren."

"Lucky?" She shivers enough for him to lift a sweatshirt from a wall hook, give it a shake, and drape it over her shoulders. "Is that how you see my life? Lucky?" she asks.

"Yes. And when you move to this beloved Stony Point, you need to do more celebrating than mourning. Especially when you see old haunts and ghosts there. Promise me?"

"Promise you what?" She holds the sweatshirt—Neil's sweatshirt—tenderly around her shoulders, her head pressing back into the bunched hood behind her neck.

"One thing." Sal's voice is close, so close to her ear. "Okay?"

Though she's looking outside, leaning on the doorframe and holding a piece of Neil's clothing, she's silent. If she listens carefully, she swears she can hear his voice once more.

"Okay?" he whispers.

She nods. Only nods. And she's sure he knows that it's all she can do.

"Promise me you'll smile, even when you're sad. Because what you have is actually beautiful, Lauren. Layered and emotionally wrought and full and vibrant. *Sorridi*, my friend. Smile."

Lauren glances up at him in the shadows of the night, with a mist rising off the sea. Standing in the timeworn shack, it's hard to tell who it really is beside her.

"You have quite a love story in your life, Ell. And though you might not always think so …"

In his pause, whoever's pause it is, she breathes. One breath of that sweet salt air, raw and alive off the sea, then another.

"I think you actually did get a happy ending."

twenty-two

EARLY SUNDAY MORNING, CELIA NESTLES sun-bleached conch shells among white pillar candles on built-in shelves, to draw the eye to the dark end of the room. The dining room walls in this cottage are paneled with knotty-pine beadboard and finished with a walnut stain, the same dark stain as on the shelving. Long windows opening to a sunny front porch line the far wall and let in necessary light.

"Knock, knock," a voice calls as the cottage's front door swings open.

She leans over to see Sal, holding a glass jar filled with summer flowers. He's wearing his new cargo shorts and a navy tee. Of course, the braided rope bracelet is on his wrist, too. She silently watches him for a few seconds as he fusses with the flowers, obviously waiting to hear her voice.

"Celia?" he asks, straightening a rogue black-eyed Susan in the vase.

"Sal! What are you doing here?" She sets down a large shell and walks over, brushing her dusty hands on her denim cutoffs.

"For you," he tells her while holding out the glass vase. "Have you ever received Sunday morning flowers before?"

"No." She takes the vase and dips her face close to the flowers, inhaling their scent. "Heavenly," she says, her eyes dropping closed for a moment. "This is the one and only Sunday bouquet I've ever received."

"Good. Then you'll always remember it." Sal walks closer and sets his hands on her shoulders, leaning in to give her an easy kiss. It's how the day has been feeling: easy, calm, relaxing. As his fingers tangle in her French braid, he tells her, "Jason says Sunday mornings with Maris are his paradise. I kind of like that idea."

"Me, too. It's sweet." Celia takes his hand and stands on tiptoe to give him another kiss, her other hand still holding the flowers. "Do you really have to go back to Wall Street?" she whispers. "Can't you stay on here?"

He cradles her face and brushes her lips with two light kisses. "I have lots of options, that's for sure." With that, he turns and looks at the cottage rooms she's been staging. "Waiter, architect assistant. Part-time beach guard."

"Stop teasing me!" The vase is still in her hands, and she pulls a stem of yellow snapdragons to the front of the arrangement. "These are so pretty. Where are they from? Your mom's place?"

"I bought them at a farm stand not too far from here. Took Kyle's wheels for a Sunday morning spin. The farm has a flower hut, an old dilapidated trailer filled to the brim with those glass vases of flowers."

"What are they, old milk jars?"

"Looks it, doesn't it? It's a charming spot, reminds me of a little storefront on Italian streets."

Celia sets the vase on a table near the doorway so that she doesn't forget them when she leaves. When she picks up a large wreath made of twigs and seashells, Sal hurries over and holds it for her as she points out a wall hook. "What a nice time I had at dinner last night. Your mom sets such a lovely table, and that deck! It was so peaceful sitting outside with a glass of wine, the stars twinkling in the sky. Thank God you were able to fix Kyle's truck and get Lauren home safely."

"I love that old truck," he tells her as he hangs the wreath on the wall and steps back, straightening it. "Someday, I'm going to buy it from Kyle."

"I have no doubt that you will, Mr. DeLuca." Celia looks around the room, then goes to the cream sofa and fluffs two brightly striped pillows. "I usually do this last-minute staging the night before an open house, so I'm backlogged this morning." A low, thickly woven basket sits on the coffee table. "I don't mind, though. It was worth it, having a late dinner together. Then walking the beach with you," she says as she sets three glass fishing floats in the basket. "Waking up with you in my cottage, the sun rising outside the window."

Sal hugs her from behind, kissing her ear. "I'll let you be so you can get your work done."

Celia just smiles, and when he wraps his hands around her waist, she holds them and leans back into him.

"I'm going to take another walk down the beach, then meet you at your place?" he asks.

She only nods, still smiling.

"Kyle is stopping by there for his truck. I told him that's where I'd be today."

"Okay," she whispers.

"I think he's bringing his kids," Sal says. "Can't wait to meet the little Bradfords."

"What are you eating?"

Jason holds out his cell phone and squints at it in the bright sunshine, wondering how his wife knows from three thousand miles away. Then, well then he takes a bigger bite of the cinnamon doughnut in his other hand. "Nothing," he says around the food.

"It better not be some sinfully gooey, rich, sweet morsel," Maris warns him. "It's been brought to my attention that you and Elsa are bingeing in my absence."

"Says who?" He sips his hot coffee.

"I have my sources," Maris softly answers. "And I really wish I was there with you right now, having a bite. Thirty-six years old, and I'm completely homesick."

"I miss you too, sweetheart."

"Even though I'm back in the States, California doesn't hold a candle to Stony Point."

"Goes without saying, Maris."

"So let's see, it's the nineteenth, and I've got two weeks of meetings here in L.A. I also need to spend time at Saybrooks' laundry headquarters working on the new denim washes. Plus presentation samples arrived for next summer's line, so those need a looking-over before I come home."

"You're busy, but it's Sunday. Take a breather, relax." And she does, he hears it, his phone bringing her sigh across the country's miles, straight to him. And what it does is make him miss their Sunday mornings together, even more. He needs her to be back, needs to be in bed with his arms wrapped loosely around her, stroking her long brown hair, their voices murmuring as they drift in and out of sleep, the sea breeze coming through the window brushing their skin. "Sunday mornings aren't the same without you here."

"I'm so mad I'm missing the summer with you." After a pause, her voice drops even softer. "I don't know how long I can keep doing this, Jason. Where are you, on the boardwalk?"

"Yes, on the end. Sitting in the sun."

"Tell me what you see. Right now, this very second, so it'll feel like I'm there."

Jason surveys the beach. It's a typical view for a mid-July Sunday morning. "Okay," he says, dunking a hunk of doughnut in his coffee.

"It's early still, just after ten. So the beach is half empty. But there's a line of umbrellas and empty sand chairs set along the water."

"Oh, I can practically see it, all those lollipop-colored umbrellas. Folks reserving their family-day spot?"

"As usual. A few people are on the beach, though, hanging out. You know how it is. A couple of kids floating in their tubes. It's a lazy morning, nice and warm, but no humidity today." He's distracted then, by footsteps and someone clearing their throat. It's the beach commissioner approaching with a handful of papers. When Jason salutes him with a piece of doughnut in his hand, the commissioner slows.

"No eating on the beach," he says. After he walks past, that's when Jason stuffs the last of his doughnut in his mouth. "Food ordinance, but I'll let it go this time," the commissioner—with apparent eyes on the back of his head—calls out.

So Jason holds up his coffee in a toast. "Wait till you meet the new beach commissioner, Maris. What a piece of work. A real stickler for the rules."

"Oh boy. Even on your job sites?"

"Especially so. Gives your aunt a hard time with different things on her property. You know, fence sections, a sign." Something gets Jason's attention then, out in the water. A splashing of some sort, a panicked splashing.

"Jason? You there?" Maris asks.

"Yeah, just watching some kid horsing around in the water. It's nothing." But still, he hurries down the boardwalk for a better view. When a woman yells for help, he steps onto the sand. "Wait, I think something's wrong, Maris. Let me call you back." He disconnects and winds through the arranged sand chairs set out in hopes of a beautiful day spent with family and friends. All the while, the commotion continues—an older woman pacing at the water's edge, then looking back on the beach. Jason trots now, trying to keep the splashing boy in his sights, and tripping on a blue tube at the same time. He catches himself, his hand brushing the sand, and sees the woman turn frantically and point to the kid.

"Shit," he says, his heart pounding now as the boy goes completely underwater, but bobs suddenly back up, gasping and wheezing. He's in deep, about halfway out to the floating swim raft. When Jason glances down the beach, he notices Sal approaching. But he's far off still, near the rocks, so Jason hooks his fingers in his mouth and gives a sharp whistle, then points to the boy.

"There's a kid in trouble. Can you help?" Jason calls when Sal rushes closer. "My leg," he says while motioning to his prosthesis. "I can't get there fast enough."

"Kid?" Sal asks, a little breathless while turning toward the cries in the water.

"Sal!" Jason shouts, this time with unmistaken urgency. "Can you swim out?"

Sal kicks off his sandals and glances quickly around, finally grabbing a boogie board he spots at a nearby blanket. Holding it, he shields his eyes from the sun and squints toward the boy.

"Jesus Christ, *go* DeLuca, before he drowns!"

A second passes—too long of a second, Jason thinks—before Sal goes in with his shorts and tee still on. He holds the board high and merely runs out instead of diving in and swimming the distance right away.

As Sal gets closer to the boy, Jason approaches the panicked woman; but he's worried, seeing how slow Sal is in the water. "It'll be okay," he tells the woman, who looks to be in her sixties, and wears a loose tee over long, khaki shorts. "He's got the board for your boy to float on."

"It's my grandson," she says, clutching Jason's arm. "He's got to hurry!"

Jason looks toward the boy again. At last, Sal is swimming—slowly, but steadily. "Call for help," he tells the woman at the same time he considers removing his prosthetic leg and swimming out, too. "Call nine-one-one, now!" Because suddenly, he's not too certain all is well. Sal seems to be struggling, at times barely keeping his own head above water. The older woman gets her cell phone off a blanket and dials instantly. As she talks to the authorities, her voice high-pitched and terrified, Sal finally gets to the boy. When he grabs him, though, scooping him under the arms, the boogie board gets away from him and floats out of reach. Which seems to set another panic in Sal, who lunges for the board with one arm and loses his hold on the boy. But he keeps grabbing for that board, and the boy goes under again, prompting the stricken woman to run into the shallow breaking waves, screaming, "*Save him! Save him!*"

Still holding the board, Sal goes under and emerges with his other arm wrapped around the boy's chest. They just float there; Sal seems to be talking to the boy, maybe calming him down before making any move. It's hard to tell from shore. But in a few seconds, right as he looks like he's about to lose his grip again, he lifts the dripping boy onto the board, holding it steady as the kid flops on it, stomach down, one leg hanging off the edge.

"He got him! He got him out!" the woman says into her cell phone, while waving a clenched fist. "Oh Lord, thank you, thank you!" When she turns to Jason again, she holds up her phone. "They're sending an ambulance, right away."

"I think he'll be okay." Jason shields his eyes against the glare of the sun, trying to see more. The boy lies on the dipping-and-bobbing board, gripping its edges, while Sal floats beside him far out in the water, hanging onto the board without making any move to get to shore.

"He's only nine, my grandson. Nine," the woman tells Jason, tears streaming down her cheeks as she walks into the shallow water, constantly turning back to explain what happened. "He's not allowed to go to the raft," she continues, suppressing another sob. "But he tries to sneak there sometimes." She gasps then, as the scary reality of what nearly happened hits her. "His mother and brothers are at the cottage, getting ready for a family picnic under the pavilion. So I brought Timmy with me, he was so excited to go in. I only looked away for a few minutes," she barely says, "setting up the chairs."

"It's okay." Jason points to Sal, who is slowly paddling to shore, keeping one arm on the board as he does. "They're coming in now."

"Oh, thank *God*," she murmurs while quickly blessing herself, tears still lining her face. "I didn't even have a chance to put his swimmies on."

Now Sal is within walking depth, and he *does* walk, slowly. Every now and then, he adjusts the boy on the board to be sure he doesn't slip off, and the closer they get, the louder the boy's crying gets. Finally, the woman wades out and lifts her grandson. In one fluid motion, she presses him to her body, cradling his sodden head on her shoulder as she rushes to shore, straight to a dry blanket. The boy sits there, sobbing and gagging on the salt water. When Sal follows behind them, carrying the boogie board, the woman turns and tries to thank him, but he waves her off, drops the board and heads down the beach, a dripping mess.

"Whoa," Jason says, hesitating while looking from Sal to the boy. He stops at the boy's blanket, crouches down and reassures him. "You took a good dunk, but you'll be all right," he says as he pats the kid's leg. "Just relax, breathe slow, okay?" When the boy doesn't look at him, Jason reaches over and tips his face toward him. "Okay? Let me see you breathe." And he doesn't let go of the boy until he does, breathing and coughing up a little water, too. "You're a trooper, my man," Jason says, standing then. "He seems okay, but have the paramedics examine him," he tells the grandmother, who is rubbing the child's back as he continues to cry. "I've got to check on my friend. You all set here?"

"Yes! And please, don't let him leave. I can't thank him enough."

Certain that the boy will be fine, Jason hurries along the high tide line toward Sal. Sal who is now doubled over, hands on his knees, his soaked shorts and tee clinging to his wet body.

"You okay, guy?" Jason calls when he gets closer. When Sal doesn't move, remaining doubled over, Jason snatches up a random beach towel and wraps it around his drenched shoulders. "Hey. Do *you* need the ambulance? They're on their way."

"No!" Sal shakes his head, but his breathing is ragged, as though he can't get a full breath, or his lungs are closing in.

"I think you need a doctor, man." Jason takes his arm. "Your breathing's not sounding good."

Sal pushes him away and takes a few steps toward the rocks. "Back off, Barlow," he says, then wheezes a deep inhale. "Give me a few minutes."

So this is something Jason never saw coming. The whole ordeal was too much for Sal; it's apparent now. He's just not sure why. And when Sal doesn't improve, Jason presses him. "We have to get you off the beach. I'll bring you to the inn."

"*No*, Jason. Not a word to my mother." Sal hikes the towel up higher, covering his neck with it and giving a good cough. "She'll overreact, it's too much to deal with her."

"But you're not well." Jason walks ahead of Sal and stops in front of him, watching him closely. "We have to do something for you."

"Celia's. Take me to Celia's." He barely gets the words out, with water still streaming from his hair onto his face. "She's staying at the Carbone cottage."

"Can you even *walk*?"

"Don't know."

"I have my golf cart here. Let's get you to the street." He puts an arm around Sal's back, and with his other hand, holds his arm to support him. Sal leans into him as they move across the sand toward the steps leading down to the street.

"You all okay?"

Jason looks up, surprised at the voice.

"Everything all right?" the beach commissioner asks. He's sitting on a bench on top of a small dune, still holding those loose papers.

Jason is clearly aware that Sal can't get a decent breath. "Fine," Jason says. "He'll be fine. But you might want to check the kid."

"Kid?"

"A kid almost drowned over there." He hitches his head in the direction at the same time an ambulance siren gets louder. "This guy hauled him out of the water. Don't you have any lifeguards on the payroll?"

"*What?*" The beach commissioner shields his eyes, looking down along the sand. "My God, I didn't even know. Was updating the community bulletin board," he calls back as he runs toward where a crowd has gathered near the water. "And we're short on lifeguards this year. Kids don't want to sit out in the sun anymore!"

Jason waves off the commissioner, and Sal remains silent, even as Jason walks him down the few granite stairs to settle him in the passenger seat of his golf cart. "You going to make it? Need anything, bro?"

Sal shakes his head and simply closes his eyes, without speaking a word.

"Try to see the cottage today, Lauren. I just got back from staging it," Celia says into her cell phone. "The agent thinks it'll sell fast." As she talks, she heads to her kitchen to clear the morning's dishes soaking in the sink. "Four bedrooms, too, so it *could* work for you guys."

After she disconnects, Celia opens the paned kitchen windows. The whistling twitter of lagoon birds makes its way inside, along with the slightest of breezes. It's the type of breeze that makes the marsh grasses whisper, often having her do a double take, the way it can sound human. Or spiritual, even. She pushes the chrome chairs snug against the table, and gets a swirled pottery bowl from the cupboard to fill with native nectarines and plums. After giving the kitchen a once-over, she heads to her bedroom to change into a different outfit before Sal gets there. Maybe a sundress today, something light and airy, and they'll have lunch on the deck.

But when she opens her bedroom closet, there's a sudden racket out in the cottage. It's at the front door, and is insistent enough that she turns quickly at its urgency: a loud rapping, over and over, followed by the locked screen door being rattled on its hinges as someone tries to get inside.

"Celia!" a voice calls out—Jason's, she's thinks. "Hurry!"

twenty-three

JASON SITS ALONE IN AN Adirondack chair on the deck, waiting for Celia. Waves of green grasses curve through the lagoon, and a great blue heron stands statue-still on the muddy banks. At the dock, Sal's old rowboat is tied up; it shifts with the currents, creaking against the roped piling to which it's secured. Seeing it here on the marsh brings memories of Jason and his brother paddling through the lagoon years ago, reenacting their father's Vietnam stories.

The cicadas buzz in the surrounding trees now, and Jason's thoughts drift to another summer day, a hot one—with temperatures nearing one hundred and the sun beating relentlessly as he and Neil paddled through the lagoon in an old rowboat like Sal's.

~

The jungle was hot, their father told them, *always hot. But one day in 'Nam, even more so.* That abnormally hot day in the jungle happened after their father had been in the war for nearly a year. *If it had happened early in my tour,* he assured them, *I wouldn't have survived the day. I would've hit the spider. But experience came hard and fast evading ambushes in the jungle, with good reason. Experience was the only way an American boy like myself could outlive the enemy,* he explained. *Experience was like gold, and the ones who survived? We hoarded it. So that one day, my unit had been patrolling, searching for enemy positions for what felt like an eternity. We'd just finished crossing a river, weapons held above the water each step of the way, and I was glad to get back into the cover of the jungle.*

It was bad enough we were weighed down with gear and ammunition; that our pants and boots were soaked and muddy, too. But that heat … Suddenly my skin started burning up, prickling even, and it got my attention. So I gave a whistle, a birdcall whistle, to warn the others, motioning for them to freeze.

Because I knew. My body burning up was from the pounding heart and increased blood pressure of pure adrenaline, and that adrenaline wouldn't have pumped unless I'd sensed something amiss, or heard something—a snapped twig, maybe—or smelled something. One of my senses triggered that adrenaline rush, and experience had me pay attention. The enemy was close at hand, so I froze.

That day in the lagoon when Jason couldn't have been more than twelve, hovering dragonflies, cruising bumblebees and flitting monarch butterflies became the tarantulas, horseflies and scorpions of the Southeast Asian jungle. Minnows swimming alongside their boat were leeches, and an eel slithering by was a viper snake. And the great blue heron? That was the enemy. He and Neil had been paddling along the saltwater inlets winding through tall, sweeping marsh grasses that whispered danger to them, because the enemy hid within the swaying plumes. When they rounded a bend, Jason pulled up the oars and the only sound came from the water drip-dripping back into the lagoon. He gave a slight whistle and Neil turned to look at him. *Don't move,* Jason barely breathed, nodding to a bank of the lagoon, where if you squinted through the sunlight, the great blue heron was barely visible. Motionless, but there.

Whoever moved first, us or them, would be deciphered and shot. At one point, a massive spider walked across my neck, but if I swatted it, I'd be dead. It moved slowly up to my face, across my cheek and toward my ear. I heard each goddamn furry leg on my skin, and I couldn't move. Not if I wanted to stay alive. So I just stood there and the only thing louder than the buzzing bugs around me was my pounding heart.

Neil didn't move, too. Neither did Jason. They hunkered low in their floating boat, sweating, letting the bugs bite and the imagined snakes swim past, while waiting out the enemy to stay alive.

Apparently someone else, an enemy soldier, was tested, too. Someone younger and naïve, someone who jumped when maybe a jungle snake slithered over his foot, or wound its way down a tree onto his shoulder. Someone who cracked first, after two hours of standing motionless to the point of cramping up. And it saved me. Shit, some North Vietnamese kid's panic saved me. When he lurched from the brush, the soldier beside me threw a grenade in that direction, one that ended a skirmish before it had a chance to begin. And I made it through another day alive, all because of the wisdom that came with living in hell—to know when to be still.

Time passed that childhood day, unending time as Jason and his younger brother didn't move a muscle until that great blue heron took sweeping flight, veering off toward the sea. After it passed over them, Neil heaved a rock he'd brought aboard their vessel, heaved it straight to where the bird had been standing, a rock that exploded in the water, effectively killing any lingering soldiers there so that Jason could set the oars in the lagoon and paddle them through another day together.

———

Now Jason jumps when Celia opens the slider and brings two coffees out to the deck. "Sal's sound asleep."

It doesn't surprise him, not after what he saw on the beach. Jason sips the coffee. "He said he really needed to rest."

"Maybe that's all it is, Jason. And he was soaked through, too. Thank God George left clothes here. It helped to get Sal into something dry. I hope he'll be okay."

"What I saw on the beach was not okay, not by any means."

"But that had to be a scary situation, and maybe he's not much of a swimmer. Plus it's hot out, so could it even be heatstroke or something?" It's obvious Celia desperately wants to find an easy answer. To not have anything be wrong. "Elsa should know, don't you think?" she asks.

Jason takes a long breath. "Let's see what Sal says when he wakes up." He looks beyond the marsh then. The sky far above it stretches over the deep water of Long Island Sound, water filled with danger—some sort of danger that reached Sal when he swam to the boy. And now? Jason glances back at the quiet cottage. Now, Sal's still, not moving, merely waiting things out until it's absolutely safe to get himself through another day.

"Technically it's a four-bedroom. So keep an open mind."

There are those magic words again, and it doesn't help that this real estate agent says it as she tugs the latch on the pull-down attic stairs. "Are you kidding me?" Kyle asks, with Evan beside him. "The fourth bedroom is up *there*?"

"Dad," Evan whispers loudly. "That could be my room!"

When Kyle starts climbing the ladder to the unfinished attic, his son is right behind him.

"Maybe Celia can put small buoys on the ladder to pretty it up?" Lauren calls from below while holding Hailey's hand.

But it's when the agent warns him to be careful of the nails in the bottom side of the ceiling beams that Kyle stops. "Back down, buddy," he says to Evan over his shoulder. "Too dangerous for you."

"But it does sit on a hill, with a slight water view," the agent tells them when they walk through the living room.

"There go our property taxes," Kyle counters.

"Well," the agent persists, "folks shell out a lot of green for that blue view."

On the front porch, Lauren remarks that the space is large and airy. Hailey sits herself at a folding table there and prances her plastic horse along, murmuring secrets to it. As she does, Kyle hears something else, something tapping on the roof. He opens the porch door and looks at two towering oak trees, their acorns already falling.

After finally touring the kitchen and one bath, both needing remodeling, they all pile into the car.

"Are we moving here?" Hailey asks from the backseat when Kyle pulls out of the driveway.

"No, princess. Not this one."

"You won't even think about it?" Lauren asks, glancing over at the empty house.

"It's overpriced and I'm underwhelmed. Even Celia's staging couldn't convince me."

"We just have to keep looking, then."

"Right. And working, to afford something better." Kyle drives along the winding roads of Stony Point, passing perfect homes, places that don't need an open mind: New England colonials with flagpoles in the front yard; pristine shingled bungalows with potted geraniums on stone walkways; sprawling seaside ranches with porch swings. None are for sale. "Let's go to Celia's and pick up my truck. I have to get to the diner for the lunch crowd. Jerry's waiting for me."

~

"How long do you think he'll sleep?" Celia quietly asks.

It's that kind of day now. Quiet. Cautious. "From what I saw, I don't think he'll be getting up anytime soon." Jason sets his coffee cup on a patio table and walks to the edge of the deck, breathing the salt air in long, slow breaths.

Minutes pass like that, in a hushed limbo, until a car door slams. Then another. He turns to Celia sitting with her coffee, her face tipped up to the sun. "You expecting somebody?"

"Oh, shoot!" She checks her watch, lifting her sunglasses to the top of her head to see the time clearly. "*Gesù, Santa Maria!* Kyle is coming for his truck, and Sal said he wanted to meet the kids, too. I'll bet that's them."

Jason feels the same prickling panic he felt on the beach; the others can't see Sal in this condition. So he grabs Celia's arm from behind just as she heads through the slider. "Don't let them inside, Celia."

"What?" She stops and looks back at him.

"No, give them a story. I don't know." Jason spots Sal's wet clothes hanging over the outside shower wall. "Tell them the shower was broken. I helped Sal fix it. Okay?" When she hesitates, he gives her arm a shake. "Okay?"

Before she answers, a blur of motion runs onto the deck. Little Hailey stops in her tracks, a plastic horse clutched in one hand, her two wispy ponytails sitting high on her head. "Hey there, Hailey-copter," Jason tells her. "Give me a high-five." After she first sets her tiny hand against his, then runs to gallop her horse across the deck railing, Jason fist-bumps her brother. "Look at that, Evan," he says, bending low and facing the lagoon. "See the egret?"

Evan walks to the edge of the deck, squinting, then turns back. "Where's your dog?"

"She's not here, I left her home today."

"Hey, hey, Cee," Lauren says when she rounds the corner of the cottage to the backyard and gives Celia a hug. "We noticed you out here when we pulled in."

"Yo, Barlow. Celia." Kyle glances at the deck. "Sal around?"

"He wanted to meet Evan and Hailey," Lauren says to Celia.

"He's getting some tools. At the inn. Workers left some on-site." Jason points to the shower. "We played plumber this morning, fixed a broken nozzle."

"I can tell you a thing or two about showers," Kyle says as he heads toward the outdoor cabana. He opens the door and takes a look at the nozzle. "See what I mean?" he asks Jason, who's standing in the doorway. "Shit, chin high. The agents always tell me to keep an open mind."

"Kyle!" Lauren calls from the marsh with Celia by her side. "We need to look for houses around *here*. It's so peaceful, and scenic. And there's so much I could paint."

Kyle salutes her, then walks out with Jason. "What's keeping your cousin? I'm on the clock and can't keep the help waiting."

"Probably got tied up with Elsa and some project. So what are you Bradfords up to?" Jason asks. "Put in an offer on the open house?"

"Hell, no. Not today."

"That bad?"

"Nails-coming-out-of-the-ceiling-beams bad. But man, we're busting out of the seams in our little Cape Cod. We need more space, especially for Lauren's studio. Her driftwood paintings are selling like hotcakes at the diner." He heads toward the dock where Lauren and Celia sit with Evan and Hailey, their bare feet dangling over the edge. "Now she thinks she wants an in-law apartment, so her mother can babysit more often," he says over his shoulder to Jason.

"That's not a bad idea."

"No. Just expensive," Kyle tells him. "Hey, Celia. Got my truck keys?"

Celia motions for him to wait as she gets up from the dock and rushes inside.

"What's the Sunday Special?" Jason asks Kyle in the meantime.

"Oh, a good one." Kyle lifts a corner of his tee and dabs his face. "Thanksgiving in July, people love it. Turkey with all the trimmings: stuffing, cranberry sauce, mashed potatoes, beans. The works."

"Make me up a platter, would you? I'll stop by in an hour for it."

"Here you go," Celia calls while leaning over the deck railing. "Catch!"

Kyle grabs the tossed keys. "Say hi to Salvatore for me. He's the man these days, fixing up everyone's life." He turns to the dock and crouches down, arms wide open. "Hey kids, kiss Daddy goodbye."

When they run over, Kyle scoops them off the ground and spins them, which is precisely when Jason meets Celia's eye and hurries to her. "I'll bring my golf cart home and pick up food from the diner. Sal could use a hot meal, I'm sure."

"Want to come berry picking with me and the kids, Cee?" Lauren asks as she walks to Kyle.

Before Celia can answer, Kyle scoops Lauren up, too, and plants a kiss on her mouth before setting her down. After ruffling Evan's moppy hair, he heads around to the pickup in the driveway, whistling as he walks beside Jason on his way to his golf cart.

"Blueberries are ripe," Lauren calls back while leading her children to the car.

"Thanks anyway, Lauren." Celia slowly walks to the front, waving goodbye to everyone.

When Kyle guns his truck engine and motions for Jason to race him with his golf cart, Jason simply gives the cart horn a toot, throwing a quick glance back at the cottage window. The one with the blinds drawn, keeping the room dark and quiet inside.

One of Celia's favorite things to do is to walk the beach streets at night, when the summer homes are illuminated. It gives her a glimpse inside, a different viewpoint for staging and decorating ideas. Night seems to be when the bungalows and cottages are fully lived in: hurricane lanterns glimmer on front porches; folks gather around kitchen tables; happy voices ring out; cool glasses of iced drinks clink together.

But tonight, driving Sal home, she sees none of it. In her car, it's all she can do to take her eyes off of him and watch the sandy roads she maneuvers.

"I'm glad you slept all day. But are you *sure* you had enough to eat?" she asks, squeezing his hand.

"Yes. It was nice of Jason to bring me dinner like that."

She glances over at Sal in the passenger seat, thinking he looks a little better now. "Still, it's good you'll sleep at home. There's nothing like resting in your own bed. Take some aspirin, too."

"Don't worry, Cee. I'm all right now."

"Sal, I can't *help* but worry. Jason and I honestly thought you were dying. If you need to see a doctor about something, I can drive you."

"You're overreacting! I'm *sure* it was just heatstroke. With some panic thrown in."

"Panic?"

"I'm not that good of a swimmer." His voice is raspy now. "Didn't actually know if I could make it out to the boy."

"Oh, Sal. It must've been awful, then." Her car's tires crunch over gravel as she turns into Elsa's driveway. Golden lamplight spills through the beach home's paned windows onto the misty night. "At least mention it to your mother? So she can keep an eye on you?"

Sal looks at her silently in the dark, pressing back a wisp of hair that escaped from her now-loose French braid. "You don't know my mother. She'd set a thermometer in my mouth every hour, on the hour, if she knew."

"Do you want me to come in with you? I can sit up for a bit, maybe we'll relax on the deck, get some air?"

"Not tonight. I'm just going to sleep, but I'm okay. Promise." He leans over and kisses Celia's forehead, leaving his pressed lips there on her skin for a long moment. "Goodnight, darling," he says before getting out of the car and disappearing into the shadows of the big old cottage.

twenty-four

WORK COMES IN DIFFERENT WAVES. Some weeks, Jason spends on the road, at job sites, meeting with new clients. Others, like this one, find him alone in his barn studio researching through Neil's scrapbooks while immersed in design work. Time passes the quickest on those days: pencil in hand at his worktable, layers of tracing paper laid out, computer screen covered with graphics, Neil's handwritten notes propped to the side in an open leather journal.

That's been his week, and except for a stiff neck from sitting still for so many hours, he can't believe it's already Thursday. Elsa needs to approve this final turret option before too much time goes by. The design requires a variance to Stony Point zoning laws, and that alone can take weeks to happen. So after pulling his golf cart into the parking area below the inn's deck, he gets out, grabs his drawing tube from the backseat and hangs it over his shoulder.

"Surprise!" a voice says as he leans into the cart for the bag of breakfast food. "Oh, it's *so* good to see you."

And he knows just who it is. "Hey there, Eva," he says while turning around and giving his sister-in-law a hug.

"Mm-hmm," she says, lingering with it. "It's great to be home again."

He steps back and also hugs Eva's teenage daughter, Taylor, standing behind her. "So how are the weary travelers? Did you have a good vacation?"

"The best," Taylor says. "It was super fun, Uncle Jason."

"We got back yesterday," Eva tells him. "And I dropped off a souvenir for Elsa."

"One of those happiness jars," Taylor explains. "We filled it with things on vacation that made us think of her."

"She's waiting for you upstairs." Eva points to the deck next to Foley's old back room. "And we're off, got so much unpacking to do." As she says it, she takes Jason's hands in hers. "How's Maris?"

"Getting homesick now," he says.

"Out of everyone here, I miss my sister the most. When will she be home?"

"End of next week. Friday."

"Oh, I *cannot* wait." She gives his hands a quick shake before linking arms with Taylor. "Ready, sweets?"

As they walk to the road leading to their cottage, Jason calls out, "Tell Matt we'll have a beer at The Sand Bar. Soon."

Eva wiggles her fingers in a wave, and Jason grabs his bags before heading up the deck stairs. The morning sun is just making its way around, but a large oak tree gives them a shady spot to sit in. He sets his drawing tube on the table and gets the food ready, opening the paper wrapping of an egg sandwich right as Elsa comes out with a carafe of hot coffee.

"I brought you food," Jason tells her.

"*Perfezione!*" Elsa pours the coffee into large mugs. "But you know this illicit diet will have to stop once your wife is back," she warns him.

"Unless we sneak around." With that, he tears open a foil packet with his teeth and squeezes ketchup onto his sandwich. "Got mine on a bagel today. Yours is the croissant."

"Good. I prefer those, anyway." As she says it, Elsa shakes salt on top of the dripping ketchup of her own melted-cheesy egg.

"How's your son? Haven't seen him around all week."

"Sal? Oh, he had a cold for a couple days, was a little under the weather. Spent some time catching up on sleep." As she says it, Elsa tucks a napkin into the collar of her tank top and bites into her sandwich. "I think that Wall Street pace does him in sometimes," she says around a mouthful of the food, her eyes fluttering a bit as she chews with a slight smile. "But he rested Monday and seems better. Been in and out since then. Tuesday … yesterday."

"Really. Where's he keeping himself?" Jason dunks half of his sandwich into ketchup on his plate. "Helping Kyle at the diner?"

"Don't think so," Elsa manages to say, motioning for him to let her finish chewing, before washing it down with a gulp of coffee. "He might be with Celia. I think they're doing some painting, fixing things up at the cottage she's staying at. Well, that and a summer romance, I'm sure," she adds with a quick wink. "He's been leaving here early with tools, paint." She picks up what's left of her sandwich and pauses, mid-air. "Even took a curtain yesterday."

"Is that right?" Jason swipes ketchup and crumbles of cheese and egg off his plate with the last of his bagel. "Well, back to work," he says as he presses it into his mouth, wipes his hands on a napkin and reaches for his drawing tube. "I brought my latest round of turret adjustments. I hope this is what you're looking for," he says while sliding the rolled drawings from the tube. And while throwing a glance off the deck in the direction of Celia's place, too.

~

"Now I'm *really* mad." Celia paces her cottage, hands clenched. "I need a cat, or a dog. Something so I'm not ranting to *myself* like a nut," she says to no one while rattling around, punching the sofa pillows a little too hard. Her guitar leans against the wall near the fireplace … and she thinks maybe she can write a song with her angry thoughts. "Something about rowboats," she muses, "tied to the dock when I leave to go to work, and *gone* when I return." She looks out the window toward the rickety dock behind the cottage, where Sal's rowboat floats serenely, tied to the piling.

He's apparently avoiding her, ever since his episode. His text messages have been cryptic, too. So what's he hiding?

"Today I'm finding out." She nods with conviction to her reflection in the seashell mirror near the front door. She'd put on a lacy tank top over her Bermuda shorts this morning, and her auburn hair is brushed back off her face. The only way to see Sal is to catch him in the act. So she snatches her canvas tote, hurries to her car and drives to a nearby vacant cottage she'd recently staged, leaving her car in the driveway. Then, well then she walks back home—to her cottage that now *looks* like it's empty, as if she'd gone to work.

And she waits at the sliding glass door in the kitchen, with a clear view to that bobbing wooden rowboat.

It doesn't take long. Sal finally shows up, carrying a large box and cutting through her backyard toward the dock. She watches from the slider as he settles the box in the boat, then starts untying the rope securing it. Which is precisely when Celia walks out to the deck, in *his* clear view, and stands there.

"Celia," he calls, tightening the rope to the dock post and getting out of the boat.

But she notices how he doesn't rush over. Instead he tips his head up to see her beneath the brim of his *Beach Bum* cap.

"They teach you any communication skills on *the Street*?" she asks, air-quoting the words.

Sal turns up his hands. "Celia, I've been meaning, well …" He gives a quick look at the big stainless-steel chronograph watch on his wrist.

She feels it, the way her mouth is set, her fists still clenched, her foot giving a stamp, all while fighting back burning tears. "I've been *worrying* about you, and you up and disappear?"

The odd thing is that he still stands on George's weathered dock. It sways with the incoming tide, and so he takes a sidestep to keep his balance.

"You couldn't even text me?" And hell, she does it, yup, not caring what he thinks. She swipes an escaped tear. So there's this change. Usually, if there were a tear on her face, it would be Sal who would gently touch it, brush it away, then kiss where it had been. Now, he just gives another—*another!*—look at his heavy watch with its subdials and date windows and tachymeter. "Would you *look* at me when I'm talking to you?" Celia yells, shielding her eyes from the sun as she steps off the deck onto the lawn, closing the distance between them.

"Celia."

Then … really? Yes, he throws her an easy smile, which only enrages her further.

"I've been busy at the inn, and around. You know. With everyone."

She stops, her hand still shielding the sun as he stands there on the dock. "Too busy for someone falling in love with you?"

"Oh, Celia." He looks out at the marsh and takes a long breath before turning back and squinting at her for a few seconds. Then he does it *again*, checks his watch. "Can you hold that thought?" he asks, walking slowly backward, glancing over his shoulder to be sure he doesn't fall off the dock.

"What? You're *leaving*? Oh … Oh!" She looks around, unsure of what she's even seeking. "You *scoundrel*!"

He still backs up, his hands turned up in apology. "How can you be mad at someone this handsome?" he asks with a wink.

"You're really annoying me lately." She walks closer, and when she spots a stone near the dock, picks it up and pitches it straight at him, such that he has to duck. "Now *I'm* turning into a hot-headed

Italian, throwing things, yelling." And more tears come then, because what the hell happened to their sweet summer romance?

"I'm sorry, Cee. I really have to go." He backs further away, then turns, gets into his goddamn rowboat and quickly unwraps the rope from the piling.

"Well ... Well I'm tired of wondering about your comings and goings, so don't you come back!" She steps onto the dock, tears running down her cheek. "I don't want your boat here anymore. Just stay away."

As she says it, he starts the little outboard engine and it begins puttering—a hazy smoke rising from it for a moment—before he navigates away from the dock and steers out of the lagoon, giving one last look over his shoulder as he turns the first bend.

Elsa couldn't be happier. Jason's turret design reached right into her heart and put it on the page. Adding a balcony to the second floor of the turret ... what a vantage point to watch the stars, celestial *and* ocean. She loves it, and after he leaves, she takes all that happiness out to her hydrangeas. It feels so good to stand there in the sunshine and water the flowers, the droplets sparkling—well, yes—like stars, too.

"Mrs. DeLuca!"

She turns around to see the beach commissioner approaching, taking off his cap as he nears. Even the sight of *him* can't diminish her happiness. Not by much, anyway. She gives a wave and keeps spraying her blue hydrangeas.

"I wanted to stop by and see how your son is doing."

"Sal?" she asks, then stops spraying. "Sal's fine, why?"

"He seemed sick on the beach the other day."

"Pardon me?" At this, she sets down the hose and pulls off her daisy-print garden gloves.

"Sunday, I think it was. Yes, Sunday. He swam out to help a boy who almost drowned, actually. Didn't he tell you?"

Now Elsa simply shakes her head. And that happiness, that fleeting happiness—damn it—it's blown straight away with the sea breeze.

"Jason was helping him. Jason Barlow? Your architect?"

"Yes, I know precisely who Jason is. He was just here, but he didn't say anything."

"Mrs. DeLuca—"

"Elsa." She steps closer, curious about what this man knows about Sal. "Please call me Elsa."

"Okay. Elsa. I know what I saw on the beach. Your son could barely walk. He was not well."

"Wait." Elsa throws a longing glance back at her beautiful hydrangeas, where only moments ago happiness sang in her life. "Would you like a coffee, Commissioner Raines?"

"It's Clifton. But everyone calls me Cliff."

"All right, then. Cliff. Coffee?"

"Now? Well, sure."

Elsa reaches out and takes his arm, leading him inside the inn while saying, "You need to tell me everything."

Jason wavers, uncertain which he likes better: nights on the beach, or early morning when the sun rises. Both have their merit, but he senses Neil more at night, beneath the cover of the stars, beside the rippling water of Long Island Sound. Especially when he's been alone for this long.

Now he walks just below the high tide line. After sitting all week at his studio worktable, the packed sand feels good on his stiff gait. A quarter moon rises and drops a swath of pale light on the dark water, illuminating the swim raft and big rock beyond it. "Elsa finally approved the inn's turret," Jason says. "I borrowed an idea from a sketch in your scrapbook."

"No shit," he hears, just as a small breaking wave hisses and froths.

"It was an old shingle-style cottage, a real grand dame, but the passage you wrote clinched it." Jason keeps a slow but steady pace, down the beach. Occasionally he picks up a stone and throws it out in the water, listening in the dark for the splash. "You said that the cottage mirrored the rhythm of the tides, the way the homeowner could easily go outside and in with several large balconies, some covered."

As Jason nears the end of the beach, the dune grasses leading to the lagoon whisper in the dark, a sea breeze rustling them. "So you worked that rhythm into your turret?"

"Added balconies to it, for a fluid feel. You know, you can stand and overlook the water outside, or recede and let the sea breeze reach you inside." Up ahead, the waves gently lap against the rocky point, and beyond, the small patch of woods rises in misty shadow. "Elsa loves it, loves anything connected to the sea like that."

"Who you talking to?"

Jason stops still and squints toward where the voice came from.

"Over here."

Someone is moving, so Jason shields his eyes and sees a dark figure walking off the rocks onto the sandy beach. "Sal?"

"Yeah, man." Sal comes closer, slowly, though.

Jason looks out at the water, then back at Neil. With that thought, he gives his head a good shake. Sal—it's *Sal*, for Christ's sake. "What are you doing out here?"

"I could ask you the same question."

"Yeah, except that no one's heard from you for days. What gives?"

"You know how it is," Sal says, joggling a beat-up fishing rod and small tackle box. "Been casting off, letting that salt air cure what ails me."

"So you're feeling better?" As he says it, Jason backs up, hoping to keep walking away and not answer Sal's questions.

"I am, guy. I'm feeling okay. Slept it off, and hey, thanks for that turkey dinner. Worked wonders." With that, he reaches forward to shake Jason's hand. "How about you, cousin? Who you talking to out here? Ghosts?"

"Shit." Jason turns and continues walking down the beach. So his gig is up. No one's ever heard him talking to his dead brother like that, no one. Not even Maris. She knows he does it, but she also knows it's a deeply private thing for him. "Neil," Jason finally admits.

"Your brother?" Sal wades barefoot in the lapping waves.

"That's right. A ghost."

"Wow." Sal stops and looks out at the moonlight glistening on the water, almost as though he's listening for Neil, the way Jason does. "You're a fortunate man, Barlow."

"Fortunate?"

"Hell, I never had a brother. Would've loved to have had that connection."

"Yeah, well." They head across the beach toward the boardwalk. "So I walk out here sometimes, usually when I can't sleep, and talk to him. Or, you know. His *spirit*, I guess. Maris would correct me and say his soul, but yeah … Maybe I'm just thinking out loud, I don't know." Jason stops walking then, and goes silent until Sal stops, too, and turns back to him. "And what's your story?" Jason asks.

"What do you mean?"

"You drift."

"What are you talking about?" Sal whips back, chin raised, ready to argue.

"Don't give me that bullshit. I see you drifting out on the water. Practically every night." He steps closer to Sal. "I *see* you out there. You know, there's something suspicious about you, hanging out here, no work. So what's *your* story, man? Straight up."

Sal hesitates. Behind him, the boardwalk's timer lights illuminate the marina. "Come on." Sal says it, but doesn't wait. He simply walks across the beach toward the boat basin, saying over his shoulder, "I'll show you my boat."

"I was using the dock at Celia's cottage, but now I'm using the little marina here, instead." Sal lifts the latch on the entrance gate. "She gets worried when my boat's gone, you know how they are," he says while swinging the gate open. "Women."

They pass several docked motorboats and get into Sal's rowboat, all while Sal tells him how it came with Foley's. "The family pretty much left everything behind. Furniture, the boat, crappy fishing rods," he says while tossing his rod aside. "So I've been taking rides, here and there."

Jason sits on a boat bench and the water sways the wooden vessel, making the piling creak as the mooring line stretches taut. The boat could use some work, maybe a sanding and a coat of paint, but all in all, it's pretty intact. Sal drops the engine in the water and they putter through the marina, navigating the channel out to Long Island Sound. Jason's not sure when he's last been on a boat at night. There was that one time in their teens, when they all stole a boat on a long-ago Fourth of July, and many nights when he and his brother would go out in their Whaler, sometimes doing a little fishing, sometimes partying with friends. One thing's for sure: You get to know the water better at night. Different senses tune to it in the pitch dark as you listen to the waves lap the side of the boat, hear the fish jump. The scent of the night-dampness is heavy with salt. And there's nothing like reaching your hand in and touching water that you cannot see into.

"I'd never been on the water at night, not until this summer," Sal says as he carefully steers the boat out past the big rock. "It's different, man. Really chill."

Jason reaches a hand over the edge and scoops a bit of water. "So you just float out here? That's it?"

"You don't understand what years on the Street do to you. It's mad crazy. But drifting here, there's little noise." He kills the engine then, and they free-float. "The boat creaks, maybe," Sal says as he settles in. "A fish jumps. A wave splashes on the boat. Nothing else like it." He leans back and looks at the star-speckled sky. "Pure quiet."

"Celia knows about this? Your drifting?"

"Somewhat. She's had a ride or two, but during the day."

"Everything okay with you guys? She was worried sick about you."

"I know." Sal takes the two oars and sets them in the water, lightly dipping them. "We talked this morning." He paddles into deeper water, then lets the boat drift, the oars dripping.

"But you've been keeping yourself pretty scarce. You sure you're okay?"

"I am. How about you? You been back to Sullivan's yet?"

"No."

"Think about it, man. Do you know what it would mean to that dude to be invited to Neil's memorial mass?"

"I'm not sure. Maybe I'll talk to Maris. She's back next week."

"Ah, the elusive Maris." Sal looks out at the beam of light flashing from the Gull Island Lighthouse. "Not sure if my cousin really gets it, though. The Sullivan situation. She ever meet him?"

"No." But what Jason knows is this: No one will ever fully *get* the Sullivan situation. There's no arguing it; it's just a painful reality. And sometimes he gets tired of explaining or justifying his own feelings about Sullivan. Now he picks up the oars and dips them in the sea, paddling. He hasn't rowed on the Sound in too long; it feels good on his arms. "Maybe you'll trade up to a better boat next year."

After a moment when Sal silently watches him paddle, he answers, "I don't plan that far ahead."

"Seriously? In your line of work? Or is it that you'll be heading to the city soon? Not staying on here, after all."

"Don't know."

Jason dips the oars and pulls back on them, listening to the creak and groan of the paddles against the oarlocks.

"When I'm out here," Sal continues, "it's like the hourglass at your place. I feel time, but each moment's smooth; it's *right*, somehow. Like your father's hourglass. Every grain of sand inside it is a moment, one moment, and you flip it and each one matters as it passes through. Ever since I was a kid, I don't take time for granted."

"Why's that?"

First, there's only the sound of the rippling sea lapping against the wooden boat's hull, until Sal quietly talks. "When I was a boy, I was sick and spent a lot of time in bed. Days, when each hour seemed eternal and I'd see sunshine out the window and want to go outside and play. Then I'd fall asleep, and time passed so fast. I'd wake up and the same window would be black; I'd slept for hours, well into the night. My mother came in one time, after a week of this, and asked—I remember her hushed voice as she touched my forehead—*What can I get for you, Salvatore?* And what do you think I said, Barlow?"

"Don't know, guy."

"A boat. I told her I wished I were on a boat. I had such a fever, and aches and pains, and I thought I'd feel better if I could float on the open sea and sail away. A day later, when I woke up feeling groggy and ill, I turned my head and right there, on my little bedside table, the medicine bottles and damp cloths and thermometer were moved aside, and in their place was a boat. It was a beautiful hand-carved sailboat my mother bought in the village toy store. Man, I'd reach for that boat and hold it for hours, imagining drifting endlessly on the water. Lying in bed, I'd pretend I was lying on a sailboat, watching clouds and stars up above, feeling the sway of the sea. It got me through those days." He shifts then, and lies across the rowboat bench, his hands clasped behind his head, his bare feet hung over the boat's side.

"What was wrong with you, being laid up like that?"

"I was a sickly thing, Jason. Fever, strep throat."

Jason paddles slowly, guiding the boat parallel to shore. The moon lightens the beach, turning the breaking waves into a silver lace.

"And this drifting," Sal says, lying there in the dark, "is exactly how I imagined drifting on that toy sailboat would feel, just watching that endless sky."

"My brother was fascinated with the sky, and told me to always remember it in my cottage restorations." Jason glances at the quarter moon far overhead now, the dark sky dotted with stars. "Said it's a masterpiece, the way it always changes."

"If you watch it long enough," Sal says, "the view can play tricks on you. That sky turns into a midnight-blue sea up above, the stars being the ripples of the waves."

Jason lifts the oars from the water, dips them back in and gives a pull. When he considers Sal again, he's still looking up, drifting on the sea, about as far away as can be.

twenty-five

ELSA MIGHT AS WELL COOK some elaborate Saturday dinner, because what else is she going to do with her anger? Banging pots and pans always worked in the past. A few lid-rattles, a few dropping pots onto stove burners and into the sink does the trick. Because there's certainly no other way to channel what she's feeling, except to shake, rattle and bang. When she turns with a copper pot in both hands, Sal is standing in the kitchen doorway wearing a T-shirt and cuffed jeans, unshaven, his hair sleep-mussed. She glances at the clock—okay, so maybe it's a little early to be thinking dinner—surprised to see the sun has only been up for an hour.

Sal walks across the room to the coffeepot and fills a big mug. "It's decaf, Ma?"

"Always, for you," Elsa says when his back is to her. "I have a question, too. What are you doing here?"

"You woke me up," he answers without turning. "Making that racket."

"No." She sets her pot on the countertop. "What are you *really* doing here?"

Now, cupping his mug, he faces her. "I told you. I'm *burned* out, so I'm using my vacation time resting and helping you with the inn. For a change of pace. *Portami al mare*, remember?"

"Your dream, yes. Take me to the sea." Elsa shuts off the flame beneath a small steaming pot on the stove, then turns and eyes her son. Outside the kitchen window, her seashell wind chime clinks in a light breeze. "But Mr. Raines tells me you nearly *collapsed* by the sea."

"Who?"

"The beach commissioner. Cliff Raines." She tucks a wayward wisp of hair behind her rolled paisley-print bandana. "He said you had a problem breathing. So come over here." She motions to the stove, then glares at him when he doesn't move. "Now, Sal. This works wonders, and you know it."

"I'm not that hungry," he says, leaning against the counter with his coffee. "Whatever it is."

"It's not food. I boiled thyme leaves, fresh from my mini-herb garden." She slides the pot onto a cool burner. "Do this for a few minutes, it'll help."

Sal shakes his head, sets his coffee down and walks to the stove. "Ma, I have to go to the diner."

Lowering her head while raising an eyebrow, she tells him, "Everyone else can wait. You need to put yourself first. And when you were a boy and would get sick, I used to do this in Italy and you'd feel better. So maybe it'll help again."

"That was when I was little."

"There's no age limit on these remedies." She gives him a large dish towel. "Hold it up, don't you remember?"

Sal snatches the towel and drapes it over his head, then bends so that his face is near the pot. "Okay."

What he can't see is the way Elsa quickly blesses herself with the briefest of prayers before taking the lid off the boiling water-and-thyme concoction. She hovers beside him and lifts the towel so that the steam rises directly into her son's nasal passages, straight to his lungs. "Breathe deep. Inhale, two, three," she says, her voice soft. "Exhale."

He does; she can see by the way his back slowly rises.

"Why didn't you tell me you had an incident?" she asks after he inhales several quiet breaths. "Why do I have to hear it from a stranger?"

"*Merda*," Sal whispers beneath his towel-tent. "I didn't want to worry you, that's all."

"Jason couldn't tell me, either? If it's such a big secret, it must have been bad."

"Don't be mad at Jason."

"Stop talking and breathe. It helps your respiration." She adjusts the towel so that no steam escapes. "Couldn't Jason have helped save the boy?"

The frustrated way Sal gulps one more deep breath before tossing the towel on the counter and taking his coffee to the table tells Elsa that, yes, this really happened. "Jason was helpless to go in, with his prosthetic leg. You know that, Ma. It was just a situation I was thrown into." He grabs a napkin and dabs his steam-dampened hairline.

"But you have to be careful." Elsa says it while emptying out the thyme pot in the sink before sitting in a chair across from Sal.

"What could I do?" He sips his coffee, then tips his chair back on its rear legs. "Let the boy drown? I'm all right. It was only a scare when I got winded, and needed to rest." He takes another long drink of the coffee, then puts the cup down and stands, turning to the wall near the doorway where his waiter apron hangs on a hook. He lifts it off and ties it around his waist. "I'm taking your car, okay? But we'll talk later." He scoops up her car keys from a basket on the countertop. "I have to go to the diner for a few hours. I promised Kyle I'd wait tables this morning."

"Celia, Jason. Now, Kyle." When Sal looks over at her, he must see the tears welling in her eyes. "You're *my* son, the one person I have left, and suddenly I'm on the outs with you here?"

Sal takes a long breath while shaking his head, her key ring still in his hand.

Celia pushes down the bicycle kickstand and turns toward the inn's front door. As she walks up the pathway, passing soaring scaffolding reaching up to the roof, voices come to her through the open windows. It's nice the way the sea breeze always wafts here, so close to the beach, and she breathes in deeply, hoping to patch things up with Sal. They'd left too many things unsaid the other morning, and maybe they can take a walk near the water now. After maneuvering around a sawhorse, she tucks her hair back behind an ear, gives a light knock on the front door, opens it and leans inside.

It's cooler in the big old cottage. The July sun hasn't had a chance to warm it yet at this early hour. Still hearing voices from the kitchen, Celia cautiously steps inside, about to call out her greeting. But the tone of the voices stops her.

"It pains me to be the last one to know these things, Sal."

"Ma! *Basta!*" A chair scrapes on the floor, as though someone slams it in to the table. "Enough!"

Why, oh why, did she ever open that door and let herself in, even though Elsa has told her to do so time and again. Celia turns quickly to slip outside unseen, but stops again when she hears Sal's raised voice.

"I'm lucky to be here at thirty-five years old! Back then, you didn't expect me to be around this long. *Nobody* did. So trust me when I tell you I'm *fine*, it was nothing!"

No one thought he'd live this long? What the hell? If silence could talk, the one that follows does. Celia is still frozen, her head turned, listening to … nothing. Elsa must be crying, which worries Celia even more. Why would she cry, if Sal's okay?

"Don't worry," Sal says. "I'm still here, it was a scare and nothing else. Maybe a touch of heatstroke, that's all. And I couldn't *not* help the boy. Come on, Ma. You, of *all* people, should understand that."

Something drops, maybe keys—Celia can't be sure—but they clatter to the kitchen floor.

"I'm late, Ma. I *really* have to get going. I'm sorry you got upset, but you're making too big an issue out of things."

"Are you sure? You're feeling okay and I shouldn't worry?"

"Yes! Just a little tired sometimes, that's all. So we're good here? I have to go."

"Oh, shit," Celia whispers. She slips out the front door, closing it gently behind her. While walking quickly away, she can't stop herself from running, then, faster, nearly colliding with that darn sawhorse but managing to evade it as she gets to her bicycle, gives the kickstand three kicks before it releases, mounts the bike and furiously pedals—out the driveway, down the road, her eyes barely seeing through her tears.

"Shh. Daddy's busy," Lauren whispers in the doorway, holding Evan's hand on one side of her, Hailey's on the other.

"Hey, hey!" Kyle looks up from the desk in his diner office. "Never too busy for my favorite customers." When Hailey runs over, he scoops her onto his lap. "Open the drawer, princess. Right there," he tells her while pointing to the top desk drawer. She does, and finds a clear plastic bag filled with miniature farm animals. "You take those to the cottage, okay?" he asks, giving her cheek a kiss and standing her on the floor.

"Open them, Daddy?" She holds the bag up high in her outstretched arms. "Open!"

"Look," he tells her while carefully taking the bag. "There's a rooster, a cow, and a horse, even."

"And a pig!" she says, pulling it out and turning to show Evan.

"Hey, buddy." Kyle hitches his head to his son. "Come on, got something for you, too. To start your vacation." He opens the desk drawer further when Evan nears.

"All right!" Evan says, pulling out a new snorkel and swim goggles.

"Latest style, and non-fogging. So you can explore the ocean floor with those." Kyle stands and gives Lauren a quick kiss then. "You headed to the cottage now?"

"We are. I can't believe our vacation's here."

"No kidding. My pickup's jammed with the sand chairs, boxes. Everything else fit in your car?"

"It was a mad-dash packing, but I think so."

"Good. I'm sneaking a few days off next week. And after that, seven days of vacation, here I come."

"Jerry's covering for you?" Lauren asks.

"Yeah, him and Rob." Kyle's distracted by Evan wearing his new gear and pretending to be a sea monster, chasing Hailey. "Hey kids, go out and grab a booth for lunch."

"How are the numbers?" Lauren nods to the ledger on Kyle's desk once the kids scoot out.

"Fantastic. Almost *too* good." He lifts the fabric of his new Driftwood Café tee and swipes his perspiring face.

"Kyle! Don't use the good shirts. Sheesh," Lauren says, grabbing one of the three-packs off a wall shelf, pulling out a black tee and swatting him with it. "Use these cheap ones."

Kyle strips off his sweaty tee and puts on the new.

"I can't wait to drive beneath that Stony Point trestle and get to the cottage. It's so nice that Elsa extended our stay as a stipend." Lauren presses out the wrinkles in his tee as she says it, her hands brushing across his chest.

"If business keeps up, we can increase our budget for a *permanent* house there. That DeLuca gets people to order food like crazy. The cooks can't keep up with him."

"Is he working today?"

"You bet. He sure is a blessing."

"I'll go say hello." Lauren gives Kyle another kiss before hurrying out to the diner, finding her kids at a window booth. She settles in with them, seeing Sal over at the far wall, draping new diner T-shirts across the fishing net hung there. When he glances over, she gives a wave. "Nice display!"

"Finally," Sal says as he walks past crowded tables, squeezes by a high chair, waves hello to a customer. He wears his waiter apron, with a pencil tucked behind his ear. "I get to meet the little Bradfords."

"Kids," Lauren tells Hailey and Evan sitting across from her. "Say hello to Mr. DeLuca."

"Oh, man. You make me sound so old." With that, Sal pulls a new yellow T-shirt from his apron pocket, gives it to Hailey and takes her hand. "You can call me Sal, and it is a *distinct* pleasure to meet you, young lady."

"That's Hailey," Lauren tells him.

"You are as pretty as your mom, Miss Hailey. How old are you now, about fifteen?" he asks with a wink.

"No!" Hailey sets a red plastic horse on the table. "I'm six!"

"Six!" Sal turns to Evan then, and hands him a blue tee. "For you, my man. A brand-new diner tee. You can wear it on the beach for a cover-up," he says, tapping the goggles strapped on top of Evan's head. "What do you want to be when you grow up? A scientist, maybe? Studying the sea?"

"No."

Lauren sees it, how Evan gets unusually shy with Sal. So Sal crouches down beside the booth seat. "No? With that awesome snorkel to swim underwater with?"

Evan shakes his head.

"Okay, lay it on me, Ev. What will you be when you grow up?"

Evan looks at Lauren, and she nods for him to tell Sal, tearing up as she does.

"A chef," he quietly says. "Just like my dad."

Sal stands up and puts out his hand to Evan. When Evan puts his hand in his, Sal gives him a hearty handshake. "I am *so* impressed, man," he says with a quick glance at Lauren. "So impressed."

Really now, who designed these contraptions? Celia takes the beach-umbrella pole and stabs it at the sand close to the water's edge. It's better to sit here, where she can take a dip anytime her anger boils over. She drops the umbrella pole, picks up a plastic shovel she found in her cottage shed and scoops out a hole in the sand. Then the shovel gets tossed and she takes the umbrella post again, trying to spear it into the hole.

"Hey, Celia. Easy does it!"

When she glares over her shoulder, strands of her hair fall across her face beneath her straw fedora. She sweeps it all back and sees Jason standing there with his dog at his side. "Swell. Might as well have everyone watch me come undone." She gives the pole another stab at the sand.

"So what's going on?"

"I'm trying to have a relaxing day at the beach." She tosses the umbrella pole and snatches up her sand shovel, falls to her knees and digs into the sand. "Except I'm finding out there's way too much drama at this peaceful little place. Thought I'd have a nice vacation here, and really?" She swipes the back of her hand across her forehead. "My blood pressure must be through the roof."

"What happened?"

"I'll tell you what happened." Celia pushes herself up off her knees, grabs the umbrella pole and stabs at the sand again. "You hear things at Stony Point that you really aren't supposed to." With two hands wrapped around the pole, she gives one good shove into the sand. "Oh, I'm so upset!"

"Celia, relax." Jason steps closer, and his dog whines, too. "It's only an umbrella."

"It's not *that.*" And the way even the dog tips its head while watching her, Celia figures she must look a complete wreck. "It's Mr. Salvatore DeLuca." Now she pounds the pole into the sand, over and over again.

"Sal?" Jason carefully lifts the umbrella pole out of her hands and gives her Madison's leash, instead. Finally, he twists the pole into the beach and mounds a pile of sand around its base.

"Right," Celia explains. "Your cousin through marriage." When she tips her hat up, she wonders how it got so hot already? Sweat lines her face. "With his God damn ready smile, then he disappears? We have a nice thing going, until he backs off? So I thought, well I *thought* he was just a player, you know? A Wall Street playboy. It's why I didn't even try with love, Jason. Who needs it?"

Jason picks up the top of the umbrella, opens it and snaps it into the pole standing firm in the sand. "What are you talking about?"

"He's *not* a player, okay? It's something else. I heard him talking—well, never mind. What I'm trying to say is that …" With a quick breath, she looks out at Long Island Sound, then slips off the chambray blouse over her bathing suit and hangs it on the back of her sand chair. "It's time for me to leave."

"Leave?"

"Exactly. To go home to Addison, where there are no surprises. No *blessed* …" Yes, she does it; she gets her fingers into curled position and air-quotes the precious word tossed around here all the time. "*Secrets.*" Then, with just the right attitude, she tosses her straw fedora on the chair. "Thanks, Jason. For the umbrella work."

"You're really leaving? Does Sal know this?"

She waves him off, shaking her head. "Doesn't matter. I'm taking a swim now," she tells him while wading straight into the cool water, "before I head back home."

"Maddy, let's go."

Jason pulls the German shepherd close beside him as they wind their way past sandy beach blankets and inflated tubes. He gives a look over at Celia swimming steadily across the water, one hand over the other, maybe a little too harshly. When they reach the boardwalk, he pulls his cell phone from his cargo shorts pocket and sits on the bench, the dog lying at his feet. The midday sun is bright, so he shields his eyes and squints out beyond the people on the beach—eating ice cream, reading books, chatting, wading in the water—to Celia, still swimming. From the tone of her voice, it seemed like she meant it, that she was really leaving Stony Point, *today*.

So not wasting another second, he pulls up the number on his screen and places the call, waiting through two rings before hearing the din of the diner in the background right before the familiar voice answers.

"Sal?" Jason asks.

twenty-six

Celia moves her chair into the shade beneath the umbrella. All around her, happy families are settled with their beach gear: Children in tubes splash in the shallow waves; books lay open in laps; sandcastles are being built; suntan lotion is being rubbed on. It's a scene straight out of a movie—just add her broken heart and it's got romantic comedy written all over it. Because isn't it *funny* that she can feel so sad in the middle of such a scene. After taking two swims already, she's drying off in the early afternoon sunshine, soaking in the seaside view one last time before packing up her things at the cottage.

They always say to trust your gut; even Kyle talked about it the other day when he stopped by for his truck. He told Jason that he gauges the houses he tours by his gut instinct when he walks through the front door, that studies have proven the gut doesn't lie. Isn't that the truth? When she first arrived here, her gut told her to simply take these fleeting summer days to catch her breath after her divorce. To rethink her future, beside the sea. To find her personal happiness again, strumming her guitar and searching for sea glass. To stay as far away from love as possible, for now. That love would only lead to more heartache.

So the studies are right. Pulling her straw fedora on over her sun-dried hair, she settles in her sand chair, ready to leave this place with its beach friends and secrets and, well … and its one particular Italian.

Wait. Its one particular Italian who, at this precise moment, is flipping open a beach towel and spreading it on the sand beside her.

Celia lowers her sunglasses and peers at him. "What are you doing here?"

"Celia." Sal looks up at the sun, settles his *Beach Bum* cap on his head and sits on the towel.

"It was Jason, wasn't it?" She whips around and scans the beach. "He called you."

"You know what they say … No secrets at this Stony Point Beach."

"It's no wonder. With all the thin cottage walls, close homes, friends always walking past, open windows … secrets waft in the damn sea breeze." She pulls her knees up and wraps her arms around them, looking out at the Sound, feeling that breeze she'd nicely cursed.

"What's wrong today?" Sal asks, his voice low.

Oh, if she could just go back ten minutes—stood up ten minutes ago and left—she'd be halfway to her cottage right now with her closed umbrella slung over her shoulder, her folded sand chair hanging from her hand, her flip-flops flipping on the sandy road. Instead, she has this: waves lapping at her bare toes and a smooth voice lulling her.

And nothing more from Sal, nothing except a touch on her skin as he reaches out and lightly brushes her arm.

So she looks at him. Doesn't dare remove her dark sunglasses, though. Not this time. Not with what she is about to say. "I haven't seen you in two days. *Two* days. I told you I loved you, and you left. So now *I* am."

Sal takes a long breath and his gaze shifts from her, to the sea sparkling in front of them. The way he takes that breath, it makes her think of the mantra everyone at this darn place always tosses around: The salt air … cures what ails you, cures what ails you. Take a breath, breathe it in. So is he trying to cure something? Some pain? Some ailment, with that salty tonic?

"You know," he says, still looking at only the water. "I never dreamt it would go this far."

"You mean, that *we* would?"

Now he looks at her, straight on. Hat removed, hand—with requisite sailor's knot rope on the wrist—dragged back through waves of thick, dark hair. And he nods. "A month ago, I was just taking you to a shindig on the beach. To cheer you up, have some laughs together. Believe me, I never saw this coming. Never thought I'd be drawn deep into every damn thing that *is* this place called Stony Point."

"Neither did I. And so I'm sure Jason told you that I'm leaving."

"Before you decide to go, please let me show you why I haven't seen you in two days."

"*Show* me?"

He nods, then pulls his cell phone from his cargo shorts pocket. "I have to check the tides first."

She waits while he scrolls his phone screen, tilting it against the sun's glare. And what that does is give her a few seconds to decide: Stay and hear him out? Or walk away. Cut your losses, stop trying, pick up your gear and go.

"If we leave right now," Sal says as he stands and puts his phone in his pocket, "we have time. I can get you there." He holds out his hand toward hers. "Come with me?"

The Sound is calm this Saturday afternoon, covered with tiny ripples beneath a beating sun. After they brought her beach things back to the cottage, Celia changed into a tank top and distressed-denim Bermudas, glad now that she threw on a thin white blouse and wore her fedora, too. She dips her fingers into the seawater that's been lapping the side of Sal's rowboat.

Once they round the turn in the coastline, he points out Little Beach. "It's there, just beyond that woodsy area. I guess there's a path leading to it from the main beach."

Celia looks over at the small stretch of sand beyond the woods. It's an untamed strip of the coast, with occasional boulders dotting it. She's heard mention of this Little Beach, another magical, secretive part of the Stony Point mystique.

After they round yet another bend where a ragged beach and scrubby dunes line the coast, Sal carefully watches the shore. Plumes of grass, green and feathery, cover the sandy hills. "I'm glad you came along, Celia." He kills the engine and sets the paddles in the water, his arms pulling back on them as he maneuvers the boat into the shallows. Finally, he climbs out into nearly waist-high water and pulls the boat in closer. When it is practically touching bottom, he drops the anchor and takes Celia's hand as she steps over the edge of the boat into low water. Sal reaches for their sandals and boat shoes while she wades toward shore.

"Where are we?" she asks. Here, a gentle breeze lifts off Long Island Sound.

"The only way to tell you is to show you." Sal holds her hand and leads her through a narrow, sandy trail that winds through the sloping dunes. A weathered storm fence leans against overgrown grasses and yellow wildflowers, some sweeping across their path. They eventually climb one last rising dune that blocks the scenery beyond.

"What *is* this?" Celia asks when they reach the top of the dune. Around her, the grasses whisper, and down below, a shabby silver shack faces the sea. Lobster buoys of white and yellow and blue hang from its shingled walls, and old, paned windows look out on the sea.

"Just a place to go." They walk down the other side of the sloping dune, and Sal leads her around another storm fence set out against more wild grasses growing behind the shack, then to the wooden front door. Its white paint has faded, and streaks of the natural wood beneath it show through. He turns the knob and with his shoulder, gives the sticking door a shove.

A moment comes then, when he stops and simply looks into the shack before turning to her. And when he motions for Celia to walk in ahead of him, she does. If she thought Little Beach looked mystical, then the only word to describe this place is enchanting. Golden sunlight pours in through the rustic windows; wood shelves gleam along the walls—shelves lined with gorgeous leather journals and scrapbooks. Glass domes of hurricane lanterns sparkle; white conch shells shimmer. Above the one front window, beside the door, a café-style curtain is hung, its white linen sun bleached.

As Celia takes this all in—walking slowly and touching a journal, a coffee mug, a tattered lobster trap—she hears it, hears his voice behind her.

"A place where no one's always watching, calling, knocking on the door."

"Damn you," Celia whispers. "Damn you, Salvatore DeLuca."

"Wait. Look." He points past her to a round table with Mason jar candles on it. "A place to sit and talk, by the sea. There's food here. A cooler to keep things fresh." He picks up two dishes from a shelf. "Plates, cups."

Her eyes drink in everything and fill with tears. "This is what you've been doing?" she whispers.

Sal nods and steps back.

"But this is fantasy. A hideaway shanty at the beach? The stuff of dreams. Of *movies*." She turns to him. "This is *not* real life, Sal."

"But it is," he insists with a knock on the wood table, with picking up a vase of dune grasses and yellow wildflowers. "It's very real."

"Damn you," she barely whispers again. Or maybe she only thinks it while realizing what he's gone and done. Her intent to leave Stony Point, to drive beneath that railroad trestle with one of three things—hers being a broken heart—has been utterly defeated.

"Shh," he says when she starts to talk. "Celia." He lifts both her hands and they stand still. "Just stay in the moment, okay? One moment to close your eyes and breathe. Breathe that sweet salt air here."

She looks away quickly, blinking back persistent tears, then looks at him again. He nods at her to do it, to breathe. And she does, closing her eyes and taking one long breath, followed by another. Which is when it happens, when she feels his lips on hers, so soft, so loving, she could just about sob. Or kiss him right back, which she does.

"Better now?" he asks as he kisses her cheek, her eyes, her mouth once again.

She nods, lacing her hands with his. Behind him, the room holds duck decoys and vintage fishing rods and scruffy chairs with comfortable throws tossed over them. Even a dusty typewriter beside a hurricane lantern. "How did you ever find this place?"

He smiles, slightly, but enough. "Your beach friend showed me."

"My friend?"

"Lauren."

"What?" Thinking of Lauren being in this space has Celia spin around, taking it all in again. "How would she know about this?"

"Ah, that's her secret to tell, Celia. Not mine."

Maybe. Or maybe it's the shack's secret to tell. Because when Celia looks around again, she sees hints of Lauren's secret: in the drumsticks, and the man's black sweatshirt hanging on a wall hook, and in the leather-bound scrapbooks. She slides one off the shelf and opens it to a photograph of Lauren in her twenties, it seems, with long blonde hair, wearing a denim jacket over a light tank top. Celia runs her hand over the image, trying to place what she's seeing on Lauren's face. It's love, of course. The eyes never lie. She thumbs through a few of the pages that are warped and dried out from the sea elements, gazing at other photos of someone she's never seen. Images of a man, his dark hair wavy and thick with sea salt, his face unshaven, a heavy silver chain around his neck, and a smile meant only for whoever took the picture. Celia looks up at Sal, who gives her a silent, but slight shrug, one that confirms Celia's thoughts.

"Neil," he says.

And so she tenderly closes the book and places it back on the shelf.

"Let's sit outside." Sal carries two folding chairs out the door and sets them in the sand, facing a distant lighthouse. Seagulls fly past, and the breeze rustles the dune grass behind the shack.

But something stops Celia from joining him. She merely watches from inside until he glances her way while arranging the chairs, and motions for her to join him. She sits beside Sal and again takes his hand in hers.

"I'm sorry I haven't been around to see you this week. But do you trust me now?" he asks. "Trust that I love you, too?"

Her thumb runs across the sailor's knot bracelet he wears. "When you stop lying to me is when I'll trust you."

"What?"

"This place," she says, motioning to the shack. "This beautiful, exquisite hideaway is not the only reason you've been avoiding me."

"What are you talking about?"

"This morning, before you went to the diner, I stopped by your mother's, Sal. She always tells me to come right in, don't knock. You know, in case she's busy cooking, or is outside watering her geranium and tomato pots. So I went there to see you, and I knocked lightly and walked right in. And I heard you."

Sal sits back in his chair and gazes at the sky before turning to her.

"Sal, I heard things I didn't understand. About you, and about being sick. But I also heard how upset Elsa was, and that? That, I understood. I understood that something was seriously wrong."

"You're right, of course," Sal tells her as he touches her face and runs his finger along her jaw. "Something *was* wrong. When I was a boy. Thirty years ago, Celia. Yes, I was very sickly, and I was in bed often. And you know mothers, they'll always worry."

So his voice explains, and she listens to his gentle inflections telling about times when his frantic parents would bundle him up and bring him, hot and feverish, to the hospital, fearful for their only child. And how he didn't want to worry Elsa yet again with his recent incident that unexpectedly winded him, an incident she learned about anyway from the beach commissioner. He assures Celia that what she overheard was exactly what he did *not* want to put upon Elsa.

And Celia knows. It all comes down to choice. She can continue to doubt him, or she can believe him. Believe him as he tells her that growing up in Italy, his health was challenged and he had to be careful, but that those worries are far away now; he's fine.

"You see?" he asks as he leans close and tips Celia's face to his.

She does, that's the thing. She sees his dark eyes and a shadow of whiskers against his tanned skin; his hair, wavy in the sea damp much like Neil's in the scrapbook photo; and she smiles, her fingers skimming his face.

"Yes," Sal says, slipping his hand beneath her hair on her neck. "There it is, the smile that lights up my days." He dips his head low and kisses her then, kisses her while the waves break nearby and a seagull caws and the grass whispers. When he pulls back and straightens her fedora, he touches her ear, her jaw. "The smile I fell in love with."

twenty-seven

ELSA'S HEARD IT TIME AND again, ever since she bought Foley's. *You are not to change the back room. Leave that room alone. Do not touch the back room.*

And when Jason finalized the inn's turret design, which includes the back room within its parameters, he reminded her once more. "Just because it's in the turret does *not* mean you can change that room. You leave it be, you hear me?"

So she spent all weekend considering how she can update it, while keeping its integrity intact. Every bit of the dark beadboard wainscoting was scrutinized, every dining booth sat in, every window looked out of. For the first time in years, Elsa pulled a ball shooter on the pinball machine, tapped the flippers as the game dinged and whistled, and still … nothing. For the life of her, she does *not* get the magic of this drab room.

Now, on Tuesday morning, Elsa sits in one of the booths yet again, seeing the old decks of cards on a shelf, the notepads, the plates and cups. Rays of sun reach in through the windows, catching dust particles that dance and twirl in the silence, making the whole room look like a dreamy apparition. If she's still enough, she can imagine the vintage jukebox playing old rock-and-roll tunes; can almost see the shadow of a teen couple dancing on the small, wooden dance area; can picture Jason's brother, Neil, maybe sitting on top of the counter, drumsticks in hand, tapping out a rhythm. Because that's the thing: Everyone's told her some variation of this room's memories, but she hasn't experienced any herself.

So she squints at the shabby space, at its floor holding close the beat of dancing feet; at its booths giving no hints to the secrets shared in them; at its walls—oh, if they could only talk—mocking her with their silence. She tries to picture the whole gang, Jason and Neil, Maris and Eva, Kyle and Lauren, everyone, gathered right here throughout their teen summers, on hazy nights, the moon low over the sea beyond, the air damp and salty.

And then … it happens. She knows exactly how to better understand this room. It's the only way, actually, and it's surprising it's taken this long to figure out. Elsa pulls her cell phone from her back pocket, sets it on the table, scrolls through her contacts, and begins typing a group message:

Please Come: It's a Party!
For: Maris and Eva's Stony Point Homecoming
When: Saturday, August 1, 7 PM
Where: Ocean Star Inn
Attire: Casual
Attitude: Happiness

—

On his day off from the diner, Kyle leans over and helps his daughter pull in her crabbing line. "You got one, princess!" he says, scooping up the net. "Drop it in here."

Hailey shakes the crab off her bait into the net, and Kyle flips it into a large bucket filled with water. A small eel hovers on the bottom, near a piece of seaweed he dropped in as well.

"Dad," Evan calls from further out on the rocks. The tide is low and several kids are crabbing, watching their lines intently, murmuring when they see a crab scurry in the shallows. "Can I go over there?" he asks, pointing to an area on the point. "It looks like a good spot."

"Just be careful," Kyle tells him. "You have your water shoes on?"

Evan kicks a leg, then takes his crabbing line and pail to a new rocky post.

"Is Mommy coming?" Hailey asks.

"No, Hay. We'll see Mommy at dinner. She's busy working, making beautiful paintings at the big beach inn." As he says it, a seagull swoops low, looking for their bait bag, he's sure. "See that pretty bird? I'll bet she's painting some of those, too."

Hailey squints up at the bird, then carefully tiptoes across the rocks to a tidal pool swirling with gentle waves and seaweed.

After a quick glance to Evan, Kyle follows Hailey, then clamps a hunk of hot dog onto her line. As she drops it in the water, his cell phone dings with a message.

"Is that Mommy?" Hailey asks while watching her baited string and holding back a wisp of blowing hair.

"I'll check." He does, tapping his phone. "Nope, it's Elsa. She's the lady who owns the big cottage where Mommy's working." He reads the invite, liking the idea of dinner at the as-yet-unopened inn. *Sweet*, he whispers. *Good times*. He texts Lauren to see if she can get a babysitter for Saturday night.

It's that kind of summer day when time moves slow and easy, when bumblebees buzz lazy, when even the robins' song is light and airy. All the windows are open at the inn, and the lace curtains waft every now and then with the slightest of breezes bringing in the salty tang of the sea.

Lauren closes her eyes for a delicious moment and breathes the scent, then shifts the foamy pad beneath her knees. As she adds green to the dune grass along one side of the stair risers, her cell phone dings. Which is the perfect time to stretch her legs, and so she walks down the few stairs and pulls the phone from her tote. And smiles, with a glance around the corner and down the hall, where she knows Elsa is sitting. She went into the back room an hour ago, and still hasn't emerged.

"Elsa?" Lauren calls out.

"Yes, dear," a voice comes from somewhere in the dark recesses of that room.

"I'm RSVP'ing. Kyle and I will definitely be there!"

"Wonderful!"

So Lauren picks up her paintbrush and dabs it into the green paint, finding herself smiling more and more here at Stony Point.

—

At Last, the cottage sign reads. The white letters are painted on a backdrop of blue waves, with a gold anchor off to the side. Celia thinks that must be what the owners said anytime they arrived, dropped their overnight bags on the screened porch and smelled that sweet salt air. *At last*, they were here at their little beach cottage.

She gives the front door a tug to be sure it's all locked up. When Eva called her and asked if she could stage *one* more cottage, really, Celia couldn't resist. Every cottage she's worked on here has its own seaside allure, from one with twinkly white lights outlining the front porch, to another with paned windows opening to the sea, to this charmer: a bungalow nestled among hydrangea bushes, with a birdbath in the front yard and seashell wind chimes clinking beside the door.

Still, she's glad the stage was mostly rearranging furniture, finished in a day. Now she can spend the rest of her time here working one-on-one with Elsa, developing a vision for the beach inn.

Okay, she thinks as the ice-cream truck drives past, a soft tune tingling from its speaker, and she might also convince herself that this *can* be, as Sal puts it, real life.

Her phone dings as she walks down the cottage's flagstone path, so she checks her message, smiling at what she sees there. And wasting no time. She texts Elsa an enthusiastic *Yes*, adding an offer to help cook for the party, too.

As she puts her bag in her bicycle basket, her phone dings again. Before pedaling back to her cottage, she settles her straw fedora on her head and reads the new message. It's from Sal. *Ciao, bella. Open mic at The Sand Bar tonight. Bring your guitar?*

Okay, she does it, after reading his message a second time. Still smiling, she pinches her own arm to believe it, that this really happens. Seaside soirees and beach friends texting sweet messages and salty breezes and bicycle rides to cottages? Oh yes, life right now is very real, indeed.

twenty-eight

JASON TOLD SAL TO MEET him at Maggie Woods' place today, the first stop on a short Tuesday itinerary. Though the Hammer Law prevents the heavy work of this teardown from beginning, he can move forward with everything else, including his vision for the new owners. Crucial to any design are varying views of the property, including how the different positions of the sun might alter it. So he walks through the now-practically-empty cottage, his footsteps echoing on the bare floors and paneled walls, before going out to the side patio. He sets his duffel on a rusted table there, noting the peeling paint on the deck railings, and the seagull droppings covering everything. It's apparent Maggie Woods never once powerwashed it to keep it even somewhat clean. The neighbors must be relieved to see the whole mess go.

"Yo, Barlow!" Sal calls out from the lawn below. "*Avanti tutta*, boss!"

"Full speed ahead, yeah, yeah. Come on up. I'm taking some pictures." Jason gets his camera from the bag and pans the scenic view, camera to his eye. Umbrellas and sand chairs are scattered across the crescent-shaped beach as families settle in for a sunny Tuesday. "Where's your hard hat?" he asks when he turns and sees Sal wearing cuffed jeans and boat shoes, with a navy linen blazer over a chambray shirt. "No gear today?"

"Nope. You mentioned it was a light day, so I thought I'd wear my blues." He gives his jacket sleeve a tug, the sailor's knot bracelet showing as he does. "Beach blues." As he says it, a cell phone dings with a message.

"That's me." Jason reaches into a flap pocket on the leg of his khaki trousers.

"No. It's me." Sal says, pulling his cell phone from his blazer.

"You sure?" Jason asks while tapping his phone.

"Think so."

"Nope, it's mine. It's your mother."

"A text?" Sal lifts his sunglasses to the top of his head and angles his phone. "I got one, too."

"Guess she's planning a homecoming party."

Sal looks up from reading his message. "Maris is back *this* week?"

"Friday."

"Hey, hey. Sweet for you, no?"

"You bet. And I guess we have plans for Saturday now." Jason leans on the deck railing and gives his phone a joggle to RSVP. "We'll be there," he says while typing.

"Yup," Sal says, fingers plucking out his message. "Me, too."

After checking his watch, Jason picks up his camera and snaps a few more pictures, noting the angles of the morning sun.

"Woods never took care of this place, did she?" Sal asks, nudging a loose piece of the patio's crumbling stone floor.

"No. She was too busy watching everybody, and lifting things, too. A sand chair here, a beach umbrella there. She even stole one of Neil's journals, filled with his writings, back in the day. Anything left out in the open was fair game."

"But why? What was her problem?"

"Insecurity. Jealousy, maybe. Wanted what everyone else had and ended up with nothing. No family, no kids. Just a bitter heart." Jason puts his camera into his duffel and hikes the bag on his shoulder.

"And now? You're dismissed, cousin. Short workday for you. I've actually got an errand to run this afternoon."

They walk down the hill to Jason's SUV. "Where to?" Sal asks.

"Personal stuff to take care of." Jason opens the vehicle's liftgate and sets his bag inside.

"Want some company? For the ride, anyway?"

"Ride?"

"To Ted's."

"How'd you know?"

"When you told me last week it would be a slow day today, I figured as much. Thought you might invite him before your wife gets back."

Jason closes the SUV's rear door and squints at Sal. The way the sunlight hits him from behind, casting him in silhouette, his hands turned up, waiting, it could be Neil standing there—always ready to tag along, come for the ride, hang out. "Come on." Jason pulls his keys from his pocket. "Let's go, then."

They stop to pick up Maddy before leaving Stony Point and getting on the highway. Traffic is light, the day warm. Jason turns on the radio and finds a Yankees game, just beginning.

"I've got a friend in the city," Sal says. "Has season tickets to the Yankees' home games."

"No shit. Season tickets? That must've set him back a few."

"It did, but not with cash. He paid on the job."

"How so?" Jason checks the mirror and changes lanes to pass a slower car.

"He's a cop. Mounted police officer, actually. But before that, he patrolled in a cruiser, and was involved in a situation where his partner was killed. Point-blank, by some lowlife. My friend—Michael, Michael Micelli—well, he took the dude out right there on the spot. Ended his life and got him off the streets for good. His coworkers thanked him with the tickets."

"That's some serious stuff that went down."

"It was, and Micelli took it hard. He's better now, and a really good guy."

Jason feels Sal's gaze on him and glances over.

"You'd like him," Sal tells him.

As he says it, Jason is driving along the sandy road parallel to Sea Spray Beach. One side of the street is lined with cottages, and across the street, past craggy low dunes, the narrow beach opens up. He parks the SUV behind Ted's place. The new cedar shingles turn this cottage into a shade of golden honey, accented with a dramatic dark roof and wide white trim detail. Big brass wall lanterns glimmer in the afternoon sunlight.

Sal gives a low whistle. "Breathtaking work, Barlow."

"Thanks." Jason unbuckles his seatbelt.

"You go in alone." Sal reaches for the leash in the backseat. "I'll take Madison for a beach walk."

"You sure? You can come up."

"No. You go." Sal gets out and opens the rear lift for the dog. "It's all good, man," he says as he clips on her leash. "You'll never regret it."

The deck table now is all teak, with a massive white conch shell centerpiece. The woven fabric on the teak chairs is covered in blue-and-white stripes.

"Quite a difference from the old webbed chairs and metal table," Jason says, tipping his beer bottle to Ted's. "Nice choice here."

"My wife loves to decorate. The décor is all her doing."

"Any misgivings about the renovations?" Jason asks.

"None at all. Well, maybe one. That I'm sorry it took this long for me to do." Ted sits back and sips his beer. "You?" he asks.

Jason stands and takes his beer bottle to the deck railing. He's been talking to Ted for a half hour now, and out on the beach, Sal's heading back with the dog—who's got a long stick of driftwood clamped in her jaw. Jason turns and looks up at the redesigned cottage. The egret depicted on the loft's stained glass window subtly wavers in the sunlight. Large windows on either side of it are open wide to the sea. The last time he was here, he went up to that loft and considered the view. That changing masterpiece of sky, particularly when it's over water, is always a sight to behold.

"Neil would've been proud of this one," he says to Ted then, raising his bottle in a silent toast to his brother. Ted does the same, from where he sits at the table. "Now I can't imagine *not* having done this job. It put me in a different place with everything."

"Me, too," Ted tells him. "Thanks to you, I find a lot of peace at the shore. My wife, as well."

Jason returns to the table and sets down his drink. It's time now. But he hesitates until a sudden sea breeze kicks up, bringing his brother's whispered voice: *Say what you want to say, already.* "Okay," he begins. "Listen, Ted. Neil's anniversary mass is this Sunday. Think you could make it?"

"Hell, Jason." Ted swipes away a sudden tear. "Of course. It would mean the world to me. But," he asks, standing. "Are you sure?"

Jason glances over as Sal walks up the deck steps with Maddy. Sal gives a slight nod, and Jason does it. He turns to Ted and extends his hand.

It'll always be there between them—Neil's death—in quiet pauses, in awkward hesitations, but now there's this, too. This distinctive waterfront home and newfound friendship built from the ruins of one day.

Ted takes Jason's hand and clasps it tightly. "I've got a brew with your name on it, once a summer, Jason. I want to see you, and have a toast to life. To Neil. Maybe walk the driftline, whatever. I don't want to lose touch with you."

Jason glances over at Sal, who gives him a thumbs-up, nodding. So he looks Ted in the eye, then steps closer and hugs him, slapping his shoulder. "There's no going back now, is there?"

twenty-nine

Even sitting below skylights in his barn studio, Jason still likes his swing lamp shining when he's in the throes of designing. Thursday morning, he wheels the mobile roll file closer and puts the turret blueprint in one of the bins. The inn renovation is by far the biggest job he's ever undertaken, and with Elsa's never-ending and ever-changing ideas, there's now a different design sketch in each of the bins: turret, varying floor plans and elevations—with additions and without. At least the turret is finalized. For now.

He reaches for a reference book on a nearby shelf, then turns to his computer. His work camera sits on the long wooden table, and one of Neil's leather journals is off to the side, near a few architectural scales. Fiddling with his pencil, Jason looks from the water-view shots on the computer screen, to Neil's journal notes, to the pages of sketches spread out. Several ideas have been simmering for the new Woods' property, and he wants to firm them up before Maris gets back tomorrow. After adjusting the swing lamp, he sets his hand on another blank paper, the straight lines quickly taking shape as he leans over the table.

Time passes easily when he works like this. A soft breeze floats in through the open windows, and outside a robin sings the same verse over and over again. From off in the distance, the sound of a boat motor rises, making its way into the studio space.

"What've you got, Jay?"

Jason's pencil hovers as he hears his brother's question, just as the breeze lifts a piece of tracing paper. "Windows, lots of windows, wide white trim," he answers.

Then, nothing. Only his pencil moving back and forth again, the lead dragging out lines and angles and paned windows, windows, windows. His hand slides across the page, pulling and pushing the shape of his ideas into a design.

Finally, leaning in his seat, he holds up the paper, that robin still trilling outside. But he hesitates. When he hears a soft footstep, just one, he turns his swivel chair toward the door. Maris stands there, wearing tattered skinny jeans and a black V-neck fitted tee, her gold star pendant glimmering against it.

"I'm home," she murmurs, not moving closer.

Jason glances away with a wide grin, then looks at her again. He still sits, leaning back and watching her. "Come here, beautiful."

Maris takes one step, then stops. "Close enough?"

He simply watches while she tucks her hair behind her ear, dipping her head as she does. "No," he tells her.

So she takes another step. Behind her, sunlight spills in through the double slider, casting a halo of light around her long brown hair. "Better?"

Now, well now he stands, still holding his paper, which he sets on the table. "No, sweetheart."

Another step, her sandaled feet brushing across the floor. "How's this?"

Jason puts his hand to his jaw, his thumb finding the scar there and dragging across it. "What are you doing home early?"

"I'm not early." Her voice is summer soft, hushed like the breeze. "I *told* everyone I'd be home tomorrow because, well ..."

"The phone won't stop ringing tomorrow?"

She nods, barely. "People will be at the door to see me."

Still, neither of them moves. Until now. Jason's eyes fill with tears while he watches Maris take one step, then another, until she's inches away from him. Close enough for his fingers to stroke her arm, her shoulder, to skim her hair. "Don't tell anyone you're back."

"I won't." She reaches for his hand that hasn't stopped touching her cheek, her hair, her neck, and clasps it tightly. "I missed you," she whispers, closing the gap between them. "I want to tell you about my trip, and see what you're working on so diligently." She nods to his worktable and the papers scattered there. "And, you know," she adds, grazing his face with the back of her fingers, "*without* the phone ringing."

No, she's not an apparition. After all these quiet weeks, his sweet Maris is home. Right here, touching him. He cradles her face, his thumb caressing her jaw, her ear, as he leans slowly in and finally kisses her. And he knows she feels the same, that she's missed him just as deeply, by the way her body presses against his, the way her fingers hook his belt loops and pull him even closer, the way, when he stops kissing her, she rises on her toes and kisses him again, once, twice, a third time even longer.

"Jason," she murmurs between those kisses. "God, did I miss you."

It's one of those late-July days when the sun cranks up the heat with each passing hour. Kyle and Lauren cross the beach after lunch, with Evan and Hailey running ahead of them. Kyle had closed up their umbrella and sand chairs before they went to the cottage to make sandwiches, and now he can't open that umbrella fast enough.

"Man, it's hot," he says as he bends and snaps it up. Beside him, Lauren drops a tote of sand toys and straightens their chairs. "Glad Jerry's covering for me this afternoon. Must be hell behind the stoves today."

"Dad!" Evan calls from the water's edge, goggles on and snorkel in hand. "Let's explore."

"In a few, buddy." Kyle peels off his tee and blots his face. "Let me digest a little."

"It's so refreshing being near the water," Lauren tells him when she sits on a blanket in her tie-dye tankini, arms folded around her knees.

Something about the moment makes Kyle want to stop the clock, right here in the sun, seaside with his family. He crouches behind Lauren and wraps his arms around her waist, kissing the side of her head as he sits close.

"Hey," she says, leaning back into him. "What's that for?" She twists slightly and gives him a light kiss.

"I don't know." He presses his face to hers, watching the waves break beyond their blanket. "Just because," he says. When Lauren throws him a puzzled look over her shoulder, he kisses her again, his arms squeezing her waist from behind. "Everything's really … good."

She strokes his arm and they sit there like that, not moving. "You going fishing tomorrow night with Jason?"

"I suppose." He touches her blonde hair, pulling it gently back. "Why?"

"Well, Maris is coming home, so they'll be busy, I'm sure."

"Damn, I forgot." Kyle sits back, puts on his *Gone Fishing* cap and breathes in the salt air. "Maybe she'll be visiting the ladies, though. You know, Elsa, and her sister."

"Kyle. Maris has been gone for a month. Do you seriously think those newlyweds are going to be apart much?"

"I'll text Barlow, he must be on a job somewhere." He pulls his cell phone from Lauren's tote and angles it, raises it, gives a shake, but nothing. "I'm going on the bench. It's higher up, maybe I'll get a signal." He trots barefoot across the hot sand, lifting his burning feet quickly, and climbs up the small ledge of rocks, through a patch of beach grass to a wooden bench where he clicks to Jason's name on his phone.

Friday night fishing tomorrow? When I get out of work? he types. And waits.

No, I'm busy, Jason answers a minute later. *Maris is actually back.*

Kyle reads the message and rolls his eyes. There goes his buddy, lost to love. *Got it*, he types on the phone. *She hooked, lined and sunk you.*

Pretty much.

Guess I'm on the outs then, he types, ending the message.

He sits there, holding his cell phone and taking in the view. Stony Point Beach is crowded with families, but quiet in the bright heat. On the boardwalk, women with strollers sit beneath the shade canopy, wheeling their hot babies back and forth. And on the swim raft, teens lie flat, sunning themselves after the long swim out there. The water glistens beneath the bright sky, and a motorboat putters past, beyond the big rock.

Which gets Kyle to thinking. He finds Sal in his contacts, considers him for a second, then texts a brief message. *Game for some Friday night fishing?*

Elsa elbows Sal out of her way and adjusts the burner flame. "I have so much to get done. Everybody's coming Saturday. Everybody!"

"And you get to practice your inn-keeping skills." Sal dips a hunk of bread in the tomato sauce simmering on the stove. "Oh, you've outdone yourself, Ma," he says around the mouthful of food. "*Perfezione!*"

"And every time I turn around, you're in my way." She dips her wooden ladle into the sauce and gives a stir. "By the way, did I hear you taking pills before?"

"When?"

"After you had that sandwich I made you."

"*Mamma mia*, that is the one thing I did not miss in the city … your incessant worrying. Isn't this salt air supposed to make you relax?"

"Well, when you went in the bathroom, I heard a pill bottle rattle."

"Oh, that. I have a headache, that's all. It was aspirin." He stuffs the last of the bread into his mouth. "And this amazing sauce is making it better."

Elsa gives another stir, then samples it. "Hmm."

"Never mind *Hmm*," Sal says while squeezing beside his mother again and dipping another piece of bread into the pot. "Leave it alone."

"Look! You're dripping on my floor." Elsa grabs a towel and swats it at Sal, while he stands there cupping the soggy bread.

"Your kitchen's too small," Sal tells her as she wipes up the sauce. "These old cottages weren't designed for modern living." He returns to the table, where he's been typing away on his laptop, tinkering with a business plan for the inn. "With a gourmet kitchen, you can justify setting competitive room rates. So tell Jason to make this room twice the size when he renovates."

"Don't worry, I did." Elsa tucks a strand of hair behind her blue bandana, then pulls a tissue from her apron pocket and dabs her forehead. "I also want a large south-facing garden window for my herbs. They need lots of sunlight." With a handheld sprayer, she spritzes water on her potted plants. "I told him the kitchen is *thee* most important room in the house."

"Absolutely," Sal agrees while lifting a paper from the table and giving it a once-over.

"Not by his standards, it isn't."

"What? *Stronzate!*"

Elsa looks over her shoulder at him and raises an eyebrow.

"Well, it is, Ma. It's bullshit. The kitchen is where the heart is."

Elsa simply shakes her head.

"Oh, wait," Sal says, laughing. "Don't tell me! It's that *room*."

"Correct. Jason said that in *this* cottage, the utmost important room is Foley's old back room. And—*and*—I am not to change it in the renovation. He wouldn't take on the job unless I agreed to that, and put the stipulation in our signed contract."

"What *is* it about that dumpy room? Everyone's so hung up on it."

"Don't know," Elsa says, cranking the kitchen window all the way open so her tiny herb pots get fresh air. She plucks a dried leaf off the basil plant and hears Sal's fingers tapping the keys of a large calculator beside the computer. "I thought you were working with Jason today."

"I thought so, too," Sal says, twisting a big silver watch straight on his wrist. "Was supposed to meet him at his place right after lunch, but no one answered the door when I knocked. Wasn't in his studio, either. So I left."

"Really?"

"I wonder if Maris is back."

"I don't think so." Elsa pulls a lasagna pan from the cabinet. "She told me not till tomorrow afternoon."

When Sal's phone dings, he slides it closer. "Maybe that's Jason now."

Elsa walks past him to the refrigerator and gets out ricotta, eggs and mozzarella.

"Did you get the good mozzarella?" Sal asks, looking up from his phone.

"What do you think? Of course I did. Who's on the phone? Jason?"

"No. It's Kyle."

"What does he want?" Elsa cracks open eggs into a small bowl and lightly whisks.

"To go fishing tomorrow night. But I don't know. I need to research your yield management so we can coordinate the inn's rates with seasonal vacation patterns."

"Sal! Please! My room rates can wait. Go fishing. Celia and I will be so busy cooking, and we don't need you getting in the way in my too-small kitchen."

"Fine," Sal says while texting Kyle back. "I'll fish. But promise me you won't say anything to Celia to scare her off, Ma."

"Me? I *like* Celia. Don't forget, she was *my* friend first." Elsa lifts the lid on the sauce and inhales the aroma, then looks over at her son sitting there in a tee and cargo shorts, when really? Really he should be wearing a fine suit, working the numbers on Wall Street. "When are you going back to New York?"

Sal pushes his phone aside. "Are *you* fishing now, too? For information?"

"Yes, I am." Elsa tosses a dish towel over her shoulder and sits across from her son. Through the doorway beyond him, she sees a glimpse of the living room and the vintage buoys hanging beside the fireplace. "Because what about Celia? You two have gotten so close."

"But I have to go back to my job. In September, I told you. After I finalize your business plan, what more can I do here?"

"Are you kidding? I'm opening a grand beach inn." She quickly gets a big black binder from the counter and rummages through a drawer for her leopard-print reading glasses. "I need you to help me run the place. That way," she says while putting on her glasses and brushing through tabbed sections in her binder, "I won't have to call these companies for grounds upkeep, marketing, building maintenance." She turns the open binder to him. "Can you do handyman work?"

"Ma." Sal slides the binder closer and looks at the contractor names and phone numbers. "You are *not* putting me on your payroll."

"Of course I would. We can keep this in the family. And it doesn't have to be just maintenance work. There's accounting, too. And what about Jason?"

"What about him?" Sal asks while turning to the numbers in several columns on the computer screen.

"You can advise him on his books, his taxes. And mine, here. And Kyle's diner books. Assist in investing. I don't know. Open a finance company." She takes a plate of meatballs out of the refrigerator and adds them to the sauce. "But honestly?" she says. "I just don't want you breaking Celia's heart. She's a special lady."

"I know she is," Sal agrees, tipping back in his chair while looking from the view out the window first, then to Elsa. "And that's a real issue, Ma."

"Once upon a time, I did it. Completely. For your father."

"Did what?"

Elsa wipes her hands on the towel still hanging on her shoulder, then nudges her reading glasses low on her nose as she peers over them at Sal. "Packed up everything to move to Italy, and said goodbye to life here in the States. To my parents, my sister. And I never looked back, Salvatore."

"I know you didn't."

Elsa puts the lid on her saucepot and lowers the flame beneath it before turning and eyeing her son again. "So which of you two will do the same?"

thirty

THEY BAIT UP THEIR FISHING rods while still docked in the marina. With Friday night's full moon, there's little need for lanterns or flashlights, except to shine in the tackle box. Now the engine putters softly as the rowboat moves through the channel out of the marina, and that moonlight bathes Long Island Sound.

"You ever open her up?" Kyle asks. "See what she can do on the open water?"

"No." Sal laughs. "Not really. Maybe we'll try when we're done. Don't want to scare the fish." He steers his rowboat beyond the big rock, over toward the reef before Little Beach. "How about that pickup of yours? Running okay these days?"

"Shit, yeah. You must have the magic touch, DeLuca. She's been purring like a kitten since your weekend jaunt."

"One day, you're signing over her pink slip, Kyle. When I'm back in the city, I'll make the arrangements and get you a bank check."

"Suit yourself." A swath of light falls from the moon, painting the night water silver. Kyle squints past it toward the coastline, looking for a good spot to anchor. "That old truck's not worth much, but if you want to fork over a couple grand, she's yours."

"You've got my word." Sal approaches the bend in the coast leading to Little Beach. The Gull Island Lighthouse beam sweeps across the Sound as he kills the engine and lifts the paddles, dipping them in as the boat slows.

"This is great, DeLuca. After being behind the stoves all day, nice to be on the water instead."

"You're on vacation now, right? I think Lauren mentioned it."

"Damn straight. Diner's been so busy, I need the break."

"How's the outdoor patio coming along?"

"Oh man, couldn't be better, Sal. Added twinkly lights under the table umbrellas, and folks line up for a seat most days."

"Ambiance. That's what I like to hear. You should post a picture of those twinklin' tables online."

"Online?"

"Shit, yeah. On your social media."

"I'm not really into that. I just have a website."

"The Driftwood Café is not on social media?" Sal asks. "You're killing me, Bradford."

"All right. I'll tell Lauren. We'll work something out."

"You better. And soon!" Sal lifts the oars and they drip seawater as the boat slows to a stop. "This a good spot?" he asks.

"Definitely. Might hook a fluke around here. And the blues are always biting at night, driving the minnows to the rocks."

Sal sits back on a bench, runs his hand along his fishing line, then casts it over the dark water. "Where is Barlow tonight, anyway?"

"In bed, I'm sure. Probably has been for the past two days."

"In bed? Is he sick?"

"Yeah." Kyle shifts on his seat and opens the small cooler. He pulls out two cans of beer, passing one to Sal. "Lovesick," he says while snapping open his can. "His wife's back. They have a lot of catching up to do."

"Ah, the elusive Maris."

"She's the best thing that ever happened to him." He holds up his can in a toast to Jason and Maris.

"Seriously?" Sal asks, raising his can to Kyle's. "I hear that, but find it hard to believe. Jason seems all right on his own."

"You wouldn't have even recognized him before Maris, trust me." The boat sways with the movement of the sea, small waves lapping at its sides. There's a tug on Kyle's line, and he lets the fish pull the drag. "Jason and his brother used to have a boat. A beat-up Whaler. When we were kids, we'd tool around on the Sound. Neil got us all fishing."

"You teach your boy to fish?"

Kyle glances over at Sal. "Evan? No, he's into crabbing on the rocks this year." His line spins quickly, so he jerks the rod back, but is too late. The line goes limp and he easily reels it back in. "Shit. That was a big one, been playing with me out there." He lifts the empty hook from the water and it drips in front of him. "Should've snagged him a few seconds earlier."

"Chalk it up to regrets."

Kyle shines a small flashlight in the tackle box and puts a new lure on the line. "You got any?"

"Regrets?"

"Yeah."

"Don't we all." Sal opens a bag of chips and grabs a handful. "I regret that I didn't go home to Milan more often. Didn't see my father enough after I moved to New York, and now? Now, he's gone. Couldn't seem to make the time, like you all do here."

"That's a tough one." Kyle casts his line and it whistles over the water. "No going back to fix it."

"Nope. Those are the worst. The regrets about someone gone."

"No shit."

"You say that like a man of conviction."

"That's because I've got the king of regrets."

Sal tips up his can to finish the last of the beer. "Going to spill it, sitting here on the night sea?"

"Hey, I didn't say I'm telling you. Just saying I have a regret. No one knows about it, except me."

"Not even your wife? No one?"

"No. And the only person who *did* know is dead."

"Oh man, no. It's Neil, isn't it?"

"Sure is."

"*Gesù, Santa Maria.* What happened?"

The light of that heavy full moon falls across them in the water, and Kyle sees Sal clearly, sitting sideways with his elbows propped on the edge of the rowboat, his fishing line slack in the water, waiting. But Kyle doesn't talk; this is one regret he never dreamt would see the light of anything, day *or* night.

"I have a friend in the city," Sal finally says into the silence. "Michael Micelli. He likes to wager all the time. On little things, you know? For fun." He digs into the bag of chips and pulls out a handful. "So how about a wager? I get a fish first, you tell me your regret."

Kyle snaps open another cold beer. "And if I hook one first?"

"Your call. But trust me, my friend." He motions his empty beer can to the star-speckled sky. "What's said under the stars … stays under the stars."

Kyle reaches into the cooler and tosses Sal another brew. Then, well then they fish. The boat drifts, rising and falling with the gentle swell of the Sound. The rocky ledge of Stony Point's beach is a silhouette, a black shadow he can make out in the distance. Just like his regret. Dark and vague, but always there. Suddenly Kyle's rod bends and his line goes under.

"Hey, hey," Sal says. "You got one."

But Kyle can tell, reeling it in, that it's not much of a fish. Still, he caught something and lifts it out, flapping, as Sal nets it.

"Looks like a striper," Sal says. "Must've been feeding over at the reef."

"It's a little guy, shit." Kyle takes the fish and gently unhooks the barbless hook from its mouth. But before slipping the fish back into the water, he holds it with both hands, then lifts the fish and plants a kiss on it before bending low and letting it swim out of his hands. And that's where Kyle stays, sitting on the side of the bench, ready to kiss off the past, to set it sailing beneath the silver light of the moon. If he looks east, he can make out tiny dots of lamplight from the houses on the bluff, one of those houses being where he last saw Neil Barlow.

"Happened nine years ago," Kyle finally says as Sal casts his fishing line out again. "I carry it every day."

"That's usually how regrets work."

"You know, I can never think of Neil and think of the *good* stuff, the good words. No," Kyle explains, still watching the bluff and imagining him and Neil out there that night, two dark shadows on the brink. "It's not Neil's thoughts about the driftline on the beach, or about a hurricane coming up the coast that I remember. Not a cottage renovation. Not how he was intrigued with the union shipbuilding work I used to do. No. It's my last words to him that I think of."

Sal doesn't move. In the dark, he simply watches and listens.

So Kyle takes a long breath of, yes, the sweet salt air that cures what ails you. Okay, so that's Neil's line, definitely. He lifts his arm and presses it against his damp forehead. "I had just found out Neil was seeing Lauren, right before I was supposed to marry her."

"Ah, shit," Sal barely says.

"That's right. We were out on the bluff, there." He points to the distant shadowy cottages on the hill overlooking the Sound. "Sitting on the bench his old man built when he got back from 'Nam. Words were said—damn, was I fuming, pacing, ready to fight—and what'd I do? I tripped in the dark, almost went over the God damn edge of the bluff. Falling to the rocks would've killed me, would've been the end. But Neil grabbed my arm and yanked me back. So you know what I did then?"

"No."

"I looked him straight in the eye, and yup, I said it. Told him he deserved that fall more than me. Wished him dead, right to his face. And two days later, he took a fall, all right. A fall off his Harley and across the pavement, man. Gone." Kyle snaps his fingers, once. "Just like that."

thirty-one

SHE MIGHT BE ONTO SOMETHING.

And on Saturday night, Elsa doesn't want to leave Foley's back room. No, she wants to sit in a booth by the window, with a sea breeze wafting in through the tarnished, torn screen, and relish the feeling. Oh, it's sublime, purely sublime, this whisper of a feeling.

So much so that she had to shoo everyone out. Her welcome-home dinner was long done, the dishes cleared, and everyone gathered in the old back room. Finally, she waved her hands at them all, her bangle bracelets jangling as she moved the crowd first through the screen door to the deck, then down the stairs. They didn't mind—she could see that—as they kept walking, red cups in hand, chattering nonstop while they headed straight for the beach.

With the cottage empty, she made one stop in her bedroom for the big binder before returning to the back room. The cherished jukebox was gone—after becoming Maris and Jason's wedding gift last August—but its absence didn't stop the magic. Tonight someone merely plugged in Jason's old construction-site boom box instead. Songs played all evening: songs about summer, and broken hearts, about the earth moving, and about boardwalks, and braided chains and love. Songs that got everyone on the small dance floor, that got voices singing along, that peeled away the years of time. For her, too.

That was the unexpected surprise. Hearing the familiar tunes and seeing everyone laughing and mingling after dinner, well damn, didn't it seem like someone else was in the room … someone who made her way through the misty moonlight, and cobwebs, and dust particles swirling in the glow of the pinball machine? Now she knows how Jason must feel, sensing his brother in these places. He said it tonight; Elsa heard him tell Sal how if he listened hard enough, he'd hear Neil keeping the beat with those drumsticks of his.

Because she felt the same, about her sister, as the welcome-home party moved from the decorated dining room to the infamous back room. When Elsa sat in the shadows in the corner, her heart so full seeing her son *here*, with Celia, and with her nieces and their friends, everyone simply celebrating a summer night … didn't she feel it, feel a young hand squeeze her fingers, telling her she loves her, still.

Yes, she could swear that her sister, June, was in the room. All it took was a little nostalgia—beach style—to do it. And so Elsa shooed everyone out so she could jot down her redecorating ideas for the back room, now that she began tapping into its vibe. She opens her black binder, puts on her leopard-print reading glasses and finds the appropriate tabbed sections. Everything will be new, brand new.

Okay, but *exactly* the same. She peers over her glasses at the room: sliding windows, stain for the beadboard wainscoting, new hardwood for the dance floor. She'll match the same old curtain fabric for new valances. Now that'll need a yellow tab of its own: *Curtains*.

But first she opens her laptop, then flips through binder pages of contractors and vendors that Jason's mentioned to her. Where is that company name? She brushes a few pages forward, then turns one back, skimming. He jotted it down, saying Celia might find staging items there. A restoration company of some sort. If she could get her hands on one particular item, maybe she'd fully understand this room. Because something's *still* missing, one secret key to unlocking the room's magic; Elsa knows it in her heart, in her observations of this space.

Her fingers stop on a starred entry. Yes! It's a *salvage* company Jason spoke so highly of. Elsa reads the name, then sets her fingers on her laptop keyboard and pulls up its website. When she finds the contact form, she begins her message: *I'm looking for a vintage jukebox, Rick. Something circa 1970s.*

Jason sets his cell phone on his dresser, then picks it up again. He turns it on and taps to the photographs. If the couple they stopped on the boardwalk only knew what they had signed on for, they might've kept walking. "Could you take a picture?" Maris had asked earlier, handing them Jason's phone. "A group shot, of all of us."

Countless tries later—after Kyle blinked; and Nick looked away; and Eva's hands were in motion; and Lauren was partially cut off; and Maris' mouth was caught mid-word, explaining how she'd spilled coffee on her own phone; and after Celia adjusted her guitar strap, then dropped her pick mid-strum—they finally did it. Yes, he has them all on his phone, every one of the photo outtakes. He scrolls through them slowly, thinking he should have offered the poor couple money for their time.

Outside their bedroom window now, the sound of waves gently splashing against the bluff comes to him. And that moon … Hell, that big *red* moon—Kyle was sure to inform them with a detailed explanation about August's haze giving it that hue—well, it sits high in the night sky over Stony Point, casting its misty glow on only memories. Jason supposes that on certain nights all his life, he'll walk on the beach when that red moon shines and hear laughing whispers, see dancing shadows, tip his head at the echo of a strumming guitar.

But for him, sweet nights on the beach also carry a price; he'd spent the past twenty minutes sitting on the edge of the bathtub, cleaning tiny grains of sand off every nut, pin and component of his prosthetic leg before drying it all off. Using his crutches now, he sits in his bedside chair, glances at Maris asleep beneath the sheet, then runs a finger across his phone screen, looking down at the images. Neil's mass tomorrow will be so different from all this night was. Or maybe it won't. Maybe it's all about what's in certain moments.

He swipes to a photo with the illicit bonfire in the distance, the flames licking the night sky while also burning the ticket they'd tossed into it—the one Nick issued them when he came upon them sitting around the fire, Celia strumming her guitar, a few of them dancing in the sand. The package of red cups is there on the sand, too, one of which Nick filled with wine when he threw caution to the wind and joined their beach party. And there's Sal in the next picture, head tipped toward Maris, assuring her that *everyone* took *very* good care of her husband in her absence, to which Jason suggested that maybe he could finally get some rest now.

A swipe to another group picture where, the second the camera clicked, Celia stepped forward and took in the length of the boardwalk when Maris mentioned the summer they were teens and had to paint its every board—the year they just couldn't stay out of trouble. *Paint it?* Celia asked. *Yes*, Kyle explained. *After we got caught stealing the boat.* To which Sal suggested that this beloved beach is more about angst and turmoil than rest and relaxation. So Matt warned him not to even ask about the moose head story.

Another swipe to a group photo where—*click*—precisely as Kyle waved his red cup of wine, warning that if he ever keeps an open-enough mind and finds a beach home here, he might snag that moose head guarding Jason's studio, just for the hell of it.

Another photo, one where Sal really couldn't help himself right as the group picture was snapped. He'd taken Celia in his arms and waltzed her along the breaking waves, her sundress sweeping around. *I think I'm finally getting the hang of this place*, he said, dancing her across the sand.

And that did it. They all scattered in the shadows, kicking off sandals, cuffing jeans and tossing a glow-in-the-dark Frisbee beyond the bonfire. Through it all, the camera-couple didn't seem to mind—telling them to *stand, link arms, be natural*—in this impromptu photo shoot. Finally they settled on the sand once more, free as the sea breeze, beneath August's glimmering stars, tiki torches and that full moon casting enough light to capture the moment.

Maris sat in front of Jason and leaned back into him, watching Celia strap on her guitar and begin strumming. *Wouldn't your brother have loved to drum along?* Maris asked. Jason folded his arm around her, pressed his face to her hair and whispered in her ear as Eva and Matt settled on the other side of him. Lauren knelt beside Kyle, wrapping her arms around his waist and resting her head on his shoulder. The sea, and the music, and longings they all must've felt … It is all there in the snapshot. Now.

Magical, no? Sal had asked with a glance out at the water. Which is what Neil always said on these kinds of rare, easy nights—that you'd almost want to bottle such moments, stardust and all. *In the city*, Sal said, *it's all work, around the clock, around the calendar. There's no time to sit beside the sea like this.* He leaned back on his hands and watched Celia strumming. *You folks are very blessed.*

And then? The click of the final picture being snapped.

Jason looks toward the open window now, then closer at the last photograph. The bonfire crackles off to the side, tiki torches flicker and the red moon hangs low over the water. A hitching breeze holds a touch of sea damp, and Celia's fingers slide over guitar strings, leaving behind wavering memories in each and every note.

thirty-two

THE NEXT MORNING, JASON CAN'T get one thought out of his mind, especially as he and Maris pull into Saint Bernard's parking lot. The church's shingles are weathered driftwood gray by the salty air lifting off Long Island Sound, the gray being the same color as a stormy sea. So there's this connection—the sea, the church. At both, he's bowed his head in prayer.

Inside, the cool wooden pews are filled, ceiling fans slowly paddle and the stained glass windows are tipped open to the sea breeze. Only last August, the happiest hours he'd ever lived happened in this very church. The scent of the sea drifted in the open windows; hydrangea flower arrangements decorated each pew; Mason jar candles shimmered at the altar where Jason stood in his black tux, watching his bride walk down this very aisle. Now, a summer later, Maris occasionally holds his hand as they stand, kneel and sit their way through the readings, prayers and responses at Neil's annual memorial mass.

And all the while, that one conflicting thought simmers for Jason Barlow in this sacred place: Life at its best, and at its excruciating worst, come together at the altar of God.

So he finds comfort in familiar faces as he scans the parishioners: Eva and Matt off to the side, Sal and Celia a few pews behind them. At the altar, there's another Mason jar filled with sand, shells and a small stick of driftwood, all of it beside a flickering pillar candle. Only one person would have quietly arranged that, and he nods when he meets Elsa's eye. Her hair is pulled back in a chignon and she wears a navy sheath, her gold star pendant—the same one Maris has—glimmering around her neck. Standing with Sal and Celia, she subtly waves at Jason.

Still, it's the one spoken line still to come that Jason always has difficulty with. Even today, nine years later, his body tenses as the priest begins those words.

"For all of our departed brothers and sisters who have gone to their rest in the hope of rising again, especially today for Neil Barlow, for whom this mass is offered, we pray to the Lord."

And while the words fill the church, as Maris' fingers squeeze his hand and she leaves a breath of a kiss on his cheek, he tries, tries to fathom what he *didn't* hear all those years ago when he was a physical wreck laid up in the hospital, critically injured and covered with road burns, while Neil's funeral was said. He imagines hearing the words he *missed*, blessed words granting eternal rest unto his brother, words asking for perpetual light to shine on Neil. Jason didn't hear a priest's low voice, the words fluid as a gentle stream flowing over stones, asking God to have mercy on Neil and bring him into His kingdom of peace.

No, he heard none of it as he lay in a hospital bed—his leg gone, his injuries dire, his consciousness medicated—during his brother's funeral. All he'll ever hear is this offering, which brings him to his knees in his best suit, head bowed, until he joins the communion procession to receive that sacrament during Neil's mass.

As the church later empties, someone taps Jason's shoulder. It's Sal, nodding to Ted Sullivan leaving a side pew with his wife. Jason looks over just as Ted turns toward him. There's nothing to say, not now, not here. But there's still a gratitude, for which Jason nods to Ted, prompting Ted to discreetly salute him in return before taking his wife's arm and leaving the church.

Jason watches them go, then turns to Maris. "Sweetheart, why don't you go on outside with Elsa."

"Everything okay?" she asks with a hopeful smile, reaching up and touching his face.

"Sure," Jason tells her, taking her hand in his and giving it a kiss. "Sal wants to light a candle."

Maris catches up to Elsa and Celia, while he and Sal approach the votive candle stand. Sal wears his beach blues today: jeans on bottom, navy suit jacket and tie on top. As they walk together, he tells Sal that Neil dressed the same way for Eva and Matt's wedding, jeans and formal mixed.

"A man after my own heart," Sal tells him as he drops a few dollars in the offering box, kneels and lights a candle.

What's surprising is that he then hands Jason the burning taper stick so that Jason might also light a candle. The tip of the wood stick is a tiny red ember, and Jason looks at Sal for a long second before selecting a candle in the top row, lighting it, then blessing himself.

"Let's get out of here," he tells Sal. "Everyone's headed to brunch at a local restaurant."

But Sal still kneels, gazing at the flickering bank of candles. "Just like the old country, man. The big funeral is like a party … dinner afterward, good cheer." He glances over at Jason. "Honestly?" he says, pushing himself up off the kneeler. "I thought this day would be more intimate. So far, this is the best part, right here. Lighting a candle."

"Wasn't always like this," Jason explains as he sits in the end of a pew, his arms resting on the pew back in front of him, hands clasped as he faces the altar. An arched beadboard ceiling soars above it. "It grew into something big, I guess, because there's a lot of people in my life now. It's changed. And I do actually miss the days of just me and Paige being here."

"Paige?"

"My sister." He looks over at Sal. "She's in Florida with her husband and kids, staying at my mother's for a few weeks. They're having a mass said down there."

"Well," Sal says, clasping Jason's shoulder. "I'm sorry about Neil. Really, guy." He turns to the altar, genuflects and blesses himself then.

"We better go." Jason stands and tugs his jacket sleeves straight. "Everyone's waiting out in the parking lot."

But there's a reluctance; Jason senses it in Sal. A window, bright with August sunshine, draws his cousin closer to it. "That crowd?" Sal asks.

"That's the one." Jason comes up behind him and sees about fifteen people gathered around, mingling, talking, laughing.

"Want to bail?"

"What?"

"Cut loose, avoid the formality." Sal glances back at Jason. "Doesn't really seem to be Neil's way."

"Are you kidding me?" Jason looks from Sal, to the window, then back to Sal. "There's a mob out there. What would they think?"

"Who cares? You can't worry about what other people will think. What's the point of that?" He puts out his hand. "Give me your phone."

Jason hesitates in the quiet church. Now that it's empty, even his own movements echo—the rustle of his suit jacket when he reaches for his phone, his footstep when he moves toward Sal.

The whole time, Sal simply watches him, even once the phone is in his hand. "You have to get right back on the horse that threw you, cousin. To move on. Seeing this," Sal says while giving a sweeping motion to the church, "it's like Neil's still here, laid out in the coffin. You're still in that day, in his funeral."

"I didn't make it to the funeral."

A couple of seconds pass with Sal still looking at him, then quickly down at Jason's phone. "I'm texting your wife. She'll think it's you."

"What the hell?"

Sal glares at him. "Hey, you're in church?"

Jason holds up a hand. "Wait. Maris' phone is broken. She doesn't have it on her."

"*Merda*," Sal says, giving back the phone and pulling out his own. "I'll text my mother, then." As his fingers fly over the keyboard, he talks the message. "Get the crowd moving and head to the restaurant. Take Maris and Celia with you, Jason and I will catch up."

The whole time Sal's voice is relaying the text message, Jason watches Maris through the window. He sees Elsa show her the phone, prompting Maris to raise her hand and call out to everyone. "It worked, bro," Jason says. "They're getting in their cars."

"Man, I've got to get me some wheels," Sal says when he joins Jason at the window again. "Get Kyle to part with that truck of his."

"What would you do with it, bring it back to the city?"

"No way. I'd leave it at the inn. You know, my beach wheels for when I'm here, so I can get around."

"Yeah, well I've got the wheels covered for today." Jason nods to his SUV in the parking lot.

"Let's wait, five minutes."

"Then what?"

"I don't know. Drift?"

Jason throws him a quick look. "Maris will kill me, Sal."

"No, she won't." He squints at him, tipping his head. "She loves you, man. She'll get it." Reaching quickly for his phone again, Sal begins typing, talking his message aloud. "Tell Maris not to be mad. Her husband and I will catch you later. For now, Ma, we're bailing on brunch."

~

If Jason Barlow had to name it, he would say it's déjà vu. Eerily so. Leaving the church, they'd stopped at his house so he could change out of his suit and into cargo shorts and an old concert tee, then fill a small cooler with a few cans of beer, and potato chips from the cupboards, and onion dip from the fridge before stacking it in his golf cart.

"Hey, this is supposed to be brunch, right, guy?" Sal asked. "Stop and get me one of those egg sandwiches, would you?"

So Jason pulled the golf cart into the convenience store where they loaded up on sandwiches, ketchup and salt packets, pepperoni sticks, cellophane-wrapped coffee cakes, marshmallow-iced brownies, and a deck of cards. Just like he and Neil would do as kids: load up the old rowboat they'd found, packing lunch and snacks before heading into enemy territory—the lagoon to some. To them? The jungles of 'Nam.

"I'm docked at Celia's," Sal tells Jason as they head back under the railroad trestle, so Jason drives to her place, leaving the cart on the side of her cottage. They carry their gear and bags out to the little wooden dock and settle in the boat, hats and sunglasses on. "Got enough chow to capsize this vessel," Sal says while cuffing his jeans. "Where to?" he asks when he unhooks the dock line.

Jason takes the oars and dips them into the calm marsh water. "Right here. If we're drifting to honor my brother, there was nothing he liked better than to navigate all the lagoon inlets." He pulls on the oars and they creak against the oarlocks as he sets the rowboat moving.

"*Andiamo*." Sal sits back, watching a swan sitting on the muddy banks, then tips his head up to the sun. "Let's go."

"Appreciate this, Sal. That mass, well, it's not like it used to be."

"I guess not. I'm sure it was once a blessed hour, just you and Paige and the other parishioners. It must have been very private for you then."

"You know it."

Jason paddles around a few bends, the tall marsh grasses shimmering gently in the midday sunshine. The tide is low. Only monarch butterflies hover, and dragonflies. A red-winged blackbird trills, and occasionally a small fish ruffles the water's surface.

"From what I saw today, it's like your brother was never set free with the beautiful sea breezes and whispering lagoon grasses that were his world. Back home, the Italians say that if you stew in your sadness, you're not letting it go. You have to find a way to celebrate a life."

Jason dips and pulls the oars, paddling away from the cottages that border the lagoon, and moves closer to the woodsy area on its far banks. He hasn't been in this part of the marsh in years, but remembers every curve of the inlets, the sway of the grasses, from the hours he'd spent drifting in it with Neil. "Drop the anchor, man."

"What's that, a blue crab?" Sal asks, obliging and looking into the shallow water.

Jason sees it, nestled against the murky bank. Its two large front claws are folded in front of it, its shell protruding from the water. "Or a toe-popper."

"A what?"

"A landmine. When we were kids, my father told us all his war stories. So for me and my brother, back in the day, crabs were mines set to maim and kill us, egrets were the Viet Cong, on the hunt, the marsh grass was jungle brush we needed a machete to get through … Because all this here?" He motions to the serene lagoon, the blue sky above it, the grasses lush and sweeping. "This was our Vietnam."

~

Jason followed behind his brother, barely dipping the paddles into the swamp water as Neil waded barefoot. Any motion would stir up the muck and conceal the landmines. "There's one," Jason whispered, pointing ahead of Neil. "A toe-popper!" His brother shined a flashlight into the dark water and caught the large blue crab in its beam. So he sidestepped it, giving those pinching claws wide berth while trudging through the Southeast Asian jungle.

The tide was low, and Neil walked along the wet banks, slowly, carefully lifting each foot from the muck and looking before he placed it back on the earth again. He wore his camping vest, the pockets filled with a jackknife, flashlight and small stones—his day's ammunition. He'd pulled their father's tiger-striped boonie hat low over his moppy hair, and Jason followed in the rowboat, his brother's lookout. Occasionally Neil lifted the toy tactical machine gun slung over his shoulder and found an egret or great blue heron in his sights, then scared off the enemy—his gun vibrating with electronic sounds instead of bullets as he pulled the trigger. With the path clear, he'd resume walking. They were very quiet, and very much aware of the seriousness of the patrol. One wrong move, one miscalculation, and Neil would either be dead, or at the very least, his leg would be gone. The area was heavily armed with booby traps and mines so they'd already lost three of their comrades.

"What's the matter?" Jason asked from the rowboat, pulling up the oars and steadying them as they drip-dripped into the lagoon.

Neil held up a hand and bent low, knee-deep near the banks and squinting at the ground ahead. Two dragonflies hovered close to him, as though watching, too. He lifted his foot and held it aloft before slowly setting it down, a little at a time, beside the sweeping marsh grass. But too late—when it hit the mud, he jumped and ran sideways, falling over the edge of the boat and grabbing onto his leg, yelling, "A toe-popper! A toe-popper! My leg, it's gone!"

All mania ensued amidst the splashing, until Jason shoved the oars back in the water, paddling furiously to get away from the mined area before anchoring their vessel and taking a look at Neil's leg.

—

"The way we imagined, the leg was maimed, right to the knee," Jason says to Sal now. His cousin sits at the other end of their anchored rowboat, his *Beach Bum* cap pulled low, his overgrown hair curling out from the edges, his legs extended. "So I got him to the medevac chopper, quick, but they couldn't save it."

"Shit, man," Sal says with a slow grin and shaking his head. "What memories you have, you and your kid brother being war buddies in this swamp. It's the stuff of novels."

"That's how we grew up, every summer. Relived my father's 'Nam horror stories. The toe-poppers were a particular nightmare for my dad. He saw too many guys lose their legs to landmines over there. Plenty of days, he would tell us, simply setting your booted foot down could end your life, or maim you at the very least."

Sal looks over the edge of the boat at the big blue crab still hunkered down on the muddy bank of the lagoon. "Toe-popper. Damn. Kind of ironic, no?" he asks, motioning to Jason's prosthetic leg.

"Absolutely." Jason picks up the dog tags hung around his neck and twists the chain through his fingers before dropping them back down, cicadas buzzing in the distant trees, tall grasses whispering, brackish water lapping the side of the rowboat. "Ain't no doubt about that."

Elsa does it; she actually takes Maris' hand when they step onto the boardwalk. The day has been long, the brunch bittersweet without Jason there. And even though Maris said she understood, Elsa thought she'd been withdrawn in the restaurant, and so invited her for a beach walk as the sun goes down.

"Any word from Jason?" Elsa asks.

Maris shakes her head. "No. But that's his way. He's not one to check in often."

The boardwalk is gritty with sand at the end of a hot beach day. Elsa slips off her sandals and sits on the edge of it, scanning the violet horizon. A nearly full moon hangs low over the distant sea. "Look," she says to Maris. "The moon is rising."

"It's lovely," she hears Maris say behind her, sitting on the bench.

And Elsa has to agree, thinking it's also a little sad, somehow. A day has ended, come what may. Whether the hours went as we'd hoped, or disappointed, or enthralled, that moon will rise just the same, giving us reason to walk outside and seek it, to quiet our thoughts.

"Will you be back to work soon?" Elsa asks.

"A couple more weeks, still, before I go back." Maris explains that Saybrooks is wrapping up her Denim Blue Sea line, waiting on final samples before bulk production. And all the while, Elsa sees how Maris also keeps looking toward the beach sunset she so dearly missed while away. The sight seems to soothe her worry about Jason, her voice dropping while explaining that her assistant, Lily, is handling many details while Maris finalizes her trip notes and ideas. "So I'll *be* working now, but here, in my studio. Jason really made my job perfect when he built that loft in the barn."

A few families linger on the beach, near the water—their umbrellas closed, beach gear packed up, but sand chairs still opened next to the breaking waves. It's been that kind of hot day, when all you want to do is stay at the water's edge. Even the evening is warm. Two young couples stroll the boardwalk, their bare feet thumping on the wood planks. They hurry past, saying hello to Maris as they do. When Elsa turns to join Maris on the bench, she notices someone sitting on the far end of the boardwalk.

"It's Sal," she says, holding out her hand to Maris. "Come on. Visit with your cousin."

They walk in his direction, the beach sand looking the same golden hue as the sunset horizon. When they near Sal, he stands, hands in pockets, dress shirt casually worn over his tee and cuffed jeans.

"My two favorite people, *a braccetto*," Sal says.

"Arm in arm," Elsa whispers to Maris as they walk together.

"Maris," Sal says, stepping toward them. "I hope you're not mad. We went out for the afternoon in the rowboat. Talked about Neil, life. You know. We ate, had a beer. Fished."

Maris simply nods. "Fished, too? Jason loves to fish."

"Cards, Maris. *Go* Fish. He beat my ass. So Jason should be home now," he assures her. "We docked and cleaned up the boat a little while ago."

"I must've just missed him." She walks closer and hugs Sal. "But *grazie*," she whispers.

"You're *thanking* me?" Sal takes her by the shoulders and holds her at arm's length, tipping his head.

She nods, looking from Elsa, back to Sal, before motioning for them to both sit on the boardwalk bench with her. "For doing what I could never do. Two years ago, Jason took me to the crash site where his brother died. He was still devastated, and all I could tell him back then was to live. Just live. It's what Neil would've wanted. And it's always been hard for him to do that on this day, but I think for the first time since the accident, he finally did, with you. He just lived."

"Oh, hon," Elsa says then, seeing the tears escape from Maris' eyes. Tears about Jason, and about missing much of the summer in this sweet place called Stony Point; it's all there.

But it's Sal who changes those tears. He brushes one off Maris' cheek. "*Sorridi, per favore*. Even when you're sad, Maris. Smile, please."

Maris does and takes each of their hands while standing. "Do you have a minute?"

"For you?" Sal stands, too. "Always."

Maris tugs Elsa up and walks between them, leading them onto the sand while heading across the beach toward the water's edge. The waves hiss as they break in a silvery lace on shore.

"Where are we going?" Elsa asks when they stop at the high tide line.

"Right here." Maris motions to the dried seaweed running the length of the beach.

So Elsa squints, wondering what she's seeing. The low setting sun casts a soft pink swirl on the sand, and the tangled seaweed meanders along above the breaking waves.

"Neil loved this part of the beach. It's called the driftline." Maris picks up a stick of driftwood and lifts some of the seaweed, exposing white shells, and green and blue sea glass beneath it. A periwinkle snail clings to a piece of damp sea lettuce. She hands the driftwood to Sal, who also browses the dried seaweed. "Neil told me it all seems like random stuff the tide brings in. But in the driftline, everything's somehow connected."

Elsa looks from the sandy beach, to her niece—the niece she'd not seen for over thirty years, and now sees almost daily. Behind Maris, the evening sky is turning deep lavender, with tiny stars twinkling far above, beginning their night's journey.

"And the thing is?" Maris continues, brushing back a wisp of dark hair as a sea breeze skims off the water. "I think Neil was referring to everyone here, too, drifting in and out of each other's lives, but intricately connected in our own driftline." She takes Sal's hand then, tearing up again. "You, too, Sal. For Jason this summer, *especially* you."

thirty-three

The idea comes to her later that week. While the eggs cook Wednesday morning, Elsa digs in a cluttered cabinet for a mini watering can. Her little herb pails need a drink this hot day. As she stands on a step stool to reach a high cabinet, she thinks to remind Jason to include a massive island in her new kitchen. Massive. So that she can prepare meals, read recipes, *and* water her herbs on the windowsill, all while having people sit and chat with her. Of course, she has the thought right when Sal breezes barefoot through the kitchen in his cargo shorts and tee, laptop in one hand, steaming coffee mug in the other.

"*Buongiorno*," he says as he keeps walking and heads out the side door to a small stone patio.

"Good morning, Salvatore," Elsa calls back, setting the watering can down to slide a spatula beneath the eggs on her stovetop.

"Working outside on the inn's business plan." The screen door closes behind him as he asks, almost as an afterthought, "Are those scrambled eggs you're making?"

"With cheese and diced tomato, fresh from my deck pots—just the way you like." Elsa flips the sizzling eggs and lets them sit, watching them and lifting the edges until a thunderous crash has her cower and drop the spatula on the floor. "*Gesù, Santa Maria!*"

"Ma?" Sal rushes into the kitchen and reaches for her hand to help her up. "What *was* that? Are you okay?"

"Yes, yes," Elsa tells him while looking around the room and turning off the flame beneath the eggs. "*You* didn't make that noise?"

"Me? Ma, it sounded like a *bomb* going off. I think it came from that direction." He motions with his coffee cup toward the side of the cottage. "You wait here and I'll go check it out," he says, already on his way.

"Oh, no. I'm coming with you!" Elsa sets her fallen spatula on the countertop and follows behind him as he rushes down the hallway toward Foley's back room. She's breathless when they swing open the door to the old, dusty space. Everything's intact.

"Nothing. Hmm," Sal says, walking past the empty booths, the pinball machine, the boom box, the dorm-sized refrigerator.

Elsa hurries to the windows. "There! Outside, Sal." She points beyond the deck as she heads to the screen door leading to it.

"Wait, don't go out," Sal warns. "It might not be safe." He comes up behind her while she's stunned speechless by a massive limb that fell from the overhanging oak tree onto the deck staircase. "You don't know if there's any structural damage."

"The deck. Oh heavens, my tomatoes!" She leans forward and peers out at her potted-and-staked plants, miraculously unscathed. "To think I was out there this morning, picking a tomato for your eggs. I could've been killed!"

"Don't say that, Ma. At least you're fine, that's all that matters."

Elsa picks up Sal's left arm and twists it around to see the time on his heavy wristwatch. "I have to get to the commissioner's office and petition for an exemption to the Hammer Law. This deck might fall down, with that limb there. Someone could get hurt."

"I'll call Jason, Ma. He can assess the damage, I'm sure." Sal pulls his cell phone from his cargo shorts pocket. "Do you want me to go with you to the commissioner's?" he asks while pulling up Jason's number.

"No." Elsa looks out at the tree limb, suddenly thankful Sal didn't have his morning decaf on the *deck* patio table. "You go eat those eggs. Be sure to add a sprinkle of grated Parmesan. Oh, and give my herb pots a little drink, too," she calls back, heading to her room to brush her hair and freshen up. "I can handle Commissioner Raines all by myself."

—

By midmorning, the sun is rising high in the sky, illuminating the August marsh grasses with a soft glow. Celia sits outside on her deck, facing the lagoon, her guitar on her lap. This is a first, the way she's being serenaded by a choir of sounds as she strums. The marsh water gurgles as it flows past in the curving inlet. Cicadas buzz from the trees in the woodsy area on the far side of the lagoon, and sparrows and robins bring in the harmony. She hums with them while her fingers move softly, and slowly, across the guitar strings.

"That sounds like one sad song."

Still strumming, Celia looks up at Sal walking around the side of the cottage toward the deck. Lifting his sunglasses to the top of his now-overgrown dark hair, he's wearing new cargo shorts, a navy tee and boat shoes. All the while, her fingers continue to pluck out a melancholy tune, and she's not surprised that her eyes are actually teary. "It *is* sad," she tells him.

"Why?"

She motions to the cardboard cartons just inside the slider. "I packed up the staging things I'm done with here. And seriously? I don't know how I'll ever leave this version of *real life*," she says, using one hand to air-quote the words, then resuming her song.

"You're not leaving yet, though." Sal glimpses into her kitchen, then sits in an Adirondack chair beside her. "You've got all month, still."

"Right. And look how fast the weeks go by." Her hand continues to rise and fall as she changes chords with her sad song. "My father's always loved sea glass, Sal. Do you know why?" And she figures it's the tears in her eyes that silence him, as he just shakes his head no. "Because sea glass tells the story of passing time. The glass, it's all worn smooth. And by what? By years and years of *time* in the sea." She quickly raises the back of her hand to blot a tear. "And I feel the same way about my time here," she says, strumming and nodding to the grassy lagoon where an egret descends from the sky and lands on a curving bank. "These sweet summer days … they softened all the rough edges of my life. Everything's smooth here, and gentle now. Like the sea glass. And I really don't know how I can ever get in my car, turn the ignition and leave."

"Cee, no." Sal reaches over and touches her hair, his fingers toying with an auburn strand.

"Yes, Sal. I think of packing, of locking the door of my friends' wonderful cottage hideaway, saying goodbye to Stony Point, and then driving under that railroad trestle out of here?" She shakes her head and blinks back more tears. "I so have the blues today," she says while looking down at her fingers picking out her song, slowing the tempo as she does. "The beach blues."

"Celia."

She stops her song and rests her open hand over the guitar strings.

"Don't think ahead," Sal quietly says, his hand brushing her chin and along her jaw. "Why bring that future sadness to this beautiful day? Come on," he says while standing and holding out his hand for hers. "I'll show you a different kind of beach blues, the kind that'll only make you smile."

~

"You'll need to fill out an Emergency Extension of the Hammer Law Request." Cliff Raines sits at his utilitarian desk and holds up a piece of paper, nodding at Elsa to take it.

Instead, Elsa glances around, finds a metal chair and drags it over to his matching desk, thinking—okay, briefly—of how she *could* decorate this trailer office to at least look beachy. The steel entry door is propped open, obviously to make the stuffy, confined inside air more breathable. "Listen, Commissioner Raines," she says with a glare at that form still being held in her direction, so she finally snatches it. "I already told you the situation. A tree limb, and a huge one, no less, fell on my deck. This will take too much time to fill out, repeating myself all over again." She gives his blessed form a harsh shake.

"Well," he says, sitting back with his head tipped in such a way that she can't be sure: Is there *always* a twinkle in his blue eyes? "You could have downloaded the form at home, from the Stony Point website, filled it out and brought it over. All the forms are clearly posted online."

"I'm sure they are," Elsa mutters before whipping her leopard-print reading glasses out of her tote and perching them on her nose to skim the form. Then she peers at him over the top of her glasses. "I don't know how your wife puts up with you." When she gets busy scanning the multi-lined form, she hears him say something. "Pardon me?"

"I said, I don't have a wife."

"Well, I can *see* why." With a quick breath, she looks at the form, then at him—again over the rim of her low-perched glasses. "You won't even give me a break, will you, Cliff? After I served you coffee and pastry when you told me about my son being ill on the beach?"

He turns up his hands, a goddamn dimple giving away—oh yes, she sees it—a *resisting* smile.

"Ooh! Don't even say it." She leans forward over his desk. "*The rules are the rules!* You Stony Pointers just don't budge, and I need to rebuild the stairs immediately. It's a safety issue. My architect is assessing the damage right now. The entire deck structure was compromised, I can assure you, and I don't need kids sneaking around there getting hurt."

Cliff Raines, with his pale gray shirt—what did he do, try to match it to that salt-and-pepper hair of his?—leans closer to her then. His eyebrows lift in question as he asks, "Did you ever think of trimming back those large trees?"

"And do *you* know how many things are on my to-do list for that neglected rattrap?"

He points to the form, and after glaring at him, she looks at it. "How would I know by *whom* the work will be done? That will all be facilitated by my nephew Jason Barlow." She whips off her glasses and leans even closer to him. "Isn't that sufficient for you?"

The thing is, the closer they get, the softer his voice—a soothing voice at that. She gasps and pulls back at the thought, just a little, and waits for his answer.

"The Board of Governors must be certain the contractor is licensed and insured. Bring the form back when you have all the answers." He stands and motions to his industrial-strength steel door. "And be sure *no* work begins until the board approves it."

"But how long will approval take?" she asks, the form still in her hand.

"That depends." Now, oh yes he does, he leans on the *edge* of his desk, even closer to where she sits. "Some board members are on vacation, but I'll get together as many as I can."

"Vacation! Then this could take weeks!" Elsa stands up so quickly, her inadequate metal chair flips backward. "And I can't be held responsible for your slow pace!"

"Elsa, Elsa," a voice says from behind her. She spins around to see Jason picking up her fallen chair. "Breathe." With a stern glare, he takes her by the shoulders, pauses, then very gently moves her to the side. "How you doing?" he asks the commissioner. Before he can answer, Jason grabs the form from Elsa, lifts a pen from the desk and stands there, bent over the paper and quickly filling in each line.

"What are the damages?" Cliff asks Jason.

"The entire deck needs to be rebuilt." Jason's pen stops moving and hovers there for a moment. "But," he finally says, "there will be *no* design changes. The new deck will be an exact replica of the original."

Of course, with those instructions, his gaze shifts to her and he doesn't write *anything* until he sees her nod of approval, which she gives him. Barely.

"I'm including names of contractors who can get right on it. It's not a big job." Jason scrawls his signature on the bottom of the form. "They'll squeeze it in for me."

Elsa steps closer to the door, and Cliff and Jason both look at her. So she pulls her sunglasses off the top of her head. Wait, were they really there while she had on her reading glasses? How does this annoying, stubborn commissioner unhinge her like that? Okay, so she discreetly shoves the reading glasses in her tote and puts on her sunglasses—double-checking by touching the glasses' frame, because that's what Mr. Raines does to her; he has her doubting herself now. "I'm leaving."

Jason dates the form on a dotted line. "Hang on!" he calls to her.

She stops, right in the trailer doorway. A doorway that can use twinkly lights around it, at least. Maybe a seashell or dune-grass wreath. Something! She stands stock-still, listening to Jason, even though his voice has dropped to a near whisper.

"Take care of this, would you?" he asks Raines, then slides the form his way.

Elsa manages a glance over as the commissioner scrutinizes every damn line, she's sure, before he catches her eye and—what? *Winks* at her? She storms out the door.

"Elsa!" Jason persists. "Hold your horses."

She hears him follow behind her, his feet stepping down the metal trailer stairs to the pot-holed parking lot. "Oh, he really gets under my skin," she says to herself while tossing her tote—too brusquely—into her golf cart.

"You okay?" Jason asks as he gets into his own golf cart, parked beside hers. "Because you seem too bothered to drive. *Hot* and bothered, maybe?"

"Jason!" She sits in her driver's seat and lifts her big sunglasses to the top of her head. "What's happened to your manners?"

"Just saying. Now follow me back to the inn. And *no* speeding. Take a breath, would you?"

Elsa does, then rolls her eyes and reluctantly takes another.

"That's better. I want to get ideas on your new kitchen and that garden window you've been pestering me about, so we'll talk there. *And* we'll have the two egg sandwiches I picked up at the store." He raises a white paper bag and gives it a shake. After sternly pointing a warning finger at her first, he pulls his golf cart onto the beach road.

Sal and Celia walk up the granite steps to the top of the small dune and sit on the bench overlooking Stony Point Beach. The midday sun pulses heat, the sand nearly white beneath it; striped and colorful umbrellas line the beach; the air is still enough that the sound of the gently lapping waves reaches them.

"I just took my coffee outside, oh," Sal checks his silver wristwatch, "must be two hours ago, and that limb came crashing down. So I'm sure my mother is having it out with the new beach commissioner right about now. That old tree did a lot of damage, and she needs to take care of it."

"Poor Elsa." Celia squeezes Sal's hand. "I'm so glad neither of you were hurt. Then I'd have some serious blues."

Sal leans close and kisses the side of her head. "Now *these* are the beach blues you need to soak in." He motions to the scene. "Blue water, blue sky, blue hydrangeas on the dune." He plucks off a heavy blossom from the nearby bush and gives it to her. "Come on, we'll walk the driftline and hunt for sea glass. What kind did your father collect?"

"Two colors," Celia says, touching the hydrangea blossom to her face. "Greens and blues, actually. Blue is one of the more rare colors."

"Excuse me," a voice comes from behind them. It's Nick approaching, ticket pad in hand, pulling a pen from his shirt pocket. "Did I see you snap a flower from the dunes?" he asks, raising his uniform cap to better see them.

"Are you kidding me?" Sal asks.

"Sure am." Nick salutes them as he hurries past. "Have a nice walk, kids."

Sal shakes his head while leading Celia down onto the sand, straight to the water's edge. And Celia's not sure if this will end up making her even more blue: feeling the cool water of the Sound on her bare feet, hearing the splash of the small waves whispering along the beach, seeing the families relaxed, the seagulls swooping low, the ocean stars twinkling.

"Hey, Celia!"

She turns to see Lauren and Kyle donned with sun hats and sunglasses, sitting beneath an umbrella. Lauren waves them over.

"Enjoying your vacation?" Celia asks them.

"Absolutely. By the sea, no place else I'd rather be." Lauren stands, leaving Sal to shoot the breeze with Kyle. "We're having a nice week, especially since Kyle took it off from the diner," Lauren says. "After this, he'll be back and forth to work and here, for the rest of the month." She waves to Hailey, wearing her ladybug swim ring and paddling in the shallows. "And the kids, well they love it. They're in a couple of Parks and Rec programs—exploring the beach, swim lessons—which is a huge help, so I can work at the inn then. You know."

"Sure," Celia says, waving to Hailey. "She's *so* cute, Lauren."

"That's Kyle's princess, definitely." Lauren turns when Kyle and Sal approach them.

"Took Evan crabbing this morning," Kyle says to Sal. "During low tide, when we could get to the tidal pools." He motions to a green snorkel rising out of the water. "That would be Evan."

"Tide coming in now?" Sal asks, shielding his eyes and looking toward the rocky outcropping and patch of woods framing the end of the beach.

"You bet. Think I'll swim out to the raft. You game?"

"Not today, man." Sal takes Celia's hand. "We won't keep you two from relaxing. Have a nice afternoon."

"Thanks. Take it easy, guys," Kyle tells him.

But it's the way he says it while lifting off his *Gone Fishing* cap, looking up at the hot sun, then resettling the hat on his head that has Celia think a sand-chair snooze is more likely than a swim today, for Kyle. Not that she could blame him as she wades ankle-deep, leaning into Sal beside her, the water so soothing on this August afternoon.

They wind their way around low-floating tubes and sandcastles being built, stopping to pick up pieces of sea glass, which Sal slips into his shorts pocket. It becomes a competition of sorts to see who spots a piece first.

"Ah! There's one," Celia says, hurrying to the sea glass glimmering pale blue amidst tiny sand stones. She looks at it closely, running her fingers over the frosted surface of the glass. "Perfect." This piece she folds her fingers around and holds onto.

"Kyle says the tide is coming in. Maybe we can beachcomb at the shack?"

"Oh, that would be perfect! I'll bet there's lots of sea glass washed ashore there."

She's not sure what triggers it, but Sal stops, just stops, and faces her as they stand knee-deep in the water. "Look at you," he says, lifting his sunglasses to the top of his head.

"What?"

"Look at you *smiling* like that. A little bit of beach blues, me and you," he says, cradling her face with his hands and giving her a sweet seaside kiss as ocean stars sparkle around her on the ripples of the Sound, "and life's good once more."

thirty-four

OKAY, SO EVEN THOUGH HIS definition of paradise is Sunday mornings lying in bed with his wife, Jason thinks this qualifies as paradise, too. Any day of the week being in bed with Maris works just fine, including this early Thursday morning.

"Stay," Maris whispers beside him, her arms reaching around his back, her fingers stroking his shoulders.

He kisses her again, feeling her smile beneath his lips. The bedroom windows are open, but no breeze comes in. The air is still, holding only the raucous cries of feeding seagulls as they swoop out over the bluff. Once the sun is fully up, the birds will quiet, but to Jason, the early caws are his signal the day's begun. He presses Maris' silky brown hair off her face and tangles his fingers in it.

"Don't go."

Her voice is so soft against his ear as he kisses her neck that he can't resist. And her touch sliding down his arm and across his belly, as light as the summer morning, has him move on top of her. Maris extends her arms on the bed, and he draws his hands down them, finally entwining his fingers in hers, their arms linked for a moment. Until he can't stop. Until he feels her mouth on his again, until her legs rise languid against his hips and he raises her arms above her head to the pillow and makes love to her once more. They do it slower this time, and sweeter; their kisses fewer, but deeper. When he finally lowers the weight of his body on hers before turning onto the mattress, he folds his arm across his forehead and drifts toward sleep. And it makes him smile, the thought of drifting and all its connotations now.

"Feeling good?" Maris whispers, touching his smiling lips.

"Always, with you." He takes her fingers in his hand and kisses them. "I love you."

Seconds pass before she tells him the same, and he knows. She's drifting off to sleep, too.

The seagulls out on the bluff have quieted, their feeding satiated. And the quiet gets him to open his eyes and lift his watch from the nightstand, then sit up. But he can't do it, can't get out of bed without watching Maris doze, without touching her long brown hair and loving its velvet feel beneath his fingers.

"Are you getting up?" she asks from behind closed eyes.

"Have to take care of my *moncone*."

"Your what?" she asks, her voice breathy with sleep.

"Mon-cone-ay," he repeats. "It's Italian, for stump. Sal says it has a nicer sound to it."

"Oh, that cousin of mine."

And that's all she says as sleep hovers over her like a mist slipping in over the sea. In a minute, Jason moves to his bedside chair and puts on the pair of cargo shorts draped there, then leans back and buckles the leather belt left on the shorts. Taking a second, he breathes in the salt air, then holds the silicone liner and sock onto the end of his amputated left leg, being particular about smoothing them out before attaching his prosthetic limb and standing.

"Want me to put on coffee?" he asks.

"No, I'm going to sleep in." More dozing seconds before Maris nearly whispers, "It feels so good to be home after running around these past few weeks."

"Okay, I've got a busy day, so I'm off." Jason walks across the room to his dresser and puts on an olive tee, partially tucking it in. "*Avanti tutta.*"

"Sal again?" her sleepy voice asks, though her eyes are closed once more.

"Full speed ahead, sweetheart. Life waits for nobody." He hurries to the hallway to go downstairs.

"Oh, hon!" Maris calls out. "Can you leave me your cell phone? I haven't replaced mine yet and I really need one today. My assistant's going to call with wash questions for next year's line."

"Lily?"

"Yes."

Jason walks back into the room to his dresser, checks his phone and sets it on the nightstand. "It's charged, so you're all set."

"I'll give her your number, but only for today."

"That's fine. And if you have to reach me, I'm meeting Matt for coffee first, so you can get me on his phone."

"Matt?"

"He and Eva want a media room in the attic. We're just talking concepts at this point. Then I'm making a pit stop at the Woods place, but there's no phone there. After that, I'll be out back in the barn for the afternoon. Lots of design work waiting for me." He sits on the bed beside her and strokes her hair. "What about you?"

"Me? Let's see, it's Thursday." She squints toward the window, then pulls the sheet up to her chin. "I have to work on my travel notes for a presentation next week. And I'm having lunch at Elsa's. My sister will be there, too."

"Okay, darling." He bends and kisses her head. "Have a good sleep-in."

~

"What does that door lead to?" Kyle asks while pointing across the cottage bedroom. "A walk-in closet?" He's lost hope that they'll ever find a place to move to, at least not in time for the kids to settle in before school. But maybe now that Eva's back and showing them homes, their luck will change. He turns the tarnished knob and gives the hollow door a shove. "What the heck?"

Lauren comes up behind him. "Are you kidding me?"

"It's the garage, off the master bedroom?" Kyle turns and glares at Eva.

"Listen, guys," Eva says. "Finding a year-round home at the beach is going to be a challenge, so it's important to consider things from all angles."

Shaking his head, Kyle closes the door.

"Come on," Eva pleads. "At least it *has* a garage, you have to give me that."

"I don't need to see any more, Eva. Thanks, but no thanks." Kyle throws a glance at the garage door and grumbles his way out of the bedroom, to the outdated kitchen, picking up a spec sheet off the Formica countertop and skimming the stats. "I'm just not stoked about this one."

"But it does have two bathrooms." Eva turns up her hands as though maybe Lauren can convince Kyle. "In this real estate market, you really have to keep an open mind!"

"Oh, no." Kyle walks out the side door, squinting into the mid-morning sunshine. "Not you, too?" he asks over his shoulder.

"What?" Eva asks. "What did I say?"

And even though Kyle keeps walking to the front yard, his ear is tuned to Lauren explaining, in hushed tones, "Every, and I mean *every* agent who showed us a house while you were on vacation has said the exact same thing. *Keep an open mind.*"

Kyle stops and turns around as they approach him, Eva holding her realtor tablet. "Eva, it's not personal. But it's been a long summer of disappointments, with most of these dumps practically breaking the bank." He holds out a hand to shake hers. "No hard feelings?"

"Of course not!" She clasps his hand before getting into her SUV. "I'll keep looking, don't worry. I have to meet another client now, but I'll see you at lunch, Lauren. And hang in there, guys. We'll find something, eventually."

As Kyle walks Lauren to the inn where she'll be painting for the rest of the day, they pass all sorts of idyllic homes. Gingerbread trim on some, stone foundations on others, paned windows on hilltop cottages, flowering vines draping from window boxes. "I give up," he says.

"Don't get discouraged!" Lauren tells him, squeezing his hand. "And don't dwell on it. Maybe go paddleboarding for a while. Until you have to get the kids at Parks and Rec, okay?"

"Yeah, I'll paddle off my frustration, I guess." He resettles the *Gone Fishing* cap on his head. In the distance, Foley's big old cottage rises against the skyline. "Elsa sure hit the jackpot with that one," he says, nodding to it as they get nearer.

"No, no. Don't compare yourself to Elsa," Lauren warns him as she gives him a quick kiss before veering off. "Stay positive!"

When a golf cart toots its horn behind them, Kyle turns and puts out his thumb to hitch a ride when he sees that it's Jason.

"Where to?" Jason asks.

"Hey, guy," Kyle says, leaning closer and swiping Jason's face. "You shave today? Looking a little shabby."

"Yeah, you know. Too hot out." He glances at Lauren. "You guys need a lift?"

"Not me. I'm going to work at Elsa's." She gives Kyle another kiss. "See you later?"

"Sure, we'll take the kids out for dinner." He turns to Jason as Lauren continues along Elsa's pathway. "I'm supposed to be going paddleboarding now."

"*What?*"

"My thoughts exactly. Feel like some company?" Kyle asks as he holds the grab handle and settles in the passenger seat, noticing too many perfect cottages to count as they maneuver the sandy beach roads. Cottages tormenting him with their unavailability and absolute shingled, front-porched, window-boxed, landscaped perfection.

—

"Quick stop here. I have to double-check some numbers." Jason parks the golf cart beside the caving-in garage on the Woods' property.

"Sheesh, got some hoarding issues," Kyle tells him with a glance into a broken garage window.

"No kidding. It'll all go in the dumpster before the wrecking ball takes the place down."

They walk across the unkempt grassy yard toward the patio, where Jason snaps a laser distance meter onto a tripod. "Man, what a hot day," he says. "Not even a breeze up here on the hill."

"Connecticut's got another heat wave going on." Kyle tries to open the rusted patio umbrella. At first, he thinks the sound he's hearing is the grit and metal of the umbrella's crank gears. But he stops and tips his head when the noise gets closer by the second. "Now there's something you don't hear much of around here."

"What's that?" Jason asks while recording the distance from the patio edge to the property line.

"Milwaukee thunder." Kyle turns around and looks down the hill toward the street. "Someone's driving a Harley."

Jason walks over and looks with him as the motorcycle engine grows even louder as it approaches. And slows. And stops exactly, precisely, right beside his golf cart. "Holy shit," he says under his breath.

Down below, the driver lifts off his helmet and runs a hand through his thick, wavy hair, then gives his head a shake and climbs off the bike.

Kyle hits Jason's arm. "Is that the Italian?"

"Looks it."

Kyle pulls off his *Gone Fishing* cap and squints down the hill at Sal, wearing an old tee and faded jeans.

"That yours?" Jason calls out as he grabs his tripod and walks with Kyle.

"Sure is." Sal holds the key ring up high in the air.

"Damn." Kyle keeps walking, right past Sal, to the motorcycle.

"I needed wheels to get around. You know, I couldn't always be using my mother's car."

"But a bike?" Kyle asks, turning around to Sal. "Seriously?"

"Why not?" Sal shrugs as he and Jason near it. "I grew up riding scooters in Italy."

"This is *not* your mama's scooter, dude," Jason tells him, stopping a few feet from the motorcycle and checking it out, slowly making his way around it.

Kyle climbs on, gripping each handlebar as though going for a ride. He can't even help himself, the way he lets out a long, low whistle at the chrome-and-black machine. "Must've set you back some?"

"Not too bad." Sal eyes the bike, then brushes off the chrome fender. "The dealer gave me a fair price, so I rode it right off the showroom floor." He turns a foot to the side, a foot in a brand-new black leather boot. "Stopped and got the footwear to go with it, too."

"You have a license to ride this machine?" Jason asks.

"Definitely." Sal pulls out his wallet and flashes them his license. "Got one in the city a few years ago."

"In New York?" With one hand on the bike handlebar, and one hand on his leg, Kyle looks over his shoulder at every bit of shining chrome detail.

"Had a small bike for a year," Sal explains. "It was an easy way to maneuver the traffic. Until I was ticketed for weaving in and out. Micelli, my friend in the city, he's the cop who pulled me over."

"The mounted police officer you told me about?" Jason asks, still keeping his distance and not touching the Harley.

"That's the one. A guy on a horse, pulling over a guy on a motorcycle."

"Well, nice wheels, man." Kyle shakes Sal's hand.

"Thanks," Sal tells him. "They'll get me by until you sell me your pickup. Name your price."

"You're so full of shit." Kyle backs away from the bike, unable to stop looking at it. "Like you'd want my bomber when you have this slick machine."

"I mean it, Kyle," Sal says while putting on his helmet. "Okay, fellas." He wheels the motorcycle off the grass and onto the street, then gets on, his feet solid on the ground. Before starting that engine, he looks directly at Jason. "Jay."

If Kyle's jaw could ever hit the ground, this is the moment. Because no one—*no one*—except Neil ever, *ever* called Jason *Jay*.

"Come on, Jay. Get on," Sal insists easily. "Go for a ride."

As soon as Jason takes a step, Sal leans over and puts down the passenger foot pegs before starting the engine. And that's all it takes—that *thump-thump-thump* of the Harley engine; it's like a siren call, drawing Jason closer, straight toward the bike.

"No way," Kyle says to himself, watching as Jason drops his tripod into his golf cart parked beside the Harley.

With Sal and Kyle waiting, Jason stands there, his hand to his face while his thumb runs across the raised scar along his jaw. Still eyeing the idling bike, he walks to it and shocks Kyle with his next move.

Because what Kyle remembers are the hours he'd sat with Jason over brews at The Sand Bar, or while night fishing. He can't count how many times Jason's said the words, again and again, when they'd talk about some trouble his stump might be giving him, or about the accident that killed his brother:

Doubt I could ever swing my leg over a Harley again.

"Whoa, whoa, whoa!" Kyle yells as Jason does just that. He puts his left artificial foot with the prosthetic limb—having lost half that leg in the mother of all bike accidents—on the peg first. With no hesitation, he swings his right leg over the bike and settles on the passenger seat with a slight bounce.

Then Sal straightens out the front fork and stands the bike upright, using a booted foot to fold up the kickstand before taking off. When they're less than a block away, Kyle whips out his cell phone and runs into the middle of the beach road, gritty with sand. The motorcycle winds around a gentle curve far ahead, Sal and Jason leaning into the turn.

Kyle pulls up Jason's number from his contacts and rapidly begins texting him, his two thumbs flying over the letters.

"Mmm, heaven," Maris says while wiping a drop of Caesar dressing from her chin at lunchtime. "This is exactly the jump-start I need for my Thursday afternoon."

"What's on your agenda?" Eva asks.

"Tons of organizing. I have to finish typing the travel notes from my trip. There's a big meeting at work next week, and I have so much to present. Then I might give Maddy a quick bath, too."

"In that case, eat up!" Elsa tells her as she pulls her chair in close.

"Thanks for asking me to lunch, too." Lauren sets a napkin across her paint-spattered shorts. When she glances at the women, she sees that each one wears the same gold star necklace, the chains glimmering in the sunlight. She's never had a close bond like that and is intrigued by it. "This food looks amazing, and … I can't help but notice how the three of you always stay connected with your gold stars."

"Four." Elsa picks up a pitcher and pours slushies into their glasses.

"Four?" Maris asks.

"I'd bought one for my sister, June." Elsa turns to Lauren. "Their mother," she explains.

"Our mother had one, too?" Eva asks. She lifts a chicken Caesar wrap off the platter and sets it beside a handful of gourmet potato chips on her dish.

Elsa nods. "I bought the first two etched-star necklaces—one for her and one for me—right before she died. Our names were engraved on the back of the pendant, and hers was going to be a Christmas gift. This way, she'd have a star here, and I'd have mine across the sea in Italy, like they were our own ocean stars." Elsa lifts her necklace and glances at it. "But I never had the chance to give it to her. So not long after her death, I decided to buy one for each of you," she tells Maris and Eva. "To keep *us* connected, forever."

"That is so sweet," Lauren says. She lifts her sunglasses to the top of her head and turns to Maris beside her, lifting her pendant and looking closely at it.

"I keep June's in a happiness jar I made." Elsa lifts her chicken wrap. "I'll show it to you when we go inside."

They quiet then. The women sit behind the cottage at an old round patio table left behind when Elsa bought Foley's. The noon-day sun is pulsing with August heat, so much so that Elsa brought outside an extension cord and fan to create a light breeze. "I wanted to eat on the deck off the back room, but with that limb down, it's not safe."

"That must have been terrible, hearing that crash," Eva says between bites, holding a napkin up to catch the dripping dressing and juices from the tomato and lettuce.

"It was, but fortunately, no one was hurt," Elsa tells them. "And *unfortunately*, I'll have to cut our lunch short because the tree company will be here later to remove that massive limb *and* take down that ancient oak. What time is it now?"

Maris slides over her cell phone and checks the time, then checks for messages, too. "Just after twelve. Will you be rebuilding the deck?"

"Absolutely. Jason said it's very unstable. He found a contractor who can rebuild it right away, Monday and Tuesday of next week."

"That's my guy." Maris raises her blueberry-lemonade slushie in a toast, to which everyone tips their frosted glasses. "Calling in his favors, I'm sure."

"You see?" Eva asks Lauren. "If we find you a home needing fixing up, Jason can recommend contractors for you and Kyle. You just have to—"

"I know." Lauren raises her hand to stop her because she really does *not* need to hear it, *again*. "Keep an open mind, oy!"

"But it's true, Lauren. When I bought this place," Elsa says while waving a hand toward her rambling beach home's scaffolding along the side of the cottage, "I had to look past so much to the bare bones of the structure." She reaches over and gives Lauren's arm a squeeze. "You'll find something, but it might take *pazienza*. Patience, my dear."

"What time are the tree people getting here?" Maris asks.

"In about an hour." Elsa lifts a few potato chips, eating one. "So please take the afternoon off, Lauren," she says around the food. "I don't expect anyone to work in the racket that'll be going on."

"Are you sure?" Lauren asks. "I can do more painting on the stairs."

"You go enjoy the beach. With Kyle on vacation this week, I want you to spend time with your family. It'll be fine, and I'm just glad that all the tree work will be done in time for Sal's surprise party."

"Wait," Maris says, putting down her chicken wrap.

"What did you say?" Eva asks, her slushie glass halfway to her face.

"Ooh, this sounds good." Lauren scoots her chair closer to Elsa.

"Shh!" Elsa says, smiling, with a manicured finger to her lips. "It's a *surprise* birthday party on the fifteenth, next Saturday. I'll be sending a group text with the details, so watch for that."

"Okay, but my cell phone's broken," Maris says. "And I haven't replaced it yet. So text Jason's." She motions to Jason's phone on the table. "I'm using his for now, too."

Eva drags a piece of her wrap through the Caesar dressing on her plate. "Sal doesn't know about this party?"

"No! And even better? His very good friend from the city will be here, with his wife. Oh, Salvatore will be thrilled! Celia's out right now, looking for a birthday present."

At that moment, Jason's cell phone dings with an incoming text message, so Maris pulls the phone close. "It's from Kyle," she says offhandedly.

"He drove off with Jason in your golf cart before," Lauren tells her.

"Well, apparently they're up to something." Maris slides the cell phone to Lauren. "I'm sure Kyle thinks he's texting Jason and has *no* clue that I have his phone."

Lauren picks up the phone and angles it away from the glare of sunshine. "Oh, crap. Sorry, Maris, for whatever trouble they're getting into."

"Trouble?" Elsa asks, leaning to Lauren.

"Yeah. Listen." Lauren clears her throat, then reads Kyle's message. "Jason, man I cannot believe you did that. Your wife is going to KILL you!!"

"Uh-oh," Eva quietly says.

When Lauren looks up, she sees it: Maris simply raising an eyebrow in such a way that anyone can figure, well, she's already got her husband trapped in whatever lie he'll cook up for her.

thirty-five

EARLY THAT THURSDAY AFTERNOON, ONCE her lunch guests leave, the tree work begins. Elsa cringes at the noise, but hopes the neighboring vacationers understand. One young mother pushing a stroller, the baby wearing the cutest frilly sunbonnet, did wave a cheery hello. Still, with a bucket truck lifting a worker to the top of her unhealthy tree; and with downed branches being fed into the grinding wood chipper; and with two men firing up chainsaws—helmets, ear protection and spiked shoes on while strapped to the upper part of the tree—well, her yard is drawing lots of attention.

Which meant it would only be a matter of time before he arrived, wearing black jeans and a khaki button-down shirt with, of course, some sort of hiking sneaker to emphasize the danger Elsa is posing to passersby. But it's when the beach commissioner, with his appropriately mussed silvery hair, raises his clipboard as he nods to her that she knows she's in serious trouble.

"Not only are you breaking the noise ordinance," Cliff Raines yells over the screaming grind of the chipper devouring oak tree branches, "but Stony Point has a strict policy regarding tree maintenance. We like to keep the environment as natural as possible." He touches a pen point to some claim form on that damn clipboard.

Elsa cups her hands and leans to his ear. "The Board of Governors granted me an emergency approval! I have it in writing, which you delivered yourself, yesterday!" Then, well then she puts her hands on her hips, tipping her head and raising an eyebrow.

"That was for deck work," Cliff says, motioning to the upper-level deck, the same one upon which a massive, jagged limb still leans. "Allowing hammering and sawing. Not tree work."

Now she does it. Yes, she stamps her sneakered foot, hoping her silver ankle bracelet remains intact with the force. "But this is *all* part of the deck job, which cannot be rebuilt with tree debris obstructing the job site. Jason explained it in our appeal."

Cliff lowers his sunglasses while surveying the tree crew. "Mr. Barlow did not elaborate on the tree work. I thought only one fallen branch was to be removed, not the entire tree."

Elsa is out of options. She can't just stand here in the blazing sun—wood dust and chips floating in the air like snow—and huff and puff. So she takes the beach commissioner by the arm and leads him around to the front of the inn. As they go inside, she explains she'll bring him to the back room where he can better see the damage. But he pulls out of her hold when they pass the staircase.

"What is this?" he asks, pausing at the seaside mural covering the stair risers.

"Please. You're not going to tell me this goes against some code, are you?"

He steps closer, bending low while tucking his sunglasses in his shirt pocket. "No. The artist has done a fine job." He looks at Elsa. "Someone local?"

"Yes." Behind him, Elsa sees Lauren's brushstrokes that created sweeping dune grasses climbing each riser, and a long-legged sandpiper scurrying across the painted beach, which leads to gently breaking waves with a distant lighthouse, and on the higher stairs, a dramatic skyscape. "Yes, a good friend of mine." Elsa motions for him to go ahead of her past the stairs.

When they reach Foley's back room, the afternoon sun shines through the old windows, catching dust particles drifting like stardust.

Which stops her, again. Because doesn't the sunlight have a way of casting a spell on the room, as though if you're very still, you might hear laughter, or see shadows dance by? After hesitating for a second, she tucks her hair behind her ear and walks to the screen door. In a moment, Cliff is standing behind her, looking out at the deck. But he doesn't say anything, not until she backs up and bumps right into him.

"Excuse me," he says, his hand lightly brushing her waist as he moves aside, still perusing the damage.

After glancing at her waist, she adjusts her long V-neck tee over her black capri leggings and clears her throat. "Now you can see from here," she says, pointing to the towering oak tree which still has two men strapped to it, working limb by limb to take it down, "that tree was neglected for years by prior owners. I certainly *was* going to wait until after Labor Day to trim it back, and then this happened."

Still, he doesn't say anything. Instead, he opens the screen door and leans out, looking at the splintered limb fallen across the deck stairs, its smaller leafy branches covering the deck floor and concealing any structural damage. "The Board of Governors wasn't able to *see* this though." He comes back inside and closes the door. "You did not include photos on your petition."

When Cliff turns to her as he says it, she notices he didn't shave that morning. Whiskers cover his chin, a mix of silver with some black, like his hair—which is nicely combed, with just the right tousle. "Oh!" Elsa says, brushing off her own distraction and walking across the room.

"What now?" he asks while setting his clipboard on the countertop.

"Hmm?" She spins around to face him, consciously not looking at that scruffy chin as she fiddles with her gold star necklace. "No, no photos. But given the dangerous circumstance, I had no choice but to get this crew here."

"You didn't observe falling sticks, or debris, prior to the limb breaking?"

"No! I'm not in the habit of tree-watching, Mr. Raines. I *am* busy with other things." She gives her V-neck tee a tug and straightens her posture.

Outside, the men on the tree start up their chainsaws again, working their screaming blades through some stubborn, half-rotten, hundred-year-old branch. But Cliff doesn't flinch. He simply tips his head and takes a step closer to her. "I only ask because if we *had* advance notice," he says, "the board would be more lenient."

That's about all Elsa can take. Advance notice? She grabs his clipboard from the counter and skims the top page, the one listing all beach ordinances. "And where on this list is there anything about advance notice? First it's my fence, then my chalk messages, and now this? I'm ready to sell this place and go back to Italy, for goodness' sake!" When she brushes aside the top sheet of paper, the clipboard pen flies to the floor.

And so Cliff does it, this new, particular, stubborn, handsome—*merda!*—beach commissioner. He bends over and picks up the pen, walks closer to Elsa and gently tugs the clipboard from her hands. Without even a glance at it, he returns it to the counter, all while his blue eyes are locked on only her. Then he very carefully puts a hand on each of her shoulders, guides her a few steps to the side, loosely pins her to the wall, leans in and kisses her. Just once, as if they've bantered *all* there is to banter so, what else *can* he do? But oh, he means it, that kiss; there's no mistaking that. Afterward, he tips his head down and looks her in the eye again, those lips smiling just enough to bring out a dimple in his whiskered cheek.

Elsa glances first to her right, then to her left, at each of Cliff's hands still pinning her to the wall. Even *she* notices how her breath has quickened. "I do believe your kiss is in violation of Ordinance 34.27 or some such thing."

Only one long moment passes until he lifts one of those hands of his and tucks her thick hair behind an ear, then moves that hand behind her neck and bends close, kissing her once more.

Who knows if it's the suddenness of his kiss, or the intensity of it, maybe. But the chainsaws continue blaring outside the windows; inside, the dust swirls around the pinball machine and faded seascape painting and secondhand restaurant booths, all as rays of golden sunlight strike the wooden dance floor where, oh does she need a jukebox. All of it is captured in her sights as her eyes flutter open for only a second, before she raises her hands to that darn sexy commissioner's scruffy face as his kiss deepens. And as her knees weaken and they slowly, leaning against Foley's back-room wall, slide down to the floor in an unexpected embrace.

After waiting on the dingy patio of the Woods' place, Kyle figured Sal and Jason must have hit the highway on that Harley. It's that kind of hot day meant for cruising the open road. He gave them an hour, sitting there on a mildew-covered wooden bench and watching for the bike's return, before walking back to his rented yellow cottage on Hillcrest Road. With Lauren working all day at Elsa's, maybe he'd sneak in a nap in this heat, before picking up the kids.

But when Kyle crosses the front porch, passing dusty conch shells gathered on an end table beside his favorite white wicker chair, he sees Lauren inside on the big striped sofa in the living room. Her blonde hair is pulled back and she's in her work clothes: paint-spattered Bermuda shorts and a pale pink tee. She scrolls through a real estate listing on her laptop computer.

"Hey, you," he says, moving aside one of the starfish pillows and sitting beside her. "I thought you were working at Elsa's."

"I was, for a little while this morning. Just enough to get my hands covered." She holds up a blue-speckled hand. "But the tree people are there making a racket, so I left early, right after lunch. Maris and Eva were there, too."

"Oh, nice."

"Maris, who had Jason's cell phone with her."

"What?"

Lauren nods, clicking on the interior images of a cottage for sale. "Hers is broken, so she has his today."

"Shit," he whispers.

"You going to tell me what kind of trouble Jason is in?"

Kyle reaches his arm behind Lauren and toys with her French braid, touching a few loose wisps. "Long story short? Sal bought a Harley."

"He did?"

"Man, what a machine. He's got some street cred with that one. And Jason actually went for a ride on it."

"Are you kidding me?" Lauren finally turns to him, tearing her gaze away from what looks like a pretty decent cottage.

"Nope. He got on, and they've been gone for an hour now."

"He got *on* the bike? What's the matter with him?"

Kyle shrugs, then strokes her braid again while leaning toward the computer. "What are you looking at?"

She angles it toward him. "Eva called me right when I got home and said this one *just* came on the market. She said it has lots of potential ... if we could keep an open mind."

"Seriously?" Kyle watches as Lauren scrolls through pictures of white-paneled rooms, a screened front porch decorated with painted slat-back rockers and tall vases of cattails, and a tiny galley kitchen—updated, but tiny. "If I hear that again, I quit looking."

"It's probably worth walking through. But I'm covered in paint." She sets the computer in Kyle's lap. "Check out the details, and I'll call Eva after a quick outdoor shower. We can see it before we pick up the kids from Parks and Rec." She hurries to grab a towel from the bathroom, drapes it over the couch while getting her robe from their little bedroom, before rushing barefoot through the cottage, out the back door to the enclosed shower.

Kyle clicks to the beginning of the cottage slide show. It's not bad: a shingled two-story with a peak on the front. The front porch needs work, new windows and whatnot, but it's one of the better homes he's seen. While he studies it, not even a breeze comes in through the living room's open windows beside him; the neighboring cottages, stacked so close to theirs, are absolutely quiet. It's no wonder. With the day's blazing heat, everyone must be planted on the bright beach, beneath shady umbrellas, hoping for any sea breeze, or sitting at the water's edge with their feet in the sea. Raising his arm to blot his sweating forehead, Kyle notices Lauren's bath towel on the couch; she'd forgotten it in her house-hunting rush, so he scoops it up and walks through the cottage, pushing the back screen door open onto the deck. The only sounds there are the cicadas buzzing, and a blue jay cawing from a low tree branch. Everything else is midsummer still.

After a moment's pause, Kyle walks around to the outdoor cabana, where the shower is running. Rivulets of water run from beneath the planked cabana walls. He stands there with the towel, looks up at the beating sun, then knocks on the cabana door and opens it enough to slide himself inside with the towel.

"Kyle!" Lauren says with a startled jump, her arms moving to partially cover her soaped-and-dripping naked body. "What are you *doing*?"

"Shh." He holds a finger to his lips. "Don't want the neighbors to hear." He reaches forward and runs his finger along the silver chain hanging around her neck, following it to where it stops, but only for a second before his hand continues to her breasts, covered in droplets of shower water.

"Kyle, are you kidding? Right here?"

He smiles and looks away, slips off his shorts, then reaches around her and cups her soaking bare bottom in his hands and pulls her close. "Just keep an open mind."

Late Thursday afternoon, Jason parks his golf cart on the lawn and goes in through the front door, dropping his tripod and duffel on the kitchen table before grabbing a bottled water from the fridge. He sees Maris in the backyard with the dog and walks over to the slider to watch them.

"Come on, let's go," Maris says to Maddy, who is lying in the blue kiddie pool, her muzzle resting on the curved plastic edge. There's a bucket of soapy water at Maris' feet, and she's wearing her wash-the-dog threads: cut-off denim shorts with an old white tank top. And Jason understands why when the dog leaps out of the pool and gives a good water-shake, sending drops flying all over Maris. But she persists and pulls the German shepherd close, talking softly and gently petting her.

"You're looking as mangy as Jason's been lately," she says to the dog, which gets Jason to run a hand through his overgrown hair. Then he swigs his bottled water and stands at the side of the slider, still watching. Maris lifts a big sponge from the bucket and dribbles warm water across Maddy's back, then adds dog shampoo. She starts to massage the dog's scruff and sides of her chest, working her fingers through the thick fur. And Jason has to laugh at the way Maddy goes completely limp once the scrubbing and lathering start. Lucky dog, getting a rubdown like that from his beautiful wife. Maddy whimpers, and as Maris bends over, a hand on each side of her massaging in the soap, the dog turns up her head and licks her across the face.

"Aww, you're too cute, Maddy." She dabs a dot of soap bubbles on the dog's nose, laughing now. As the bath continues, though, the dog gets anxious, whining as though pleading for this to be over soon. "But see how pretty you are now?" Maris reassures her in a soothing voice. "So, *so* pretty. I could use you in my new denim campaign, you can walk with the models." Finally she picks up the hose and gently rinses off the soapy shampoo, pushing the lather with one hand while spraying the German shepherd's coat of fur, trying to keep up with her as Maddy slowly takes steps away, wanting nothing more than to shake off this sweet-smelling soap.

While they stand there finishing up the bath, Jason sets down his water and slides open the screen door. As he does, he runs his hand through his motorcycle-windblown hair again, two times. "Hey, darling," he says, walking outside into the bright sunshine. "Good day to wash the dog, cool her off."

After a moment when Jason wonders if she even heard him, Maris calls out, "I was too mad to do anything else, including typing up my fashion notes from Europe."

"Mad? Why?"

Maris looks over from rinsing Maddy and swipes at a loose strand of her hair. "Did you even bathe her at *all* while I was gone, for all those weeks?"

"I didn't actually get to it," Jason says as he pulls out a chair at the patio table.

"Why not?" Maris uses the back of her hand to dab a drop of water from her forehead. "The way everyone babysat you, you must've had plenty of time."

Jason glances over his shoulder at her. "What are you talking about?"

"Well, everyone fed you in my absence. I'm supposing they clothed you and cleaned the house, too?"

Jason throws a look at the house, then at her, turning up his hands.

"No, wait," Maris says, dribbling hose water down Maddy's soapy fur. "The house was a *mess* when I got back from my trip, including all those wedding gifts still lined up along the hallway. Gifts that you promised me *two* times you would put away. So what, did you just leave everything for me to do in my *free* time?" She drops the hose then and bends over the dog, working the remaining lather down her legs toward her fidgeting paws.

Jason walks to the deck stairs, stops, crosses his arms and eyes Maris, her hair pulled into a low ponytail, her gold star necklace glimmering as she bathes Maddy. "Okay. This is *not* about a messy house. What's up?"

"You tell me. I'll bet it's quite a story, too."

"Would you stop beating around the bush, for Christ's sake?"

With her arms elbow-deep in dripping, soapy dog water, she nods toward the patio table. "You got a text message while you were out."

Jason notices his cell phone there, in the shade beneath the open umbrella. He picks up the phone, reads Kyle's text and drops his eyes closed.

"I saw that, Jason!" Maris stands there, the hand on her hip holding a big soapy sponge dripping down her bare leg. "I saw the way you closed your eyes."

He deletes the message and puts down the phone. "It was nothing."

She bends over and picks up the hose, pointing it in his direction. "Spill it, or I'm turning the hose on *you*!" When the dog gives a thorough water-shake beside her, she doesn't flinch.

"You wouldn't," Jason says, walking down the deck stairs to try to calm her down.

Maris gives the hose nozzle a shake. Strands of her brown hair have escaped from her ponytail, the fringe of her short-shorts are wet from bathing the dog, as is half of her white tank top, clearly showing her black bra beneath it.

"Maris," Jason patiently says, turning up his hands. "Come on. Sit down with me." He hitches his head to the deck.

There's no smile on her face, and no relaxing her hold on the pistol-grip trigger as she turns the dial on the control knob, then squeezes the handle so that a high-pressure stream of water reaches him in an instant.

Jason looks down at his drenched tee. "You didn't!" As he's saying it, brushing the water off his shirt, more cold water hits him on his head. When he looks up into the glare of the afternoon sunlight, the spray of water shimmers thousands of silver droplets—aimed exactly his way, causing him to duck and sidestep, to no avail.

Maris shifts her stance and doesn't let up on the water. "Talk, Jason. *Why* does Kyle think I'm going to kill you?"

"Don't know," Jason lies, ducking again and picking up a potted geranium to shield his face.

"What did you *do*?" Maris persists, adjusting the spray to a pulsating stream now.

Holding the flowerpot up high, Jason sidles over toward the kiddie pool, which causes Maris to move away from it, exactly as he'd hoped. He quickly puts down the clay pot and picks up Madison's soapy bucket, tossing the dirty bathwater out of it and scooping up clear water from the pool. Then, well then he eyes Maris and steps toward her.

"Oh, no you don't." She backs up, pulling the nozzle trigger again and dousing him but good, so that now water drips off his hair onto his face. Madison lets out a yip and runs in a circle behind her, then stops, her front paws down, rump in the air, tail swinging.

But Jason watches only his wife. He's got a plan now, one that'll leave her too stunned to move—and then he'll give her a taste of her own dousing. "I went for a ride on a Harley today." He takes another step as she freezes.

"You went on a bike?"

The way she winces at him, her eyes give away her hot anger. So he cools her off, holding the bucket but jolting it so that a splash of water catches her on the shoulder and some of her hair. "Who says I can't?" he asks, walking closer.

Maris glares at her dripping shoulder, which gives him enough time to toss another splash of water her way, making her jump when it hits her directly. "Ooh!" She gives him a spray of hose water, soaking his shirt and most of his shorts. "You bastard!"

"Listen, sweetheart," he says, the half-full bucket tipped her way. "At least I told you and didn't keep it a secret."

"What?" She backs up, hose in hand. "How could you get on a bike, after all you've been through? I mean, with your leg? And losing your brother? Oh, I *really* can't believe you did that."

This time, when she pulls the sprayer trigger, he dodges it and moves even closer to her. "It was with Salvatore."

"Sal?" Water drips from the nozzle, which she now loosens her grip on. "He has a motorcycle?" The dog has given up fidgeting and moves into her kiddie pool, laps the water, then sits, watching them.

"It just happened, Maris." Jason dips his hand into the bucket and sprinkles a handful of water her way. "He pulled up and the next thing I knew …"

"Don't give me that." The nozzle is reined in and she gives a quick shot of cold water his way. "As if you had no control. I *saw* what you've been through coming to terms with that accident, and riding Sal's bike is unacceptable."

"I know." Jason swipes his hand across his dripping forehead while trying to get near her. "But if you could have seen him. It was like Neil sitting there."

"Stop it!" She sprays him directly, keeping the stream coming even when he turns sideways to deflect it. "Don't talk about your brother like that. Neil's gone."

The only way he can get her to quit spraying him is to heave half the bucket of water her way, which he does, high in the air so that water droplets fall on her from the head, down. "Just *listen* to me, Maris, would you?" The thing is, she doesn't say anything. And when he looks away, then at her again, he can't tell if those are tears on her face, or drops of the water he pitched. "Listen," he says, setting the bucket down. "Sal said something. It came out of left field, he didn't even realize it."

"Oh, this should be good." She slowly raises the nozzle. "What did he say?"

Jason turns up his hands. "Jay. He called me Jay."

With a long, defeated breath, Maris closes her eyes.

"I'm telling you, it felt like *Neil* said it, wanting me to fully make peace with everything." As he admits it, Jason finally reaches her and puts his hands on her soaking-wet face. He looks at her drenched hair, lightly moves strands off her face and kisses her, just barely. "I won't go again. But today? It's like I was riding with my brother, on a hot summer afternoon. I got that back for a little while, cruising the dusty roads, feeling that wind."

Maris suddenly drops the hose nozzle she'd been fiercely gripping. Then she drags the back of her fingers across his whiskered face. "You're looking as shaggy as the dog lately."

"So you're not mad?"

Her hands slide to his waist and slip beneath the sopping olive tee he'd put on hours ago. They move behind his back and tug him closer before she rises on her toes to kiss him.

Relieved, Jason cradles her face and deepens their kiss. Having her in his life like this is enough, it's his happiness; but he feels like there's more to be said, so he pulls away, still holding her face. His thumb strokes the drops of water on her cheek. "I did *other* things while you were in Italy, besides clean house. Like, well, I won a clamshell toss on the beach and have a voucher for free ice cream."

"So you want to go for ice cream?"

He nods.

"All wet like this?" she asks, her hands settled on his drenched hips.

"Sure." He dips his head and kisses her cheek, her ear, her mouth. "Ice-cream truce?" he whispers, his fingers stroking her wet hair.

He feels it then, as she kisses him back. Hears it, too, a small sob of love, and grief for him, as she kisses him at the same time that her hands are unbuckling the leather belt he'd buckled that morning. Slowly, she drags it off and he feels it slip through each belt loop. At the same time, his hands drop to her wet tank top, his fingers moving beneath the drenched fabric on her shoulders, slipping the straps down her arms. He stops then and simply looks at her, her soaked tank top half off and revealing her lacy black bra beneath it, his belt hanging loose in her hands, water still dripping from both of them.

And he knows, as he puts his arm around her, adjusts her tank-top strap and walks her toward the house. Yes, he knows without a doubt, as he tips her chin up and his mouth meets hers while they walk inside, that the ice-cream truce won't be happening for about an hour or so.

thirty-six

FRIDAY EVENING, ELSA SWINGS HER front door open. "Celia?"

Before talking, Celia peers into Elsa's dimly lit cottage, then sets her guitar case and duffel on the stoop. "I don't want to impose," she says in the dusky light. "I know we're going shopping tomorrow for those pretty garden lights you wanted."

"And still are, I hope? They'll be nice at Sal's party next week, and we could buy some streamers and balloons, too." Elsa throws a concerned look at Celia's bags. "You're not leaving, are you?"

Celia can't help it then; she laughs lightly. "No! I'm actually arriving. I was wondering if you have a room I can stay in for the weekend?"

As though her words were a magical *abracadabra*, the front door sweeps wide open and Elsa reaches out to pick up the duffel, prompting Celia to grab her guitar case. "Of course!" Elsa assures her. "What happened? Is everything okay at your cottage?"

As Celia follows Elsa inside, she explains how her friends Amy and George wondered if they might stay in the cottage this weekend, with Amy's daughter, Grace. That Amy's parents are visiting and Grace really needs a seaside break before starting nursery school in a few weeks. "They insisted I stay," Celia continues. "But I thought they might want some family privacy and hoped you would have extra space for me here?"

"Wonderful!" Elsa tells her as they head up the stairs to an empty bedroom. "You'll be my very first customer." She drops Celia's duffel on the end of a bed made up with a pale blue quilt edged in a seashell scallop. "I'd love to practice my inn-keeping skills with you."

There's no mistaking, though, that Elsa's already begun—so apparent by the lovely happiness jar on the bedside table. The Mason jar is partially filled with beach sand and tiny seashells, and a note beside it instructing guests to fill the jar with happy souvenirs from their stay at the Ocean Star Inn.

"I was hoping you wouldn't mind," Celia says when she unzips her duffel and pulls out two new pairs of flip-flop slippers, along with a new nail polish color. "And I brought some fun things to do?" Elsa still looks concerned, standing there with a rolled bandana tying back her thick hair, and wearing a light cardigan over her outfit. So Celia gives her a hopeful smile and holds out the yellow slippers.

"What about Sal?" Elsa asks, taking the fluffy flip-flops. "Wasn't he with you?"

Celia shakes her head. "He's waiting tables at The Driftwood Café, on the outdoor patio. Kyle extended his weekend hours for the summer and of course since he took the week off, they're mobbed at the diner. When I called Sal, he was so busy with the Friday night crowd, I didn't even tell him I'd be here."

~

Foley's back room seems even more atmospheric in the evening. Elsa brought a table lamp and plugged it in at their booth. They sit across from each other, Celia sideways in the booth seat, wearing her pajamas: silky polka-dot shorts with a matching button-down top. Naturally, they both wear their fluffy flip-flop slippers. The windows are open and a soft sea breeze makes its way into the shadowy room.

"Here," Celia says, extending her hand across the table. "Let me paint your fingernails."

Elsa does, relaxing and enjoying this beach chat with her friend. She sips from her glass of white wine, then dips a biscotti in the wine before taking a bite. "I have a secret," she says around the food.

Celia glances up from her nail-painting, but only for a second before dragging the brush of silver along Elsa's nail, beneath the lamplight.

"Promise not to tell anybody?" Elsa asks.

"You know it, girlfriend." She holds out a hooked pinky. "I see Maris and Eva do this. Pinky swear?"

"Oh, yes!" Elsa briefly hooks Celia's pinky with her unpainted one, then leans closer over the table. Light jazz music plays on the old boom-box radio on the counter, and outside, lights come on in the neighboring cottages. "Now you *cannot* say a word, Cee."

"I won't."

"Well, the thing of it is … I finally *get* the magic of this room."

"What do you mean?" Celia is bent over the polish, diligently edging Elsa's nails.

"You know. Foley's, Foley's. Everyone acts like it's such a beloved beach shrine where great things happen. And it is. I was kissed in here, yesterday."

"What?" Celia sits straight and looks her dead-on. "By whom?" she asks, reaching for her wineglass.

In the pause, wisps of jazz fill the room, soft and easy, like a summer mist. "The beach commissioner. Clifton Raines."

Celia does it then, she lightly slaps Elsa's arm. "You can't stand the man!"

"That's what I thought, too. But all of our bickering, well, it was something else, I guess. Hiding something neither of us wanted to be the first to admit."

"You *kissed*? Where?"

Elsa points to the wall near the doorway into the room. "There." She even gets out of the booth in her nightshirt and light robe, flip-flopping across the lovely, beautiful, dusty old floor. "Right here," she says, standing in the exact spot. "At least, that's where we started, when Cliff pinned me to the wall."

"Elsa!"

"Oh, it was all in good fun. But we only stood here until …"

"Oh my gosh! Until what?"

Elsa wraps her arms around herself and closes her eyes for a long second, saying, "Until my knees gave out." Then she twirls around and slips back into her booth seat. "Imagine? I'm in my fifties, having a fling."

"Sounds more like a summer *romance*!" Celia picks up Elsa's other hand and begins painting those nails, dragging the wet brush along each one.

"I don't know about *that*. I'd been prattling on when I was with him, you know, about inn violations … mostly that tree. Sometimes I wonder if he kissed me just to finally *quiet* me."

"*What?* No way. More like he couldn't resist you."

"I'm not really sure where Cliff and I stand, Celia. To be honest? It was a little awkward, afterward. He seemed flustered and left right away." She gazes over at the wall where it happened. "But one thing's for sure, I *never* dreamt I'd discover the magic of this place right here, being *kissed* in this room." When Celia looks up from her painting, Elsa throws her a fun wink.

"Well. Since we're sharing secrets …" Celia says.

"Wait." Elsa pulls the silver nail polish bottle closer. "I'll paint your nails while you spill your juicy secret."

So Celia gingerly sets her hand on the table and Elsa adjusts its position for painting, all the while Celia is silent until Elsa raises an eyebrow at her. "This is a good one, Elsa."

"Tell! Tell me!" She drags the brush over Celia's fingernail as she says it.

Celia leans closer and drops her voice. "I think I'm falling in love. With your son."

It surprises Elsa how her eyes instantly fill with tears. Happy tears. Because of course she suspected as much, but to hear Celia say it, she's purely over the moon.

"Elsa?" Celia whispers.

Elsa looks up at her, smiling, and gently moves a wisp of auburn hair from Celia's cheek. "This is the best news I've heard in months!" When she half stands, Celia does the same and they reach across the table, both in their light pajamas, and hug each other—careful not to smudge their nails.

"Oh, Celia," Elsa says as she sits again, holding Celia's arm. "You're the finest thing to happen to Salvatore. He's been so burned out lately. I catch him napping on these warm afternoons and see how tired that job's made him. But the way he's also exploring his options here, looking at a different way of life—one that includes you—I wonder if he'll stay on at Stony Point."

"Nothing would make my heart happier, Elsa. I only have a few more weeks here, but the drive to Addison isn't bad, forty-five minutes at the most. So it could work." She sets down her other hand for Elsa to finish up painting the nails. "Do you think he'll ever make that move?"

"Here's the thing about Sal." Elsa dips the brush into the nail polish and drags off the excess. "When he's doing busywork like waiting those diner tables, or driving shotgun with Nick on his security runs, he's really doing something else."

"He is?"

Elsa nods. "He's *thinking*, coming up with something. Which makes me wonder if he's trying to find a feasible way to move his life here." While she paints the last of Celia's nails, the sound of a motorcycle grows closer. "There he is now."

"What?"

"He didn't tell you? He bought a bike."

"Are you *kidding* me?" Celia whips around and looks out the window toward the parking lot below, where all the tree debris has been nicely removed. The motorcycle turns into the lot. "He said he had a surprise for me. Was *that* it?"

"I'm sure it was."

In the next few moments, Elsa hears Sal open the front door, hears his booted feet coming down the hallway, hears him calling out *Ma?* And what she feels is this: all the magic of this blessed dump of a room, especially when Sal walks in, a motorcycle helmet folded in his arm, the love of his life sitting across from Elsa.

"What's going on here?" Sal asks, spotting Celia in her silky pajamas, then briefly shifting his gaze to Elsa.

"We could ask you the same question, Salvatore," Elsa says, capping the nail polish bottle. "We heard your motorcycle, and I'm wondering if maybe you're having a midlife crisis?"

"Could be, though I'm not quite at midlife yet. So I'm not really sure."

But Elsa knows it's not a crisis; it's more like love, and it's written all over her son's face. Because the whole time he's stood there, Sal's only had eyes for Celia.

"Don't suppose anyone wants to take a ride?" he asks, holding up the helmet in their direction.

Okay, so if this were a scene in one of those romantic-comedy movies she likes to watch with her best friend Amy, it would definitely be leaning heavily toward the romantic. And Celia would have the starring role, sitting at their little umbrella table behind the ice-cream stand, a saltwater marsh in the distance beneath a starry sky, a triple-scoop banana split in front of her. She can't believe it's already been a month since Sal first brought her here in Kyle's old pickup, and now it's become *their* place.

"Once you drive beneath that railroad trestle and arrive at Stony Point, you will *never* leave the same," she tells him while stabbing a chunk of fudge-covered banana.

"How so?" Sal asks, a spark in his eye as he holds a dripping spoonful of his strawberry-shortcake sundae.

"Well," Celia begins, leaning close, "according to Lauren—and she has it on good authority—you will always leave Stony Point with one of three things that you did not have when you arrived: a wedding ring, a baby, or a broken heart."

"Interesting selection." With that, Sal touches his ice-cream spoon to hers in a toast. "Cheers," he whispers.

Now, sitting on the back of his Harley-Davidson—wearing her cuffed jeans and a pair of Elsa's sneakers, but still in her polka-dot silky pajama top, with the requisite helmet on her head—her arms reach around Sal's waist as he slowly maneuvers the roads, playing her romantic love interest. She leans into him, watching the night sights flashing by as they return to Stony Point.

Cruising beneath the railroad trestle on his motorcycle, the breeze fluttering her silky pajama top, her body against his, Celia imagines the movie director considering the atmospheric illumination at this hour: golden lamplight spilling from screened porches, and a quarter moon casting a hazy glow on the streets. Far above, starlight twinkles. *Roll camera!* the director would yell as Sal veers left onto the winding, narrow Sea View Road. *And ... Action!*

Celia takes it all in as though looking through the lens of that movie camera. There are stories to tell on lantern-lit front porches of New England cottages, where ornamental dune grasses and hydrangea bushes are mere shadows in the night. Illuminated living rooms and tiki-torch-framed outdoor decks hint at families lingering with this August Friday, maybe after turning keys in cottage doors, arriving for a weekend escape.

When the imagined camera shifts to filming her, it captures an exquisite summer still playing on. The salt air brings the scent of the sea, with its waves lap-lapping along the beach—where Sal heads the bike now. His shirt ripples in the wind, and Celia's auburn hair blows beneath her helmet. After parking, they sit side by side on the boardwalk, the moonlight dappling the dark water gold, a foghorn's low call drifting over the misty sea, the scene fading out tenderly when Sal's hand reaches to her face and his mouth covers hers in a kiss as sweet as this night's whispering sea breeze.

And when the movie pans forward years in time and finds Celia lingering over old photographs, *this* is one of the moments that'll have her bring her hand to the fading photo and touch it lightly, the summer moment never completely gone.

thirty-seven

"WHAT DO YOU GIVE A guy who's got everything?" Jason Barlow asks the following Wednesday. Beneath a mere sliver of a crescent moon, there aren't even shadows on the beach; there is only darkness. And the tiny stars are too far away to illuminate the night. Jason walks along the packed sand beneath the high tide line. Ahead of him, Maddy runs with her nose to the damp seaweed, her tail swinging, her collar jangling. The oppressive Connecticut heat's been hanging on—Jason's sure Kyle could give him some explanation about the dog days of summer. And yet, the beach is eerily quiet this mid-August night, the way it gets in September, when the seasonal cottages empty out. Maybe folks feel autumn's closeness now. Sal's surprise party is close, too. It's days away.

"You out there, Neil? Because when I say the guy's got everything," Jason continues, "what I mean is that if he *doesn't* have something, he's damn sure got the money to buy it."

"Like that bike?" he hears whispered right as a warm breeze lifts off the water. Maybe that's what signals summer is waning. In July, a hot day like this would never end with a sea breeze; the air would be stifling.

"Oh, that bike. Man, it's sweet." Jason stops and looks out over the water. The dark sea blends with the horizon, so he can't place where they meet. "That was something I never thought I'd do again, Neil. Swing my leg over a hog and cruise."

A gentle wave breaks and hisses along the beach. "Was surprised you did."

Jason bends down and scoops up a handful of small stones. "Quit bullshitting." He throws a few far out into Long Island Sound. "You were there, too, and you know it."

There. He said it. Said what he's felt since that afternoon on Sal's bike. And now, he stands still. Words are coming, words he desperately needs to hear in order to let go of the guilt he's felt *since* that ride.

"I was, Jay."

Sudden tears fill his damn eyes, and he swipes at them. As though she senses his distress, Madison lopes down the beach toward him, so he bends to scratch the scruff of her neck. "Good girl, Maddy." He pats her flank as she turns her attention back to the driftline. At some point, she'll drop a stick of driftwood at his feet to begin a game of fetch. But not yet.

A couple approaches; they walk slowly, barefoot in the sand, nodding to him as they pass by. That sea breeze suddenly ripples Jason's T-shirt and it feels like the warm wind on the Harley. "I *thought* you were there," he whispers. "So you know what I mean," he continues once the couple's out of earshot. "And I'm stuck on a birthday gift. The guy has everything, but when I'm with him, it's like he's got nothing. It's just him, laid-back and casual." Madison is scrambling over the rocks now, so Jason gives a sharp whistle for her return. "Maris is in the city for a few days. Said she'll look for a gift there."

"Nobody has everything." The words are so quiet, Jason's not sure if they're simply his own thoughts.

Then, nothing. So Jason makes his way back across the beach, sticking to the firm sand that always eases his gait. "I thought he traded in his tie and cuff links," he finally hears, as though his brother is still contemplating this gift dilemma.

"For the summer, anyway," Jason answers. "He's drifting for a while. Figuring out his future. Which apparently includes Celia now."

Walking alone, Jason thinks of the bike ride, and how when they stopped for a beer a few towns over, Sal asked him a question. *If you could have one thing, anything, what would it be?* Of course, Jason said he'd want his brother back.

"How about you?" he'd asked Sal.

"It's the same answer anyone from the Street would give you. Time. More time." With that, Sal gave his heavy wristwatch a shake. "Time's an obsession on Wall Street. The jobs are so huge, so encompassing, we find any way to pad a few more minutes onto every hour, every day. Flagging a cab when I could walk. Takeout when I could cook. Using a credit card instead of thumbing through cash, just for a *blessed* few seconds. Every minute saved is a minute to live."

To which Jason tipped his beer bottle to Sal's.

Suddenly the dog is at his feet, paws prancing, a wet piece of driftwood clamped in her jaw. Jason takes it and teases her, making like he's throwing it, then hiding it behind his back as she spins around—this way, then that—looking for it. "Where is it?" he asks. "Where'd it go?" When she gives a playful yip, he throws the stick far down the beach, watching the German shepherd give chase.

"Kind of ironic, don't you think?" he hears then as the dog's feet kick up the sand.

"What is?" he asks his brother's spirit, drifting back and forth over the beach much like Sal drifting aimlessly in his rowboat.

"In order for you to have the one thing you wanted, me being back," the voice murmurs as the foghorn wails, "we needed the same thing Sal wants. A minute or two."

"Shit," Jason whispers, running his hand through his hair, feeling the seaside dampness in it tonight. "Time."

Celia reaches up and touches Sal's face. "You sure you don't want to take a beach walk? It's early still, just after nine. We could sit on the boardwalk again and listen to the—what does your friend in Manhattan call it? Boat talk?"

Sal opens his eyes and first strokes her face on his chest, then folds his arm behind his head. With blue-and-white striped pillows propped around them, they lie together on the sofa, still and quiet in her little cottage living room, listening to the few lagoon noises outside the windows. "Not tonight."

What he doesn't know, as she's felt the length of his body alongside hers, is that she's been worrying more than relaxing tonight, keeping an eye on him in the dusky room and suspecting him of actually dozing every now and then. "You look so tired, Sal."

"I am," he says. "Not sure why. Had an easy Wednesday, just helped my mom measure the back room windows for new curtains. And the crew finished up rebuilding the deck while I was there this morning, so it looks great."

"She must be so glad it's done." As she says it, Celia drags a finger along his other arm, down to the sailor's knot rope on his wrist.

"She is, beyond words. I can't seem to get her out of that back room these days, and now the deck, too. We even had lunch in that dingy space before I made some phone calls to New York. Then Ma kicked me out of the house, so I took a long bike ride. Stopped by and chewed the fat with Jason out in his studio."

"Wait. Your mother kicked you out?"

"She's so cooking up something for my birthday. For her, it's a national holiday."

"Really? For thirty-six? It's not like you're hitting the big four-oh."

Sal closes his eyes again, arm still folded behind his head. And it's like he's time travelling, the way his voice gets distant as he explains. "Every birthday's a spectacle, trust me. In Italy, the celebrations all happen on your Saint Day, which is far more important than the actual birthday."

"I've heard that. It's nice."

"Not for my mom, though. Don't forget, she *is* an American, so it's all about the candles on the cake."

"Well." Celia shifts beside him. "That *is* what mothers do."

Sal sits up and takes a sip of iced water from the glass on the end table. "She must have some surprise shindig in the works."

When he looks over at Celia half sitting, too, she draws her fingers across her closed mouth. "My lips are sealed," she whispers.

"Come over here so I can unseal them."

Celia waits as he lies down on the sofa once more, then she leans down and kisses him. His touch on her skin is soft, and his fingers stroke her hair falling forward around them. She cradles his face, feeling the whiskers beneath her hands, her thumb sliding along his jaw as she kisses him once more, pressing back his getting-shaggy dark hair. "You look tired," she says again, still leaning close and studying his face. "I'll play you a tune, okay?"

"That'd be nice." He resettles on the sofa, both arms crossed behind his head as she lifts her guitar from where it leans in a far corner, next to a wooden heron statue, its head turned up toward the sky. Sal hasn't been this beat in a long time, maybe since he rescued that boy. His skin is sallow, and there are faint circles beneath his eyes. So she settles on the other end of the sofa, and her fingers pluck out a very slow, bluesy tune.

"I recognize that song," he says from behind closed eyes. His voice is soft, almost far away. "But I can't place it."

"Listen." Celia's fingers move easily, but slowly, as she plays it again, in a different key.

Sal shakes his head, his eyes still closed. "What is it?"

Since her divorce, music's become very important, connecting her with her feelings as she strums the guitar and writes her own songs. And what she's learned is this: Simply slowing down songs has a way of saddening otherwise hopeful tunes. Now she picks up the song's pace so it's not as sad sounding.

"Twinkle, twinkle," she finally tells Sal.

"Little star."

"No, not the way I sing it." She watches his face in the dim lamplight, his eyes closed but his senses tuned to her. And so she can't miss his smile when he hears the very first line. "Twinkle, twinkle," she sings in a breathy voice, "ocean star."

Seeing him react, and how he relaxes further with her take on the song—it all makes staying in tonight special. She continues moving her fingers over the strings, now and then working the slide noise of her fingers on the fret right into the melody, as though the sound comes from her fingers sighing while changing chords.

Twinkle, twinkle ocean star … How I wonder what you are.

Floating on the sea, so light … Like a diamond, shining bright.

Twinkle, twinkle ocean star … How I wonder what you are.

The gentlest of sea breezes ruffles the lace curtains as she sings, the crickets chirp steady outside the window, while her fingers move like shallow, shallow waves, and the song beckons the magic of stars above, and atop the sea.

thirty-eight

It's the guitar that does it again, Saturday night in Foley's back room. Everyone in the crowded booths stops—midsentence, mid-drink—and turns toward Celia's sudden, quick strums. She sits on a stool near the dance floor, her long gauze skirt sweeping the top of her sandaled feet, a beaded necklace draping against her fitted tee, while the guitar rests across her lap. Above her, crepe streamers crisscross the ceiling, and off to the side, a bouquet of blue balloons rises. Even the pinball tournament in the corner quiets—the flippers stilled, the ball-in-play hitting a mushroom bumper before steadily rolling down the drain.

But the clapping begins when the lights dim and Elsa enters the room, wheeling a cart topped with a massive birthday cake all aglitter with tall, thin candles and a flickering sparkler on each corner.

"Ma," Sal says, setting down his glass of water near the pinball machine and walking across the room in his suit jacket over cuffed jeans, boat shoes on his feet.

But he stops when Celia strums the opening notes of *Happy Birthday* on her guitar. She pauses to point to Lauren—who is walking across the room, wearing a denim vest over a sleeveless floral-print dress, a crescent tambourine in her hand. Lauren moves just behind Celia and waits until Celia gives her the sign, pointing to her again, to begin.

"*Tanti auguri a te,*" Lauren sings, her voice soft and soulful, the words coming slow. "*Tanti auguri a te.*"

Jason, standing at the pinball machine in the back of the room, crosses his arms in front of him and grins. From the tune Lauren is perfectly carrying, accompanied by Celia's strumming, there's no doubt that the song is *Happy Birthday*, in Italian.

"*Tanti auguri, Salvatore,*" she sings, lightly jangling the tambourine. Celia improvises a few bars on the guitar, her fingers moving over the strings in a way that brings tears to several people, until she stops and glances at Lauren with a slight nod. "*Tanti auguri a te!*"

At first, Jason thinks the sharp whistle breaking through the applause is from Kyle, until he turns and sees it's actually Sal's friend from New York, Michael Micelli, his eyes moist, his smile wide.

"Come on, everybody," Elsa calls out. "Gather round."

"Hell, I already know I want seconds," Jason's brother-in-law, Vinny, says while heading for the cake, its white icing edged with strawberries and blackberries atop puffs of whipped cream. "I mean, that pastry is friggin' sinful."

"Get in line, after me," Nick tells him. "Didn't you hear the new beach rules? Security guards get to cut."

Kyle gives Vinny's gut a faux punch. "Looking fit and trim there, Vincenzo."

"I'm telling you, Kyle. It was so hot in Florida, I need a vacation from my vacation. I must have sweat off five pounds."

Coming up behind Sal at the cake, Jason swings an arm across his shoulders. "Make a wish, man."

Problem is, the way the thirty-six candles burn, each flame flickering in the dimly lit room, he'd almost need a strategy to blow them all out. When Sal bends with a deep breath, Michael moves closer to help, motioning discreetly for Jason to join in.

"All right!" Eva says while snapping a picture of them huffing and puffing. Then she gives Sal a birthday hug. "What'd you wish for?"

"Can't tell," he says with a wink to Celia beside him. "It's a secret."

"A secret?" Kyle shakes his head. "You know what that means around here."

"What's that?" Michael asks.

Kyle looks him straight on. "There *are* no secrets at Stony Point. So whatever Sal's secret wish is, we'll all know it within two weeks."

It's quick, when it happens. But Jason sees it—the way this Micelli throws the briefest glance at Sal, who catches it and gives him a slight shrug in return—leaving Jason wondering just what it is the two of them know.

~

"Please, the guest of honor—my son—sits here." Elsa motions to the center booth. "And Michael," she adds, "you and your lovely wife, Rachel, please join Sal and Celia."

Before they do, Michael taps Sal's shoulder. "Come on, guy," he says, and when Sal slides out of the booth, Micelli embraces him, slapping his back as he does. "Many more, my friend. Many, many more."

"It's a deal," Sal agrees with a firm handshake as they take their seats. "I can't believe you made the trip from the city. Damn, what a surprise."

And this is what Elsa likes about serving the cake; she gets to mingle among the booths and hear all the banter, and birthday wishes, and fond memories.

Remember the setback tournaments? And the time we swiped the moose head? How about planning Eva and Matt's shotgun wedding? Oh, my parents were so mad! Eva recalls. Or that Fourth, when we got half lit here before stealing the commissioner's boat? Commissioner? Jason asks. Don't even talk about beach commissioners. This new one's a real piece of work.

"He's not that bad, is he?" Celia asks now from her seat beside the open sliding window.

And Elsa knows, as she sets down their plates of cake, that on some level, Celia's coming to her defense.

"Just ask Elsa," Jason suggests. "She'll tell you a story or two."

"Oh, I'll bet." Celia raises a forkful of cake to Elsa in a toast, not even trying to hide her smile.

"Yeah, but the worst memory?" Lauren interrupts. "It has to be two summers ago when Scott showed up here."

"Scott?" Celia asks from the booth behind Lauren's.

"Who's Scott?" Sal asks Maris, who is sitting with Jason in two chairs pulled up to his booth.

"My fiancé at the time." Maris sinks her fork into a piece of cake. "I was living in Chicago, but staying here for a month or so to settle my father's estate. Scott surprised me with an unexpected visit."

"And that was a *bad* thing?" Sal asks.

"You don't know the half of it," Kyle adds from the booth behind him as Elsa sets down an extra-big piece of cake for him. "We were partying right here in this room that night. Illegally, I might add."

"And Maris was practically sitting in Jason's lap when Scott and I walked in," Matt manages around a mouthful of cake and berries and icing.

"Oh, *merda*!" Michael says, shaking his head. "What the hell happened?"

"Let's just say the best man won," Jason tells them all, lifting his beer bottle in a toast.

It's these raucous good times, like the laughter and wolf whistles that follow Jason's pronouncement, that keep Elsa smiling. That, and her own personal memory in this room now, too. All she has to do is glance at the wall near the doorway to feel tingles of giddiness.

But it's the gifts for her son that move her the most. Elsa squeezes in at Eva's booth when Vinny offers her his seat, and she sits beside Paige, Jason's sister. She has a clear view to Maris handing Sal a present from the stack of gifts, but leans across the table and quickly asks Eva, "Where's Taylor tonight?"

"She's babysitting at Lauren and Kyle's."

"Tell her I missed her." The gifts get her attention then, as Sal works on opening the first.

"For a toast to the good life," Rachel says when Sal unwraps a bottle of Italian wine from her and Michael.

"It's the finest prosecco, to toast some special occasion," Michael explains. When he stands and leans over the table, so does Sal, and they hug once again. "Crack it open on a day to remember."

"Life has been *very* sweet lately, so it'll be hard to pick one special day," Sal says when he sits again and opens the next gift, from Celia. "And with this," he adds about the portable sun canopy for his row-boat, "everything's made in the shade."

Sitting beside him, Celia whispers, "Love you," before giving him a kiss. A kiss that Sal keeps going, his hands rising to her face and slipping behind her neck.

"Get a room, kids," Matt calls out, which starts the whistles up again. "And I guess Elsa can arrange that now!"

And Elsa sees it, the way Eva slaps her husband's shoulder, before entwining her arm through his and leaning close.

"Now we're talking," Sal says while peeling the wrapping paper off his gift from Lauren and Kyle.

"You need your own equipment, man," Kyle tells him. "You like it?"

"Like it? Awesome." He gives a mock cast of the brand-new fishing rod. "Really awesome. And this lantern?"

Elsa's not sure why, but Sal catches Lauren's eye when he holds it up. "Perfect. Absolutely what I need for cruising on that rowboat of mine, exploring the coastline's hidden nooks and crannies."

But the next gift takes the cake, the way it gets everyone buzzing as they all want him to pass it *their* way: a large driftwood-framed photograph of the friends, gathered together around a bonfire on the beach. And Elsa thinks it could only come from Maris, with the way she cherishes family after missing one for most of her life. Sal gets out of the booth and walks to Maris, taking her hand as she stands, too. "Thank you, cousin." He kisses her cheek and she just nods, teary-eyed. "And you, too, Jay."

Jason looks quickly to Maris, then stands and hugs Sal. "Happy birthday, Salvatore," Jason says. "I'll never forget that day you arrived. Shit, you were so damn arrogant and cocky as hell, getting out of that cab."

"Some things never change," Micelli says. "Like when I pulled him over on his scooter in the city a few years back. Thought he was king of the streets." Michael raises his beer bottle to Sal. "Wall Street, anyway."

"Now that was a long time ago," Sal says, laughing. "Before this salt air settled me down."

"Speaking of time," Jason says. "I've got a little something for you, too." He walks to the gift table and brings over a tall, wrapped box. "Careful, guy. It's fragile."

Sal takes the present and stops, staring at Jason. "You didn't." And when Jason merely nods at him to open it, Sal sits again and slowly tears off the giftwrap. But it's when he lifts out an exquisite pewter hourglass that the entire room goes silent.

Until Maris reaches for Jason's arm. "Jason?"

"It's okay," he whispers to her, putting his other hand on top of hers and giving a squeeze.

Sal tips the hourglass over to get the grains of sand flowing, then sets it on the booth table, just as Michael lets out a long, low whistle. "But your mother gave this to your dad," Sal says, looking over at Jason. "After 'Nam. It belonged to him."

"Not anymore." Jason lifts his drink, holds it up in a toast, then takes a swig.

"You have no idea what this means to me," Sal says, touching the pewter hourglass. "Time."

"For the man who has everything," Jason explains. "It's yours."

"And now it's time to christen the back room's newest addition," Sal announces. "Maris, I'm so happy to have met you and Eva this summer, the best cousins ever. And I'm allowing you both the honor of choosing the very first song on my mother's new, vintage jukebox—delivered in the nick of time, no less."

"You pick, Maris," Eva says from where she sits cozying up to Matt. "You and Jason."

So Jason takes Maris' hand and leads the way to the golden light of the jukebox. Looking through the glass dome at the record selections, Jason hears the talk, and especially the bursts of laughter, in Foley's back room. Standing beside Maris, his eyes close while listening for Neil, too, for the clatter of drumsticks on a tabletop as his brother grows impatient for a song to begin. Instead, he hears Matt waving off Kyle's arm-wrestle challenge, telling him again that Kyle's *twice* the size of him, prompting Nick to take the dare. And the women's voices—Lauren, Rachel and Elsa—deep in conversation about sketching beach scenes, apparently a serious hobby of Michael's wife, Rachel. All of it hovers like a mist behind him, evoking decades-old images he'll never forget, and that he'll always have, here.

"Babe, it's our song." Maris points to a selection behind the glass. "*Glory Days*."

Jason pushes the buttons, and when the record drops into play, he takes Maris in his arms with the opening licks, the drum picking up the beat. In the dark room strung with twinkly lights for Sal's party, that song is the magic that gets every booth to empty and the friends all on their feet. For Jason, it's the song he fell in love with Maris to, fourteen years ago, dancing on Foley's deck.

Which gives him an idea. He motions for Maris to wait, then grabs a small cast-iron anchor statue from the counter, which he uses to prop open the screen door to the deck. The deck to which he then sweeps Maris when he takes her in his arms again. She had said on that long-ago night that they were living out a memory they would always have. And here it is, come around again, in the stomping and swinging and touching and changing dance partners—Sal to Maris; Jason to Celia; Matt, Eva, Kyle and Lauren all switching it up. Out on Elsa's new deck beneath the stars, nostalgic beach memories come alive with talk about the old days as they relive those endless nights.

And just like those old days, they all join Springsteen, their voices rising in a rocking *Oh yeah, all right*, over and over again until the song ends and folks drift back inside—Matt challenging Sal to a pinball tournament; and Kyle setting up a tomato-sauce taste-off with Michael, warning him that Elsa will want in on this competition, too, with her deck-pot tomatoes.

But not Jason. Someone cued up the next jukebox song—something about sweet lovin' and leaving it all behind—and he's not too keen on letting go of his wife yet. He missed her all summer, thinking of moments like this: slow songs playing, Maris in his arms.

Nick stands in the propped-open doorway, holding a beer bottle. "I do believe a noise ordinance was violated," he yells over the music and talk.

"You really going to start up with that?" Jason asks over Maris' shoulder.

"To quote our new beach commissioner, *The rules are the rules*." Nick holds up his bottle in a toast to the night. "And I'm *off* duty, man, not able to enforce them."

Jason brushes him off, then gently places one hand on Maris' hip, raises her arm with the other, and spins her easily, then pulls her back close.

"Why don't you get yourself a girlfriend and pipe down?" Vinny says to Nick as he waltzes Paige out onto the deck, dancing past them all beneath the summer sky.

~

"Barlow, over here," Kyle calls out later, waving him to the back of the room. "There's only one guy left to beat your score." When he steps aside, Michael Micelli is at the pinball machine, his hand on the plunger, ready to play.

"Hang on," Jason says, leaving Maris with the women chatting over wine spritzers in the center booth. Everyone knows a challenge hangs in the balance. He approaches Michael, standing there in his cargo shorts and NYPD tee, his dark hair showing gray at the temples, his face shadowed, city swagger dripping from his look. "Got a feeling something's riding on this one," Jason tells him.

"What do you have in mind?" Michael asks as the room quiets with the duel.

"Name it."

"This oughta be good," Kyle adds, holding a bottle of beer.

Michael steps back and considers Jason. "I hear you're the best. Word on the street, even in New York, is that you're the architect to snag."

"Is that right?" Jason asks.

Kyle swigs his beer, noting the sheer poker face on Jason. "Remember," he reminds the New Yorker, "you're taking on the Stony Point champ."

"Okay, then." Michael raises his own beer bottle and takes a hit. "I'm wagering a ferry ride."

"A what?" Jason asks.

"Ferry ride. I own a summer cottage across Long Island Sound. At Anchor Beach. A little place a lot like your beach here. Would love to hear your thoughts on a modest redesign."

Jason squints through the dusty light at him. "Well, if the price is right, food is good and dogs permitted."

Michael extends his hand in a shake. "You're on."

"Wait!" Kyle clasps their shaking hands. "I want in on this."

"Me, too," Vinny says, coming up behind them.

"Count me in," Nick says, plate of cake in hand.

"Matt?" Kyle calls out, to which Matt nods. "Five dollars each," Kyle says. "My money's on Barlow. You New Yorkers are pups with pinball."

"What the hell?" Nick asks around a mouthful of cake.

"It's true," Kyle explains. "I read that pinball machines were banned from New York for over three decades. Back in the forties, LaGuardia considered them a form of gambling and ousted them."

When every head turns to Micelli, he begrudgingly nods in agreement.

"So you amateurs have only been playing since the mid-seventies." Kyle lifts his arm to his damp forehead. "We've got a few years on you this side of the Sound."

"Well, let the game begin," Vinny says, just as Micelli pulls the plunger and sets his hands on the flippers, sending the silver pinball into play.

"Ma, do you have a bell?" Sal asks, leaning over the table where she sits with Eva and Maris.

"A bell?" Elsa looks up from her booth seat. "What kind of bell?"

"Do you mean, like, a timer?" Maris asks.

"No." Sal glances at Celia beside him, then holds up his hand as though jingling a handbell. "A bell!"

"A cowbell?" Eva asks, squinting to decipher his charade.

Finally Sal throws up his hands—muttering, *Basta!*—and leads Celia through the room to Jason. "What's the verdict here?" he asks.

"Your pal whipped my ass," Jason admits, shaking Micelli's hand as the guys pay the cop their five-dollar wagers. "Great game, fair and square," Jason says to Michael. "I can maybe get out to your place mid-September."

"That'll be perfect," Maris murmurs, sidling up behind Jason now and slipping her arms around his waist. "I'll be in the city, too, for fashion week."

"Hey, man," Sal tells Jason. "Give me a whistle. I have an announcement."

"That right? What's up, guy?" Jason asks.

"Just do it." Sal motions to Jason's hand. "Whistle."

And so Jason does, hooking two fingers in his mouth and giving a sharp whistle, quieting the room and stopping Kyle and Lauren from heading out to the deck with their drinks.

When Sal's arm lightly comes around her waist, Celia senses this is something big. Sal walks with her toward the glowing jukebox in the front of the room, beneath his birthday streamers, past the Mason jar candles on the countertop, up to the balloon bouquet, where he turns to face everyone. All eyes are riveted to him standing there, a line of perspiration on his temple, his dark hair pushed back, his face—if Celia had to say so—still tired.

"Thank you, everyone, for an amazing birthday. I don't want the night to end without sharing an announcement with you all." Another whistle breaks through the dark, making Sal hold up his hand for silence, the sailor's knot bracelet showing beneath his jacket sleeve. "You people are very special, what a summer it's been," he says. "I don't know if there's something in the salt air here, but Stony Point's changed my life. So much so, I want you to know," he says, pausing to touch Celia's face before continuing, "that I'm moving here. Permanently."

Celia steps back, unable to take her eyes off his face while his words sink in.

Amidst woots and cheers, Sal calls out, "I already put in my notice at work, and just have to finalize some things in the city."

"Sal?" Celia takes his hands in hers. "Is this really true?"

"Absolutely, darling. My plans for what I'll do here are loose still, except for the first year when I intend to make the Ocean Star Inn *thee* most popular bed-and-breakfast on the Connecticut shoreline."

"Wait!" Elsa squeezes past Eva and slips out of her booth. She rushes to Sal and hugs him, tears running down her face. "Why didn't you *tell* me?"

"I *am*, Ma. Right now." Sal bends and kisses his mother's cheek as Eva and Paige come up behind her, giving hugs all around.

Elsa merely nods, laughing through tears and unable to say more as Eva and Paige take her arm and lead her to the kitchen. Elsa's enthusiasm was only the beginning, and it's spreading through the room. Celia has so many questions, but the excited voices calling out prevent her from saying *anything* to Sal.

"After you get the inn established," Kyle yells from where he sits, his arm around Lauren's shoulder, "I have an apron for you at the diner. You can wait tables anytime, goombah."

"No way," Jason says, standing quickly and pointing to Kyle. "*I've* got a tool belt with Sal's name on it already."

But it's Maris' words that finally bring tears to Celia's eyes. Something about the way she says them hits home. Maris walks up to Sal, her arms extended, and takes his hands in hers, looking at him until a hush falls over the room. "Someone once told me," she says then, throwing a telling wink at Kyle, "that Chicago does *not* hold a candle to Stony Point. And I'm assuring you, Salvatore DeLuca, that neither does Manhattan." When she hugs him, only Celia and Sal hear her emotional words. "Welcome to our little corner of the world."

As Maris says it, Celia wipes her own tears. Elsa comes back into the room then, pouring champagne, filling flute after flute with the sparkling wine. After Eva gives everyone a glass, Celia sees each one being raised high, the liquor glimmering in candlelight.

Sal tips his glass to Celia's, saying the words she's been waiting to hear. "You're my true reason for staying, Celia. My one and only," he whispers as he bends and kisses her. "I love you, too."

When the jukebox starts again and the needle touches the vinyl, Sal takes her in his arms and only the two of them slow dance, their bodies close, the folds of her skirt swirling. Someone shuts off the lights—Jason, she thinks—making the strung twinkling lights look like starlight.

And Celia never wants to leave, never wants to walk out the door of Foley's old back room again.

thirty-nine

Elsa's cottage is quiet on Tuesday morning. Celia walks through the living room hearing the swish of paintbrush bristles as Lauren adds coastal details to the staircase mural. "Have you seen the measuring tape?" she asks Lauren.

"No. Sorry, Cee. Maybe it's in the kitchen, in a junk drawer?" Lauren suggests, still painting.

But Celia already checked the kitchen when she jotted decorating notes there. She walks through the living room holding her clipboard and goes out the front door to find Elsa. It's surprising how warm the morning has already gotten, with the air inside the cottage cooler still.

"Hey, Elsa," Celia calls out when she spots Elsa on her knees, writing an inspirational chalk message on the stone patio. "What's the thought of the day?"

Clutching a thick piece of chalk, Elsa's hand moves in a grand cursive. "The gentle sea breeze," she says while writing, "keeps life at ease."

"Beautiful!" Celia watches as she finishes up with a blue swirl of chalk beneath the words. "Listen, I wanted to take room dimensions for my decorating notes, but I can't find the measuring tape. Have you seen it?"

Elsa sits on her haunches, eyeing her handwritten message, a finger to her face. "I remember Salvatore had it, getting a window size for Jason." In the bright sunshine, she squints over her shoulder at Celia. "Check Sal's room, it's probably there."

"Will do." Celia hurries inside to the upstairs bedrooms, stopping on the way to chat with Lauren. For the first time, Celia notices one of the seaside views in particular and realizes it might be the view from the secret shack. "Your painting is so realistic," she tells her. And from her beach friend's soft expression, it's apparent that personal memories inspire much of this artwork. "I love what you're doing here, Lauren."

"Thanks, Cee." Lauren shifts her kneepad and adjusts her position. "I've never painted anything this large scale before, so it's been challenging."

"And gorgeous. Elsa loves it, too. She sent me up to Sal's room," Celia says while climbing the stairs. "The measuring tape should be in there."

"Oh, good!"

"Where are your kids today? With Kyle?"

"No, he's back to work this week, and it's crazy busy with the outdoor patio in full swing. The kids are at Parks and Rec, taking a beach-exploration walk this morning."

"Nice, it's a good day to be close to the water." Celia continues up the stairs. "That sun is so hot." She heads down the hallway then, toward Sal's bedroom. The measuring tape is right where Elsa said it would be—on his dresser. Celia sees it as soon as she's through the doorway, where she stops and takes in the darkly paneled space. A red-and-cream checked quilt covers Sal's bed, which is under the slanted ceiling of an eave, the ceiling accented with wood planks and beams. A lamp and wristwatch are on a plain bedside table, along with the inn's printed business plan.

But as she goes quickly to his dresser for the measuring tape, something else distracts her. Grabbing the measuring tape, she begins to walk away, then turns back. All the while, a voice in her head admonishes her, *No! No! Don't do it.*

Problem is, there's no way she can listen. The temptation to look is too strong. Beside Jason's pewter hourglass on the dresser, there's a little velvet box—and maybe it's that tiny size that intrigues her—small enough to take a speedy peek inside it. For a moment, she merely holds the box in her hands, her eyes closed as that inner voice still whispers a warning.

A warning disregarded when she lifts the box lid and gasps, never quite expecting what she sees.

—

"Gallaghers' have a nice home," Jason says as he pulls the golf cart into their driveway. The two-story Dutch colonial sits on a big yard, with the marsh spread out behind it. "It's a work in progress, though. I've been doing small jobs here and there."

"Wow, what a grand old place." Sal gets out of the golf cart, the hammer and pliers and wrenches and chalk line and screwdrivers in his tool belt clanking and creaking as he takes in the view.

"Hey, guys," Eva calls from the front porch door. "Come on in."

They follow her inside as she leads them upstairs, past a large, scrolled mirror on the wall, to the pull-down attic ladder. "Matt *really* wants a media room here. Well, he *calls* it a media room so that I'll agree to it."

"So what is it really, then?" Sal asks when they climb the ladder.

"Sports room, guy. A genuine man cave, which I wholly support. Not to mention," Jason adds, throwing a wink to Eva, "it'll get him out of your hair."

"That's right. And I'm sure this'll be a sports *shrine* by the time you two are done with it." She squints at her watch in the dim attic space. "Hey, it's Tuesday, right?"

"Last I checked," Jason tells her.

"Which means I have to show a cottage. So Matt gave you the room details, right?"

"Got them all here." Jason pulls a tablet out of his leather tote. "You'll want to replace that ladder with a staircase, so it meets the building code."

"Definitely." Eva turns to leave. "Can you guys let yourselves out?"

"Go ahead," Jason says, waving her off. "I'll take a few measurements and be out of here in no time. We'll lock up for you."

"Great," she calls back while rushing down the steps. "Oh, and Jason?"

He looks down the ladder to where Eva's stopped at the bottom. "You can drop the dog off Friday morning, before you hit the road. Okay?"

"About eight sound good?"

"Perfect."

"What's happening Friday?" Sal asks once Eva leaves.

"Maris and I are going away for the weekend," Jason says, noting ceiling height and a possible new dormer in his media room file. "It's our wedding anniversary, remember?"

"No shit."

"And the next weekend, I've got an expo in Boston, for business. Barlow Architecture needs to stay up on the trends."

"You're busy, man. You ever take time off?"

"No rest for the weary, Salvatore. And with that Hammer Law squelching construction, I squeezed in the trip."

"So I won't see you after this week. Not for a while, at least."

"Really?" Jason looks over at Sal. "You leaving already?"

"It's the end of the month, good time for me to square things away in the city. You know with my apartment, my job. I'm taking the ferry back Saturday morning."

"You'll be gone long?"

"A few weeks at least, Jay. Got a mile-long to-do list of things to close out, moving arrangements to be made. Lots of paperwork, red tape."

"A shame you'll miss the teardown on the hill, then."

"*Damn* it. I will, won't I?" Sal glances toward a window, as though picturing the Woods' cottage from here. "Shit. It's ready to go?"

"I've been finalizing the design all summer. The new cottage will be understated, with classic cedar shingles, peaks, three levels to capture the water view. And the focal point? A stone-sided lower level, picking up the same stonework in a massive chimney."

"Right. Understated."

"You'll see it is, the way I've drawn it up. The mason's using New England granite, and also building a low stone wall facing the water, almost as a fortress against the ocean elements. I'm meeting the demolition foreman there tomorrow morning for a walk-through." As he talks, Jason notes the Gallagher attic's existing windows on his tablet while sidestepping boxes, a table lamp. "As soon as Labor Day's done, down she goes."

"Pity. Would've liked to witness that." Sal opens a dusty trunk and lifts out a pair of brass candlesticks. "Hey, where you taking your wife this weekend, anyway?" he asks while holding the candlesticks up to the light coming in the attic windows.

"North, to Vermont. Same place where we honeymooned, a rustic chalet up in the mountains."

"Sweet, man. You and Maris deserve it." Sal returns the candle-sticks and walks around the attic space, his work boots heavy on the wood floor as he passes taped cartons of Christmas ornaments and blankets and forgotten knick-knacks, as well as old pieces of furniture covered in sheets. "I'm thinking these aren't the only things going to be covered in sheets. Just so you know, Barlow, if a child happens to be conceived on this romantic getaway … I'm calling dibs on being its godfather."

As he says it, Jason looks up from his tablet, gives Sal a shove, then walks past him with his notes.

First, she hears someone clear their throat. Second, Elsa smiles, all while crouched on her garden kneepad, tugging weeds growing beside her hydrangea bushes. Smiles because, somehow, she can tell exactly whose shadow is falling over her.

"Elsa," a voice says.

And now, before she turns, her eyes drop closed as she calms her nerves. *Nonchalant*, she tells herself. *Be cool, Elsa.* Then she looks over her shoulder and lifts her cat-eye sunglasses to briefly peer at him. "Oh. Hi there," she says to the beach commissioner. It's funny how quickly she formulated a plan-on-the-spot. When he nods, she simply lowers her sunglasses again and turns back to her weeding. Let's see how *he* likes being ignored, she thinks, knowing that more than a week has passed since their … kissing escapade. That's right, she's counted the days.

"How've you been?" Cliff asks, stepping around to better see her.

So she sets down her hand cultivator and dabs her forehead. "Fine, thank you." Then, a glance at the bright sun as she stands and presses the wrinkles out of her denim capris.

"Is something wrong?" he asks.

"No." Elsa quickly looks at him and tugs her striped garden apron straight. His silvery hair is nicely mussed, she notices, and he's wearing a red polo shirt over new cargo shorts—anyone could tell they're new by the sharp creases in them. So, he put on a spiffy new outfit to come see her? "Why would something be wrong?"

"You seem much quieter than usual."

"I beg your pardon?"

"Well," he continues with a glance at the cottage scaffolding, "usually you're jabbering on about this or that." As he says it, as if to make a point, his one hand motions this way, the other that way.

To which she says nothing, making him uncomfortable enough to still those hands.

"So your quietness makes me think something's wrong," he explains.

"Hmm. Wrong. Well, if you call *this* something wrong." She points a garden-gloved finger at him. "We actually kissed, remember?"

"Of course."

"So we kissed, and then … nothing. Just business as usual, you stopping by to fine me for some beach violation? Did that kiss even *mean* anything to you?"

He glances away again, no dimple, no twinkling eyes. "As a matter of fact—"

"Oh, my word! You know what? Scram. Leave. If that's how you feel, I'll have Jason forward any necessary correspondence to you." With that, she puts her hands on her aproned hips and tips her head, thankful that her dark sunglasses hide her almost-tearing eyes.

"Elsa," he softly says, more serious than he's ever been. "Whatever you do, stay calm and do *not* move."

"What?"

"Please." He takes two steps closer and leans in. "Shh," he says, slowly leaning even closer, right before he takes a long breath and blows a stream of air directly on her shoulder.

"Good heavens!"

"Elsa." He reaches out a hand to her arm. "You were about to get stung! I'd been watching a yellow jacket on your shirtsleeve the whole time. They say to puff a breath of air on them to move them along, being careful not to spook them."

"Well, why didn't you *say* something?"

"You would've jumped and startled it."

She looks at her bee-less tee's short sleeve.

"I swear," he insists.

She glances at her arm, then twists around to try to see the back of her shoulder.

"Now careful," Cliff says. "Just come here, slowly." He holds out his hands and she places hers in them. "Let's be really sure it's gone." He tugs her, gently.

Elsa walks closer so he can bee-patrol the back of her shoulder, too. He brushes the fabric, then puts his arm around her and turns her to him.

Now? Well now it's all there: the dimple, the twinkle in those blue eyes. "Cliff?"

He reaches a hand to her face and lifts her sunglasses to the top of her head. "You did it again."

"Did what?"

"Didn't give me a chance to get a word in edgewise. Or the bee didn't." His finger brushes her cheek. "That kiss meant the world to me, and I'm here hoping for another." With that, his hand slips behind her neck and he leans in and kisses her, standing near her inn-spiration chalked message about life being at ease beside the sea.

She's not sure if it's the sea, or the way this man is kissing her, deeply. Deeply enough to get her knees weak again. "Oh!" she says, pushing away. Because sure, life is at ease if you're being kissed—*without* an audience.

"What's wrong? Is that bee back?"

"No." Elsa glances at the cottage windows. "But my friends are inside, Lauren and Celia. They might see us."

Cliff reaches up and brushes her shoulder once more. "At least you're safe from that bee." He checks his watch then.

"So that's it?" Elsa asks.

"No. It's just that, well." He takes a quick breath. "Have you had lunch yet?"

"Lunch? It's only after ten. And I'm gardening. I mean, look at how I'm dressed." She motions to her garden clogs and dirt-stained capris. "And my hands, they're chalky. You know, with that graffiti thing I do here," she says, pointing to her chalked message. "And the hydrangeas need a drink, as do the geraniums out back. I bought a new hose, you know. One of those crinkle ones?"

His grin says it all as he simply shakes his head.

"Oh dear. I'm prattling, aren't I?"

He shrugs. Still smiles, too, and that dimple! Beneath those light whiskers covering his cheek. "How about lunch tomorrow, then?" he asks. "I'll pick you up early afternoon and we'll go someplace nice. Indoors … where there are no bees."

~

"Whoa, whoa!" Lauren says. The noise is so sudden and loud, at first she thinks Celia's *falling* down the stairs instead of, well, *flying* down them—the loose blouse over her tank top billowing behind her. "Slow down, girl," Lauren warns when Celia reaches for her.

"Come here." Celia grabs Lauren's arm and rushes to the bottom of the staircase. "Hurry up!" she says, tugging Lauren's hand while heading to Foley's back room.

"Wait, Celia." Lauren pulls away. "Let me put down my things." She holds up her hand and the wet paint from a brush there drips along her wrist.

"Okay." Celia's voice is a harsh whisper. "But quick. *Quick!*"

Lauren sets down her brush and wipes her hands on a rag left on the stairs before meeting Celia in the back room.

"Shh." Celia holds a finger to her mouth, her eyes sparkling.

"What the heck is going on?"

"I have such a secret to tell you!" Celia paces back and forth—past the booths, the jukebox, the pinball machine—glancing out the rusting sliding windows as she does. "Oh, it's a huge one. Promise, *promise* you won't tell anyone?"

Lauren hoists herself up to sit on the countertop. "I promise."

"No, I mean this is a *real* secret." She points a finger at Lauren. "*Not* a Stony Point secret that everyone ends up knowing."

"Okay! I swear, I swear. Now spill it."

Celia cups her hand over her mouth, trying to refrain from laughing, or smiling, or saying too much. Trying to refrain from something, but all the while her eyes give away sheer delight. "I think Sal bought me an engagement ring."

"What!" Lauren jumps off the counter and takes Celia's hand, searching for a ring. "Where is it?" she squeals.

"Shh! Isn't it exciting?"

"But how do you know?"

Celia pulls her over to one of the booths and they sit across from each other. Sunlight streams through the cloudy windowpanes, catching dust particles floating in its beams. Lauren reaches over and slides their window open to let in a waft of warm air.

"Okay, listen." Celia sits back, holding her hands up, palms open. "I was in Sal's room to get the measuring tape, and I saw a tiny little box on his dresser. I wasn't snooping, I swear!"

"Oh, no. Of *course* not," Lauren says with an exaggerated nod.

"No, really. It was just, well, it was *there*. Right in front of me." She leans close over the table. "So I peeked inside." Again, she clasps her hand over her smile.

"A ring?"

"Yes!"

"Well, what did it look like?" Lauren whispers.

"It's sea glass. Blue sea glass!"

"Sea glass? Are you sure it isn't, like, sapphire? The guy's loaded, you know."

Celia nods. "It's absolutely sea glass. Sal knows how much I adore it, we go collecting on the beach all the time. But it has diamonds around it, and the way it shines, oh! You *have* to see it."

"When?"

"Now."

"Can I?"

Hatching an illicit plan, they both look out the window together. "The thing is," Celia says, "I'm not sure when Sal will be back. He's with Jason for a while today."

"Just sit here and keep a lookout. Where's Elsa? I don't need her walking in and catching the help snooping."

"She's down there." Celia motions to the front stone patio. "Pruning her hydrangeas. I'll watch and let you know if anyone's coming."

"Really?"

"Yes! Go! Go!"

Lauren does, running quietly up the stairs—careful to avoid smudging the wet paint—and finding Sal's room at the end of the hallway. She turns in and looks from the bed beneath the eaves, to the window with a straight wooden chair beneath it—a pair of jeans tossed over the chair back—to the dresser, to the tiny box. She clasps her hands together while tiptoeing closer, then stops.

"Okay," she tells herself. This is *so* wrong, and her pounding heart clearly reminds her of that, the pounding the same as when she'd had an affair with Neil all those years ago. "But I'm doing this for *Celia*. Really."

With that, she picks up the box, feels its weight, then looks to the doorway. Nothing. So she lifts the lid to see the frosted surface of a deep sea-blue stone. Her finger lightly touches it, just for a second: a blue *sea-glass* ring, surrounded by diamonds, set on a platinum band.

When her finger slightly skims the lovely blue glass, she swears she can feel it … the very salt of the sea on her skin.

forty

It strikes Jason as ironic. Once the demolition foreman leaves on Wednesday morning, he walks through the Woods cottage alone. It's almost empty; only odds and ends remain, things to be tossed, or free for the taking—an end table, a few dishes, a couple of chairs. But the irony is that the structure is stripped to its bare bones, the same way it began as a bare-bones architectural drawing, years ago. He shuts the door behind him and heads down the hill to his SUV.

At the same time, a familiar golf cart—Elsa's—parks right beside it. With the glare of the morning sun, Jason shields his eyes and squints at the cart, laughing when Sal gets out. Especially when he notices the full construction garb: yellow hardhat, heavy tool belt over Sal's shorts, solid work boots on his feet.

"I thought I wasn't seeing you anymore this week," Jason calls to him.

"Change of plans. Because it's a beautiful day to break some rules, don't you think?" Sal asks as he reaches into his mother's golf cart.

"What are you talking about?" Jason crosses his arms and leans against his SUV.

"Here's the thing, cousin." Sal hands Jason a take-out coffee, doing a quick switch when he mistakenly passes him the decaf. "In my line of work on the Street, I never get my hands dirty. Today? Today, I am, with a tip of my hat to you." He pulls a sledgehammer from the golf cart. "I want the first hammer swing on this very important job." He reaches into the golf cart once more. "*After* we christen it," he says over his shoulder, then turns holding a bottle of wine. "The finest Italian prosecco will work just fine." He gives the sledgehammer to Jason, before retrieving a crowbar from the cart, as well as his own coffee.

"Hey, Sal," Jason says, nodding at the prosecco. "Isn't that from Micelli, the bottle he gave you for your birthday?"

"That's right. He said to save it for a special occasion." Sal hitches his head toward the cottage as he begins walking through its yard. "This is it. I wanted to do this with you before I left for the city."

Jason—holding the sledgehammer in one hand, his coffee in the other—walks with Sal alongside the gray cottage. He points out termite damage in some rotten wood, a broken window, moldy shingles from a roof leak. "But I don't do the demo, Sal, or the construction. I just manage the job if the client hires me as architect *and* general contractor, which this one did."

"I understand that. But under the circumstances, we surely can do a *little* pre-demo work." They get to the patio, where Sal sets down his tools before turning to Jason. "So where do we begin?"

"Let's go inside and finish this coffee first. Too hot out here in the sun." Jason opens the slider—gritty in its tracks—steps into the screened-in room and sits on a threadbare chair.

Sal follows him in and walks around the room, looking out at the view through the sliding windows. "These yours?" he asks, lifting a pair of black binoculars from a wall shelf.

"No, those were left behind."

"So old Maggie Woods was a bird-watcher, then?" he asks, putting the binoculars to his eyes and scanning the beach.

"Bird-watcher?" Jason asks with a short laugh. "She wouldn't know a snowy egret from a great egret. Maggie was nothing more than a busybody. She'd use those binoculars to spy on folks on the beach."

"That right?" Sal adjusts the lens focus and trains the binoculars on families settled beneath umbrellas on the sand. "How do you know?" he asks then, doing some spying himself.

"We'd *see* her while sitting under our umbrella. If the sun hit just right when you'd glance up at the houses on the hill, there she was, huddled off to the side in this very room, those binoculars trained right on us."

"Sheesh, what a creeper. Why'd she do it?"

"Couldn't mind her own damn business. It gets worse, too. Last summer, Maris and I liked to sit on the beach to chill a little, before the wedding. One day when Maris was sketching in her fashion journal, that Maggie actually sent her sister down to spy on us, maybe get her hands on Maris' work."

"You kidding me? She'd *bother* you guys like that?"

Jason shrugs. "Her sister dropped her crappy old beach gear two feet behind us, wheezing and huffing, all out of breath from hauling it from the cottage. The beach was half empty, but she planted herself practically on top of us, watching our every move. Take a look." Jason pulls out his cell phone and scrolls through his photographs. "Here," he says, handing the phone to Sal. "We got in a few pictures, always recording bothersome things like that."

Sal swipes through the images. "Why didn't this Maggie just leave people alone and live her own life?"

"Don't know, and don't care. But rest assured, I have this shit all documented, in case I ever had to press charges."

"Well, come on," Sal says as he gives the phone back and picks up the wine. "This fine Italian liquor will bring good luck and positivity to the new owners."

"Let's do this." Jason opens the rusty slider and motions for Sal to go out ahead of him.

Outside, Sal glances at the dilapidated cottage, then down to the beach. "This is a good spot, right here." He walks to the front corner of the cottage, sets the wine down and pulls heavy gloves from his tool belt, along with a thick mesh bag that he slips the bottle into to catch the glass debris. "Right in view of the beach."

"Go for it, man."

In his own christening routine, Sal holds the bottle up high, then lowers it with his gloved hands and gives it a kiss. He joggles it and turns to Jason. "For you, Jay. For your health and happiness as you work through this project, bestowing the same upon the honest new residents who will live here. May the stars always shine upon you … *Salute!*"

Jason holds up his coffee cup in a toast as Sal swings his arms back. With both hands on the neck of the bottle, he carefully brings it around to hit the corner of the cottage, where the glass shatters and the fine prosecco sprays on the property. "The best to you, Jason," he says, setting the bagged bottle pieces on the patio. "Now let me take the first swing at something inside. If that commissioner tickets you with a noise violation, you put it on my tab."

Jason picks up the sledgehammer and they walk back through the doorway. He follows Sal into the cottage, past stripped-down walls, exposed studs and bare floors.

"Holy wood paneling, Barlow. Is this a cottage or a cabin, man?"

"No shit. Lots of wood, and extensive termite damage, too. That's one of the reasons it's coming down—it's rotting from the inside."

"I'll have to stop home and shower after this demolition shift," Sal says, eyeing the brick fireplace filled with debris and charred embers. He takes the sledgehammer from Jason. "Because I'm having dinner this afternoon with your best man."

"With Kyle?"

"He wants to thank me for helping out at his diner. It'll be hard to connect after this week, I'll be back and forth to the city."

"Really?" Jason pulls out his phone and checks for messages. "He must've texted me, too."

"Early-bird special. He and Lauren got a babysitter." Sal runs his hand along a dusty wall, contemplating his first sledgehammer target. "You coming, then?" he asks, looking back at Jason.

"Huh." Did his best man not include him? Jason checks his voicemail, his text messages. "No, wasn't invited. I guess I'm not on his list." He puts the phone back in his pocket. "Where's Kyle taking you?"

"The Sand Bar. Says I'll like the lobster dinner."

"Ain't nothing like the seven ninety-nine special. Good grub, but seriously? Get ready to be bibbed."

~

The jukebox at The Sand Bar is always playing some bluesy tune, so when you're settled in a dark booth, the time of day doesn't matter. To Lauren, it could just as easily be nine at night, instead of two in the afternoon.

"There he is," she says to Sal, pointing toward the propped-open door where the one hint of broad daylight makes its way inside. Standing in front of that dusty shaft of light, completely silhouetted, is her husband.

"Hey, guy," Sal calls out, twisting around in his seat.

Kyle saunters over and sits beside Lauren, then shakes Sal's hand. "Thanks for coming, what a summer it's been. The Driftwood Café's never been busier."

"My pleasure." Sal clasps Kyle's hand. "Always glad to help out."

"I see you've got the Harley parked outside."

"I do," Sal says, lifting his helmet from the seat beside him. "A bike's fine, but only in good weather. What I really need is a vehicle, and that would be your pickup."

Kyle nods to the waitress as she sets down a seltzer water for Sal and a pitcher of beer.

"I don't get it, DeLuca," Kyle argues as he takes the pitcher and fills Lauren's glass. "You keep pestering me about that truck, but come on, you can buy anything with your bloated bank account, I'm sure."

"Apparently I *can't*, though. You're holding back on the one truck that I want. I'm still waiting for you to name your price."

Kyle waves him off, then clinks his glass to Lauren's before taking a sip.

"Cheers," she whispers, holding her glass up to Sal's, too.

"I'm toasting your truck," Sal says. "Because all I want is to roll around town with those wheels, nice and easy." He takes a swallow of the bubbly water. "When I get back from the city, I'm bringing a bank check with your name on it."

"I'll be waiting for it."

"Seriously." Sal points to the far window along the front of the bar. "I swung through the dealer lot across the street. They had a few decent trucks that were sharp, guy. You can trade up, you know? Being a family man, you need something respectable, and safe."

There's truth to that, and Lauren figures Kyle knows it, so she nudges him. "He does have a point, Kyle."

"All right." Kyle stands and takes his glass with him. "All right. I'll go have a look."

"So, Sal." Lauren sits back in the booth, her two hands wrapped around her glass. "I worked on the stair risers, today."

"I saw. That mural is definitely coming together. Almost done?"

"Pretty soon. I'll be staying at the beach until Labor Day, so hopefully by then. But Sal? *Celia* was at the inn today, too."

"Is that right?" He checks his watch. "I'm picking her up later, maybe take a boat ride to the shack."

"Listen, Sal," she says in a harsh whisper as she leans across the table. "I'm just saying, there are no secrets at Stony Point. You know that, right?"

"So I've heard. Why?"

"Well, especially when someone—Celia—is looking for the *tape* measure?"

He turns up his hands, shaking his head.

"And Elsa sent her to *your* room to find it, your room with a small velvet box on the dresser?"

"*Gesù, Santa Maria!* I didn't put it in the drawer?"

"No."

"Damn. Did you see it, too?"

"Of course! She wouldn't let me leave without sneaking a look."

"I figured as much." He glances over to Kyle, standing window-side, checking out the trucks across the street. "Beach secrets really *are* public information here."

"So when are you asking Cee?" When he doesn't answer, all Lauren can do is raise an eyebrow at him until he caves.

"Okay," he says, wiping his hands on his shorts as though they're suddenly sweaty with nerves. "Okay. I'm proposing when I get back from New York. I want it to be special. And I *thought* it would be a surprise."

Lauren leans even closer. "By the way, the ring is *gorgeous*. But …" She looks to the doorway when Jason walks in. "Good luck picking your best man. There will *so* be a duel for the honor." She nods toward the far window.

Sal turns around to where Jason now stands beside Kyle, who's pointing out some vehicle that's surely caught his attention. So Sal grabs his glass and excuses himself to join his bro friends, apparently having had his fill of wedding talk.

Which gives Lauren the perfect opportunity to whip out her cell phone and text Celia: *Proposal plans in the works. Do NOT let on when you see Sal.*

"Hey, hey," Sal says, putting one arm around Jason's shoulder, the other around Kyle's. "Anything catch your eye?"

In Kyle's wildest dreams, it would be the silver king-cab pickup he points to. "She's a beauty, man."

Sal lets out a low whistle. "Sweet. And how about you, Barlow? Couldn't resist the seven ninety-nine special?"

"Nope. Figured this would be a good party for me and Maris to crash."

They head back to the booth where Maris is already sitting, so they push over another table for more room.

"Ready to order?" their waitress asks, pad and pencil in hand.

"No, wait." Maris interrupts. "Matt and Eva are coming in. I saw them in the parking lot."

"You called them, too?" Kyle asks Lauren.

"*I* did," Maris tells him, "when Jason told me about this party."

"Party?" Sal eyes Jason. "How'd you make a party out of a thank-you dinner?"

"Good enough reason for me," Jason says, clapping Sal on the shoulder. "And where's your girlfriend?"

"Celia? She's doing some work for the inn. I'm seeing her later."

"How about another pitcher in the meantime?" Kyle asks the waitress. "Now that the whole gang's here."

"Refill on the seltzer, too," Sal says, holding up his empty glass.

Eva and Matt hurry in, Eva tucking her sunglasses in her tote while Matt pulls over two chairs. At the same time, Kyle stands and pours drinks all around.

"Wait," Eva says as Kyle sets down the pitcher. She nods to the doorway. "Two more."

Everyone turns at once. Then? Well, then you could hear a pin drop. "What are *they* doing here?" Kyle asks upon seeing Elsa, wearing black capris and a white tie-front blouse, standing with the new beach commissioner and squinting around the dimly lit bar.

"No way." Jason looks again. "Are they a *thing* now?" he asks Maris.

Maris shrugs, hands turned up.

"*Ciao,* Ma!" Sal calls out while waving them over.

When Elsa spots the crowded table watching her, Kyle can't believe what he sees and leans close to Lauren. "She's actually blushing."

"What's up, lovebirds?" Eva asks, sneaking a wink to Elsa as the couple nears.

"What?" Elsa throws a quick glance at the commissioner. "No. No, it's not *that*." She takes his hand and turns to him, then back to the still-riveted gang. "You all know Cliff Raines, from the beach."

"And he's looking mighty dapper, too," Kyle whispers to Lauren.

Clearing his throat, Cliff steps forward. "It's business, folks. Discussing broken ordinances filed against Mrs. DeLuca's inn."

"I'm sure you are," Jason tells him while giving him a wary once-over.

Kyle leans to the side and drags another chair closer. "You're just a cheap date, Cliff, booking the seven ninety-nine special." He motions for Elsa to have a seat.

"I honestly didn't think *anyone* would be here at this hour," Elsa explains as she sits beside Kyle at the pulled-over table. "I mean, it's two-thirty, kids!"

"Well, our secret's out now. And so's yours. So grab a seat," Sal tells Cliff, nodding to an empty chair. "Join the party."

"What are we celebrating?" Cliff asks as he gets comfortable beside Elsa, his hand discreetly taking hold of hers.

"The last supper," Kyle explains, "before Salvatore heads to Manhattan to close up shop there."

"Since Jason and I won't be around this weekend to see him off, today's the day," Maris explains.

Sal checks his watch again. "Fair warning, I can't stay too long. I'm meeting up with Celia afterward. Taking a beach walk tonight, which is why a two-thirty dinner suits me fine."

"And I've got the late shift at the diner, have to get back there," Kyle adds.

Sal nods, then motions for the waitress.

"So you're headed to the city," Cliff says to Sal. "Catching the train?"

"No. I'll take the ferry across the Sound. My friend Michael, he's picking me up on the other side. He'll drive me in."

"Oh, right. Michael of the *Best Garden in Queens* fame?" Kyle asks, air-quoting the words. "I've got some frozen tomato sauce for you to bring back to that dude. I'll put it in a small cooler. He needs to know exactly *whose* sauce is boss."

"And that'd be mine," Elsa chimes in. "I'll send some over."

"What?" Kyle squints at her. "Mine's better, I'm sure. Don't even waste your time."

"Oh, Kyle," Sal says under his breath. "No. Don't go there, don't."

"*Better?*" Elsa asks, sitting up straight and tugging her gold star necklace. "Why don't we have our own tomato taste-off? You and me."

"You're so on," Kyle tells her, tipping his glass to hers.

"Pasta dinner with everyone at the inn," Elsa says. "Sometime in September, when Salvatore's back. I'll text you all with the details."

"We'll be there," Jason says. "Wouldn't miss this one for the world."

"Here we go, folks," their waitress announces while setting down a handful of napkins and silverware. "Ready to order?"

"Sal, you're my guest today," Kyle says, nodding to him and raising his glass in a toast. "For lending a hand at the diner this summer." After glasses clink and cries of *Hear, hear!* ring out, he tells him, "You order first."

Sal reaches across the table—the sailor's knot bracelet on his wrist—and picks up a menu. "A good friend told me I can't go wrong with the lobster special."

And Kyle can tell one thing by the way Sal says it; it's obvious by the smiles and easy quiet then. Every person sitting crammed around the pushed-together tables in that dark bar—with vinyl-padded booth seats, and a jukebox always playing while piecemeal traffic sounds make their way past the propped-open door—each one of them believes that *they* are that very good friend.

forty-one

I LOSE TRACK OF TIME with you."

Celia feels the way Sal squeezes her fingers when he says it. They walk barefoot along Stony Point Beach that evening, the setting sun's rays turning the sand gold and pink. Gentle waves lap at their feet and a seagull swoops low, caw-cawing as it skims the water. It's true, she knows it: Time somehow idles when they're together. "I can't believe you're leaving for New York in just a few days."

"It'll take a while to wrap things up. My apartment, banking, post office notices, the whole routine. But I hope to be back early fall. It'll be beautiful here, Celia. Our own private paradise."

"*Perfezione.*" Celia reaches up and gives his cheek a quick kiss. "How nice that everyone showed up at your dinner with Kyle."

"It was a surprise, let me tell you. Though I suspected all along Jason would crash it. But seeing my mother there, with a date, no less, that took the cake."

"Elsa's so cute."

"And more than a little embarrassed to be caught red-handed, going out with the commissioner!"

They continue strolling the beach, and Celia looks out at the horizon. "I can never decide which I like better," she muses. "Sunset, or sunrise."

"Hmm. If I had to pick, I'd go with sunset."

"Really?"

"It's the close of another day, good or bad. A sunset's like a gift, giving us time to pause and reflect on our choices. So that the next day, we live without regret."

"Oh." They walk along quietly. "I like that thought."

Sal cuffs the sleeves of the faded denim shirt he wears over a tee, then picks up a few flat stones and rinses them in the lacy froth of a breaking wave.

"But I'm still torn," Celia continues. Shades of violet turn the distant sky inky. "The colors are deeper in the evening. But in the morning, when the sun rises over the sea? Oh, the way those ocean stars sparkle on the surface!"

"My mother's favorite time of day, absolutely." He moves behind Celia and wraps his arms around her as they face the sea. The Gull Island Lighthouse beam sweeps over the Sound, catching a slow-moving barge in its path.

"Knowing Elsa's story, I'd have to side with her. As beautiful as this is, there are no stars. Not in the sky, *yet*, and not on the sea. So I choose the stars of sunrise."

Sal does something then, giving her a perfect summer memory—mostly because it's blended with the salty air, and the sea breeze blowing wisps of her auburn hair and brushing her skin. He presses a kiss on the side of her head, arms still around her, such that she turns her head to his, kissing him at the water's edge. A beach kiss.

"Here," he tells her when they're drawn to that setting sun once more. He drops a few stones in her palm, then circles his finger over her skin there. "Let's skip a stone and make a wish." Giving a side-arm throw, he skips the first. It skims the dark water with only two small jumps. "Kyle says anything over three skips is a *guaranteed* wish come true."

"Do you believe him?" Celia asks while throwing a stone, which plunks into the water.

"Believe Kyle? Of course I do. That's the magic of life, beach stones and summer wishes and sunsets." He joggles another stone in his hand. "Got my wish ready," he says, then throws the stone low over the water, squinting to count the skips. "Three. Not enough. Your turn."

Okay, so Celia looks up at the sky to make a wish, then gets into position, turning sideways, bouncing on her slightly bent legs, her bare feet pressed into the damp sand. She hooks her finger around the flat stone, pulls her arm back and gives it her best.

"*Gesù, Santa Maria!*"

"Oh, wow. Look, Sal!"

"I am, I am."

Her stone flicks along the rippling surface of Long Island Sound as though skating across it. As it does, the water behind it sprays up in a small silver plume, trailing behind the skipping stone. "A star," she says, surprised at the tears blurring her vision. "It's like a shooting star."

"I hope it was a good wish," Sal tells her as he adjusts the cream-colored cardigan draped over her shoulders. Then he takes her hand as they continue walking the crescent-moon-shaped beach, where a lone cottage stands on the far end—its windows gold with lamplight, a family sitting on the deck. "Because that one's definitely coming true."

Her voice is quiet and her step slows when she makes out his rowboat floating in the distance. "I think it just did." The boat's anchored very close to shore and filled with a small cooler, an illuminated lantern and a light blanket.

"The tides are high, darling." As he says it, she slips her bare arms into the sweater sleeves to keep off the sea damp, then shifts the sandals looped around her fingers to her other hand. Sal helps her wade out in her denim cutoffs and steadies the boat as she climbs aboard. And though the tide is high, the sea is calm—like it's gone tranquil just for them.

Sal starts the engine and the boat putters out deeper. When it rounds the bend past the rock jetty to the woodsy area of Little

Beach, he turns off the engine and paddles beyond it, the rest of the way. The oars creak, the water drips, and Celia doesn't think anything can be more peaceful.

"I'll be returning to Addison right after Labor Day," she says. "Fall is a busy time of year for me, the staging jobs are already lining up before the holidays."

"Addison is close, not even an hour away, so it won't be bad driving back and forth. We'll make it work, Cee."

"We will, I know. A couple weeks ago, the thought of leaving made me so sad. But now? Having Elsa's beach inn as an ongoing project, and knowing that you'll be here soon, I couldn't be happier."

Sal dips the oars and pulls back on them. After he anchors the rowboat in shallow water, he hops out first, his distressed denim shorts rolled enough to not get too wet. He hooks the cooler strap over his shoulder, lifts the lantern to light the way, then helps Celia ashore. His hand never leaves her arm, guiding her through the small waves splashing at her ankles.

But it's on the dune trail that a certain misty magic settles. The low sun casts its final light on the wild grasses as they walk the winding sandy path. A whispering comes from a breeze moving through the yellow wildflowers and cascading grass pressed against the old storm fence. It's that pastel time artists capture on canvas, each brushstroke sighing like the wind.

Time does stop for Celia then, when they crest the final dune. Down below, waves break on the twilight beach. She pulls her cardigan close, feeling Sal's hands come around her waist as she does. The secluded path opens to the gray shack, where clustered lobster buoys hang from its weathered shingles. Seagulls soar on a wind current coming off the water, and more sweeping dune grass rises alongside the hideaway.

After a moment, Sal raises the illuminated lantern and moves in front of her—his dark hair windblown, his denim shirt loose over his tee—then turns back and reaches out his hand for hers.

forty-two

Though calm seas rarely make a skilled sailor, Elsa is quite content with her smooth-sailing Stony Point life. No waves jarring the boat, no strong winds setting her off course, no turbulent waters to fight through. Sparrows and chickadees twittering outside the kitchen window are the perfect soundtrack to her Friday. Lord knows, days like these are few and far between. But that's how she's felt since Sal left for New York, knowing he'll soon return: that life's suddenly become smooth sailing. In fact, when he gets back, there's one thing she wants to do: go out for a ride with him in that old rowboat. He seems to love toodling on the Sound, and she hopes to join him on a clear September evening, maybe paddle through the marsh to see the swans. That marsh is so special at this time of year; it was September the last time she was there with her sister, June, and all the fireflies rose, twinkling like stars from the whispering grasses.

But for now, she gives her windowsill herb pots a quick spritz and checks her watch. Jason called from Boston earlier. He wants to meet her next week to show her the latest cedar-shingle samples from the building expo. *I'm loaded down with coastal brochures, Elsa, which I'm sure you'll dog-ear extensively for the inn*, he'd said on his voicemail. *Get back to me with a time good for you.*

So Elsa sets her big daily planner on the kitchen table and opens it to the day: Friday, August twenty-eighth, a week since Sal's left.

And he won't be back for a few more weeks, so anytime Monday or Tuesday would work to look at Jason's hefty haul. They can sit out on the new deck, and maybe she can convince him to stop at the convenience store first, for one of those grilled hot dogs with cheese spread and pickled jalapeños.

"You must've read my mind," she says when her cell phone rings, thinking it's an impatient Jason. So when she picks it up off the counter, she's surprised to see that it isn't.

"Salvatore? Your voice is music to my ears on this beautiful day! How are you?"

"Hey, Ma," he says. "Are you busy?"

"No, not really. I was about to call Jason; he has last-minute inn plans for me. I can't wait to see them and get on with this reno." She sits at her table again, her finger tapping the twenty-eighth. "How's the packing going? Okay? Do you have enough boxes?"

"Ma."

And she knows. Her heart drops and her eyes close for a long second when she tries to hold onto the morning's ease. *Smooth sailing*, she convinces herself.

"Ma, I meant are you busy for the next few days."

"Days?" Elsa asks. "Why?"

"Okay, listen. And I need you to listen without panicking."

"What? Now you're scaring me, so that's impossible!"

"No, no. Wait, because I have to be honest with you."

He stops then, just stops, enough for her to hear his breathing. "I knew it," she whispers. "It was all too good to be true. You coming to Connecticut for the summer, and living at the beach, and the inn. Everything. I just *knew* it." As she says it, she stamps her foot while her eyes fill with tears. "You're not well, are you?"

"Things have happened, Ma, but I *can* be. Except it's going to be a difficult road getting there."

"Damn it, damn it, damn it." She swipes at her tears. "What can I do to help?"

"Okay, here's the thing. Come to New York."

"What?"

"Yes, Ma. Please come, as soon as you can."

"How will I get there?"

"Have Jason bring you. You and Celia."

"Celia?"

"Yes. She's the love of my life, you know that."

"Of course. When, Sal?"

"Right away."

"But Jason's not here. He's in Boston until Sunday, at an expo. Maris tagged along, too."

"*Merda*, I forgot. And I really wanted him here. But okay, just you and Celia, then."

No, no, no. The words expand and fill every thought. "We can't wait for Jason to get back?" she whispers. "It's that bad?"

"Not sure yet."

"Oh no, Salvatore. This isn't sounding good."

"The sooner you and Celia get here, the better. You can catch the Cross Sound Ferry. Remember my friend Michael?"

"Yes."

"I'll ask his wife, Rachel, to pick you up when you arrive. I'm sure she'll do it. They want to help, too."

Everything stops, then. There are no birds chirping, no sunlight glancing her mini-potted herbs, no planned rowboat rides, no Jason, no inn. Nothing. "Sal, this is serious, isn't it?"

"It is. So call Celia and see when the two of you can get here. Tomorrow would be good, actually. For all of us."

"Okay." She glances at the planner on the table, when five minutes ago, each day was bursting with possibility. "What about Jason? I can track him down …"

"Leave him be, Ma. He and Maris have enough on their plate. And it would take too long."

"Are you sure?"

"Yes. Until I know more, I'd rather not worry them."

"Okay, I'll just leave word that I'm helping you pack in New York. But Celia?"

"Celia needs to know. Everything. You can tell her on the ferry ride over."

Change is in the salt air; it's undeniable, moving Celia to slip on a blouse over her tank top and frayed denim shorts. That end-of-summer feeling permeates her cottage like a seaside mist, making her want to—as Sal told her—lose track of time.

The best way to do that is with music. So she sets aside her vision board of inn photographs and magazine clippings, after tacking on one last photo of the infamous Foley's hangout room. She'll get back to decorating ideas later. For now, her guitar beckons, so she straps it on and walks barefoot to the backyard, bringing her cell phone, too, in case Sal calls. The morning sunlight shines on the marsh water, sparkling on the flowing ripples, and the lagoon grasses are more gold now, rather than green … another sign of summer's waning.

Somehow, though, she doesn't mind. Because autumn is promising so much more—of life, of Sal, of inn design work, okay, and of change. She's not certain how much longer she'll actually call Addison home, and the thought scares and thrills Celia at once.

But her mission on this one Friday is simple: to stop time. So she takes a chair from the cottage deck, carries it across the backyard and sets it on the rickety dock. Sal's rowboat is still tied there, the old dock post creaking as the boat rises and falls on the gently flowing water. Beyond the boat, cattails rise on the banks of the marsh, and a yellow finch perches on one of the brown spikes for a moment, before flitting off into the sweeping grasses.

Now it's just Celia, her guitar and the view. She settles on the chair in the sunshine, guitar in her lap, and draws her pick across the strings. The sight of the lone rowboat evokes sweet memories of her and Sal in it, floating on the Sound. Right as her fingers strum *Twinkle, Twinkle, Ocean Star*, her phone rings.

It's an interruption she welcomes, hoping it'll be Sal, checking in the way he does. She picks the phone up from the chair arm and presses it to her ear. "Hello?" As she says it, the happiness in her own voice has her smile.

"Oh, thank God I caught you, Celia."

Silence follows for an alarming second when Celia swears she hears a muffled cry first, then, "It's Elsa."

On Saturday morning, Celia sits with Elsa at a small table on the upper deck of the Cross Sound Ferry. Beneath the golden late-August sun, there's a salty breeze blowing off the water, and Celia takes a long breath. *Cures what ails you*, she remembers, closing her eyes briefly. *If only, if only*. Her sandwich is barely touched on her plate; her coffee grows cold between sips.

"It's interesting the way people are drawn to the water," Elsa tells her. A rolled paisley bandana holds back her thick brown hair as she leans close. "Look."

Celia glances to where several ferry passengers lean on the deck rails, wearing shorts and light jackets and sweatshirts, taking in Long Island Sound before them.

"There's something about journeying on water that's so mesmerizing," Elsa softly says. "You can see it in their faces, the way they're somewhere *else* when they gaze out at the sea like that."

"Oh, Elsa," Celia says. "How I wish *we* were going somewhere else. Or going to New York for *different* reasons."

"It won't be easy, dear. But good things are never easy to attain in this life." Elsa squeezes her hand. "There's a photograph of my mother I'll show you one day. It was taken when she left Italy and sailed to America. She was only fourteen at the time, imagine? And someone snapped her picture as the boat neared Ellis Island. A heavy, long coat hung from her shoulders, and she wore laced high-top boots. It must've been damp on the water, a misty day, because a scarf was draped over her hair and around her face."

"That photograph must mean so much to you."

"It truly does. Maris actually has the picture; she showed it to me recently. And the name of that ship my mother was on? It's right in the image, painted below the rails of the upper deck. It was called *Evangeline.* Eva's name."

"Eva's named after the ship? What a beautiful sentiment."

"And full of meaning, as you can see, beginning my mother's journey across the sea. June, that's my sister, she named *both* her daughters after that image. Maris, meaning of the sea, and of course, Evangeline."

"Maris and Eva," Celia whispers.

Elsa nods. "In the picture, I could always see the hardships Mama endured on that journey—it's in her face. Her eyes are dark, her expression tired … stern, even. Or, I don't know, maybe it's a determination. Because I always, *always* see something else in Mama's dark eyes when I look at the photo." Elsa stops and leans across the table, clasping both of Celia's hands in hers, running her thumb over the sailor's knot bracelet. "There's a spark in her eyes, too, and that spark is one thing and one thing only. It's simply hope, for the life she's sailing to."

"No, don't say it, Elsa." Celia fights back painful tears, the same way she's been fighting them since Elsa called her yesterday. "You're scaring me."

"The life we're sailing to today, Celia, it will be difficult. But for Sal, he has to see that spark." Elsa reaches up and touches Celia's face. "It's a very powerful thing, please remember that. *Hope.*"

forty-three

THE DAYS ARE GETTING SHORTER, especially now that it's September. Sitting at his worktable in the barn studio Wednesday evening, Jason glances at the skylights, gauging the time by the color of the sky: bluish violet. Must be about seven-thirty, the blue hour. He rolls his stool over to the Woods' drawings and pulls his calculator from a desk drawer. The teardown has been tentatively penciled in for the week after Labor Day—first up, window and glass removal. But it won't happen until Jason double-checks things with a final walk-through as project manager. Nothing moves forward without his okay. So this is the point when he reviews all the dimensions on the finished plans. One math error here can cost a lot of money to fix once construction begins.

"Is that yours?" he calls to Maris, mid-calculation, when a cell phone dings with a text message. She's ripping a razor across denim, so a slashing noise comes from her loft, as do thuds from Maddy maneuvering a rawhide bone up there. It's hard to tell whose phone dinged.

"No, yours."

He rolls his chair back to the other end of the big L-shaped desk Maris insisted he buy for his studio, and reads the text. "It's from Elsa," he says, scrolling through the words. "Group text. Did you get it, too?"

"Don't know. My new phone's in the house." More slashing fills the studio space as she continues distressing some pair of jeans that will no doubt be included in her next line. "I thought she was helping Sal pack up in the city for a few days."

"That's what she told me last week, when we were at the expo. Looks like she's back. Maybe she wants to review the brochures and samples."

"Oh, great! Can't wait to see her."

Jason angles the phone beneath his swing-arm work lamp. "No, wait. It's an invitation. She wants a meeting tomorrow. On the boardwalk with everyone."

"What time?" Maris calls down, leaning on the loft railing now.

Jason glances up, seeing the way her brown hair falls forward as she waits, her stained glass wave window shimmering behind her. Was it only a year ago that he surprised her with the wedding gift? "I'll come up and show you," he says.

"No, babe. You stay there." When she rushes to the staircase, Madison does, too, and runs down first—collar jangling.

"Madison," Jason scolds the dog with a scratch on the scruff of her neck. "Where's your manners? You almost knocked over my wife."

Patting the moose head as she hurries down the steps, Maris trots to Jason's worktable. "Let me see," she says, reaching for the phone.

"Look." Jason points out the other recipients. "Matt and Eva are invited. Lauren and Kyle, too."

Maris rests her hand on Jason's shoulder as she stands beside his stool. "Can you make it?" she asks. "Any appointments tomorrow?"

"None that early." He lifts his hand to hers on his shoulder. "We'll go together, and bring Elsa one of her favorite egg sandwiches."

"Seriously? I *don't* believe she likes those."

"You'll see." He glances at the phone again, then to the dog standing at the glass slider now. "I wonder if Sal's back, too."

"You think so? Could be."

Jason walks to the wall hook and grabs his black sweatshirt, slipping it on as he talks. "I'm taking Maddy down to the beach."

"Everything okay? Is your leg bothering you?"

"It's fine, sweetheart. Just haven't moved around for a couple hours."

"Okay. Can you swing by Matt and Eva's after? Eva made fresh eggplant parm and froze a serving for us. Dinner … saved by my sister!" She motions to her design loft. "This way I can call Lily and tell her I'm working here tomorrow, and will be in on Friday. We have to go over whose collections we'll be seeing during fashion week."

"Will do." He checks his pockets. "Do you have the key to the shed?"

"It's over there," Maris says, pointing to a narrow table near the double slider. "Why?"

"I need the push broom, to sweep off the boardwalk for the morning meeting."

Lauren partially closes Hailey's bedroom door. Here in the cottage, her daughter needs her seashell nightlight on and the door open at bedtime. A few more days and, unbelievably, they'll be heading home to Eastfield and their regular routines. The summer flew by so fast. She knocks on Evan's door next. "Lights out, Ev."

"In a minute," he calls back.

When she opens his door, Evan's sitting up on the bed, and, no surprise, some paperback guide to beach life is propped across his knees. "What are you reading about?" she asks, just as her cell phone dings in her back pocket.

"Seaweed, and what lives in it."

She looks at him, all of eight years old and more curious by the day, his hair thick and moppy from a month at the shore. Maybe Kyle can take him to the barber for a trim before the first day of school. "Okay, one more chapter." As she says it, she shuts his door and finds Kyle—a loose button-down shirt over his black tee, his phone in hand—sitting on the living room striped sofa.

"Did you get the text?" he asks over his shoulder.

"I did!" Lauren sits beside him and reads her own phone. "Ooh, I love Elsa's morning meetings. She's always got something fun planned. Can you make it?"

"I'll call Jerry and ask him to open the diner. If he can't do it, I'll try Rob."

"Good." Lauren scrolls through the message. "I wonder if it's another inn announcement. I finished her stair mural and already have ideas for her new sign. *Ocean Star Inn.*" Cool evening air wafts in the living room windows, bringing a touch of fall; but always, always, the salty tang is in it, too. "Or maybe Sal's back?"

"You think so? He's got a lot to do before moving here. The text could just be about our tomato-sauce taste-off."

"Wait." Lauren reads further. "When Elsa sent me an email last week telling me where to find the hidden key while she's away, she *did* say Celia was going with her to help pack." She sets her phone in her lap. "I'll bet Sal proposed! What a ring he bought for Cee."

"Ring?" Kyle looks down at Lauren, reaching his arm around her shoulder and gently twisting a strand of her hair. "What ring?"

But Lauren's too distracted with this early-morning boardwalk invitation to explain. Until Kyle gives her hair a playful tug. "Oh, that engagement ring. It's a beauty. Blue sea glass, surrounded by the most amazing diamonds." She looks up at Kyle and gives him a quick kiss. "But it's a secret, so don't say anything."

"Fine." Kyle pulls up Jerry's number on his phone and calls to ask him to cover his morning shift at the diner. "Some big news planned here at the beach," he explains with a glance at Lauren beside him. "Might be a wedding announcement."

forty-four

Thursday morning, Jason and Maris are the first to arrive. The September sky is golden with the rising sun; the Sound blue and beginning to sparkle. As they step onto the boardwalk, waves lap along the sand.

"Look, it's so quiet," Maris says. "No one's even on the beach."

Jason lifts his sunglasses to the top of his head and takes a long breath while seeing the wide expanse of soft sand and smooth water. "Love it like this."

They find a spot on the boardwalk to sit and set down their coffees and take-out egg sandwiches. As they do, Eva and Matt arrive with a folded card table and an overstuffed tote bag.

"What do you think's going on?" Eva asks as she snaps open the table legs beneath the shade pavilion.

"It's got to be something with the inn," Maris muses. "Maybe Sal's going to manage it full time."

Matt sits beside Jason. "Yo, Barlow, what's in the bag?"

"Sandwich for Elsa. I would've gotten you one, but I figured you'd bring your own food."

"We did. Eva brought raspberry Danish to go with coffee." He points to his wife divvying up the pastry on paper plates.

"Just get out of work?" Jason asks, lightly hitting the State Police emblem on Matt's uniform sleeve.

"No. Going in, after this meeting. Got the day shift for the time being."

"That's good, man. Keep you off the streets at night." Jason hitches his head to Kyle and Lauren approaching from the far end of the boardwalk.

"Hey, guys," Lauren calls out, her patchwork gypsy skirt billowing in the sea breeze.

"How's it going, dude?" Kyle asks Matt while shaking his hand. "Residents behaving themselves in this fine state of ours?"

"They try, that's for sure. Most of them, anyway." Matt stands when Eva motions for him to help distribute her plates loaded with fruity pastry pieces. "Want one?" he asks Kyle before heading to the shaded card table.

"Depends on what Barlow's got in that bag." Kyle and Lauren sit in the sun beside Jason. Maris, on his other side, leans forward and waves hello to Lauren.

"Never you mind, it's for Elsa." Jason moves the bag to Maris' lap. "Didn't you bring any grub?"

"Just coffee." As he says it, Kyle raises his take-out cup. "Ate at the cottage."

"Yoo-hoo! Lauren!" Eva calls from her shaded bench seat while holding up a plate. "Want something sweet? I brought pastry."

"We'll split a piece." Lauren hurries over, grabs a napkin and the raspberry-swirl Danish, and brings it back to her spot. She tears it in two and gives some to Kyle, who bites off half in one mouthful.

"What a beautiful day," Lauren says to them all. "Oh, that sun feels *so* good." She leans her head on the seat back. "I can't wait to hear Elsa's news! Another Stony Point wedding may be in the works, you know …"

"I still think it's the tomato-sauce taste-off announcement," Kyle says around his mouthful of pastry, wiping a crumb off his chin.

"Look!" Maris calls quietly. "I think they're here."

All heads turn to the far boardwalk steps as Elsa climbs them first, followed by two others. Jason squints, then lowers his sunglasses, uncertain about what he's seeing.

"I *knew* Sal would be back," Maris says, squeezing Jason's hand. "They must've finished packing already."

Jason is still watching the others approach with Elsa. "It's not Sal."

Everyone looks more closely, making out Elsa wearing a long, black eyelet tunic over her tank top and white clamdiggers. Celia is in a sundress, her fedora on her head, her arm looped through Elsa's. Off to the side, a step behind, is Michael Micelli. And no one else. Not one of them is smiling.

"Jason?" Maris whispers. "What do you think's going on?"

"Not sure."

Celia and Michael sit on the boardwalk bench while Elsa walks closer, looking briefly at each face. And Jason knows something's wrong, as he guesses they all do. Really, Elsa doesn't have to say a word.

"They call it rheumatic fever."

Elsa pauses after saying it, giving a silence meant for only the waves to splash onshore. They all wait, taking cues from Celia and Michael, who are sitting just beyond Elsa, watching her intently. Jason sees that the past few days have taken their toll, particularly on Celia. Her posture is defeated, her expression drawn, and he's sure that beneath those big sunglasses, dark circles shadow tear-rimmed eyes.

"When he was a boy growing up in Italy," Elsa continues, "Sal came down with rheumatic fever after a serious episode with strep throat. Recovering from strep is one thing, but the difficulty of rheumatic fever is that it damaged his heart, particularly his valves.

So throughout Sal's life, symptoms would come and go like the sea breeze," Elsa says, motioning to the blue sky, "but were mild enough for him to tend to. And I thought—all summer—I *thought* he was managing, with his medications and monitoring. This year, though …"

Elsa stops then, and raises her hand to her mouth—pressing back some difficult emotion. When she does, Jason feels Maris briefly squeeze his hand as Elsa collects herself. "This year, those symptoms worsened considerably," Elsa explains after taking a deep breath. "You could wonder if it was from the pressure of working on Wall Street, but Sal *loved* his job. Thrived on it, actually. So was it fate? An inevitable lifelong deterioration of health? We can't be certain. But Sal's symptoms were serious. Chest pains, palpitations. Breathlessness, which Jason and Celia witnessed when he valiantly saved a boy from drowning here. And fatigue. Which is ultimately what brought him to Stony Point, the fatigue."

When a cawing seagull flies low over the beach, Elsa turns toward the sea. Jason follows her gaze. They all do, seeing the waves lapping on the sand, and a full constellation of ocean stars twinkling on the sea's surface.

"Even I didn't know anything about his deteriorating condition," Elsa goes on then, still looking at the sparkling sea. "Sal kept it all to himself, so as not to worry anyone. Until last week, when he may have sensed something and doubted that decision. Out of the blue, Sal called and asked that Celia and I come to New York, quickly." She walks over to Jason and embraces him. "He *really* wanted you there, too. But you and Maris were in Boston, and so busy. He hoped for the best and let it go."

Elsa paces then, walking slowly on the planked boardwalk while obviously fighting tears. "Sal finally told the two of us everything," she says, patting her heart while looking over at Celia, "last weekend. Which was that after many tests and consultations done privately over the years, the treatment for his compromised heart valves came down to him needing surgery." She takes a long, shaky breath. "Valve replacement surgery." Then she looks to them once more. "But he was tired from working long hours while his health suffered, and when his employer granted Sal an extended medical leave, he came *here.* Apparently, he wanted to spend the summer at the shore to gather his strength and stamina for the operation, and of course, fell in love with everything about this place. But his restful summer wasn't enough. The operation was Tuesday," she says, her voice wavering, prompting Michael to stand behind her, a hand on her shoulder. "Salvatore did not survive the surgery."

With those words, she shakes with grief, her tears follow a sob, and Michael puts his arm around her, walking her to the bench seat and sitting her beside Celia. He bends low, a hand on each of Elsa's shoulders, and speaks quietly to her, after which she simply nods, prompting him to turn to everyone gathered there.

"I'm so sorry to be here under these circumstances," Michael begins, walking closer. "Each and every one of you meant the world to Sal, something he never saw coming. His original plan was to rest up, have the valve surgery, and resume his city life for a while longer before making changes. But then, well, he'd call me with incredible stories of your lives here, and I saw, as the months went on, that New York was losing him to Stony Point. Your magical beach cast its spell on him. All of you did. Celia," he says, turning back to her, "especially you."

"Why didn't he say something?" Kyle asks. "We could've helped. And I never would've let him wait tables."

"Exactly, and that's why he kept it private. He didn't want to put his issues on you, or on all your relationships. If you knew he had health problems, think how different the summer would have been. He didn't want that. Didn't want sympathy, or worry. He just wanted a happy beach summer—that elusive, simple life he was always after. For everyone."

But Jason knew. Damn it if he didn't know all along; he sees that now. Ever since his brother died nearly a decade ago, Jason's tuned in to body language, reading a person's looks and gestures more than their words. It's a tendency stemming from the last horrific moment that he knew of Neil, alive, sitting behind him on a motorcycle—the pressure of Neil's body hitting against his back as a car barreled into them. Though Neil's body was propelled over Jason's head and shoulders, the sensation of the first impact on his back remained, as though Neil had tried, *tried*, to hang on.

Since then, what Jason knows without a doubt is this: What you remember of someone is what you had last.

So now it all spins out of control, every thought of Sal's secret clues: the fatigue; drifting in his rowboat at night; being winded; his obsession with time; the way he disappeared on days when Jason's sure, now, Sal must've been sick. It all comes straight at him, just like that vehicle growing larger in the bike's rearview mirror the day he lost his brother.

Jason looks out to the sea then, where the sun rises higher in the sky. A sun that turns white, glaringly white, with the force of Sal's death hitting him. During the summer, he got to recapture life with his brother; this time, through Sal. Through Sal and his hard hat and construction belt; through an epic motorcycle ride on a blue-sky day; through paddling the lagoon and fishing on the rocks and bullshitting 'Nam. But damn it if there wasn't something else always coming up behind Jason, moving closer, until it finally hit.

And now it's here, Sal's death, as Michael's voice explains. *He had no idea he would fall in love with this place* … Perspiration drenches Jason's body … *Loved you all very much* … His pulse pounds … *Funeral will be at St. Bernard's Church, Saturday* … His breathing is labored when all goes silent. There's nothing, nothing except Jason's hands over his face, pressing against his closed eyes as his world goes absolutely still and silent. Nothing.

"*Jason,*" Maris finally whispers, turning to him and resting her head on his shoulder, her arms holding him close. "Oh, Jason, please." She rocks a little, her arms tightening around his neck, her damp face pressing against his. "*No, no, no,*" she murmurs as though she knows—touching his face—knows that he's fighting a flashback of his brother's death. "It's okay, hon. You'll be okay. I'm with you."

Jason nods, hearing his wife's voice pulling him back, hearing the waves lap again, and the engine of a motorboat out beyond the swim raft and big rock. Hearing approaching footsteps. It's all he can do to stand when he sees it's Michael.

"Jason, my friend," Michael says, extending a hand, then pulling Jason into an embrace. "I couldn't be more sorry that we're meeting like this today."

"I know. Me, too." Jason backs up a step and considers Michael. He looks beat, the story of the past few days clear in his tired eyes. All of it—the hours spent in a hospital waiting room, the moment the doctors brought bad news, the time spent with Sal at the very end—it's there, in the darkness, in the fatigue. "Thank you for coming, Michael, and for helping Elsa, too. Elsa and Celia."

"No problem. I only wish I could do more." They sit side by side on the boardwalk bench. Beyond the sand, the ocean stars sparkle like he's never seen before. Maybe it's because of the September-blue sky with its billowing white clouds, all reflected on the Sound. Or maybe it's the way the waves ripple with the breeze. "You have to know," Michael is telling him, "Sal and I talked the other day before Celia and his mother got there. And he said something to me."

"What's that?"

"That you were like the brother he never had."

And Jason says nothing. He just looks at the water, exhausted and nearly unable to hold himself together. When he glances down the boardwalk, Lauren is hugging Celia, and the others are gathered around Elsa. There are tears, and only sadness. Jason grips Michael's arm first, then lets go and takes Maris' hand. Together they walk to Elsa.

The odd thing is that Elsa seems to know it, the way she moves back from the crowd, her hands turned up as she watches Jason. Are her hands waiting? Are they giving in, resigned to her son's death? Are they seeking divine answers?

But as they approach, there's more. Beneath the tears and sadness on Elsa's face, there is a smile of love and pain in one, as though she hears her son's whisper, somehow—in a memory, in imagination, in spirit. Sal's voice would be soft, and meant only for her.

Oh, Jason knows that look; he can see it, the way Elsa hears the voice and complies, so loyal to Sal's request, whether it was given during their last moments together, or now, carried on the sea breeze. It's there, in her tear-filled smile.

Sorridi.

forty-five

By SATURDAY, KYLE'S WORRIED. FROM the way Jason got through Sal's funeral—holding it together the entire time, his posture rigid, his face dry in a church filled with tears—Kyle can't help but be concerned. During the mass, ceiling fans paddled above, while on a table beside the altar, Mason jars glimmered with seawater in some, flickering candles in others. Kyle's not sure how Jason could look at that seawater and not think of the time he spent drifting on the sea with Sal, and more worrisome, not show any emotion at the memory.

Now, the room Elsa reserved at a local restaurant, serving a catered buffet brunch to the mourners, is bustling. An elegant hydrangea floral spray spills from a white urn near the doorway, beside a large framed photograph of Sal. The seats at each long table are filled with people familiar and not: the extended beach gang; Celia's family, along with her friends Amy and George; Sal's coworkers and city crew; the beach commissioner sitting with Elsa; neighbors and acquaintances; Paige and Vinny. Before the buffet begins, Elsa announces that both Michael, and then Jason, will offer words of remembrance for her son. But still, Kyle has never seen Jason like this, almost detached in his formality.

Standing at Elsa's table, Jason reads from his notes. His hands are steady, tugging his shirt cuffs before starting, holding the paper without any shake. And his voice is nearly monotone as he talks of Sal's assimilation into Stony Point life, showing up at job sites in a hard-hat and tool belt. When Jason speaks of a rowboat ride through the lagoon, Kyle wonders if maybe the quavering voice, the disruption of trembling hands and sad tears came the day before as Jason wrote these words. Did he sit at his dining room table, beneath that big lantern-chandelier, and wipe his eyes after certain sentences? Did he suppress a sob of grief, even for himself, at this deep loss? Did he struggle to find the few small truths that all the mourners would recognize?

Kyle listens as Jason rubs his knuckles to the scar along his jaw while sharing memories with the crowded room: *Sal's ready smile as he fished with me and Kyle; his fondness for mega-watches; his lapsing into Italian at just the right moments.*

Still, Kyle does not *get* how Jason could put his words together and not think, at the same time, that he never had the chance to do this for Neil. Did it feel unfair?

Lauren notices, too, when she leans close to Kyle once they're eating. "Is Jason okay?" she whispers.

"Why?" Kyle whispers back.

"I'm not sure." She glances over at Jason talking to Michael and his wife, Rachel, at the buffet station as Jason adds something to his plate. "Maybe he's *too* calm?"

Kyle looks again. Jason has on his best suit and converses quietly. To anyone who doesn't know him, he would seem fine. But Kyle does know him.

After brunch, Lauren waits in their truck while Kyle winds through the cars in the restaurant parking lot. "Hey, man," he says when he catches up to Jason from behind and puts an arm around his shoulders. "Where you off to now?"

"Home, Kyle. I'm beat."

"Yeah, what a day. So damn sad."

They walk side by side in the bright sunshine through the parking lot, leaving Maris to walk with Elsa. As Jason opens the door to his SUV, he turns to Kyle. "Think I'll close my eyes for an hour."

"You mean, take a *nap*?" Kyle looks away, then closely back at Jason. "Really?"

"Shit, yeah." Jason gets in the vehicle and puts his key in the ignition. "The women are coming by later. Elsa and Eva. You know. To be together and whatnot. Maris and I have to straighten up the house, put away some wedding gifts."

"What?" Kyle sets his hand on the roof of Jason's SUV and squints in at him. "Wedding gifts? From *last* year?"

Jason shrugs. "That's how life's been. Then I'll lie down and rest before getting some takeout for them."

"I'm coming with you." Kyle watches Jason, and doesn't waver in his stare.

"Fine."

"No. Seriously. Don't you be bullshitting me with your *fine*," he warns, air-quoting the word. "And then not show up. What time?"

Jason starts the engine when Maris waves off Celia and Elsa before opening the passenger door. Jason waves to them, too.

"Hey." Kyle gives three sharp raps on the roof. "What time will you pick me up, dude?"

"Where are you going?" Maris asks from the front seat.

"Lauren's going to her mom's to get the kids later, so your husband's taking me with him to pick up dinner."

"Oh, that's so nice of you, Kyle. Jason?" she asks, her hand stroking his arm. "About three, maybe?"

So three it is, with Jason promptly pulling up to Kyle's rented cottage ten minutes early. The cottage they're supposed to vacate by Labor Day, so Kyle steps around packed boxes and luggage on his way out. "Where to?" he asks when he settles in the SUV's passenger seat.

"Ronni's Pizza. Getting a half-dozen grinders."

But Kyle can't miss it, how quiet Jason is. As they drive the winding beach roads and head out beneath the railroad trestle, they barely talk. "Your leg bothering you?" Kyle finally asks.

"Eh. You know. It acts up when things are tough."

"Yeah. Calling today tough would be putting it mildly." Kyle glances out the window. "It's just that I noticed your crutches in the back. Like you might have to rest your, what'd Sal call it? Mon-cone-ay?"

"Stump, Kyle. It's just my stump."

"Okay, then. Stump. Sorry, bro."

When Jason throws him a look, Kyle keeps the talk going and asks him about Elsa. "How's she holding up?"

It's an awkward question, obviously, one that has Kyle run his hand along his damp hairline. Because, hell, anyone could figure Elsa's devastated—the day when she said goodbye to her only son nearly impossible to get through. And Kyle guesses now that Jason's casual shrug is as much of an answer as he's getting. The shrug that comes right before Jason pulls a cigarette from the armrest console.

"Holy crap, you back to smoking *again*?" Kyle asks. "You gave those things up last year, for Christ's sake."

"Yeah, it's just for today. Felt like a smoke."

When they get to Ronni's, they wait inside at a window table while the grinders are being wrapped. The restaurant overlooks a view of scrubby grass and railroad tracks. East Bay glimmers just past the train tracks, then endless Long Island Sound beyond. And wouldn't you know it, by the time the food's ready and they walk across the hot parking lot to the SUV—when Kyle notices Jason favoring his prosthetic leg—Kyle does it. Sitting in the vehicle with the windows down and a sea breeze coming in, he reaches for that pack of cigarettes. And as a train blows past on its way to Boston, screeching and creaking on the tracks, the vibrations carrying in the air, yes, Kyle picks up Jason's lighter and flicks it, then takes a long drag of a cigarette.

"You, too?" Jason asks.

"We'll quit together," Kyle says through a slight cough, wincing at the smoke rising past his eyes.

"Suit yourself, man."

"Listen, Jason." Kyle taps an ash out the window, then takes another drag of his smoke. "How about we do some fishing tonight? Sit on the rocks and remember Sal that way."

"Nah." Jason turns the ignition and pulls out onto the main road. "I'm crashing at home."

"Come on. It's been a helluva day." He holds up his half-smoked cigarette and considers it. "We'll finish your cigarettes, have a few beers, toast the guy. The way he would have liked it. Do the Italian proud, sitting by the water, casting off."

"Another time, maybe."

In his tone, Kyle hears it: Jason's done with today. Straight-up finished, as he drags his folded knuckles along that faded scar on his jaw. Still, there's something too stoic about his friend and no way does it sit right with Kyle. But hell, maybe that's how Jason handles stress.

Until Kyle decides otherwise. Until only a few seconds pass of remembering times like Jason's emotional breakdown on the boardwalk two summers ago, or his rage at finding Kyle messing with a twenty-six-year-old broad when he and Lauren hit a rough patch last summer, not to mention Jason's own tear-filled wedding vows to Maris last year.

It's all enough for Kyle to tell himself *one* thing as Jason drops him off at his cottage, and as Kyle stands there in the yard beside the big potted geranium, pressing his arm against his perspiring forehead and watching Jason drive off.

Jason Barlow, stoic? *Like shit.*

forty-six

THAT EVENING, THE FOUR OF them walk along the water's edge. Elsa carries a bouquet of beach hydrangeas, and Celia holds a large Mason jar. Eva's and Maris' jeans are cuffed; Celia wears a chambray blouse over her sundress; Elsa removes her sandals and walks barefoot in denim capris, a long crocheted cardigan over her tee.

"Come on, ladies," Elsa says as they near the water. "I'd like to think this is symbolic, a way to set Sal's spirit afloat." She gives them each a large blue blossom. "Please, toss it to the wind and let the sea carry it away." With her words, Elsa gently throws her blossom first and watches it drift with the current. The others do the same, first pressing the flowers to their face—Celia actually kissing hers lightly, then brushing her fingers across it. In no time, the four hydrangea blossoms float away, bobbing slightly, their lavender hue deepened by the late-day rays of sun.

Celia watches the flowers shimmer on the water, her sundress fluttering in a gentle breeze. "I've cried so much these past days, I'm plumb out of tears."

"All I can think of is how Sal always said to smile, even when we're sad," Maris says, giving Celia's hand a squeeze. "It's a beautiful thought, though nearly impossible to do."

"You know, Sal had me smiling since our first date." Celia thinks back to that June day as the four women begin walking toward the rock jetty at the end of the beach. "When he took me to the Summer Shindig here. Did that ever even happen?"

"Oh, Celia. I'm just glad that my son got the chance to fall in love, if only for the summer. He was never happier than when he was with you." Elsa takes the Mason jar from Celia. "That's why, today especially, I want to make a happiness jar in his honor."

"I remember decorating Maris' Mason jar candles last summer," Eva says then. "We found the best sand—so soft and flecked with shining mica—right over there, near the rocks." With the setting sun casting a pink glow on the sand, she bends and scoops up a double handful. "Here, Elsa, let me pour it in."

And that's how Sal's happiness jar begins, as they resolve to decorate it with good memories now, spreading out and doing a little beachcombing, a little thinking of Sal. Celia had been collecting pieces of sea glass the entire time and meets up with Elsa. "For Sal," she whispers, cupping one hand on the Mason jar in Elsa's grip. She sprinkles in her frosted green, white and blue sea glass, her eyes welling at the sight of the sea-glass engagement ring on her own finger. Sal would have added that ocean-hued stone to his list of beach blues: the sky, the shimmering Sound, the satiny blossoms of the wild dune hydrangeas. Simple things to make her smile. "I guess I do have a few more tears left."

Without saying a word, Elsa softly dabs the back of her fingers on Celia's cheek before they continue their search for happiness mementoes on the beach. Finally, Elsa picks up a dried stick of driftwood.

"Let me help." Celia takes the Mason jar and holds it for her.

"Salvatore loved to float in that wooden boat on the water. He'd always mention that to me. So this driftwood, which floated in to shore, is for that memory." Elsa stands the stick inside the glass jar, pressing it into the sand for stability. Then she gently tucks in the last hydrangea blossom she'd saved, just for this moment.

Eva and Maris jog over to them then. "Oh, I have the perfect thing for your happiness jar." Maris holds her hands behind her back as she tells a Sal story.

And Celia sees how, for each of them, tears come fresh with their memory retelling.

"Sal always listened so closely to us." Maris gives Elsa a hopeful smile. "He made us feel special, like he really wanted to *know* us, with the way he listened and drew out our secrets—usually secrets that he spun his own thread of happiness, or wisdom, into. So I'd like to add this." She shows them the pure white conch shell she found near the rocks. "Conchs are for listening," she whispers while holding it up to her ear. "To hear the sea."

"That's beautiful," Celia says as she holds out the jar while Maris sets her conch shell off to the side, nestled in the sand.

"I have one just like it at home," Maris explains. "Jason gave it to me two summers ago, before we even started dating, and it's really special. I hear the sea every time …"

They all wait as Maris pauses. But before she says more, a sob escapes and she cups her mouth.

"Oh, hon." Eva wraps an arm around her sister's shoulders. "What's wrong?"

"I'm so worried about him."

"About Jason?" Elsa asks.

Maris nods, tucking her hair behind an ear. "I honestly think he considered Sal his second brother. They were *that* close, hanging out so much. And he is *not* taking the news of Sal's death well."

Celia steps closer. "But he seemed so strong at the funeral, and held it together during his speech at brunch."

"Exactly," Maris explains with more tears. "And that's just not Jason. I've seen him at his emotional worst. And I also know he's completely devastated by this, yet he's not reacting. No anger, no tears, sadness. Nothing."

"Let's go to your place, then," Elsa says. "Maybe we can talk to him."

Celia puts her hand on Elsa's arm. "I can't," she whispers.

"That's right." Elsa turns to her. "Your friends are waiting at your cottage?"

With regret, Celia looks at Maris. "Oh, I'm so sorry. But my best friend from back home is there, and my father, too. I told them I wanted to join you all on this sunset walk, so they're waiting to have dinner with me."

"I understand," Maris tells her, giving her a hug. "Don't keep them waiting."

After they drop off Celia, Elsa walks with her two nieces across the beach, toward the winding footpath up the hill to Sea View Road. Eva links arms with Maris, and Elsa notices Maris hurrying her step the closer they get to her stately home on the rocky bluff. The shingled house with tall windows sits back on a large yard, with trees towering on either side of it.

Maris breaks away and crosses the yard to her front porch. "Jason?" she calls out while opening the door. "We're home!"

The house is dark inside, with only a lamp left on in the living room, casting shadows on end tables and upholstered chairs and the massive stone fireplace. Tucked into a side alcove is the original Foley's jukebox, its glass and silver trim glimmering in the low light. But Maris keeps going. She leads them down a paneled hallway where several gifts, some still with wrapping paper partially attached, line the floor. They head into the dining room, and Maris turns on a big lantern-chandelier hanging over a painted farm table.

"We'll eat in here, if you want to put your things down first," Maris tells them before continuing into the kitchen. She opens the refrigerator and breathes a sigh of relief.

"Everything okay?" Elsa asks, coming up behind her.

"Yes! I see Jason got the food, so that's good." She walks over to the deck slider. "He must be out in the barn." But when Elsa and Eva crowd around her, they can plainly see across the backyard that the barn is pitch black. "Oh, well. Maybe he took Madison for a walk. Got some fresh air."

"Of course," Elsa assures her. "Let's start with something to drink maybe, no? Calm us all down while we wait?"

Maris nods and gets a bottle of wine from the countertop while Eva grabs wineglasses from the cupboard. In the dining room, Elsa clears Maris' sketch pads off the table and sets them on the sideboard, then spreads a blue-and-white striped tablecloth over the tabletop. As Eva begins pouring the wine, Maris places Sal's happiness jar in the center of the table, beneath the grand lantern-chandelier, and lights two pillar candles set on wide, silver-metallic candlesticks.

Elsa sits on one of the cushioned, wooden farm chairs. It feels like she's lost everyone she's ever loved: her sister June, her husband, and now her son. "Don't mind me," she says as tears line her face. "My sadness has a complete mind of its own today. Really, I'm not sure how long I can stay …"

"Oh, Elsa. Dear Aunt Elsa." Maris leans down and hugs her. "Shh. It's okay. We'll have a little wine first," Maris says, "and eat later." She presses back a wisp of Elsa's hair and stands there until Elsa gives her a teary nod.

"Maybe a bite to eat will help," Elsa says, moving the happiness jar closer to the flickering candles.

Maris walks around the table and sits across from her. "It will. And remember," she says, lifting her own gold star pendant, "we still have each other, the three of us. We all wore our stars today. You, me, and Eva. Nothing can break our connection."

Eva returns with the last wineglass and pulls out the chair beside her sister. "Maris," she says, slowly sitting. "Oh boy. I'm not sure if this is good or not."

"What's the matter?" Maris asks.

Eva hands her a piece of paper folded in half, with Maris' name written across it. "This was on the breakfast bar. It looks like Jason's handwriting?"

"I'm sure it's nothing." Maris glances at the paper, flipping it over, then back again. "Probably his note saying where he went."

Elsa watches from across the table as Maris opens Jason's note. Candlelight falls on the paper, and on the sideboard behind Maris, a summer bouquet of marsh grasses and cattails spills from a tall ceramic pitcher.

"*Dear Maris,*" her niece reads, then looks up at them. "Oh, I *knew* it." Maris swipes at a tear, and when those tears don't stop, Elsa imagines that Jason's words are swimming before her now. "This isn't good."

"Want me to read it, hon?" Eva asks, leaning close.

"Maybe you'd better," Maris whispers while giving the paper to Eva. "I can't even see straight."

Eva clears her throat, fidgets with the braided chain of her star necklace and slowly reads the words Jason wrote privately, for his wife. "*Dear Maris,*" she says, glancing up as Maris blots her eyes with a linen napkin that Elsa hands her. "Are you sure you want me to read this?" Eva asks.

Maris nods, the napkin balled in her fingers.

"Okay." Eva scans the words, then begins again. "*I'm sorry, but please believe me when I say I can't stay here right now. I need some time to myself after everything going down these days. And you know that I can't tell you this in person because you'd also know just the right words that would convince me to stay.*" Eva stops then and reaches over to squeeze Maris' hand before continuing. "*You'd whisper them and I'd look at you, and touch your hair, and see your eyes looking into mine—and I'd give in. But it would be wrong. You have so much to handle with your work and the last thing you need is to see me come undone, again. Because that's the truth of it, sweetheart. Right now, the way I feel, I'm no good to you.*" Eva looks up at both of them, silent tears streaming down her face as she sets down the note.

"*Jason*," Maris whispers, her voice filled with disbelief as she reaches for the paper.

"That's it?" Elsa asks from her straight-back chair. "You mean, he left?"

"Apparently. I knew he was having a hard time with things." Maris takes a long swallow of her wine. "My God, what am I going to do?"

"Do you know where he might have gone?" Elsa asks.

Maris scans the note, then sets it down. "I don't. *This* is his fortress, right here. This big old house, the bench on the bluff, his father's barn. I mean, it's his entire world."

"How about if I take a ride in my golf cart? I can buzz up and down these streets looking for him," Elsa says as she stands. "And it'll give me something, *anything*, to do to keep me busy."

Maris is shaking her head, no.

"No?" Eva asks her. "I can go with her."

"Jason won't be anywhere around here. He's long gone, trust me."

"Oh, Maris. If only he got the chance to see Sal at the end, it may have helped." Elsa sinks slowly back down into her chair.

"Please don't think it's your fault, Elsa." Maris reaches across the table and touches Elsa's fingers. "You tried, you really did."

"Well, you should at least call him."

Maris only gives her a small smile. "I know Jason. With that note? He won't answer."

Eva lifts up Jason's note again, skimming the words. "I'll call Matt, then. He's a state cop, so he can get a few of the guys to keep an eye out for him."

"Would they do that?" Elsa asks.

"As a favor to Matt, they would." She grabs her straw purse from the sideboard and digs out her cell phone.

"Wait!" Maris puts her hand on Eva's arm. "Wait."

"For what? The sooner they start looking, the sooner they'll find him."

"No. Don't call, Eva." Maris looks her sister straight on. "For me, please don't do it. Not now, and don't go behind my back and ask Matt to do it when you get home. Promise me."

Eva can only implore her sister with a long look, saying nothing. The candlelight flickers in the dimly lit room, their eyes locked on each other.

"*Promise* me," Maris insists.

"Okay," Eva reluctantly gives in. "Okay."

"Maris?" Elsa asks. "But why not? If the officers look for him, it's for Jason's safety, too. Are you certain about this?"

"Yes." She looks past them to the living room and is quiet for a moment.

And Elsa wonders what her beautiful niece is seeing. What memory is playing out of Maris and Jason, maybe dancing slowly to that old jukebox on dark summer nights, candles glowing, wisps of a sea breeze blowing in through the lace curtains, their words hushed, their touch intimate. Elsa and Eva cautiously await her next move.

Finally, Maris looks at them once more, her brown hair tucked behind an ear, her eyes sad. "Let him go."

~

Jason waves to Nick on guard duty, then drives beneath the railroad trestle, away from Stony Point, the sun setting in the western sky behind him. The SUV windows are open, and Madison stands in the backseat, snorting the sea air as he drives. There's something Jason can't get out of his head, all day now, ever since he spoke at Sal's brunch. They're Neil's words that he found last night while skimming his brother's leather journals. He thinks back to when he spoke those words today—standing at the table in his suit, seeing flowers and memorial photographs in the banquet room. Elsa and Cliff sat at his table, with Maris, and Eva and Matt, as well. All the guests watched him silently from each long table, hands on their drink glasses, jackets tossed over chair backs, handbags set on the floor.

My brother said it's easy to hear sadness in waves breaking on the beach, as though the waves are done, and dying. But you have to remember that the energy of the sea can't just stop. When those waves break, their energy shifts into the air, the earth. Neil believed energy that strong simply changes course, always moving, always there, like the tides. I think the same is true of people we've lost.

He told them what they wanted to hear, but the reality of it? It's all bullshit. Fucking bullshit. No one's there. No one's ever there once they're dead and gone. He squints at the dark, winding road ahead. Lord knows, Neil's spirit sure as hell hasn't shown up these past days; no voices came in the wind, no whispers from the lagoon grasses. Gone. Sal's gone, too.

Jason drives along a curve and passes a roadside farm stand boarded up for the night, then a few small homes where lamplight fills the paned windows.

All the while, he drags his father's dog tags along the chain around his neck, feeling like he's been battling demons all day. His father used to tell him and Neil that fighting in the war was a true hell, but he learned shit there, too. Survival things his sons needed to know. Things like, when he was stationed there summoning the courage and smarts every single day to survive the jungles, the swamps, it was the nights that he actually lived for. *Yes*, he assured his sons, *and the darkest nights in 'Nam were the best.* Even with the incessant sound of insects, with his pant legs tied to keep out leeches, and with feeling creatures walk across his body in that blackness, still he appreciated the dark. *Because what I learned*, he'd often say, his voice low, *lying there, glad to be alive yet another day, was this: The darker the night, the brighter the stars.*

Years later, when he sat with Neil and Jason out on the bluff at night, he pointed to the sky over the dark sea. *And when I could somehow find those bright stars through the trees in the jungle, or see them so high above as I lay in the brush, it was the closest I came to feeling at home. Glittering in the black sky, they looked the same as if I'd been in my own Connecticut backyard. Sometimes I think it's those stars that saved me, keeping me going till I could see my home stars again.*

Jason keeps his eyes on the road with the thought, but refuses to glance up at the night sky taunting him now. The darker the night? Well, nights can't get much darker than his. The road he's driving is narrow, with few streetlights, and as he resists looking up at those God damn stars, he fights the pull of some coiled emotion. But the more he resists, the stronger the pain, blurring his vision with tears until he's forced to quickly drive onto the shoulder of the road alongside a small forest, black with shadows. His SUV lurches over the grassy area until it comes to a stop. Jason shuts off the engine, still not, not, *not* looking up at that *blessed* sky. No, no, not tonight.

But the scary part is that fighting it only brings on heaving sobs that keep coming, wave after wave—there's no controlling them. Here, alone in the dark, grief takes him on like an enemy in that jungle, strangling his breath, wrenching his heart, coating him with perspiration, attacking him at his weakest—inflicting agony into his missing limb. All he can do is fold his arms across the top of the steering wheel, press his head into them and fight the pain from the inside. How did his father do it? How did he fight off the enemy, sidestep the mines, escape skirmishes unscathed? Return home to his own starry skies, to his life, to his wife?

It's all Jason wants to do, return home to Maris.

But not like this. Not with this anguish she'd witness. He can't bring this sorrow to his home beneath the stars of the sea, and have it become a memory of theirs. No, he has to rid it from his life, alone.

So the decision helps him. He takes one hesitant, deep breath and eyes the whining German shepherd with her slowly wagging tail, warily watching his distress from the backseat; sees his crutches leaning in the corner of that seat, and the suitcase on the floor; reaches into the duffel beside him; feels around his notebook and case of pencils before pulling out the framed photograph. Maris smiles casually at the camera, dipping her head and tucking her hair behind her ear. After a long look, he slips it inside the duffel, draws the zipper closed, and still he persists.

Pulling his vehicle back onto the winding road, Jason won't look at the night sky. His eyes stay only on the dark road, with each passing curve, each passing mile, each passing town. Behind him, Stony Point diminishes the farther away he gets. The seagulls crying, the silver-tipped waves lapping along the beach, it all ebbs until he has to tilt his head and strain to imagine it. Sal's wooden rowboat creaking against the old dock, the sea sloshing into the bluff, the grasses whispering in the lagoon, everything quiets until it goes silent.

More miles pass beneath his tires. As they do, the shingled cottages, the painted bungalows, the seaside sunrises and sunsets, they fade into shadows. The sandy boardwalk, the rocky ledge at the tree-framed end of the beach, Neil's beloved driftline, all of it blurs into the mist until he has nothing left.

The miles erase it all—miles when Jason won't raise his eyes to the starlit sky—not until he can, one day, find his way back to the sea.

Also by

JOANNE DEMAIO

The Denim Blue Sea

Blue Jeans and Coffee Beans

True Blend

Whole Latte Life

Wintry Novels

Snow Deer and Cocoa Cheer
Snowflakes and Coffee Cakes

For a complete list of books by *New York Times* bestselling author Joanne DeMaio, visit:

www.joannedemaio.com

About the Author

JOANNE DEMAIO IS A *New York Times* and *USA Today* bestselling author of contemporary fiction. She enjoys writing about friendship, family, love and choices, while setting her stories in New England towns or by the sea. Joanne lives with her family in Connecticut and is currently at work on her next novel.

For a complete list of books and for news on upcoming releases, please visit Joanne's website. She also enjoys hearing from readers on Facebook.

Author Website:
www.joannedemaio.com

Facebook:
www.facebook.com/JoanneDeMaioAuthor

Made in the USA
Columbia, SC
23 June 2018